I0692892

Windy With Hell

by

Patricia Grigg

Grigg Publishing, LLC ~ Arizona ~ USA

Grigg Publishing, LLC
P.O. Box 6154
Peoria, AZ 85381

ISBN-13: 978-1-62555-004-0

This story is a work of fiction. Names, characters,
places, and incidents are either a product of the
author's imagination, or used fictitiously. Any
resemblance to actual persons, living or dead, events,
or places is entirely coincidental.

Printed in the United States of America

First Edition, 2019
Edited by Dianna Grigg
www.griggpublishing.com

Children of the Nothing Girl series:

Book One

Windy With Hell

Book Two (coming soon)

Nobody's Hero

Other books by Patricia Grigg:

The Nothing Girl

This book is dedicated to my children who have been willing to face down Officials and Hurricanes to reach me.

To John Andrew Grigg, Theresa Ann McClure, and Joseph Orien Grigg.

ACKNOWLEDGEMENTS

So many people have stood in my corner that I'm certain I will miss quite a few.

Certainly foremost are my children who have always been positive and supportive. They are the joy of my life.

Many others have been here in the background. My friend Ray Bilcliff deserves a hug and many thanks for all the wonderful butterfly covers he has been so generous in letting me use. You can visit his website at: https://raybilcliff.com/ And I don't want to forget a dear friend of mine Susan Young who has been so helpful and supportive.

Then there are two places I go for lunch. These two spots are like old friends with so many warm people working in them, from the supervisors all the way the crew who maintain the equipment. A warm thanks to McDonald's on Nelson Road and to Wendy's on McNeese Street. McDonalds' people have been patient with me for many years as I've sat reading during lunch. Wendy's is now my weekend lunch spot. They have shown me warmth and friendly faces. A big THANK YOU to both companies and to all the people I consider my luncheon friends.

To all of you many thanks.

Chapter One

THE SUBJECT

All he wanted to do was lose himself in a good book and enjoy a cup of coffee. There was a man with a fancy latte sitting two tables over. He kept clearing his throat as if to get someone's attention then wiping his mouth. Sighing, Ritter put a bookmark in the book he was trying to read to mark his spot. Not that he needed to since he hadn't been able to relax and get beyond the first couple of pages of that book. He glared at Mr. Latte and was ignored as the man glanced up and cleared his throat again then wiped his mouth, again. The uptight latte guy was watching someone and looking a bit green. It was as if that person was making him feel sick. What the hell was wrong with that idiot? Ritter did a slow-track in the direction the guy kept glancing. Finally, he saw a woman sitting at a table eating. From the almost empty plate he thought it might be chocolate cake. Sipping from a steaming cup, she sat reading her book. She hid it well, that look of annoyance when the idiot guy cleared his throat again.

She wasn't an attractive woman. Being a bit overweight with no makeup on, at least none that he could see, and a smear of chocolate over her lips. The woman scooped up the last bite of cake seeming to inhale it with a content smile. She looked over at Mr. Latte, smiled, and wiped her mouth before gathering her book up to leave. What was interesting was the fact she didn't carry a purse or bag. That struck Ritter as more than odd. She stood and walked away, never looking back. He was quick to scan the area where the woman had been sitting, looking for anything she may have left. Nothing. Nothing to set off his alarms. Nothing that should have made his mind go on alert. Yet, as he got up as if to leave, he managed to drop his book when passing the table where the woman had been sitting. Bending to pick up his book he did a quick scan under the table and the chairs around it. Nothing. Then why were his alarms all going off?

Stop it! He did an internal shout at himself. The Doc told you to relax. Relax! Yeah, right, just lay down and die why don't you. Not going to happen. You aren't dead yet. You still have a couple years, maybe. He wasn't ready to face the death sentence given him by the doctor. Ron was his friend, his buddy, and the guy who told him he was going to die. Ritter stopped his internal ranting. He was grateful to Ron for telling him the truth, and for keeping his condition secret. All Ritter had was his job. It was the only thing that gave him a reason to live. It was the truth. If he couldn't continue his work, laying down and dying wasn't a bad choice. His phone vibrated bringing an end to the funk he was slipping into.

"Ritter," He growled into the phone.

"Protection detail, sending the info now. Hogan will be the alternate. Good luck on this one," his superior said, giving his usual short briefing.

Ritter thought he heard his boss laughing as he hung up and that wasn't good. Spoiled brat most likely. He thumbed up the page outlining the subject's name, address, and occupation. Middleton Whiting was a rookie cop on the night shift. Ritter pictured a tough butch guy with a hound dog face and buck teeth. As it had for the last couple of protection assignments, his phone refused to download the enclosed photo. His next question was why did he need protection? Bingo! President Whiting's family, viable attacks attempted in the past. Protect at all cost... national treasure... valuable resource... and on and on. No way he could be all that, and if he was, then why was he allowed to become a cop? Whatever. They felt the guy needed the best sending him for the job. Good, he still had some worth. The world still needed him for something. Ritter checked his watch. He had time to eat a quick meal. Maybe even read a few pages of his book before heading to the cop shop where Middleton was stationed. There you go, Ron, I'm going to relax, he thought.

Ritter cruised around the cop shop to learn all the exits and the best places to park. He would be ready to leave immediately on the tail of any cop car his charge was assigned. His first duty would be to take over security from the present agent. Then, he would introduce himself to his charge, while he made certain the locals knew he was on the job so they didn't finger him as a stalker. Cops were sensitive about someone following them so it was best to be upfront with them from the start. He parked after spotting Sawyer, the man he was to relieve. Walking up to Sawyer he nodded at the man, who looked anything but happy at the moment. "Any pointers?" Ritter asked with a sarcastic grin.

"Yeah, watch the subject close, this one is slippery," Sawyer said putting his car in drive. "Oh, and I think the subject is inside. Good luck," he said as he drove off.

He thought! You don't *think*, you *know*. So that was why the boss had laughed, he had an escape artist to protect. Great, just great.

Walking into the cop shop he went to the desk and showed his ID to the duty officer. "I need to speak with your Captain and Officer Whiting," he said.

The duty officer looked up with a scowl on his face. "You'd be the next sucker. I'm going to tell you like I told the previous fiddle, Whiting is your responsibility, not mine. If you lose your subject, that is on you. Don't come storming in here harassing us over it. Got it?" The officer snarled at Ritter.

"You bet. Now point the Captain out," Ritter said, his eyes cold, giving this Officer Prick his death stare.

"Through the door and straight back, he'll be the one with no hair, probably yelling," Officer Prick told him.

Sure enough, when Ritter entered the door there was a bald-headed man. He was dressing down some frumpy female officer. Ritter waited at a respectable distance for the Captain to finish with his shouting. He kept his ears open to catch what offense the officer had committed.

"This was the last time I want to hear that you took a guy down for peeing on a wall. Hitting the man was completely uncalled for. One more incident like this and you are out of here, I'll transfer you to sewer patrol, *on foot*!" As the Captain yelled in the officer's face, the officer kept a straight face. All the guys in the office looked as if they were going to burst from holding their laughter inside.

"Sir, I did not hit that man, he fell over when a strong wind whipped the urine back into his face. I was at the end of the alley. The man is just embarrassed that I saw him with a face full of pee," the woman said.

"No! Don't try to weasel your way out of this! *You are on notice*! Got it!" the Captain said, poking a finger in the woman's chest. For a moment the woman seemed to vibrate, then she turned to walk off without a look back.

Ritter stepped up to the Captain. "Captain, I'm Agent Ritter. I am here to shadow one of your officers a Middleton Whiting. I wanted you and your men to be able to identify me. I don't fancy being shot as a stalker. Will you be so kind as to introduce me to the officer in question?"

The Captain smirked at Ritter and yelled out, "Whiting, your babysitter is here," before stomping off.

Ritter's face became cold and hard, he didn't even look around to see if the other officers were looking at him. One laugh bubbled out of someone before the whole room noticed Ritter's look. Silence. Everyone in the room went back to business, or pretended they were busy. That is, all but the female officer. She turned back around and stormed back to Ritter. For the first time, he saw her full face. Cake Girl. Cake Girl got right in his face, well as close to his face as her five foot two inches could manage. "I don't need any damn babysitter. You tell my grandfather to quit sending want-a-be idiots," she said, staring up into Ritter's cold eyes.

"Tough shit, Cupcake, you have me now," Ritter said while trying not to laugh in her face. She was a spitfire for sure. He watched as she turned around and headed out again.

"Fuller, I'm driving," she called out.

"Like hell, Rookie," A beefy older officer growled, holding tight to a keyring.

Ritter ducked out of the station and went to his car. He had the car running and his eyes tracking the subject and her training buddy by the time the pair were ready to leave the parking lot. The old guy drove and Ritter had no problem at all keeping the pair in sight. He stayed close enough that he could gun it to aid the subject, or bail and beat the shit out of a perp. Although he didn't expect trouble, he didn't rule it out. Most of all he didn't count on the fact she had the older officer with her to keep her safe. Safety was his job. He checked everywhere for someone tailing them. He checked for vans or out of place vehicles on side roads, shooters on buildings, the odd person standing or looking in the direction of the subject. One reason he was the best was that he never dismissed anything around his subject. Letting down your guard because the day should go without an instance, didn't mean that would be the case.

Middy was so irritated at the man following her. She had the last one trained to only sit in his car and leave her alone, now she had to start training all over again. This new guy riled her more than any of the others had over the years. She was going to get rid of him fast. Up ahead was a man standing by a building reading a newspaper. Middy rolled her window down and smiled when she heard a car braking hard behind her.

The newspaper had been a bad break. It had covered his windshield and caused Ritter to have to lean out his window to keep an eye on his subject. He had managed to get hold of the newspaper and shove it into his car. Yet, one sheet had escaped and almost caused an accident behind him. That had irritated him to no end. His job was to protect, not cause harm. Fortunately, no harm was done, but that didn't make Ritter feel any better about it happening. He swerved the car as an empty trash can blew off a curb into the road. If he hadn't been on the job, Ritter would have stopped and placed the can back where it had come from. His job was to protect another, make certain a near accident didn't happen to anyone. On the job, he didn't let anything distract him. Distractions could get a subject killed, even one riding in a police car. It went like that all night the wind kicking things on and around his car. Ritter was more than relieved when the pair driving ahead of him finally parked at the station. Ritter rubbed at the knots which had formed on the back of his neck throughout the day from constantly dodging trash blown on or in front of his car. He kept the Whiting girl in his sight while she entered the station. He slipped in the entrance of the station behind her noticing her back go ramrod straight when she saw him. Tough luck, Cupcake, get used to knowing I'm here, he thought.

Her report finished, Middy did a sweep of the area to see where the want-a-be had parked to watch her. She hadn't been able to distract him during her patrol tonight. That didn't mean she couldn't get away from him on her off time. Her shift was over in five… four… three seconds. Free! Now to really be free, all she had to do was shake the new security nut. Without a second glance at the new security guy, Middy went into the locker room. She changed into her street clothes. She traveled light, never carrying a purse or anything else to encumber her movement. She needed her hands free at all times because you never knew when a stiff breeze might come in handy. Going to the window in the locker room Middy stepped on the box she kept under the window and scooted out the window. With a smile on her face, she slipped away from the station.

Five minutes. He had given her five whole minutes to change her clothes and come out. That is all she is getting, Ritter thought, slamming open the locker room door. Just as he had thought she was gone. This, honey, he fumed, was your one chance to prove I can trust you. Now I have your number and I am done with your games.

It had taken Ritter less than ten minutes to locate Middleton. She was there in the coffee shop reading and drinking some tea or coffee with an empty plate in front of her. Taking a couple of deep breaths to calm his urge to storm into the coffee shop and read her the riot-act, Ritter stood a moment watching the woman who he was to protect with his life if needed. There was a look of contentment on her face as she read her book. Okay, Cupcake, change of plans. You are going to hate them, he thought as he walked silently up behind the frustrating woman. "Sweetheart, you started without me. Shame on you," Ritter said, putting a hand on her shoulder and bending down to kiss her cheek. "That is okay, I wasn't hungry anyway, dearest." Ritter almost laughed when the woman's eyebrows shot up and her mouth scrunched to the side. He stroked the skin of her upper arm and managed to wiggle his fingers under her top to rub her shoulder.

"Are you nuts? I want to see your ID, now," Middy barked in her best officer voice. Her eyes went to slits when the man sat down and took her hand, holding it in both of his.

"You know I love it when you get all bossy that way. It turns me on," Ritter said, suppressing the grin he was feeling. She was sort of cute in a frumpy way.

For once Middy felt speechless, nobody had ever said such outrageous things to her. This guy was crazy. Finally, she found her voice, "Then take a cold shower, or keep it up and find out how it feels to be behind bars." She stood, grumbling under her breath, "Leave it to an idiot to spoil my downtime."

Ritter sat watching his subject stomping off, he smiled to himself. Fool me once, sweetheart, never again, he thought. He pulled the handheld tracker out of his pocket. He sat watching the blinking red dot showing his subject's movements. The device he held looked like a cellphone but was so much more. Ritter had a friend who had made the device for him. He had also created the tiny skin patch tracker Ritter had placed on Middy's shoulders. She probably would never notice the little patch and it would stick on through showers or sweat for several weeks. Ritter's buddy was going to make a billion once he started to market this little jewel. He stood and bought himself a coffee to go before following the flickering light on his handheld. Where are you going, Cupcake? He wondered.

A sense of peace settled over Middy as she slipped away from the coffee shop. The idiot didn't follow her. Perhaps he had finally gotten the message to leave her alone. She knew the man was only doing his job, but that didn't stop her from feeling smothered, and hindered by having him constantly following her. He was a big boy, he could lie like the rest of them and say he always had her in his sight. Middy sighed, in her mind, she could see the look on her mother's face when Middy was a little girl. Middy had lied then about being hurt by her aunt Julian. Okay, she'd ease up on the man, she'd try to ignore him if she could. Her shoulders slumped in defeat, beaten by her own consciousness. As tired as she felt after working all night Middy had things to do before she could find her bed and rest.

Ritter followed the subject, the cake girl, at a distance, close but not so close she might detect him. Funny how he now thought of her as Cupcake instead of 'the subject'. He had never allowed himself to become close to a subject under his protection. In his mind, he referred to them as 'the subject'. He kept them at a distance, not as a person, but more a thing to protect with his life. Few of them were worth protecting. Yet he did it anyway. Because that was who he was, the protector, the meat shield. The one who took the bullet intended for some political or rich creep. This one was young and full of herself thinking she could handle anything that came along. Just like the rest of the subjects he had protected she was wrong.

The scent of hot food filled the van Middy drove through the run down neighborhood. The area looked about as decayed as a fallen tree in the forest. She pulled the van to the curb in front of a tiny house. Blooming in patches along the cracked sidewalk leading to the door were pink petunias. With a smile, she picked up the first delivery from the back of the van. She quickly walked up to the door and gently knocked on the paint flaked green door. "Miss Grace, do you mind if I come in," she called out.

The early morning hours seemed to pass too fast for Middy. She would have loved to linger and talk. She could talk for hours with any of the elderly shut-ins whom she delivered hot meals to early in the morning. This, along with her personal trips among the homeless to pass out sandwiches was her outlet after a trying day. After any day really. She was happy too that she hadn't seen the want-a-be during the time she was delivering food to the elderly. Now she could go home and just sleep until time for her shift.

His eyes followed her as she parked the delivery van and went into the office to turn in the van's keys. Ritter didn't know why he was surprised to learn she delivered food to the elderly. But it was something he hadn't expected. His forehead creased as he mulled over this new information. He watched the tracker on Cup... the subject. She was heading to her home. Ritter had checked out the house early on and noted it was secure. Still, he stayed alert. He listened for sounds of distress from the bugs he had planted when he had investigated the house. He heard her phone ringing as she walked into the house.

"Eric? Is something wrong? Have you seen something?" Middy asked when she saw her brother's number on the caller ID. While she listened to Eric, her heart started to beat fast as concern flowed to her over the phone.

"Wear your vest every time you go on patrol, Mids. I saw officers being shot and killed. You knew them. I saw you crying Mids alone on the sidewalk with bodies around you. Promise me, you have to promise me, or I'll come there and follow you around," Eric said, taking a gasping breath. "Tell your security guy. Have grandpa send more help. Do everything to keep safe, Mids, I can't lose you."

Middy did what she always did with Eric,

she soothed him and protected him from his fears. "Okay, don't worry, I'll take every precaution. Don't upset the family. I'll call you every morning as soon as I get home. Okay?"

"And before you leave, so I can remind you to wear your vest. I'm not going to be happy if I don't hear from you. I'll call Mother and Dad. Do you want them to come to visit you? If not you had better call me, Mids," Eric demanded

"Okay, don't freak out on me. And don't call Mom and Dad. I give. I'll call you before going to work too. You can be such a pain," Middy said with affection.

"You too," Eric said.

They talked for a few more moments before hanging up. Middy ate her dinner and went to bed. She worried. Never had she known one of Eric's visions to not come true. How could she protect the men here when she knew they didn't respect her. Maybe she should be more like her mother and father. Why did she always aggravate everyone? She just hadn't been able to take the put-downs from the guys as she should. Mother would be so disappointed in her. With that thought, Middy fell to sleep.

When Middy woke she resolved once again to change her ways. No more beating the guys up with words, or wind. No more giving Fuller a heart attack with her driving. If Eric was right some of the guys could be dead and then she couldn't be nice to them. And the security guy, she'd stop being a pain in the ass to him too. Where was he anyway? Middy hadn't seen him since he called her sweetheart at the coffee shop. Nobody ever called her sweet anything. It had been… nice. She didn't do nice… Oh, wait, she did nice now, before it was too late.

Two weeks, that was usually the time limit on one of her brother's visions. When he had one if they couldn't figure it out and stop it within two weeks then they had failed. This time Middy couldn't fail, she had to take steps to protect her fellow officers. She needed to get them all wearing their vests. The only problem was she knew that she had no voice over what happens day to day. Worry caused her face to become the stony image of her mother's face. She couldn't enjoy her chocolate cake at the coffee shop before going in to work. With half her cake still on the plate, she stopped eating and looked up the number of a local donut shop. Dialing the number she waited, twirling her fork over her uneaten cake. "Sweet Treats, what is your pleasure today? We have our jelly donuts and donut holes on special today. Buy two dozen and get a dozen free. The chocolate dipped donuts are to die for today. I'd be willing to let you have those included in our special if you buy two dozen," a chipper voice said in Middy's ear.

"That's great, I'll take two dozen of each of your offers. Please deliver them to…," Middy gave the station's address. "And add twenty or so coffees." There, she had taken the first step to buttering up the guys. Pushing her cake away Middy stood and gave the coffee shop a quick search. Where was her security? Wouldn't you know the moment she needed the guy he was a no show. She'd have to call her grandpa, Middy cringed at the thought of calling him. He'd go overboard as usual, and probably call Mom and Dad. No, she'd hold off calling anyone. She had to try and get hold of her security. Then, have him find a way to influence the Captain. Make the Captain order the guys to wear their vests. Somehow, someway she had to get the job done.

Middy punched speed dial number three on her cell phone as she approached the station. She hadn't even heard a ring before Eric answered. "Middy, wear your vest!" he said without saying hello. "Okay," she said, "Only call me if you see anything more."

"Will do." Was the short reply. They never needed to say much to each other. It had always been that way between Eric and her. It was what made him easy to talk to, to understand. Because they were always on the same wave link. And able to fill in unspoken words without long explanations.

Middy hung up and entered the station just as the donut delivery arrived. As the donuts and coffee were being handed around the situation room Middy paid for the delivery. Then gave them an order to do the same tomorrow. She shrugged her shoulders as her fellow officers gave her a searching look. "Don't get your panties in a twist," she snarled at the guys, then snatched up a couple of chocolate covered donuts and a cup of coffee for herself. She was relieved when they laughed and gave her the one finger salute. Middy couldn't help glancing around one last time for her security, he wasn't in sight. Now she was worried about him on top of worrying about the guys.

As the briefing ran down there was still no

sign of her security. She'd just have to concentrate on keeping the guys safe for now. Later she would have to find where Mr. Cupcake man was hiding and give him a piece of her mind. Noticing Fuller lay the car keys down to reach for another coffee to take with them on patrol, Middy snatched the keys up and headed out to their vehicle.

Fuller was on her tail so quick she almost laughed, but she didn't as she was too worried. "No way are you driving, Whiting," Fuller was shouting at her back as she approached the car. Only she didn't try to beat him to the driver's side of the car. Instead, she went and open the trunk of the car pulling out two vests. She went up to the older man and shoved the vest at him. "I'll make a deal with you, Fuller. You wear the vest and I'll let you drive. Make your mind up, going once, going twice...." Fuller snatched the vest out of her hand and slipped it on, then held out his hand for the keys. She smiled at him and placed the keys in his hand. "Good boy," she said, patting him on the head, unable to stop herself in time to keep from teasing him. He snorted at that and got in on the driver's side of the car. She slipped her vest on and slid into the passenger side of the car.

He sat slumped down in the seat of his car so his subject wouldn't notice him. Ritter watched the interaction between the old officer and Cupcake. Something was up with her. He mulled over the evidence.

1) She hadn't eaten her cake today.
2) She bought donuts for the whole station.
3) She tricked her partner into wearing a vest.
Yep, something was up with her. But what?

Ritter had been careful to not let her see him since planting the tracker on her.

For two weeks each day that passed, Middy marked off her calendar. Worry over the impending doom that was hanging over her like a storm about to let loose. Every night she had donuts and coffee delivered to the station, then bribed Fuller into wearing his vest by letting him have the car keys. She thought she would be able to keep at least one of them safe as long as she could get Fuller to wear his vest. The other men she worried constantly over.

There were some positive outcomes from her new way of treating the guys. For one Fuller mellowed towards Middy treating her more like a partner rather than a pain in the butt. It was becoming part of their beginning shift ritual to bargain over the car keys. A joke just between partners. The rest of the guys were starting to treat her a little different. Looking at her a bit more as if she was their tomboy little sister instead of someone who didn't belong at the station. A couple almost had an interest in her, and would occasionally cast glances her way.

Ritter saw it all, all the changes in the men around Middy. If sometimes his lips thinned or his hands formed fists, he didn't seem to notice. He told himself the frumpy cake eating girl was growing up before his eyes. Funny how he still remembered that smear of cake by her lips. Maybe he was just feeling like a father watching his kid growing up, he lied to himself. Regardless of what he may or may not be thinking he was there to protect the cake girl. If one of her fellow officers stepped over the line he'd be there to straighten the guy out, and maybe step on him a bit.

Chapter Two

MAN DOWN

The alarm blared jarring Middy awake. She slammed the offending clock with her palm to shut it up. Today was the last day of the vision, she hoped. If she could keep Fuller and everyone alive today. Then maybe tomorrow, and the next day to be certain they should all be okay, maybe. She rubbed her forehead where a constant headache was building. The need to stir the air was growing. It always resulted in a headache when she didn't release the energy building inside her. That, plus not having seen the security guy these two weeks of hellish worry had her head throbbing. Where was he? She missed watching him go all red in the face with her. Feeling somewhat depressed, Middy dressed and walked to the coffee shop.

Standing so he could watch her and the street Ritter waited for Middy to pass far enough up the street. He wanted to move while still staying in range to rescue his subject. He was in work mode, alert, ready for anything that might happen. She was heading to the coffee shop. He knew the route she took well now, had every nook where danger might lurk mapped in his mind. Each building where a sniper may hide was the target of the quick random flicks of his eyes. He tensed and ran fast to a building when something appeared in an upper window. A toy fire truck fell on the sidewalk and Ritter immediately switched his focus forward. He checked to see where his subject was in regards to possible ambush areas. This was his job, he took it seriously even if the subject he was protecting did not.

A breeze caressed Ritter's cheek and it felt good on this still hot day. Ritter's eyes caught a smile flash briefly upon Middy's face for a moment, he was relieved seeing her smile. His little frumpy spitfire had been worrying him. Something was off with her, and it wasn't good. His gut felt it wasn't a good thing whatever was going on with Cupcake.

He was there! That brief sighting of the elusive Ritter made Middy feel light-hearted. He was the most frustrating man she had ever had shadow her. And for some reason that caused her to miss him. She sent a gentle breeze out to touch his face before she was able to stop herself. That was so unlike her. Middy smoothed her face going into mom mode. She tried to fight the flutter of excitement inside her at having spotted Ritter. Still, she could not stop the feel good that settled upon her as she entered the coffee shop. She felt so content.

"The usual, Mickey. Oh, and add some whipped cream to the cake," Middy said, for the first time in two weeks she felt hungry.

There was no reason he should be watching her eat that chocolate cake. Ritter jerked his vision away from Middy's mouth as she took another bite of cake, and made a sweep of the area. Mr. Neat was having his usual fit of throat clearing and mouth wiping. The guy needed to sit facing away from his subject if he didn't want to see the chocolate smudge on her mouth. Ritter suspected she did it on purpose when Mr. Neat was there. His gal was a bit of an imp. He smiled, remembering how she had gotten in his face that first morning. A spitfire. He saw her glance around as if looking for someone. Ritter's forehead furrowed. Was she expecting one of the jerks from the station to meet her? Ritter made a sweep to see if he had missed seeing anyone, then heaved a sigh of relief.

You think you are hiding, Middy thought having at last spotted Ritter's hiding spot. It was as if the sun had come out along with her suppressed mischief. She flicked a finger at a ribbon book-marker hanging from a display. Ritter seemed to be studying the ribbons, and it flipped up and flapped in his face. Laughing inside she watched him snatch the ribbon off the display. What surprised Middy was the sudden smile on Ritter's face. Even more of a shock came when he bought the ribbon and stuffed it in his pocket. How odd.

The boys were in high spirits when Middy entered the situation room. The donuts had arrived. West saluted Middy with his coffee cup before biting into a jelly donut with a wicked smile upon his face. His eyebrows wiggled with a suggestion Middy

ignored. It was becoming annoying that several of
the guys seemed to be flirting lately. She might have
wanted them to loosen up around her, just not in that
way. She missed her brother and younger sister. The
truth was she missed her family something fierce.
One more day, she told herself, one more day and she
could start to relax.

Watching the tracker, Ritter stayed in sight
of his subject. Ritter fingered the book-marker in
his pocket. It reminded him of her when she had
jumped into his face trying to rip into him over
his job. It was soft and smooth…. He pulled his
thoughts back as he saw the light on the tracker
stop. He had almost driven up on the squad car.
What was up? Seeing where the squad car stopped
Ritter realized this was a meal break. He pulled his
own bagged lunch closer ready to settle in for a few
minutes while his subject ate. Ritter felt pleased
with how things were going. The little she-devil had
tried several times to lose him. She was completely
unaware of the tracker patch stuck on her shoulder.
This assignment was now a piece of cake. Cake,
he chuckled to himself as he bit into his bologna
sandwich, that gal sure did like chocolate cake. He'd
kiss that chocolate smear on her lips right off…
WHOA… clear your head man, no kissing the
subject not now, not ever.

Ritter could see her through the storefront
windows. She was smiling at the teenager fixing the
sandwiches for her and Fuller. Did she even realize
she was flirting with the guy? There was a sense of
innocence about her, even with her tough-gal display.

Being the rookie Middy had the task of going into the subway shop and getting their meal. She teased Fuller as she opened the door of the squad car. "A veggie sub with diet coke, right?"

"Hell no, Rookie. I said rice cakes and water," Fuller grumbled.

"Fuller, you cracked a joke, you old fake." Middy leaned over and kissed Fuller's cheek.

"I'm a fun guy," Fuller said poker-faced, "Or it could be all those donuts making me sweet."

Laughing, Middy climbed out of the squad car. What a great day, she finally felt like part of the team. She entered the sandwich shop with a smile on her face. Middy winked at the skinny teen behind the counter taking orders. "Two meatball subs with extra cheese and toasted. Two chips and two Cokes. Make those subs your special way. You know you are the best at it," Middy said. Letting the kid know how much she appreciated his talent for making the best subs in the area. The guy blushed. His hand flying over the sub buns adding a touch of this and a tad of that to the extra meatballs and cheese he put on the buns. The kid had a knack for creating something so tasty a person just sighed in pleasure at the first bite.

Middy took the cup holder and the nice warm sack of subs and chips after paying and giving the kid a large tip. She winked at him before turning to leave getting another blush from the teen.

Walking around to Fuller's side of the car she passed the bag and cup holder to him. Then walked back to the passenger side of the car. Opening the car door Middy started scooting into the squad car. That is when it happened. Suddenly Fuller lurched in his seat, blood spraying over Middy. The shock was shaken off quickly. Had it been any other rookie officer precious moments could have been lost with the initial shock. Middy had been well trained by her parents, the moment the blood hit Middy she sprang into action. Opening Fuller's seatbelt, she began pulling him towards her with one hand. With the other hand, she began thumbing the call to headquarters.

"Officer down! Shots fired" Corner Subs!" She barked as she dumped Fuller on the sidewalk on her side of the car. She heard gunshots exchanged. Her own weapon was in one hand while the other hand was pressed to the wound on Fuller trying to stop the flow of blood. "Officer down, need medical immediately. Shooter engaged." It was then she saw the barrel of the gun in the window across the street from the squad car.

Crouching down by a trash can was Ritter firing at the shooter. He was keeping the guy busy and motioning back towards her to stay down. Like hell! Middy put her knee on Fuller's wound and switched hands with her weapon. She could see the shooter's gun so he had to be there. Her adrenaline was so pumped it didn't take much. Just a hard flick of her hand and wind hit that window so hard the glass shattered inward.

"Fuck!" That was all she heard right after her wind blast. Ritter was up running into the building before the glass settled inside the shattered window. Middy wanted to take off after him, only she had to keep Fuller alive.

Car doors began to slam as help arrived.

Middy got on her shoulder walkie talkie, "My SS went inside after the shooter. Don't shoot him by mistake. I need help with Fuller, he is bleeding out. Hurry guys, his life is in the balance." It was times like this Middy wished she could heal like her mother. All she could do was keep the pressure on and help the guys with clear info. And Ritter was in that building with a guy who would kill him. Middy cooled her face not to show any emotion, any of the worry, the fear. Her desire to keep Fuller alive was enough to overpower her urge to run in after Ritter.

Cops were all over the place and the shooter was long gone. Ritter took a quick look at the rig set up by the shooter. The guy must have already been on his way out when the window was broken. Clearly, the last shot had been from the rigging. If that freak wind gust hadn't broken the window, they might all believe that the guy was still here shooting at them. His subject had been in harm's way. If he had reached them a second earlier, maybe he could have prevented the old guy from taking a bullet. No time for this what-if bullshit he needed to get to Cupcake.

She stood watching an ambulance blaring "Urgent, Urgent" in its wailing siren voice as it took her partner away. Blood covered her upper body and her pant leg. She didn't even turn when Ritter went up to her. "Cupcake," he said softly.

She looked at him then. "Let's catch this monster," she said and stomped off towards the building the CSI was busy marking off.

"I'm with you on that, Cupcake," Ritter said staying close to her. It was going to hit her at some point and he wasn't going to let her face it alone.

Hours passed with Middy going over every detail of what had happened. The Captain and the detectives assigned to the case grilled her over and over. As far as the police were concerned all the stops were out. The only case they cared about being Fuller's case. Fuller was well known and liked by everyone. Men kept asking to be included on the task force. Each and every one of the officers stopped in to assure Middy they would find this guy. Middy sat through all the endless questions and the reassurances. The guys came patting her on the back while Middy kept a determined look on her face. She didn't break down or raise her voice in anger, she absorbed it all waiting to be free, to go find a monster. She had experience with monsters.

It was early dawn when word came that Fuller would pull through. Middy nodded at the news saying he was too tough an old bird to give in and signed out at the end of her shift. Ritter stuck with Middy the entire time, only leaving her side to be debriefed. She hadn't spoken to him or acknowledge he was there since reaching the station until she was standing at a bus stop.

"Where are you heading?" Ritter asked Middy as she stood waiting for a bus to take her to see Fuller. She had been tempted to call her mother to come to heal Fuller. Only the fear of her mother being taken away for experiments stopped Middy.

"To visit my partner," she finally answered.

"I'll take you. I want to see him also," Ritter said, almost reaching out to take her hand. He didn't touch her. She wasn't ready to be held. She had steel and determination in her eyes, not the lost look of needing comfort.

"Okay," Middy said, turning to follow Ritter to his car. Part of her felt like the Secret Service guys were an extension of the family. That part of her needed family. Yet she was the strong one, the one others turned toward. So she kept herself on point, ready to solve the problem.

"Hand me your phone," Ritter told Middy as they settled into the car's seats.

Maybe it was the shock of having her partner's blood spray over her face. Whatever the reason, for once Middy didn't buck being told to do something and handed Ritter her phone. She watched as he entered some numbers into her contacts before handing the phone back to her.

"I've given you my personal contact info, also my superiors contact info. Call me first. I'll come to you no matter where you are, I'll come to you. You want cake you call me. I'll get it. Okay?" Ritter said, handing the phone to her.

Almost meekly Middy nodded, her mind wasn't processing what he was saying. The only thought in Middy's mind was Fuller, his blood spraying over her. She had to see him for herself, to know he really was alive.

Ritter gave the nurse blocking Middy from looking for Fuller's room his death glare. She looked at him and back at Middy, then fiddled with her clipboard. "Alright, you may look in on him, but don't get him worked up if he is awake," she said trying for a stern look at them.

The man lying so still with IV tubes running

down to his arms didn't look like the hard-nosed man Middy knew. She almost backed out of the room thinking a mistake had been made. Ritter's hand on the small of her back was the only thing which stopped her from exiting the room. His hand the only warmth in that cold hospital room. It moved her forward until she was standing looking down at Fuller's pale face. Fuller was asleep.

Middy nearly gasped when the warmth at her back left her. She looked up at Ritter as he walked around the bed and began to examine Fuller's bandaged neck. He gave a small nod as if agreeing with himself on some thought.

Ritter went back around the bed to where Cupcake was standing. She looked as pale as the guy laying on the bed. He knew she was in shock. There hadn't been enough time for her mind to process what had happened. Speaking low, Ritter told her what she needed to know so she wouldn't blame herself for Fuller being shot. "You saved his life, Cupcake, by making him wear his vest. The shooter was at the wrong angle. He intended a heart shot only he didn't count on your partner remaining in the car, or wearing a vest. I checked the vest and his wound, sweetheart. The vest deflected the round so it hit his neck instead of plowing into the heart. You saved him."

The hand on her back warmed Middy enough, she was able to gather the strength to speak. "But I didn't get the guy. I have work to do." She stated in a flat voice. How she wished her mother was here to fix Fuller. Why hadn't she learned how to heal? Agonizing over her failure wasn't getting the monster off the street. Middy turned and walked out of Fuller's room, making her way out of the hospital. Ritter stayed at her side with that warm hand on her back.

Desk duty, they put her on desk duty! Her body practically vibrated with the disbelief that was shaking her plans to track down the shooter. What the Captain told her was that it was not her job to work on a murder case. She was a patrol officer, and at the moment, a desk jockey. All the guys swore they would find Fuller's shooter. They made promises to her and walked quietly when around her assigned desk. The whole thing stank. She felt they were treating her like some fragile bit of glass work. She! Was! Not! Fragile! Her family had seen the underside of people's bellies and had survived. Middy stirred the air and caused the paperwork on the chief's desk to fly off scattering on the floor. Instantly she regretted her action. Why was it she acted before she thought when aggravated by someone? Mother would be so displeased if she had seen Middy wreck havoc on the Captain. She settled down and start going over the paperwork before her.

The tedium of working at the desk was wearing Middy out. By the time her lunch break rolled around she was crawling the walls. She was looking forward to taking a break, maybe having some cake with her meal. Cake always cheered her up. She'd buy some take out and go to the coffee shop to eat. Their cake was decent enough, not like aunt Emily's cake, but still good. Thinking of the coffee shop Middy looked up to see where her SS guy was hiding. It surprised her to see him in plain sight. He was sitting where he could see everyone entering the station and her. What shocked her was the dark shadows under his eyes, as if he hadn't slept before his shift of watching her. He could be needing cake too, she thought, and smiled to herself at the thought of the stern SS guy with chocolate on his face. Mr. Neat Freak would go bonkers over that. She walked over to where Ritter had been sitting. Of course he stood the moment she showed signs of leaving the station. "We are having lunch. We'll get take out. How does a pizza sound? And then we will take it to the coffee shop. You can shoot Mr. Neat Freak for me." Middy announced, as she opened the station's door.

The worry lines on his brow couldn't get any deeper as Ritter followed his subject down the street to a nearby pizza shop. He was worried his subject was coming on to him. He needed to think of a way to discourage such behavior. Once before a teenage subject had decided that he was her love interest. That… that had been really messy. Since then he had been careful with women as subjects. Yeah, he had overstepped a bit with this one, but she was such a firecracker, managing to get under his skin. No more calling her Cupcake. She was Ms. Whiting or Officer Whiting. He refused to walk beside her instead he stepped back to trail her as his job required. This was the freaking President's granddaughter. A very quick way to kill his career was to let her form an attachment. No way. No way would he let that happen. She was his frumpy subject, nothing more than a job.

It was clear her SS guy was not going to join her at lunch. Middy scooped out half of the pizza from the box sitting on the table in front of her. Dumb SS guy was at another table pretending he didn't know her. She got up and walked by him flinging the pizza box at him as she passed by. Grabbing a handful of napkins, she went back to her own table and sat down. Take that dumb SS, she thought. Just to make her mood all the better Mr. Neat Freak walked in and did his usual order then sat at his usual table. She wasn't even in a mood to tease him. Dumb SS guy! Through her childhood the SS had been at the farm, they ate with the family and helped with the chores. They were family. Not this dumbass. Oh no, he was too good to mix with the farm gal turned cop. Well, let him suffer. It wasn't his job to please her, she knew that. Still, it hurt. For just a moment she had thought of him as family, someone she could count on and could talk to. Not his job. Just like catching Fuller's shooter wasn't her job, but she was going to do it anyway. She was so busy ranting about Ritter in her head that she never noticed how Mr. Neat Freak was freaking out over the pizza sauce on her chin, or the worried looks from the man she was berating in her mind.

Mr. Neat Freak appeared to be about to have a heart attack. Ritter watched the man's face go purple at one point as he frantically wiped his own chin while staring at Cupcake. The man had some serious problems. Chewing on the last slice of pizza, the very pizza Cupcake had practically thrown at him, Ritter figured he had done the right thing cutting off any budding romantic feelings the girl might have started to stir inside her. His job was to keep her safe and he couldn't do that if she was emotionally involved with him like some horny teenager. Old Man Whiting could be dangerous when someone stepped on his toes, and Ritter was not about to become one of those men who the Old Man squashed like a bug. He was the best at his job and he planned to be the best for a year or two to come. If he couldn't do his job, protect the people, make the world a little safer even if it was for rich spoiled people, then… what reason did he have to live?

Feeling hurt and disgruntled, Middy cleaned up her pizza mess and threw the waste into the garbage. She didn't even look to see if the SS idiot was finished eating as she stomped out of the coffee shop.

Shift change wasn't the way it might appear at any other business, when you were an officer of the law. People didn't commit crimes or have trouble on a schedule. Nope, shift change was more of a few here and a few there. With the incoming officers arriving while the outgoing officers straggled in a few at a time, finishing whatever weird or dumb thing they were having to solve before tiredly heading home. The desk jockeys were the only ones with anything resembling regular hours.

Middy grumbled to herself as she packed up the files she had been looking through while typing up boring reports on drunks, hookers, and domestic violence. Just the same old people taking everything personally and blaming the world around them for what most believed were slights to them. If they would just stop caring about what others thought and did what was right. Honor, the truth had been replaced with rudeness and lies in the world. She glanced to where her SS was waiting patiently for her shift to end. She wouldn't let him stop her from finding Fuller's shooter. Reluctantly, she filed away the case files on people Fuller had put away over the years. Fuller had an impressive record. Every arrest he had been involved in had been a clean arrest. She found notations where Fuller noted some of his arrests were decent people who just needed a break. Often he left himself a note to give the person a contact which might help them with whatever problem was driving them to drink or violence. He was a good man as well as a good officer. Most often you didn't get both in one man. Time to go home, rest a couple hours, then begin questioning the people on the street from Fuller's address on file.

Not even giving Ritter a look Middy push out the station's doors to head off to her apartment. Twice fellow officers stopped her to ask the latest on Fuller. He was home now, on medical leave, he would reach retirement before he was physically fit to return to active duty. Fuller would be on a desk for light work if he decided to push being active again before retirement. After the first two officers stopped her to talk others gathered around to hear the news, some wanting to hear there was progress on the case, all of them patting her shoulder now and then. Middy stood calmly letting them express their determination to catch Fuller's shooter, while all she wanted was to escape the attention and get some rest so she could start the search on her own. She was about to lose what little patience she had when Ritter grabbed her around the waist and pulled her behind a police car. "Gun!" he shouted as he covered her body with his own.

The gunshots started then, rattling of automatic fire. Men who had taken a second too long to respond to Ritter's warning went down like rag dolls, lying limp and still as blood covered the concrete they lay upon. Others began to return fire, while behind them all the station's doors were filled with officers rushing to give aid. Only aid was not being allowed, the shooter wounded or killed anyone who attempted to get to or from the station. All the while Middy was fighting to get Ritter off her. She needed to see where to send her wind. Soon she heard the chopper and a S.W.A.T. truck squealing to a stop. S.W.A.T. officers with shields and padded up like a bomb squad started helping the wounded into the station building. It was slow going and those of her fellow officers still able kept up a constant volley of shots at the spot they believed the shooter to be. The shooter was firing now in short bursts, failing to hit anyone. Ritter got off of Middy but still kept her low with one hand on her shoulder. "He is gone," he barked at the S.W.A.T. team working their way to the building the shooter had been in. Seeing the disbelief in their eyes, he added, "It is a rig, like with Fuller. This guy plans his escapes." One S.W.A.T. guy rushed in on Ritter's words, within moments the shooting stopped.

Middy knelt among the bodies of the men who moments ago had been talking to her assuring her that they would find the shooter. Instead, the shooter had found them. So many of them, fresh-faced kids along with lined veteran faces of experienced officers, all dead. She knelt in their blood and screamed at the shooter now long gone as tears streamed down her face. "I'm going to find you! You can never hide deep enough that I won't find you."

Ritter wanted to get a look at the rigging left by the shooter, only he could not leave his subject. The moment the gun began to shoot in short bursts in a loop he knew it was the same ploy the shooter used last time on Fuller. While Middy had been giving her fellow officers the latest update on Fuller Ritter had scanned the area over and over. The moment the barrel appeared in an upper window of a building across the parking lot Ritter had slammed Cupcake to the ground. This time he had been in time to save his subject. His warning registered a bit too late for some of the men surrounding Middy. They reacted to the word gun but failed to dive for cover fast enough. Guns were drawn, but they had first looked around for the shooter. By then it was too late, they were dead. The S.W.A.T. team was due a huge amount of respect, they had come ready to take the impact of ammo in order to get the wounded to cover. Ritter could tell this team had been practicing since Fuller's shooting. If only they weren't needed again.

Hours passed, and questions were asked. Shocked fellow officers stared at the blood pools left on the concrete of the parking lot. People in command were lost for words, scrambling to get back some sense of order, make some sense of it all. Only there was no sense to it, no sane sense. The monster had accelerated, taking more lives than the station had lost since it had been built. Why? That was the question which haunted everyone. Who hated them so much? With Fuller's shooting, they had thought it was someone he had arrested. Only Mike, the fresh face rookie had been on his first day on the job, he hadn't arrested anyone.

The news media was all over the story of so many officers being killed at their own station. Somehow a photo of Middy kneeling among the bodies of her fellow officers with her face raised became a media focal point for all of one day before SS had it removed. Middy was tight-lipped, standing up to the endless questioning without breaking down. Ritter, Ritter watched everything. The moment the picture of her had come out he was on the phone to the head office. There would be no exploiting his Cupcake. He had that killed before the media could protest. It did not stop that brief flash of the picture over the national news. Middy and Ritter's phones went off at the same time. Ritter answered his while scanning, always scanning for danger. Middy's shoulder straighten when she saw who was calling her. Ritter noted the reaction and leaned a bit closer to find out who had her sitting up so tense.

"Mom, I'm okay. No, don't send Dog. No, I don't think coming home will solve anything, I have to get this monster. Okay, I'll call if I need you. Tell the family I love them."

Her family Ritter sighed. Not a threat. He, however, had an angry President on the phone. Fortunately, he wasn't angry at Ritter. He wanted his granddaughter removed from the area until the danger was over.

Middy heard Ritter trying to assure his caller. She realized he was being told to get her out of harm's way. Grandfather! Middy snatched the phone out of Ritter's hand. "Grandfather, I will not be hidden away like some prize statue. You will tell Ritter you have reconsidered and to just do his usual job, something he excels at by the way. He was the one who spotted the shooter and covered me. Oh, and tell him to let me up next time so I can do my thing." For a moment Middy listened to the sputtering on the other end of the phone call. "You forget I'm a grown woman. I have the right to live my life, and this is my life. I'm a police officer, I will be in danger from time to time. You have no say over my life, understand, Grandpa?" There was a sigh at the other end of the phone before her grandfather hung up.

Ritter stared at Cupcake. Had she just told the President off? A smile spread over his face. Spitfire, he thought. My kind of woman. Thoughts he should never have stirred inside him. His pants grew tight, that was when he shut those thoughts down. She was his subject, his frumpy subject. That didn't mean he couldn't admire her as he kept her safe. He just couldn't let it get personal.

Eleven people were dead, two of those, not official police officers. Kandy Kane and partner Twinkles had been on the way out of the station after bail had been posted for them. The pair were female impersonators who had been in a bar fight when some guy had gotten fresh with Twinkles, then discovered he was a man. Videos of the pair's act were played over and over on the news, the pair had reached stardom in death. Their bodies were not among the caskets in the long line of black limos making their way to the cemetery.

It was an endless train of cars which followed those nine caskets, with the largest police escort in the history of the city. It stretched for miles. The route had been carefully mapped out with all side streets blocked off. There was not enough room for all the cars which followed in the procession to park near the line of freshly dug graves. Nearby streets had been cleared for the overflow to park. S.W.A.T. snipers were on rooftops watching, ready to take down anyone who should show up with the intent to take out more of their own. The funeral service had been held in the local park instead of a church as there was not enough room in any of the buildings to accommodate such a tremendous turn out of people. It was the saddest day ever for the city, businesses closed, flower shops were emptied. Criminals went into hiding, knowing the police now had hair-trigger fingers. Some even attended the funerals having known one of the dead officers. Middy was among the men in blue watching, looking for anyone who might show up to admire their deadly work. She had a fire in her eyes, a determination in her stride, Ritter at her side. The air held grief and anger, shock and fear. Wives sat closer to their husbands wearing a vest of protection, children held tightly, eyes always searching, searching for the glint of a gun barrel. Despite their fear, the people came to pay their respects, to honor the fallen.

There was a coldness in Middy's heart. She couldn't even appreciate the fact that Ritter was sitting beside her during the service. Nor did she think about his rejection of her kindness. Nothing was on her mind except finding the monster who had killed her fellow officers. This was her monster to find, to put away, and she would find him. She watched the crowd of mourners searching their faces one by one, looking for any hint of satisfaction. Women and men with tears in their eyes, many of them waving little flags. Middy briefly wondered where they found so many of those tiny flags. Someone was making money off dead officers. That thought soured Middy's stomach. Bloodsuckers, the thought throbbed in her mind as she looked at each face. It was that which sobered Middy and pulled her out of the deep darkness that had been taking her over. She was becoming like them, the haters of the world. Sure, she had always been cynical, well, cynical since all that had happened. Duke trying to kill her father. The monster trying to kill her mother. Julian being so hateful to her mother for no reason other than the fact her mom wasn't rich. Those were also the reasons she became a protector of the people. To feel such contempt for a whole crowd of strangers simply because they were trying to honor her fellow officer by buying little flags to wave, that wasn't like her at all.

A butterfly flew towards her dancing over her before briefly lighting on Ritter's knee. Mother had told her this was the butterfly's way of giving approval of a person. It was when her mother's blue butterfly had given approval of her father that her mother accepted him as someone to listen to and allow into her life. He became her soul mate. This time, however, the butterfly was wrong. She knew Ritter could be trusted with her life, but he could be nothing more. He had made that very clear. Still, the butterfly gladdened her heart by reminding her of her mother and family. There was good in the world. She just had to keep her mind open to that good. With the conclusion of her thoughts, as if realizing that Middy's mood had lightened, the butterfly flew away.

The flags were being removed from the nine coffins. They would be presented to the families of the fallen officers. As the last flag was folded and the honor guard turned to face the families, a gasp went up from the crowd. Several guns were drawn when that gasp was heard, snipers readied looking for targets. The honor guard stepped forward and knelt before the families presenting the flags to an officer's mother, wife, father, brother, sister, grandparent, or child. Soft words were spoken by each presenter to the person being given a flag. As one, the honor guard stood and saluted before resuming their positions guarding the dead.

They came then, swirling down in front of each coffin, spreading out and settling on the coffins, covering them in a rainbow of colors. Butterflies of every color, large and small, gracing each coffin, paying homage. It was something beautiful for the families to remember on this day of sorrow.

When the last song had been sung, and the echoes of 'Amazing Grace' played on the bagpipes brought tears afresh from the crowd the butterflies rose as one. They filled the sky like a burst of fireworks. One broke free. A news camera followed that lone butterfly as it danced its way over to one of the officers in the sea of blue uniforms. The officer held out her hand and the butterfly landed on her palm. The female officer's lips moved as if she had whispered something to the butterfly. The butterfly joined back to the cloud of colorful butterflies, it was as if the display of color burst and the sparks were blown away by the wind. The people sighed with the leaving of the butterflies, turning they began to leave following the directions of the guards, wonder filling their minds, mumbles starting about how the dead officers had been blessed by God for their service to man.

Chapter Three

MEDIA MAD

Every channel in the state broadcast the funerals over and over. Cameras covered every possible view of the caskets, the families, the officers from the station. The butterflies covering the coffins held much of the attention and imagination of the public. Then there was the shot of Middy thanking the butterfly with the caption 'Officer Thanks The Butterflies'. Speculation ran wild over who the woman officer was that spoke to butterflies. A media frenzy stalked the front of the police station watching for the 'Butterfly Whisperer' as Middy had been labeled. The butterfly episode brought to the front the old news video of Felith and Fred's wedding when the butterflies had become a rainbow train for Felith on her walk down the aisle. Ritter was so uptight over it all. He felt like he was protecting some musical teenage star. Immediately he worked out alternate routes for getting Middy to the station and home again. There was no attempt by him to not be seen with Middy. He, in fact, insisted on driving her to and from the station taking great care to disguise her and prevent the cameras from taking her picture. She, for her part, scoffed at the attention, refusing interviews and appearances on talk shows. The idea of sneaking out to go to work chaffed her.

Then a single officer was shot and killed. It was like the other shoe had dropped and the killer had lifted that shoe up high making sure it made a loud thud on the floor so everyone knew he was there.

In a way, Middy was relieved that the attention was taken off of her. The endless attempts to get her to make a statement had become ridiculous and tiring. Perhaps now she would be allowed to do something besides paperwork. Only, all that happened was the whole horror story was gone over and over again from the start to the point where they were at this moment in time. It was clear there would be no relief from the media until the monster was caught.

It was on a Wednesday that the only break so far came. It was in the form of a message sent to the station addressed to 'The Female'. A lid was clamped immediately on the message. The note had come in the regular mail and might have been dismissed as just another crank letter addressed to Middy, as the prominent female, if the guys weren't having a laughing fit over 'The Female' title, and if Eric hadn't called at that moment.

Middy answered her cell phone knowing that the guys were having some joke at her expense. Even though they had all become overprotective big brothers after seeing her kneeling among their fallen comrades on television, they still had to break the tension now and then. Middy stepped away from the laughter so she could hear her brother. Eric was speaking so fast and with such a frantic tone to his words that at first Middy couldn't understand him. "Slow down and repeat what you just said. It came at me so fast I didn't take it in, Eric."

"Stop them! They are destroying evidence," Eric said in a raised voice so much unlike her shy brother. Stop who? The guys! The guys are destroying evidence. A cold chill ran down Middy's back as she whirled back to the group of guys laughing and waving an envelope around.

"Put the damn letter down!" she barked in her most official voice, her phone still to her head. "You are handling a bit of evidence from our shooter. Put it down and start praying you haven't completely destroyed any trace that was on it." Middy watched the shocked expressions on her fellow officer faces as her words sank into their brains. One of the guys produced an evidence bag and the envelope was placed carefully in the bag while. Meanwhile, the trash was looked through to be certain there was nothing in it they had missed. There was no laughter only silence as each man stared at the bagged bit of paper. What was running through their minds only they knew as they stood around the desk in stunned silence.

"Thank you, Eric. We have it bagged. Did you see anything to indicate who sent the note?" Middy asked Eric, hoping he had seen something in his vision to give a hint that might lead them to this monster.

"No, just them pawing at the envelope and knowing it was important to your case. I hope it helps." The two siblings mumbled words of love you, and hung up.

The Captain was the first to break the silence. He gave Middy a sour look before speaking. "How the hell did you figure out this was from him?" he growled.

Keeping her face in a serious expression Middy could not resist the comeback. "Female instinct, sir. Pure woman know how."

With that, the tension was broken and the guys got down to serious work. Forensics was called, the post-delivery man was tracked down. Already the postmark was being sent through every examination known. It was, of course, local and their only hope was the mail sorting room at the post office having someone remember the letter when sorting it from the place it was picked up. Officers were sent to the post office immediately with photos of the envelope to question the people there and take their fingerprints. The envelope had as of yet not been opened. They were going slowly, trying not to miss any hint, any trace that might lead them to the killer. Handwriting experts were called in, all stops had been pulled out over the hope that these bits of paper would be the break they needed to find their shooter.

Once the envelope had been thoroughly examined forensics opened it up carefully sliding out the message inside to catch the most minute bit of trace evidence. They caught nothing. The message had one line written in neat, precise lettering. "Filth must be cleansed."

Middy and the Captain spoke at the same time. "What does he mean by 'filth'?"

The two looked at each other. The Captain with questions about Middy in his eyes, Middy with anger in hers. She fumed, just who did this creep think he was calling filth? The very idea set her teeth on edge. She was so angry she almost didn't hear the Captain's question. "Why would this guy say you are filth? I want a straight answer, Whiting. If there is something in your past that this S.O.B. knows that we don't it could lead us to who he is."

Arching a brow, Middy looked at the Captain as if he was crazy. "Sir, if there was anything in my past the newspapers would know about it. Hell, the world would know about it. You know I live under a magnifying glass. There isn't a moment I don't have one of the SS on my tail. Not one moment I'm not under someone's eye. I would live my life clean even if that wasn't the case because to do otherwise would disappoint my mother and father." Middy spun on her heel and stalked away. Ritter moved from his spot following her giving the Captain a pointed glare.

Middy stomped out of the station fuming at the Captain questioning her past. What she needed was a huge slice of cake. It wasn't until she was sitting at one of the small tables in the coffee shop with a huge chunk of chocolate cake in front of her that she was able to relax. The very thought of her commanding captain thinking she had somehow hidden something in her past fumed inside her.

Middy didn't even take time to note where Ritter was standing watching everything around them before digging into the huge slice of cake. The sweet taste of sugar and chocolate melted in her mouth and she sighed in contentment. The cake was probably why she wasn't a slim trim figure of a woman. Her ample flesh did not upset her at all. This was who she was a woman who enjoyed her food.

Every so often, Ritter's eyes would settle on his frumpy girl eating her cake. The girl sure loved that cake. It was good to see her relax. To date, her life had been one crisis after another. He admired her fortitude. Most young women he had seen would be a weeping lump by now and totally useless in a crisis. Now was not a time for him to let down his guard, however. The note proved this crazy person had singled her out for some reason. He knew she most likely was marked for death by this guy. For the first time, he considered calling in help with an assignment. One thing for certain, he was going to stick like glue to Miss Frump from now on no matter how much she protested. Only Middy didn't look as if she was going to protest anything. She was totally unlike her usual self, more compliant, letting him walk closer than ever when they left the coffee shop. It worried Ritter to see that spark that was all 'her' seeming to be tamed. She had eaten her cake, thrown her trash away, and walked out of the coffee shop with the usual chocolate smear on her upper lip. Normally she would clean her face when she was done. It was like she might be a slob while eating her cake, but once she was done, she reverted to Middy the cop, all proper and prepared to take on the world.

That brash sureness wasn't there as she left the coffee shop.

It was as if the whole world she lived in was perched on Middy's shoulders. She was the one responsible in some manner for all her fellow officer's deaths. How could she live with that knowledge hanging over her? Middy was seriously wondering if she should quit the force. Would the killing stop then? Trouble was, she knew they stood a better chance of catching this monster if she stayed in sight. How was the question? All the way home, she worried about the problem with no answer leaping out at her. What she needed was one of Eric's visions. Middy thought about calling Eric, only she knew that pressure put upon her brother was one sure way of blocking him up. Middy thought briefly of bringing Susan to the city, but nipped that thought right off. Susan was too sensitive. Sure, she could reach out and find the murderer's mind, but at what cost to herself? No, she couldn't involve either of her siblings in these troubles which were her own to solve. She just needed to find the strength inside herself to find this monster and stop him. Her mind made up the day was brighter for Middy. She saw Joe's BBQ place and smiled. One thing that was almost as good as chocolate cake to comfort her was Joe's smoked ribs. Joe smoked his meats the old fashion way in a smokehouse. The scent wafted through the air, making her mouth water.

A rack of ribs later, Middy was content for the first time all day. She took a deep breath when she and Ritter stepped out into the street. The air even smelled more refreshing. That night she slept soundly for the first time since this whole thing had started. For some reason, her mind was at peace with what she felt was to be her fate, death.

Middy entered the station with a burden lifted from her mind. She marched into the Sour Pusses office and plopped down in a chair facing him. The man sputtered, his face turning red as he prepared to blast her for daring to enter his office in this manner. Before he could bring his anger under control enough to speak Middy began to lay out her plan. "I want you to fire me in a very public manner. Call me all the vile things you are thinking right now and point your finger at the door ordering me out. If you can arrange for some reporters to witness the whole thing half the war will be won. What we need is for this monster to believe I've been kicked off the force in disgrace. You need to make it look real. Don't tell anyone else so the whole department believes this is real, understand?"

For once the old man was struck speechless. Slowly realization dawned on him. "You want to draw the menace away from the department," he stated. Something flashed briefly on his face, it could have been respect, but Middy was not able to believe it. The old man just had to be relieved she was the one asking to be fired. "Okay, but you have to check in daily and let us know your plans for the day. I'll set someone to shadowing you. Don't worry, you won't know they are there."

Shaking her head Middy looked at him as if he was completely stupid. "You know I'm shadowed day and night as is. You pulling a guy off duty to follow me will just complicate things. How about I have my

SS check in with you during the day. He can keep you up to date on a secure line."

The old man shook his head, there was that look in his eyes he got when he was about to yell at her for something he thought she had done. Middy stood up. "Then it is settled. I'm going to smear some fingerprint ink on my uniform, maybe pull out my shirt tail. That should give you a good starting place. Perhaps call the press and say I am willing to give a short interview. I'll show up a sloppy mess, the rest is up to you." Middy knew she was setting him up to look the fool, but then he already thought she was a joke.

The whole office could hear the old man on the phone with the press. "She isn't a butterfly girl," he was insisting, "I have convinced the officer to give a brief statement to the press. If you will gather in front of the station I'll have her brought out to talk. I warn you she isn't happy with having to do this talk but has promised to be on her best behavior. This will be your only chance to talk to her. Be here in 30 minutes."

Eyebrows raised around the office, you could almost see the guys exchanging a 'this should be very interesting' look. In the meantime, Middy worked at being her frumpiest self. She pulled her shirt out of her pants in one spot, fiddled with the fingerprint ink smearing some on one cheek and wiping her hands down her uniform. She hitched one pant leg up over her sock looking more like a drunk off the street than an officer of the law by the time she was done. The guys rolled their eyes, knowing there would be a blowup when she went out to meet the press.

In his spot by the doorway, Ritter watched it all. He wondered what she was up to, what diabolical plan she might have stewing in that mind. He wasn't prepared for what happened.

A gaggle of reporters gathered in front of the steps to the station. They rushed to set up equipment trying to get the best spots before others arrived. A podium with microphones was ready when the Captain came out of the station. Flashbulbs were lighting up the area like flashes of lightning. When Middy came out the crowd erupted with questions thrown her way. The Captain stepped up to the podium and there was sudden silence as they waited for him to introduce Middy.

"You have all been curious about the female officer on which the butterfly landed at the recent funerals of our fallen comrades. Let me state this was pure happenstance nothing more. Officer Whiting is just a patrol officer, a rookie who screws up more than others."

The crowd of reporters laughed at that remark, chuckling among themselves as if they knew the type of person the Captain was speaking about.

"Now if you are ready… Officer Whiting, please step forward." Middy took her cue and sort of stumbled into the Captain. Laughter rang out. The old man grabbed Middy and straightened her up. He looked her up and down and it was clear he didn't like what he saw. All the media were capturing images of the frumpy woman officer and the red face of the Captain. There was no doubt they thought the whole thing funny, that is until the Captain blew up.

He didn't bother to keep his voice low as he cut into Middy. "You are a disgrace to the whole department. This is the last time you will make a fool of the brave men who have given their lives to protect the good citizens. Hand over your badge and gun, then go clean out your locker. You are fired!"

A collective gasp came from the reporters, flashbulbs all but blinded the Captain and Middy. She pulled her gun from its holster and removed her badge handing them over to the Captain. Middy gave a mock salute to the Captain and sort of stomped away entering the station. Men in blue, who had been glued to the windows, quickly pretended they had business elsewhere.

Nobody looked at Middy as she stomped into the locker room to clear her things out. That is, nobody except for Ritter. He was glued to her side, a dark scowl upon his face. He watched Middy change into her civilian clothing. He had managed to contain the fury that was boiling inside him from Middy throwing away her career. How long he could keep from saying something he knew he would regret Ritter had no idea. He felt as if he was the only thing standing between his subject and a mass killer. What the hell had she been thinking to throw her whole future away?

There wasn't much in Middy's locker mostly just a change of clothing, a few candy bars, and a picture of her family. Grandfather wasn't in the picture. She knew how badly her father's parents had treated her mother and she was not as forgiving as her mother. Of course, her mother was not very forgiving either, a person had to prove themselves as trustworthy and honorable to stay on mom's good side. Her aunt Julian was constantly considered as a person not to trust. Mom merely tolerated her presence for Uncle Robert's sake, but she would never give her aunt an assignment, a chore to do. Chores were for those she held close to her heart, people she could trust. Middy made it clear when she didn't like a person. She sought out revenge, whereas mom thought of the person as dead. Maybe they weren't so different. Middy laughed to herself, all these years and she had thought the one difference between her and her mother was the ability to forgive. How stupid was that?

Ritter went ahead of Middy when she approached the doors out of the station. He checked the area, holding up his hand to halt Middy. "You stick right behind me. There is a media mob out there just waiting for you to leave. Anyone tries to touch you I break their arm. Understand?"

Again Middy laughed. It was so funny, he thought he had to protect her from a crowd of reporters. She could make a wind strong enough to sweep them out of the way. Yet she wouldn't. Staying hidden, keeping her powers secret had always been difficult for Middy. There was so much she could do with wind. After all, hurricanes could drive a two by four through a telephone pole. She had become so strong in her wind power there were few things she couldn't do with it.

Neither of the pair walking out of the police station felt they had to worry about themselves. Ritter moved his hand in a make way motion at the crowd. The expression on his face said it was death to anyone who did not move. The crowd parted before that death glare, making room for the pair to walk with ease away from the station. That didn't stop them from trying to throw questions at Middy, or flashing the cameras until she couldn't see from the flashes. The wind picked up suddenly causing pictures to miss their target. It was all Middy could do to keep from sweeping the whole bunch of reporters away. She kept the breeze blowing long after she and Ritter were clear of the reporters. This was something she had learned was a must to keep people from believing she was the cause of the mysterious winds that occasionally plagued the city. Talk shows had decided a large amount of concrete had something to do with these random gusts of wind. Something about heat rising off the concrete causing the air currents to go crazy. Middy had laughed about that one too.

The news channels and papers would not let go of the news Middy had been fired. Film clips and photos of all the events leading up to her being fired were constantly being shown. Events were analyzed, torn apart, and pondered. A protest went up from the citizens of the city. Somehow they found out about her feeding the homeless. The people saw her as a grieving woman. The shots of her bloodied on her knees among her fellow officers were so popular, a person couldn't turn on a television or open a newspaper without seeing the grizzly scene, despite attempts to have the picture removed.

In the meantime, Middy felt imprisoned by all the attention. Ritter was a grumpy bear lurking like a shadow nearby. He had called for back up and been denied. It seemed there was a crisis going on in D.C.. Notes from concerned citizens, flowers, and even teddy bears kept arriving at the post office for Middy. Every item sent had to be vetted before it could be sent on to her. Ritter was nearly ready to abduct his own subject and take her out of the country. The only reason he didn't was because he knew she would hate him forever for it if he did. She was too stubborn for her own good. People like her need a silent caretaker to look out for them. Someone as stubborn as they were to keep them safe. Ritter was the person for the job. So he watched over her, saw she had chocolate cake now and then, reamed her out for each and every reckless chance she took, and shielded her from the media. He was weary to the bone of this media feeding frenzy.

"WHAT IS TO BECOME OF THE BUTTERFLY GIRL?" An entire hour special was presented on television on the subject of Middy's fate. People called in live to give their opinions on the subject. The mayor gave an appearance assuring the public, they were trying to contact the girl to discuss her future. Many job offers were called in, as well as people who were angry about what was termed her disgraceful behavior at the press conference. In the last fifteen minutes, a show stopping call came into the station. "Good evening. You are live on 'The Public Talks'. What do you think will happen to this remarkable butterfly whisperer?"

The voice over the phone was altered, sounding eerie and chilling. "She is going to be squashed to a bloody pulp." The click of the phone call being terminated seemed to hang in the awkward silence that followed.

For all of twenty seconds, the host of the show stared at the phone, then began frantically motioning for a commercial break. The audience was left with commercials running for five minutes. The lines to the show were bombarded with calls, which were ignored as the show involved the police, and tried to figure out what to tell the public. Finally, the show replaced the endless commercials.

"For those of you just tuning in to 'The Public Talks' we received this horrifying call just moments ago." The call was played once more. "What you just heard was a death threat aimed at The Butterfly Whisperer. It shows how deranged this murderer has become. We can only surmise this person has latched onto our local hero because she is so popular with the people of our fair city. Must she suffer because the people love her? Is this what the world has come to? We ask you to not feed this maniac and his delusions. This channel, for one, has made the decision not to feed into this deranged individual's need for attention. On that note, I thank you all for your participation in tonight's show and ask you to send up a prayer for this brave young woman. Thank you and good night." The screen went to commercials once more.

Middy hadn't been watching television because so much of it was about the shootings. She lived those deaths and did not need the daily reminder of her fellow officers lying dead at her feet. So she was not prepared for the persistent knocking at her door. Ritter was at the door by time Middy went to answer it. He had installed extra securities measures which included hidden cameras showing whoever may approach the door. The monitor showed two uniformed officers, a fresh-faced rookie, and a grizzled veteran.

Resignation settled on Middy's shoulders as she opened the door to the officers. "So you two drew the short straws. Go on, tell me how much you guys hate me, how the guys are disappointed in me. I'm a big gal, I can take it."

"No, ma'am, we are your protection detail. Rosco and Eddy will be the alternates. Haven't you heard the news tonight?" the older officer asked.

Ritter stepped in front of the two men. "Tell me everything," he demanded.

Frankie looked Ritter up and down as if asserting his role in the world. "SS," he muttered aside to Albert. It was a moment before he said more. "On some talk show, the killer called in and issued a direct threat to Miss Whiting. We were informed, and the mayor told us we would protect Miss Whiting. He insisted."

The shift in Middy stance was so slight only Ritter was aware of it. He rounded on her. "You will control your temper. It wasn't these men's doing."

She gave Ritter a cool glance before facing the two officers. "So let me get this right. It took a threat from the mayor to get you to send a protection detail?'" she raised an eyebrow waiting for an answer.

"No, ma'am. We were already figuring out our schedules as to who would be off and what time slot they would fit," Frankie said.

Albert thumbed his chest, a big smile on his

too young face. "When it went official we drew first watch," He said proudly.

Middy's face became a blank surface, then she did something so out of character for her. She grabbed both men and gave them a brief hug. Turning, Middy stomped to the bathroom before she appeared weak in front of everyone. Behind her, Frankie did his best to hide a smile, while Albert fairly beamed. "Cows really do fly," Frankie mumbled to himself. "I think you mean pigs." Ritter replied. "No, cows." Repeated Frankie. "Definitely cows."

It was so boring leading an ordinary life. The only interesting activity was playing video games with Albert. The boy was an internet gaming wizard. Middy was hard-put to keep up with Albert. Often they partnered as Albert showed her how to play a game, once in a while Middy was able to beat the master. His moans when she did were comical. Middy called him Moaning Al in the games, at which he would laugh and counter with Ruthless Mids. It was the only thing keeping Middy from going nuts through the long boring days. Albert only played with Middy for two hours before his shift. The pair of officers had split the night and day shifts between them, Frankie days, Albert nights when her protection detail was reduced to the two of them after the Captain blew up over the waste of manpower on the detail. Ritter was a constant, ever on the alert, watching, watching.

During the day Middy went over what little they knew of the killer. He hated Middy, didn't leave any trace elements, and was a crack shot. Not much, yet profiles were made with less. If only she could see what made this guy tick. She bounced thoughts off of Ritter and Frankie. Nothing connected in her mind, something was missing, some vital bit of information.

It was a Monday, the time was 12:01 P.M., Middy knew because when the doorbell rang, the surveillance tapes recorded the time. She wasn't expecting anyone, nor had she arranged a delivery. Frankie was the one watching the monitors. All he saw was a skinny delivery boy walk up and set a box on the entry way. The boy wore gloves and a hat, and kept his head down so his face was never visible. He rang the doorbell once and left. It was clearly suspicious.

Ritter became all agent the moment the doorbell rang. Someone had dropped a package at the door and left. "Frankie, take Miss Whiting into the bathroom. Lay her down in the tub and place a blanket over her. This could be a bomb."

"Now just a gall darn minute. I don't need to be shuffled off at the first sign of danger. This is my call, Mister." Middy said, rather loudly.

"So you are going to tell my bosses that I failed to protect you, the person whose protection is my job, the whole reason I'm here? You want me to be put on detail at the South Pole, or Russia, is that right?" Ritter asked calmly.

Middy sputtered, finally letting Frankie lead her to the bathroom to be hidden away like some silly scared rabbit. She just knew nobody on the force would let her live this down. Her anger boiled to the surface briefly and she punched Frankie in the nose.

"What did you do that for?" He asked, dragging her by her arm like a resisting arrest.

"So you can tell the guys I fought like hell before you could get me in that stupid tub," She said, glaring at him.

Frankie stared at her a moment, then solemnly nodded his head. "I wouldn't have told them otherwise anyway. You'd be surprised with all the crap we give you, but, honey, we know you are one tough gal."

Ritter used the landline before he opened the door and stepped out closing the door securely behind him. He didn't want to use his cell phone in case this was a bomb with a trigger related to a cell signal. Caution was the key to doing this right. There were so many ways a bomb could be triggered in today's age. He studied the box while he waited for the bomb squad to arrive. It wasn't hard to determine the package was from the sicko stalking Middy. The writing was the same, and it was addressed to 'The Female Slut'. Ritter heard the bomb bunch pull up and he stepped back from the package. "It is all your's boys. Be careful, this is from that same guy shooting all of you."

The heavily decked out bomb tech nodded approaching the package as if it might blow up just from him looking at it. "Sir, have you evacuated the house?"

"My subject and an officer have been secured in the bathroom," Ritter replied.

"That won't do. Get them out of the place.

And any neighbors must leave also. Get to it," the tech told him.

"Certainly," Ritter said, going inside to rush Middy and Frankie out of the building. He had them help him in rousing the neighbors in making them leave their homes knowing Middy needed to take some sort of positive action to soothe her anger at being ordered about. She instantly took charge of the evacuation, ordering people about like a drill officer with new recruits. She had them organized and grilling hot dogs for the kids in no time at all. Middy was like a mother hen with her clutch of chicks making this more of an outing for them than a serious event.

The bomb squad was slow and careful in handling the package. So it was almost two hours before they declared the package explosive free. The boys in blue moved in then, like a swarm of locust they searched the neighborhood and surrounding area. Middy's little abode was trampled through over and over as every inch of the doorway was powdered and prints lifted. In the meantime, the package was slowly opened in case some sort of powder trap was waiting inside to be inhaled by a careless opener.

Fear set in when the package was finally opened. More than one man went to the bathroom to throw up. There insulated and weighted down in chunks of ice sealed in a plastic baggy was the little finger of a person. But whose? A note was enclosed sealed in its own plastic baggy. The message clearly pointed at Middy.

"Something borrowed from something blue.

He'll only live with the death of you."

Albert's finger, as proved with the print, had been well cared for and preserved in ice. This immediately started a search for Albert, who had not shown up for his shift to watch over Middy. This was more personal than all of the other deaths caused by this madman put together for Middy. Albert's fate hung like a leaden weight around her neck. She had to block everything else out and think only of Albert.

Ritter stuck close to Middy, a frown upon his face, and dread in his heart. He feared she would go off the deep end and set off on a rampage of revenge. The thing was he still didn't understand her. The more pressure she was under the cooler she was in her actions. And right now she was running very cool and calm, like an iceberg with the tip showing and all the hard damaging parts beneath the surface. She was more dangerous when cold and calm than when showing her hot temper.

Chapter Four

SAVING HIM

It was early the next morning before the note arrived for Middy from the madman. Two hours passed before the message was given to Middy. The force had gone over the message with a fine tooth comb and then a microscope before they allowed her to see the message. Middy held her temper in tightly as she thought of all that time wasted when she could have been saving Albert. Reading the message she knew she would follow it to the letter if it meant Albert would be released.

"*Come where the dust is abundant, the concrete solid, to get your fellow officer. I'll be waiting.*"

He, the madman, was waiting for her. At last a showdown with this stinking evil. She would crush him with the wind, blow him through the air and suspend him there, while making him spinning so fast his insides would rupture. The guys were adamant that she was not to try to face this guy. They needed time to set up a trap for taking him down. Only Middy knew a trap would not work with this sick mind. She had to be the one to stop him, in person.

With Ritter dogging her heels and Frankie fuming, Middy set off for the old concrete factory. It had been abandoned for many years, not even the crows came to the place anymore. The silence of the place was profound. Ritter wanted to scope it out first, but Middy was having none of that. She was at the moment a force to be reckoned with, strong and unbending. So Ritter ended up following her into the factory's yard.

A huge slab of concrete laid bare to the world. All the many blocks and shapes that use to be stacked around the area were long gone, sold as a bulk lot to another company. This made the figure bound and gagged lying on the far side of the slab stand out like a beacon on that vast wasteland of concrete. Albert. He lay as still as death with the only sign of life being the rise and fall of his chest.

Ritter didn't like it. To him it looked like Albert was bait in some unknown trap. His head swung left, right, back and forth searching for the hidden danger as he and Middy crossed the concrete slab to Albert. He could not see a sniper's nest, or obvious signs of danger. That made him even more suspicious of the surroundings. Something was up, but what?

He saw it too late to prevent the trap from being triggered. The moment Middy stepped on the trigger device the trap was sprung. Suspended over their heads on a huge crane, so much a part of the landscape it was hardly something that registered in their minds. Above them, a huge concrete block. Down it came with the force of gravity making its journey swift and unforgiving. Ritter shoved Middy trying to push her out from under the danger. "Get Out! Roll! Roll!" He had noted the crane, and the object hanging from it, but it was like an optical illusion seeming further away from them than it was in actual fact. He rolled to his back and braced his arms and legs to catch that block of concrete, perhaps to hold it for that fraction of a second it would take his subject to get clear.

Ritter shoved Middy at the same time as something crunched under her foot. In the fraction of time, it took from his shove to the crunch under her foot her mind registered the block falling towards Ritter. She rolled from under the block all the while flexing her hands as rapidly as she could to create wind. As the block hit Ritter and the awful sound of his bones snapping, shattering into a million bits, she managed to create a lifting force under the block of concrete. It took all her concentration to keep the force of her wind holding that block up enough to spare his vital organs. She just needed to lift it a little more and she would be able to push the block off of him. Middy called the force of nature to her with all her strength, the wind whipping around her, blowing Albert a few feet away from where she battled a block of concrete for Ritter's life. Sweat ran down Middy's face, her will draining the strength from her legs into the turbulent force of the wind. Still, she had to try to walk into that storm to push the block off Ritter as she saw it rise just a tiny bit. She shoved the block with her hip while throwing more and more lifting wind under the block. It wouldn't budge, but then Ritter did move.

The force of the wind began to move his body inch by inch from under the block. She didn't know if he was clear when her strength gave out and her legs buckled beneath her. Middy couldn't, wouldn't, allow her body to give into the approaching blackness, her job wasn't done yet. With hands fumbling and trembling so much, it was near impossible to punch in the number she needed. Middy called for help.

"This is Officer Whiting," her shaking voice said into the speaker. "I have an SS man down and Officer Albert. We need rescue and trauma immediately. Be aware of a possible sniper in the area." She left her GPS blaring away as darkness claimed her for its own. They could make what they wanted out of the scene when they arrived, was her last thought.

The blare of sirens screaming emergency, emergency woke Middy from the darkness. "Ritter? Albert?" she managed to get out before a hand tried to calm her down.

"Albert will be fine. I can't say about the SS man, trauma team has him."

Yes, trauma team, Middy remembered getting the call out. Bitter bile threatened to cause her to vomit, but she wouldn't allow it to happen, not in front of these men she had to work with in the future. You never show weakness, never. Plenty was the times she had wanted to break down. Only once had it overcome her to the point of showing. For the rest of her life, she would be haunted by the picture of herself among her dead fellow officers crying. No weakness, not now, not ever. "I need to give my report," she said, trying to maintain a calm voice.

"They can come to the hospital to take it, you've managed to have a severe sugar low. I've never seen anything like it before. You should be dead," the man attending her said.

"Yes, it should be me," she mumbled as he knocked her out with a sedative.

She understood what they were saying to her even though they looked at her as if she wasn't taking it all in, or understanding one word they said. What it boiled down to was that Ritter would die, if by some rare chance he managed to survive, he'd never walk or use his arms again, too much damage had been done. They continued to talk in low voices about all the damage to Ritter's body, the way he had been crushed, his extremities crushed as he had tried to hold the weight off long enough for her to crawl out from under it. He had managed… just… just long enough that Middy had rolled free. She could still hear his bones shattering, the awful crunch as his leg bones were smashed, and the silence. The silence had been so loud. She pulled out her cell phone and hit one number. It didn't take long for the call to be answered. "Middy?"

For a moment Middy couldn't talk, the sound of her mother's voice brought her back from the black gulf that threatened to overwhelm her. "I need you. It is bad, really bad. My SS is going to die."

"On the way." Those words were all her mother said before the connection ended.

Middy went back to watching the still form of Ritter laying on the hospital bed in the critical trauma unit of the hospital. The pain she was feeling, the guilt of it being because of her that he was dying could not compare to the hurt she had felt when he had finally spoken to her once he became conscious. "Get out. I don't want to see you, ever." She had left the room, her mom face on, the one that showed no emotion. Inside, she was hurting, hurting big time. It was outside the room while watching the doctors trying everything they could think of to save Ritter's life that she realized his only hope was her mother's touch. She'd have to go back into that hospital room when her mother arrived, she was one of the batteries. Eric, her dad, and Susan were the other three people who were capable of giving their energy to Middy's mother. Susan wouldn't come, of that Middy was fairly certain. Her power just wasn't good to have in hospitals. Middy felt for her sister. She had been such a joyful little child. Now, there wasn't a day that went by that Susan didn't suffer when around people.

The doctors were still talking in low tones, saying it might be a relief for Ritter to pass rather than to perhaps live being so totally crippled and in pain for the rest of his life. Middy's eyes flashed with anger, yet her face remained calm and smooth with no emotion, a look that always graced her mother's face. She interrupted the doctors, holding up her hand to get them to stop speaking. "Gentlemen,

I suggest you begin to prepare the room. We will need a second bed, crash cart, IV setups, a table with a full meal of high protein foods. Warming blankets, several of those, say five. You will need to clear everyone from the area and set up screening so nobody can see into this room. I'm sure the SS will have more instructions when they arrive. If you will excuse me, I wish to take a shower and eat before my family arrives. See you in a bit." She walked off, not giving the doctors a chance to argue with her instructions. Middy knew what Dr. Andy was going to order as soon as he arrived. The sooner things were set up the quicker mother could begin healing Ritter.

Ritter couldn't move, not one of his muscles would obey him, except a couple in his neck. He knew he was dying, all he had to do was look at the figures working around him to know they didn't hold any hope of him recovering. His biggest regret was having to hurt Cupcake. He had just known she would stick with him out of guilt if he survived. Ritter didn't want that, didn't want to strap her down with a cripple who couldn't even feed himself. After all, he was going to die anyway. The doctors had thought he couldn't hear them as they stood across the room talking softly about what life would be like for him if he lived, he had. So he had sent Cupcake off to live life, to have a man she could love, to be with someone whole. His life was over anyway. He'd never be able to do his job again. Never work, never. Ritter prepared himself knowing he had done his job one last time. He had saved her not only from death but from a long life of misery looking after him. He was ready now, no need to hang on any longer… only he could see her standing out there talking to the doctors and… no fair, they were knocking him out again with painkillers. He just wanted to watch her for a little while, before she left for good.

After Middy left, the doctors argued over whether to do some of the things she had ordered them to do. She was just a stupid rookie officer so why should they listen to her. Someone mentioned that she was the person the SS agent was protecting, so must have some pull in the world. Only that didn't make sense to anyone, and they decided to ignore the dumpy looking woman. That is until a group of SS descended upon them. Quickly the entire unit was isolated from the rest of the hospital. Not only were the items the rookie officer had ordered brought in, but also another ventilator, four lounge chairs and, of all things, a dog bed. To say the least, it was crowded in the hospital room.

The staff were grumbling by the time the SS were satisfied. That was when Dr. Andy showed up. "Listen up everyone. None of you will be allowed in the room once we all enter it. You may all clear the area now. Expect…" Andy held up a hand to stop the protest. "The head of this department. For you, sir, I have more instructions." Andy waited until the room had cleared before continuing. "Neither you or any member of your staff are to touch Mrs. Whiting. You may see her seem to faint. If so, do not interfere. Keep foremost in your mind the danger of touching her. That is most vitally important. Do. Not. Touch. Her. Also, you will have to sign some documents stating you will never reveal, report, speak, or communicate in any form what goes on in this room. Any violation will see you imprisoned for the rest of your life. Are we clear?"

The department head nodded as he watched strange looking IV bags being brought into the room and set up on the IV poles. The aroma of something delicious wafted through the room as one table was stacked with covered dishes. A box of some sort of protein type looking bars was next to go on the table. Finally, Dr. Andy looked around and nodded at the SS agents. They seemed to fade into the woodwork, silent sentries. "Tell the family we are ready," Andy said.

All the bustle around the room kept waking Ritter, the drugs they were giving him weren't working anyway. He kept dreaming about the trap laid for Cupcake, seeing her trip the trigger which released the weight. It came crashing down and all he could think to do was try to stop it. "Get out! Roll! Roll!" he had screamed at her and braced to catch the cement block. His hands and feet were crushed instantly, only by sheer willpower had he held the weight for mere fractions of a second. It was enough. His Cupcake was clear. He tried, oh how he tried, to make his body push himself out from under that weight. Only his head made it, just his head. He could still hear his bones breaking, and Cupcake's anguished cry. For just a second he thought he saw her before he blacked out. Now there were people in his room disturbing his last moments on Earth. What the hell was going on?

It was painful opening his eyes at first, a crust

had started forming over his lids, but then someone smeared a cool gel over his lids and he was able to open them. The first sight that filled his vision was a beautiful black girl. He wanted to tell her she was an angel and couldn't understand why she quirked her mouth at him as if she understood his thoughts. "Mom, he is awake," the angel said softly.

"Your mother still has to eat more, I won't let her approach him until her tummy is as full as possible." That was a man's voice, a commanding voice. "Andy, ready that special IV now." A rustle of something being torn open and the voice continued. "One more bite, honey. Andy will hook you up and you can start. I know you want to get started, but I'm not going to lose you. I love you, woman!" It was such a strange conversation that Ritter thought maybe he had died after all and this was a wake for him.

Turning his head Ritter saw all the extra equipment in the room, the table with food and a very thin woman sitting stuffing her face. A doctor stood by her inserting a catheter in a vein. There was a skinny man standing back by the door talking to someone Ritter knew, Bobby Jay. Had they replaced Ritter already?

Then he saw her, Cupcake. She stood at the foot of the bed, her expression giving away nothing. "Go," he mouthed. She shook her head no. When she spoke, he wanted to weep at the joy of hearing her voice again. Still, he mouthed, "go" again. "I'm here for her." Cupcake pointed at the thin woman. "She is my mother and she is going to save you. You have no say in this. You will be healed and I will leave." She turned from him, then helped the doctor bring a chair along with an IV pole to place next to his bed.

Ritter closed his eyes again. He didn't want to watch her leaving again. It was too much. He could hear them, hear them coming to his bedside, all of them were coming. He didn't care, let them watch him die, he wasn't going to object to dying, he gave his life for her, that was worth all the pain. For a moment he wished he hadn't pushed and kept his head from being crushed. A warm hand on his forehead made Ritter open his eyes. The thin woman was touching him. He felt such warmth. No, more than a warmth, it was a feeling of contentment. "Don't you dare kill yourself, darling. Do it in stages, enough to keep him living, then rest and take in more. We are here, giving you extra strength. Think of the kids, you know this will drain them too." The dangerous looking man, with his hands on the thin woman's shoulders, kept talking to her, urging her to not do too much. Ritter couldn't help himself, he looked for Cupcake and there she was along with the black angel and the thin guy. They too had placed their hands on the thin woman. The thin guy seemed to be paling before Ritter's eyes.

"Stop healing, Eric." The thin woman's voice was strained, weak. "My instinct is to heal you, dear. Don't drain yourself." The thin guy, Eric, pulled his hands back. A doctor pushed some sort of drink into Eric's hand.

"You should take a break too, Susan." The doctor told Ritter's black angel. She nodded and broke contact accepting the drink. Only Cupcake and the dangerous man were left touching the thin woman now.

Middy poured her strength into her mother and thus into Ritter. She couldn't heal him herself, but she would make certain her mother had all the strength needed to heal. She still was so hurt he had told her to go again. He didn't want her there. Too bad, she was going to see his life saved and him whole again. Behind her, she heard Eric lay down on the bed that had been brought in. She knew he could heal and had done some repair himself draining his own strength faster than he would have just being a battery. She loved her brother for that. She loved her family. They had come, all of them, even Susan, who had to be in terrible mental pain being here.

It seemed an eternity, but only minutes had passed before the thin woman lifted her hands and leaned back against the dangerous man. "Take a nap, Love. You too, Middy. All of you put the warming blankets on and curl up in your chairs. Andy, you are in charge while we drink and take a nap. I don't have to warn you about the security, guys." That last comment was directed to the SS guarding the door. They nodded, one of them double checking the screening, while the other stood firmly against the door.

Ritter could hear them talking as they settled in to rest, even though it seemed more like a dream to him than anything else. As they spoke, he could swear he heard the thin woman referred to as Middy's mother. "Her mother is here?" he thought to himself. And the younger man, Eric... did he hear that right? He is her brother? "Is her whole family here?"

Ritter was about to fall asleep himself when Bobby Jay stepped up into his line of sight. Bobby gave a worried glance over to Eric. "Don't worry, you'll be back in shape in no time. You owe these people your life, man, make sure you appreciate their sacrifices."

Odd words, the whole thing was so odd. The best thing was Ritter could actually breathe without pain. Maybe his body was shutting down, closing off the pain centers, giving him a little peace here at the end. Ritter smiled as his eyes won and closed on him and he heard a gentle snort, Cupcake snored.

It may have been years, yet was probably hours or days. The warm hand would touch him and Ritter would feel the warm peace seep into him. He lost count of the number of times Susan and Eric were sent to eat and sleep. Cupcake stayed until her mother was forced to stop and rest. There came a point when his black angel's SS was told to take her to the hotel. She didn't object looking weak and ready to fall down as her SS scooped her up and carried her out the door. The one they called Dr. Andy kept sedating him making it harder for Ritter to keep time straight in his head. All he knew for certain was he felt a little better every time he woke up.

"Go home, Middy. Your father will be enough for the final healing." Ritter opened his eyes, but the sedative Dr. Andy had been giving him was still strong in his system, and all he could do was look through slits at Cupcake and her mother at the door. Middy wrapped her arms around her mother hugging tightly to her. Cupcake's eyes were closed, but Ritter could see the tears running down her cheeks. Then she was gone out the door, some new guy on her tail. Gone, gone from his life. He let the sedative take over, sinking into a dark place he didn't really care if he ever came out from. Still, he heard voices in that dark place. The dangerous man and Cupcake's mother talking. "She is going to make herself sick blaming herself," the man mumbled. The woman soothed him. "She loves him, even I could see that." There was the sound of the man kissing the mother. "He is her one, neither of them knows it yet. It is why she risked us all to save him. Not guilt, but love. I just hope they don't lose each other to stupid pride."

At last, Ritter woke with a clear mind. He lay still, listening hoping to learn what went on before letting his eyes open. Silence. There wasn't even the annoying beep of the heart monitor. Then he was dead, he had to be for them to have turned off the machines. Only he didn't feel dead, he hurt too much to be dead. Still alive, of all the damn luck. He rubbed his eyes and sat bolt upright. He rubbed his eyes! He wasn't paralyzed, his hands worked. Did his legs? Ripping the covers off his body, he looked down at himself. His entire body was horrible shades of bruising. All his muscles felt sore which he expected if he was alive. But his bones were straight, not mashed up pulp. How was that possible? That weird dream of Cupcake and all those strange people. Bobby Jay! Bobby had been in the dream. Ritter looked around the room. It looked like an average hospital room, no extra bed, no crash carts, not one lounge chair or an extra blanket. It had really been a dream, not something real, no Cupcake coming to the rescue, no strangers. He was insane. It was the only explanation, he was insane. Locked inside his own head thinking he could use his hands and that his legs were whole. The memory of his arms and legs shattering was there. The sound of his bones cracking, being shattered into pulp vibrated in his mind. Insane.

The door to Ritter's room opened as the horror of being alive, but insane, ran like wildfire through his mind. Bobby Jay stood there watching Ritter. Bobby's mouth formed a grim line on his face. "Eric said you would be waking up now. Guess you are wondering what the hell happened. You're alive and whole, well, except for the bruising. They didn't want to risk Mrs. Whiting on doing the bruising too. She fixed your organs, nerves, muscles, bones, and the veins in your whole body. You were a freaking mess. Frankly, I was worried about my boy helping out. He isn't very strong. Susan sent me. She is the baby of the family and is a freaky scary girl to be around. Anyway, she was worried about you, so here I am. Ask your questions."

"So I'm not dead or insane?" It was the first thing that had popped into Ritter's mind, that maybe, just maybe he was okay. Only how could he believe anything if he was insane.

"No. There is some concern over possible blood clots. Eric tried to do something about that, but we have no idea if it worked. You'll need to stay in the hospital a few more days to monitor your recovery. This, from what I understand, is by far the most damage Mrs. Whiting has healed on a single person." A look of awe flashed on Bobby's face for a moment.

"Who was the guy that exudes danger? He SS?" Ritter had noted him the moment he saw him, the man was dangerous, not someone to mess with.

"President Whiting's son, Fred. He is scary. Ritter, don't ever, ever touch his wife. Don't even shake her hand. I mean it. She is the woman who did this miracle healing. That is what she does, heal. Eric, my subject, can heal some too. Mostly he has visions. Sees things that are going to happen, and we try to figure out where it will happen to prevent a death, or whatever," Bobby smiled wondering if he should mention Eric's cat.

Ritter held up his hand to stop Bobby. "That proves I'm insane, Bobby. You are just some figment my mind has thought up to try to explain its insane thoughts. Go on, leave me alone. Let me die in peace."

"You. Are. Not. Dying. That gal of yours decided you are worth saving and risked her whole family to save your ass. So stop feeling sorry for yourself. Let me say this and you had better remember it… if you break the trust that has been placed in you, if you so much as breathe a word of what happened here at this hospital… I WILL personally kill you. And if you think killing me first will save you, there have been SS assigned to this family since your subject was a little girl and Susan was in diapers. Every one of us will die for this family, EVER ONE OF US. Don't mess up Ritter. Get your head straight." Bobby turned on his heels, obviously angry at Ritter now. He was out the door before Ritter's shock at being threatened by one of his own released his mind.

Since Susan was in diapers. She was his black angel from the dream, the young girl who was nearly a woman, or was she fully grown? The one Bobby said was freaky scary. A family with powers, like in some damn science fiction movie, or horror show. What about Cupcake? Was she weird too, some freak? Was this the crazy part of his mind going for broke? Or was this real? There was only one way to find out and that was to get out of this hospital, this crazy place.

The pads of his feet hurt the most. Ritter ground his teeth and hobbled around the hospital room searching for some clothes. Nothing, not even a toothbrush. Well, there was a toothbrush in a sealed plastic wrap unused, not his. This place didn't hold one thing that was his. Of course, it didn't, they had expected him to die. Why keep clothing for a dead man, or a wallet? But then, what did they do with his stuff? Ritter was considering using a sheet to cover himself when his door opened again. His black angel walked into the room, closing the door firmly behind her. "My sister thought you would be upset that your belongings are not in the room. She sent me to give you this bag. I can see she was right in that you will be leaving the hospital. I suggest you get over yourself. Middy is hurting enough without you behaving as if your world has ended. You are alive, deal with it." The black angel tossed a paper bag at him and spun on her heels in much the same manner as Bobby Jay had.

These people were all crazy, Ritter thought as he searched through the bag his angel had thrown in his face. Not only was his identification in the bag, there were clean clothes too. And at the very bottom sitting there as if it accused him too of some crime he wasn't aware of having committed was a slice of chocolate cake. Why did it make him feel something that felt like guilt? He had done everything right, protected his subject from the bad guy and made certain she wasn't saddled with a cripple. He had done the right thing. Hadn't he?

He didn't have shoes, but he managed to catch a taxi to his place where he had an extra pair. To tell the truth, he wasn't certain he was up to wearing shoes on his battered feet. Perhaps he should have listened to the people at the hospital and stayed there a while. No, he had things to do. He had to prove himself capable of doing his job if he was going to hold on to it. At the moment he couldn't even open a bag of chips to eat. He gave up and ordered a pizza, maybe not the best for a newly reconstructed stomach, but it would be hot and taste good.

That night was the worse night he had ever had, other than being crushed to death. Ritter kept dreaming of the concrete block falling. Every time it fell, he failed to save Middy. Somehow he would be miraculously clear of the block and he'd see her under it, her head and one arm sticking out. Her eyes would be glazed with death staring at him as if accusing him of failing her. Over and over he woke in a cold sweat. That didn't happen, he told himself, you saved her. But who saved him?

In the first rays of light announcing the new day, Ritter was making his way to the site of the crime. He needed to see that concrete block for himself to understand how he had managed to escape being crushed to death. Ritter had expected to die right there on that spot, the one covered by the concrete block. Traces of his blood had seeped out from under that massive weight. Seeing that blood gave him the creeps. How had he survived? Not one idea was plausible. There was just no way he could have pushed himself out from under that block with both his legs and his arms crushed to a pulp. It was impossible. He could remember the sound of his bones breaking, that awful sound constantly haunted him. Then the rushing sound, like water, or a hurricane. It had been that moment he had known he was dying. For a second he had thought he was floating, flying in the air. That was before he blacked out completely.

There were no answers here for him. He might never understand what happened out here. Never had he felt so lost. He was without purpose. Nothing was left to guide him, give him a reason for living. It was his own doing. He had sent her away thinking to spare her. There had been no crystal ball to tell him everything was going to be okay, he'd live. Only it wasn't okay. He had ruined it all. Only then, when he admitted to himself he had made the mess, did he realize he was rolling around in self-pity. He reached down mentally and pulled himself up by his bootstraps. Ritter was a fighter, the man who got things done even when it seemed hopeless to everyone else. It was time he put away the pity party and got on with his life. There was a subject to be protected, a killer on the loose, and a stubborn girl to wrestle to the ground. Most of all there was a huge need to redeem himself in that girl's eyes.

Pulling out his phone, or the replacement for his phone, Ritter contacted his boss. "Ritter here, I will be going back to work today. Call in your temporary sitter."

"Ritter, you have been relieved of that duty. Report to D.C. for reassignment," The voice at the other end said.

"Like hell I am!" he clicked off his phone. No way would they take his gal from him. She was a witch, but she was his witch. He wondered when he had begun to think of her as his. From the first time she poked her finger in his chest and got in his face he realized. Middy had sparked his interest and never let it wane with her stubborn determination. Ritter swore he would not be relieved from this assignment, this after he was ready to walk away for fear of being a burden to her, was perhaps the most revealing thought he had.

Sitting in her home, Middy fumed, she still wasn't allowed to be a police officer. That didn't stop her investigating. Her ire was up. This monster had nearly killed Ritter and chopped off the finger of a fellow officer, all to get to her. He was going down. Someone, someone she knew, or nodded to in the street was after her, wanting to make her suffer, to bring misery to her life in any manner he could. This monster had caused enough death, enough pain to the people of this city.

Her thoughts were interrupted by a pounding

on her door. She glanced at the monitor for the door, prepared to shoot right through the door if needed. Ritter! What was he doing here?

"Open the door, Miss Whiting. I'm here to resume my duties."

He sounded angry. Too bad, she was angry too. He had tossed her aside, making her feel foolish for liking him. She had already made certain he was no longer assigned to her as security. "You are not my SS any longer. I'm certain you have been notified of the recall by now. So, go away. Attend to some rich pampered person that is more your style."

Ritter closed his eyes and leaned his head against the door. She was pissed at him. A pissed off Middy was a dangerous woman. How do you calm a rabid dog, or more likely a wildcat? Time. He needed time to get her to believe in him again, to trust he was here to stay. She was going to spit and hiss, maybe try to scratch his eyes out, or shoot him. He didn't put anything past her, not while she was angry with him. "I refused to be relieved of my assignment. You might as well accept that I'm here to stay. I know you are pissed at me, and, honey, I'm sorry. I just wanted to protect you from being saddled with a cripple all your life. Surely you can understand that."

"Then do it from a distance, all the other SS guys keep their distance, so must you. Go, stand across the street, sit in your car and play games on your phone. You are not to approach more than fifty feet. Get!" Middy said in her mother's calm, yet commanding manner. She would not be made the fool more than once.

A smile tugged at Ritter's lips. There was his feisty girl, ordering him around, putting him in his place. All was right in his world once more. Fighting to not yell out a whoop of happy cheer into the air, Ritter retreated to the far side of the street. This was a start on winning her back to his side.

Chapter Five

SEARCHING

For the thousandth time, Middy asked herself how do you find a killer? Trouble was this guy didn't leave any clues. No trace evidence, nothing. He was too dangerous and unpredictable to try to set a trap for him. He had to be someone whose path she had crossed. Albert. Albert was the only person who had come in contact with the killer. She had to talk to Albert, the sooner the better.

With trying to save Ritter Middy had done nothing but stick her head in Albert's room while he was being checked out of the hospital. All her focus had been on Ritter. Now she turned to Frankie to find out where Albert was hiding away. Middy felt guilty for not having spent more time visiting Albert. The man had lost a finger. He had to suffer many nightmares about that precious part being cut off. Guilt ate at her when she thought about what Albert must have gone through.

"Frankie, I need to know how Albert is doing? I know he didn't spend much time at the hospital, but I was so involved in Ritter's wounds that I neglected Albert. How is he? Is he being taken care of, seeing a head doctor? Is he still able to play his games?" She had a lot of questions, but she stopped in order to give Frankie a chance to answer.

"Miss Whiting, you put me in a difficult position here. I'm not supposed to tell you anything about the case, anything at all. Lord knows you have seen enough horror with Ritter, you don't need to be worrying about Albert too. The captain would have my head if I told you Albert was in a safe house. Or that he managed to get some DNA off the guy. And captain would probably shoot me if I told you that Albert asked repeatedly to see you. You are not to be involved in this case, understand, little lady?" Frankie shut up then, made like he was locking his mouth with a key and throwing the key away.

"Then I guess you should do the right thing and not tell me anything, Frankie. I thank you for being honest with me, and setting me straight." There was a long pause in the conversation before Middy continued. "If a girl was to go out for a long walk what would be the best route to take?"

"Well, some of the neighborhoods are a tad rough, I'd take that new SS guy along if I was you. If you just want to stretch your legs you could go left on Duncan till it T's, then take a right. I understand there are some pretty run down places along there, some of the fences are broken. Nope, you should just stay here, we can jog around the building for a couple of hours."

Middy smiled to herself and gave Frankie an unexpected hug. "You know under that gruff exterior you are a pretty nice guy, Frankie."

Red spread upon Frankie's face. He cleared his throat and looked away for a moment. "I'm going to make some coffee. You stay here, then we'll go jogging, understand?"

Sure, she understood, he was giving her the out to escape his watchful eyes and go find Albert. She nodded, blew him a kiss and grabbed a light sweater. Before Frankie was in the kitchen, she was out the door jogging off down the street. With any luck she would shake Ritter's replacement and be free to go have a chat with Albert.

It wasn't long before Middy remembered why she didn't jog every morning. Walking or fast walking was more her style, jogging was a pain. She slowed down to a fast walk. The feel of a constant shadow behind her was getting on Middy's nerves. Was the SS guy still back there? She had thought she lost him way back. He wasn't as good as Ritter at tailing her. Mentally Middy kicked herself. She needed to stop comparing everyone to Ritter. He was out of her life. It wasn't easy to forget him, for he had impressed her with his stubborn too bad approach to keep her from losing him. Nobody had ever stayed at it for as long as he dogged her through life, and she had wasted a lot of different SS guys over the years. Still, that nagging shadow was someplace behind her. Was it Frankie? Or, a chill went down her back at this next thought, the killer?

Middy always thought of herself as bulletproof, even though she knew that was an

unreasonable thought. This guy, this killer was
doing his best to prove her wrong. Mostly she felt
angry when she thought of him. He was one of the
monsters in the world who didn't care one bit about
anyone else. Since witnessing Ritter being crushed
she knew this guy might be more than she could
handle. It was very likely he would kill her before
she could find him. Her thoughts turn to her family
and what they may have to go through if she died.
Susan would probably not show emotion, although
she would feel it deeply. Eric would be so torn up
he'd need help overcoming his grief. Middy could
see her brother and sister teaming up to come to
catch the killer. Her parents would be wounded
through the heart grieving in silence and there for
Susan and Eric. She doubted very much that anyone
else besides her aunt Emily and her grandparents
would be upset.

Determination filled Middy. She had to catch
the killer before he got to her first. So she circled
around coming up behind her stalker. Seeing him
she stopped and let out a long breath. Ritter. She
was tempted to call up the wind and blow him into
the next neighborhood. Seeing how painful it was
for him to walk stopped her from doing anything.
Let him think he was being useful, for now.

She approached Albert's safe house with
caution. His guards might be trigger happy, eager
to shoot the man who had killed so many of their
fellow officers. After observing the house for several
minutes she decided to take the bull by the horns, so
to speak. Determined, angry and being just plum fed
up with being left out of the loop had her marching

straight up to the front door and knocking. Just in case, she called up her wind building up a small forceful gust.

The door of the house swung open, only nobody was there. The greeter was a gun pointed at Middy's chest. "Well, I like you too," Middy said.

From deeper in the house, there was movement and Albert's voice. "Miss Whiting? Is that really you?"

A smile graced Middy's lips for a moment. "Yes, Albert, I came to see you. You knew I'd track you down, Moaning Al. I missed our games. You do still play?" She kept her voice level, calm and even as if this was an everyday visit. One thing she learned from her family was keeping a cool head often won the day. The gun motioned her inside.

Albert ran over to Middy then stood there as if uncertain of his greeting. Middy grabbed him and pulled him into a hug. Releasing Albert he staggered backward for a moment before seeming to catch his balance. "Mids, I hear that I almost got you killed, and Ritter is dead. He took the blow meant for you, didn't he?"

The guy looked so hang doggy that Middy couldn't let him go on blaming himself for what that monster had done. "You were not the reason Ritter was hurt, hurt understand, not dead. You can't believe the rumors. I'm telling you to ignore all rumors, understand?" She gave Albert her best stern look and watched him squirm trying to come to terms with something he had felt was totally his fault.

"He isn't dead? Are you sure?"

Middy laughed, "Of course I'm sure. He is out there stalking me right now. The man will not admit he is no longer my security. He has a few sick days coming, and then he is being reassigned. They sent me Dull Connor. Believe me when I say that man couldn't follow a blind man in the rain." Middy and Albert both laughed at that.

Relief swept over Albert and his knees became weak from the overwhelming emotion. He stumbled backward until he was sitting on a rather ragged couch. Gradually he gathered himself together and turned a solemn face to Middy, who had joined him on the couch. "I begged them to let me see you. I wanted to tell you everything while it was still fresh in my mind. It is still hard for me to believe I was so careless as to let that creep take me. He came up from behind and placed a cloth over my mouth and nose. It had something on it and I was out before I could do more than bury my fingers into his arm," Albert paused in his narration as if remembering those moments of helplessness. "The… the first thing he did was cut my finger off. It didn't hurt, Mids. I was so out of it, I didn't feel a thing. I think he was gone for a while because I started waking up. It was then my hand started to throb. You know what? I couldn't tell what was wrong with my hand at all. The whole time he had me, I was groggy and unable to think. I vaguely remember thinking I had to protect the evidence beneath my nails. And trying to smell anything around me. He had me blindfolded. That was more terrifying than the throbbing in my hand. It meant he could be someone I knew and would recognize. It is scary to think someone you see every day capable of such madness."

"When he came back he was talking to himself, so I heard his voice. I'll never forget that voice, sort of whiny and high pitched. He was ranting about how he finally was going to be rid of the filthy slut. He came and stood over me, I could almost hear his breath. 'You make excellent bait.' He told me. I've heard of a person's blood running cold, but never had experienced it... until then. After that, I was knocked out again, and didn't wake up until they were loading me into the ambulance.

"They were talking about Ritter, how he was a dead man. Mids. I'm so sorry."

For a moment it looked as if Albert was going to break down and cry, but he cleared his throat and sat there as if waiting for the gavel of judgment to fall on him.

Middy turned her head, and, as if in stealth mode, wiped her eyes. When she was able to speak, she asked the most burning question inside her. "What did you smell?"

Albert looked confused for a moment before closing his eyes to think back. "Cleanser, as if the whole place had been washed and scrubbed. I remember wondering if he had cleaned the place where he planned to kill me. Once, when he was breathing in that fast rushed way of his, like he was getting off on holding me, I could smell something that faintly reminded me of my grandmother. Sort of a minty something. I thought it might be a breath freshener or mint candy. I can't think of anything else, just those two things. It was weird. I mean, who cleans a place and freshens his breath to kill you?"

"You told the others about this, right?" Middy asked.

Albert's face turned red again. "I was afraid they would think I am crazy. Besides, they got the DNA and were whooping it up. I didn't have the heart to confuse them with smells. You know how the captain can be. He is old school. You bring up something like minty breath and you are on garbage patrol for the rest of your life." he said scrubbing his good hand over his face as if trying to wipe out the idea of garbage patrol. "I should have. I should have told them. Who knows what might break the case open," Albert said, then muttered more to himself than to Middy, "For lack of a nail the shoe was lost. For lack of a shoe..."

"The horse was lost. For lack of a horse..." Middy too couldn't stand to finish the quote. Details were what made or lost a case. You had to prove a person guilty, not just assume they were. Good police work required all the little, sometimes useless details. "Call the Captain now and tell him you just remembered the smells," She told Albert. He nodded approaching the phone, resigned to taking his whipping from the Captain.

"Hold it! You know the rules, no calls out. Ever," One of the two security men barked as if cracking a whip over their heads.

Middy was in his face in a flash. "This man has vital information to hand into the captain. You stop him now and the sniper may end up taking out more of your fellow officers. Do you want to be responsible for that happening?" She was poking him in the chest with her finger as she spoke, an avenging angel on a mission. Well, one would hardly call her an angel, not if they wanted to keep their teeth. Still, she had made her point and the rough, tough security man backed down.

"Give me the information and I'll relay it to the captain in-person. We are due to change shifts, so I'll be free to report what you remember." He said, not an apology but more a concession.

For the first time, they had something to go on in finding the killer. The latest theory was the killer was a woman, even though Albert swore it was a man. A pair then they said, a man and a woman. This whole bit was based on the smells of cleanser and mint. These were considered womanly scents. It was difficult keeping her mouth shut and staying out of the action. Middy tried, she really tried. It just wasn't in her nature to stand on the sidelines and let someone else do the work.

Middy began to form a mental list of all the women who she had pissed off over the years. Not counting her aunts there was quite a list. Mrs. Burrows her old landlady had thought she was immoral because of her SS guys hanging around. Dixie Rhodes the checkout at the grocery had hated her for no reason Middy had ever figured out. She was just one of many who thought Middy was a spoiled brat and didn't deserve to live in their world. People often assumed things about her that just weren't true, like that she dated older men all the time, because she was escorted everywhere by the SS guys. She had come to dislike having them around, after all, it wasn't as if she couldn't defend herself. A well-placed gust of wind could take out the largest aggressor. Only, very few people knew of her wind power. It wasn't something she could allow the rest of the world to know about. She'd be locked up in a loony bin if people knew. She smirked at herself at that thought, wouldn't the people that hated her feel justified in that hate then? She thought back and regretted some of the tricks she had played on people who annoyed her or gave her grief. Sure, they had been harmless little things, newspapers blown into a person's face, garbage cans blown over, little things that could never be attached to her. Mostly, she had to admit, her tricks were directed at SS guys that tried to boss her around.

When did she turn so bitter about being protected? The day someone called the SS her babysitters, that's when it all came to a boil inside her. That day grandmother had added fuel to the mix by degrading her manner of dressing. There was nothing wrong with being comfortable. Those prissy dresses grandmother tried to make her wear just weren't functional. Try taking down a criminal in an evening gown. How impractical was that? As she thought about her reasons for resenting her SS guys Middy knew they were stupid. These were people just doing their jobs. In her heart, she knew any of them would take a bullet for her regardless of how badly she treated them. That alone humbled her to the point of vowing to never be mean to them again. No more little tricks of wind to aggravate them. With a sigh, Middy realized she had made this vow before with other people who had annoyed or angered her. Hopefully this time she could change her ways.

Over the next few days, Middy gathered a variety of cleansers and minty candy to have Albert smell. If she could pinpoint the items he had smelled she would be that much closer to finding the killer. She would track down whatever cleanser Albert identified to the buyers of that cleaner. She vowed to investigate them all, see if any of them used something minty. These were the only clues she had and she intended to follow them to the killer come hell or high water.

At the store, Middy looked at all the sprays, liquids and powder cleaners with a feeling of hopelessness creeping into her resolve. So many different types filled the shelves, she wondered how anyone made a choice. What worked, what was just a waste of money? How was a person to know without trying them all? With quiet resolve, she bought one of each in the first third of the cleansers shelving. She bought the smallest container of each one, knowing the person in charge of her financial funds was going to have questions about so many cleaning products. It didn't matter, she would go blow them down if they complained too much. Middy was at war with a ruthless killer, and she intended to win.

Getting the cleaners to Albert was the next hurdle to leap. Middy was afraid that if she went to see Albert again the killer would latch onto his hiding place. She did not intend to put him in danger again. So she set up a relay of sorts. Frankie would take a few each night to his place. When he had enough of them to make a decent package he'd messenger them to Albert. It was a roundabout method, but Middy felt it might protect Albert. Frankie agreed. Frankie became a mule in operation 'Sniffing Al'.

In the meantime, Middy paced and thought, and thought until she thought her head would explode from just trying to figure out who was the killer. It seemed so hopeless. She couldn't see any of the people she had aggravated over the years going to such lengths to punish her for whatever they held against her. Was she that evil that someone would kill others just to hurt her? Middy hoped not. The thought that she was to blame for all the deaths ate at her, gnawing at her insides like a flesh-eating disease. So she pushed herself pacing and thinking, and thinking. Not once did she even go out for a slice of cake.

From his vantage point, Ritter watched over Middy. She is going to make herself sick, he thought. Funny how the moment she ignored him, his interest charged full force to the front. Ritter wondered what that said about him. Or was he just coming to his senses, seeing what he had thrown away drifting farther and farther from his grasp? You never knew what you had until it was gone, he thought. Ritter was determined to do better, to make Middy trust him again. If he could just earn her trust, then perhaps loving him would follow.

Ritter was the furthest thing from Middy's thoughts as she paced the floor going over the possibles in her mind. It was so hard to imagine anyone hating her as much as this killer seemed to hate her. Yet she knew monsters lived among normal people. Hadn't her mother's monster proved that when she was a child? That night, the night the monster came to take her mother was forever burned into Middy's mind. Then, it had taken her whole family to bring down the monster. Yes, monsters lived among us all. Mother had her monster, now Middy had her own monster to deal with. Could she let the monster live the way her mother had let the monster in her life live? Middy just didn't know if she could allow the monster to go on living when he had killed so many.

On Saturday Middy began to visit people she thought might be pissed off at her for whatever reason their minds might conjure up to be angry over. Her old landlady was the first person she visited, knowing the woman thought her immoral had put the landlady at the top of her list. Pasting a plastic smile upon her face Middy knocked softly on Mrs. Burrows' door. Someone shuffled to the door as if weary or having arthritis. A crack, no more, appeared and Mrs. Burrows' voice barked, with all the authority she felt was her due. "Who are you and what do you want?"

"Mrs. Burrows, I've been meaning to visit you and see how you are doing. It has been a long time since I lived here. How are you?" Middy said. She straightened her back prepared for the dressing down the old woman would give her. To her surprise the door swung open wide and two thin arms grabbed her in a hug.

"You poor girl. It is just terrible what has been

happening to your fellow officers. Come in and have some tea. You are safe here, dear," Mrs. Burrows said, dragging Middy into her living room. She continued to babble on as she prepared the tea kettle and arranged cups upon a tray. "It was wonderful and so touching what you did at the funerals. I know it had to have been a blessing for the people who had lost their loved ones. Amazing actually. I'd have never believed you capable of such a generous deed. But then, I guess I've always judged you harshly. You should have told me all those men were your private security. I'm sorry, really sorry for how I treated you back then."

Torture, pure mental torture went on for over one hour before Middy could extract herself from Mrs. Burrows. She crossed the woman off her mental list of suspects. She thanked Mrs. Burrows for the tea and made her escape.

Dixie Rhodes was next on Middy's list. Her encounter with Mrs. Burrows made Middy leery of just walking up to someone else. She thought perhaps talking to Dixie at her workstation would put a buffer around them so no matter if Dixie laid into her or went all gushy Middy could back out fast. Making up a shopping list Middy headed to the grocery store.

So many women were still not shopping unless their men were with them. They were afraid of being shot down like the police officers had been. It seemed to Middy, for the most part, that was an unfounded fear as the police had always been the target of this monster, and yet she understood why they were afraid. There was no telling what a madman might do.

Dixie looked bored checking out a little old woman who was slowly placing each item she had one at a time up on the counter to be checked. It was not the best time to approach her. Middy busied herself shopping for enough groceries to feed Frankie and the new night shift man. Despite the horror they had been through Middy wanted to continue the tradition. She remembered her mother feeding all the SS guys who had shadowed the family over the years. She could do no less. Except Ritter wouldn't be there. Middy pushed that thought out of her mind. You couldn't hang on to someone who didn't want you around. It was best to move on.

Middy was depressed by the time she went to check her groceries out. If not for her stubborn determination Middy would have passed on questioning Dixie until another day, but she had her mother's glue and would see this through. "Dixie, I have noticed you don't like me. I'm wondering what I ever did to you to cause this dislike," Middy asked outright.

Dixie's mouth puckered as if she had just sucked an extremely sour lemon. "You want to know why I don't think you are God's gift to the world? Because you have everything handed to you. Men cater to you as if you were a supermodel. You are so dumpy I can't figure out why so many different men fall all over themselves to be with you. I doubt you have ever had to do what you didn't want to do. Now you are the golden girl of the whole city all they do is talk about you. There is nothing special about you, yet there you are on the television. On every talk show all they do is talk and talk about you."

Envy. One of the many downfalls people fell into without knowing the why of things. Middy closed her eyes for a moment, trying to think of how to explain things to this disgruntled woman. "First the men you think are fawning over me are men hired by my grandfather to keep me in line. There is not a moment in my life I'm not watched. I have no freedom except what I snatch by trying to do what I've always known was my lot in life. Even then they are there ready to grab me, and cart me off from any place they think unfit. Now, now the media have joined in on making me a prisoner in my own home. You do not know the amount of trouble it has been to just get free to come shop…," Middy glanced around, sure enough there was Ritter watching her. She pointed her chin in his direction. "I see that I didn't get as free as I thought. I'm certain a lecture will be waiting for me when I take the groceries home."

"You seem to think I'm privileged and don't work. Let me tell you what being the only female officer at the station means. It means every dirty job there is, the trash picking runs, running in to get lunch for the guys, anything that is degrading or dirty falls on me. I'm teased, pokeed fun at, and considered open game for any cruel remark. You know why I put up with it? Because all my life I've been a protector. The one that gets between the weak and the bully. I wanted to make it official. So I work my ass off doing everything asked of me, put up with the remarks, the attempts to gross me out, the name calling. And being told my babysitter

is there. If I could I'd walk away, but then I'd be a
failure in my own eyes. I can take others looking
down on me, take the snarly remarks and all the
rest, as long as I don't let myself down, or give up
on what I've been put on this earth to do. And I
apologize for the lecture. Sorry." Middy put down
her payment, grabbed her groceries up and left. She
was sorry, indeed, sorry for making a fool of herself,
for dumping on Dixie.

Chapter Six

WHAT DO YOU KNOW?

You'd think she had shot Frankie's dog from the aggrieved expression on his face when Middy entered the house. "You want me relieved from duty, right? That is why you work so hard at losing me every day. Do you know I've been called on the carpet for your visiting Albert? Now you go off and disappear for a whole day. I might as well hand in my resignation tonight and get it over with…," Frankie said in an amazingly calm voice, for a man whose face was so red it looked as if his blood vessels were about to explode out of the tissue.

For once Middy had the good sense to look as if she was very sorry for having caused him trouble. "Point taken, sir. I apologize for the grief I have caused you. From now on I will strive to make certain you are with me. My only excuse is I was hot to interview two of the women suspects on my list. Unfortunately, I've ruled both of them out," Middy said. She had to do better and stop aggravating everyone around her. There had been too many deaths because she had aggravated the wrong person. Every one of those deaths was stacked on her head, her fault, all her doing regardless if someone else pulled the trigger.

The look on Frankie's face was priceless. He looked long and hard at Middy as if she was something from outer space invading the house disguised as Middy. "Who are you, and what have you done to Miss Whiting?" he finally asked. From his look, he was totally serious.

"Okay, was that a bit too strong? I'm new to this being nice to people bit, Frankie. Truth is I have to change my ways. All this trouble, all the deaths are on me. I'm responsible for each and every one of our companions who won't be going home to their loving families tonight. Because of me, because I managed to piss off the wrong person they are gone. Don't you see, if I don't change the way I talk to people others are going to die?" Middy said before going into the bedroom to shower and change.

When Middy returned to the living room, Frankie was standing with his legs spread and arms crossed. He pointed to the armchair. "Sit," he barked. Middy felt like she was back in her training class. Still, she sat, crossing her legs, and placing her hands demurely in her lap. "First of all, you are not to blame for what this insane killer is doing. He used you as an excuse. If he hadn't latched onto you, he would have picked someone else, maybe a teacher. You know what that would mean. Kids would be shot down in the schoolyard. We go out each day knowing that some freak might be the end of us. May heaven help a small child who is faced with the deaths of his or her classmates. I would rather be the one on the line than see one child put through that trauma, wouldn't you? Stop thinking like a victim and start acting like a police officer. Now, while I order pizza, you write up this list of yours and let's talk strategy. You are not in this alone."

The dark depression, which had been blanketing Middy lifted some. Frankie was right, it was time to go on the attack. They needed to find this creep or creeps.

Only a red flag was thrown into the mix with the phone ringing. Frankie answered and handed the phone immediately to Middy. "Middleton, this is your grandfather. You have someone there at your station running DNA on a person who isn't to be known to any of you. You must see that this breach in national security is stopped. I don't want to have to call your Commanding Officer and throw my weight around. I know how much you hate that sort of thing, so I'm giving you a chance to put a stop to this. Lose the DNA, lose it now."

Immediately Middy went on the attack. There was no way her own family was going to kill this investigation and let a serial killer go free. "No. I will not lose the DNA. In fact, since you seem to know who this individual is I think you better tell me now, immediately, Grandfather," she put a bit of power behind the grandfather bit to let him know she was very serious.

"No? Are you refusing to handle this bit of a flub up on your department's side? Middleton, you will do as I ask or I shall come there personally," her grandfather threatened.

"No, you won't, Grandfather. This person you are trying to protect is the man trying to kill your granddaughter. How are you going to explain to my dad that you let a killer go and kill his daughter? Don't you ever check the news? It is all over the place, media I didn't know existed have it up. Thankfully, they don't have my name. But you know I will not hesitate to let them know who I am if you buck me on this. So spill," Middy said, knowing she had him over a barrel of sharks.

There was silence on the other end of the line. Middy knew her grandfather was frantically trying to find out what she was talking about. He was gone only moments, but when he came back to the phone his tone had changed, gone was the leader of the country and in its place was the humble grandfather. "You may expect the General at your place by morning. Do not leave your place until after he arrives. I want to talk to your SS man."

Oh, crap, Middy thought, it hits the fan now. Still, she turned to Frankie and told him to have Ritter come in. They just needed to get this over with.

Ritter entered, throwing a wary look Middy's way as he did. Middy held out the phone to him mouthing the word grandfather to him. His look became grimmer as he took the phone, he figured this was her way of getting rid of him once and for all. "Sir?" he asked, waiting for the ax to fall on his neck. Instead, it was his turn to say 'no' to the President of the United States. "No, that isn't necessary. You know she will react badly to something like that. I have her, she will be safe with me, sir," he had remembered to tack on that sir thankfully. "No, sir, you might order me to come in, but I will not abandon my subject. This is a critical time for her, her very life is on the line here. She isn't even allowed to go to the station. Isn't a police officer anymore because of this madman. You send more agents in and I just might end up shooting them by mistake, sir. Yes, yes it is. I'm totally serious here, and you know my reputation," he didn't add the sir at the end since he was in attack mode. Nobody was taking his subject from him, nobody. He listened for a moment and agreed to something he knew Cupcake wouldn't like at all. Finally, he handed the phone back to Middy watching her face intently as her grandfather talked to her. He saw the moment President Whiting told her how things were to go, the brief flash of anger on her face and then the acceptance. When she hung up the phone, she didn't even look towards Ritter. He knew then she still hadn't forgiven him.

Ritter was in the house now. He was to even sleep here in her place of living. That fact did not go over well with Middy. This was her home, the only place of privacy she had. Now, where was she to find peace? And soon her home would be invaded by that bungling General her grandfather had been using as a go-between for his grandchildren and himself. Her sister Susan did not like the man, Middy tended to agree with Susan's feelings on the subject. He would blow in here and try to throw his weight around.

Middy wouldn't let him do that, she was the one in charge of her life, not some bungling fool. Almost as if she conjured him up, she saw staff cars pulling up in front of her place. Showtime. Middy squared her shoulders, took a deep breath, and waited for the knock on her door.

Ritter was at the door the moment he saw the staff cars pulling up in front. He opened the door as the General and his escort approach. "General," he said, stepping aside to let the man inside. The General looked him up and down as if searching for some hidden agenda, then spoke. "Boy, you are like a breath of fresh air. That hard-nose Tex has always made me wait until President Whiting verifies my ID. I tell him every time, you saw me last time, you know who I am. But he holds me at gunpoint until he gets the callback."

It was Ritter's turn to look the General up and down a frown forming on his face. "Do you call ahead?"

The General sputtered for a moment before shaking his head.

"There you go. Fortunately for you this time President Whiting informed me last night you were coming today. Otherwise, you might have a bullet in you right now." Ritter turned his back to the General, a clear sign of disrespecting the man.

Red of face, the blustering General turned to Middy. "Middleton, how are you, dear?"

"Cut the bull. You have information on our killer, your job is to fill me in so I can catch this monster. So spill," Middy told him, already disgusted with the pompous ass.

Frankie had been hovering in the background, now he came forward, ready to be briefed on this man they had been hunting, this killer of his fellow officers, as Middy said 'this monster'.

The General noticed Frankie and made a negative motion with his head. "Only you and your SS man may hear this, it is highly classified. Whomever this is he must leave now," He said indicating Frankie.

"General, this man is here to protect me from the very person you are protecting. Have you seen the numbers, how many people have died because you have allowed this madman to remain free?" Middy shoved a newspaper clipping with a list of the dead officers on it under the General's nose. "Read it. Then tell me this is too classified to be heard by Frankie." She watched as the General's face slowly paled. The picture on the front of the article was of her kneeling among the bodies of her fellow officers.

The General looked up at last from the article. "How close has he come to killing you? Do you think we need to double the guard on Miss Susan? How about Eric, is he safe? Is this a plot against you three?"

Middy used Susan's signal for silence and attention raising her hand in a stopping motion. "He is only fixed upon me. All these deaths are my fault. I've pissed off the wrong person. Now it is time to catch this monster and blow him into outer space."

There was a long silence before the General spoke again. "Middleton, you can't do that. You can't kill someone outright like that. He has to be processed, judged guilty. You and your siblings have to hold yourselves above such petty revenge."

Middy fumed. This pompous ass was actually lecturing her. Her voice became soft, more deadly than the rattle of a snake. "You know what I'm capable of, don't you? Have you ever known me to lose it, to just out and out kill someone?"

"N… no." Came the weak answer.

"Have I had a reason to do that, to kill someone?" She asked.

The General's look became lost as if he was trapped with a bomb that was about to go off. He seemed to finally pull himself together. "Yes, you have had a reason, but you were just a kid then, still learning how this thing worked. Now you have become strong. You could do some real damage to another person. You have to control yourself even more now than when you were a little child. If people knew what you are capable of, there would be all sorts of restrictions put on you, you know that. You know what your mother went through. They'd want to experiment on you, Middleton, take you apart. Miss Susan and Eric would be taken to some secluded place and made to do their thing. Do you want that to happen?" the General reasoned.

He had her there Middy thought, she'd never let Susan or Eric go through that torment. "Then I'll just crush him a little like he did Ritter.

"Like he did Ritter? What happen? He looks fine now. Did your mother come to heal him? Why wasn't the President informed?" the General was firing off questions like a machine gun.

Ritter wanted to step in and handle the General, put him in a headlock or goose walk him out of there, but he knew Middy would resent any attempt on his part. So he watched this little drama unfold, his hands itching, his jaw clenched.

"We don't need to go into that now. Right now you need to tell me what you know. What is it you are hiding?" Middy said, her arms crossed, her fingers twitching.

It was the sight of those fingers twitching back and forth that had the General getting down to business. "You'll never catch him. He is a ghost, no, not a ghost, but a bit of mist so thin you can't even see it. His job was to infiltrate and take down his target, then disappear until needed again. He was very, very good at his job. He leaves no trace of himself, nothing for anyone to use to point a finger at us or him. He could be standing next to you and you'd never know it. He is that good. He went rogue about five years back. We figured some little kid saw him when he was leaving after his kill. Whatever the cause, he killed everyone, the women, the children, old men and women, everyone. He started picking his own targets, killing and killing. We tried to recall him. Tried to hunt him down, but he went underground, a ghost, only appearing when he wanted to kill again.

"We didn't know he had surfaced, Middleton. I swear we didn't know," the General stopped talking looking down at his hands as if he expected to be judged for the crimes of a madman.

"You don't know what sets him off?" Frankie asked.

"No. It could be a scent, a color, the backfire of a car, fireworks, anything could be the trigger.

Anything at all," there was that lost look on his face again as he spoke. This clearly was something out of his league.

Frankie's next question had the General gathering himself again. "You brought a picture of him? If we know what he looks like we can zero in on him. There is software which can search for facial similarities," he said.

"Sketches, all we have are sketches, he is too smart to have a photo taken," was the reply.

The sketches the General provided were of little help. It seems this guy was both fat and skinny. Seeing as how it was easier to fake fat than to fake skinny they went with skinny. The facial features have also been of several extremes. The one point which was consistent on the face were the eyes. Eye shape is hard to alter, so even though the brow may appear thicker the eyes were still spaced the same distance in all the sketches. It wasn't much to go on, but it was better than what they had. A sketch was made then compiling everything they could gather from the sketches made. The person looked slightly familiar to Middy, only she couldn't quite put her finger on who it resembled.

She couldn't think straight with Ritter in the house. If it was up to her he'd be back in D.C.. Only Middy didn't want to give her grandfather a stroke. It had been scary enough when he had the heart attack when she was a little girl. Her mother had fixed his heart and died again for the effort. Suddenly Middy realized that she held that against her grandfather. If he had kept calm he wouldn't have had the heart

attack. All these years she hadn't realized before
how that instance had stuck with her, causing her
to resent her grandparents. They had not been nice
to her parents, especially her mom back then. Even
after her mother had saved grandfather they still
didn't believe in her. People, Middy thought.

The doorbell rang. Middy didn't have a
chance to even see who was out there as Frankie and
Ritter moved so fast she felt her head spinning. For
a moment Ritter seemed tense, then his shoulders
relaxed. He motioned her forward, feeling that she
should be the one to let this visitor inside. Curious
now, Middy came up to the door. Soon she was
smiling and flinging the door open to throw her arms
around Albert. The lad blushed a beet red managing
to pat her on the back as she squeezed the life out of
him. Finally, Frankie cleared his throat behind her.
"Let the boy breath, Miss Whiting," he said, grinning
from ear to ear as he patted Albert's back.

"I wanted to be in on the kill," Albert said.
"They refuse to assign me to you again, so I told
them I was taking a prolonged leave to get my head
on straight." He tilted his head to the side. "See, it is
off center."

Middy laughed, even Ritter may have chuckled
a bit before his oh so serious face came back on.
Frankie belly laughed. It was something they all
needed, that laughter.

"Well, it is about time you got off your lazy
butt and gave me a hand," Frankie said, all smiles.
"Pizza, we need pizza. Put an order in, boy, you
know what we like."

"Slave driver," Albert mumbled as he headed

to the phone.

For a few minutes they laughed together, and relaxed. All the tension came rolling back when the doorbell rang again. The four of them were up and ready to take on whatever was on the other side of the door. Two shadows fell across the camera before Fuller and Rosco showed in all their grumpy glory. Fuller still looked a little worn from his hospital stay. Officially, he was on the retirement list, still, he carried himself upright and looked all officer. Fuller was first in the door once Ritter opened it. "They don't have much use for me at the station, so I came to join your little group here. Where are we in this investigation?" He said by way of greeting.

Instead of answering Middy turned to Rosco, "And you?"

Rosco jumped as if he hadn't been expecting to be questioned. "Well, I had a few free hours so I thought what the heck, go let Middleton boss you around for a while."

"Good choice," Albert said. "We were just about to have a pizza party."

Slowly off-duty officers drifted in until the pizza party had more officers attending than were at the station on duty.

Finally, they got back to planning their approach in searching for the killer. Middy divided the city into squares giving each team a section to search, looking for the guy pictured in the sketches. She was going to start along with her usual route on a work day to see if anyone looked familiar. Her theory was, she had seen the guy somewhere she frequented. The whole time Ritter's face showed disapproval. He could keep her safe if she was to stay in one spot. He didn't suggest she stay home because Ritter knew it would only make her more determined to go out.

"Remember to check the eyes more than other features of the face, the eyes are the only thing he can't change the shape, although he may change the color of his eyes," Middy said as the groups began to disperse. There were heads nodding and mutters in agreement. Trying not to let Ritter notice Middy took a deep breath as if preparing for what lay ahead. Her wind was strong and so was her will, yet there was this hole inside her which wouldn't be filled up until justice was done for all her fellow officers, Albert, and most especially Ritter. She had to find this killer and bring him in. In her heart, she knew that finding him would mean death for him, for nobody would do less than the death penalty for such a killer. That too played inside of her, like a wound that wouldn't heal. For the first time, she would be responsible for killing another being.

Middy started with the elderly to which she delivered meals. She followed her old route, stopping briefly to talk to some of the people who were sitting outside. Their complaints were numerous since it seems the new person missed days at a time and often delivered the meal in a mess as if they had been dropped or turned on the side. Middy took careful notes on each complaint fuming at such gross neglect. It was a pet peeve of hers when the elderly were neglected.

Listening to all the complaints took most of her day up so there was very little else she did before the guys began to call in saying they would meet her at her home. Reluctantly, she decided to do more the next day. Right now she needed to hear what, if anything, the guys had found.

Shadows, they were chasing shadows. Over fried chicken and the fixings, the mismatched group of investigators compared notes. Several had taken pictures of everyone and anyone who might in the slightest be their suspect. One wall in Middy's home was stripped of any decorations and the furniture moved to expose the entire wall. Here the printed out pictures were tacked up. Next to each group of photos a description of the area covered was posted. They needed to be able to keep track of where a possible suspect might be located. It was the start of a long search for someone described as a ghost. Could they hope to find a person even the CIA and FBI couldn't locate? All they could do was try.

One by one Middy went over the pictures of the people she passed on the street every day. None of them jumped up and yelled: "I'm the killer" to her. By one in the morning Middy's eyes were blurry and a headache was beginning to throb in her temples. It was like looking for one particular piece of straw in a haystack. If only she had deductive powers she might be able to figure out what made the killer tick, but she was the muscle, the one who took the bad guys down on the street. She looked around at the few guys who had stuck it out through the night. Bring him in my sights, she thought to them, I'll blow him clean off the Earth. Of course, she could not use her wind in public, always, always she must be sneaky in using the wind. Often she would appear to have a nervous movement of her hands when actually she was tripping someone running from her and her partner. Her power was more powerful than the gun but handicapped with secrecy. Sometimes she just wanted to let loose and knock a runner to the ground. Instead, she created a small gust of wind to hinder the runner and let Fuller take them down. Sometimes Middy wished she had a different power. If she could just heal there were so many lives she could save. Neither her sister Susan or herself had ever been able to heal. Still, she didn't wish to trade places with Susan or Eric. At least she didn't suffer just being around other people like Susan, or have horrible nightmares the way Eric did. She might be going nowhere with her wind still, there were several bad guys behind bars because of her.

Someone was shaking her shoulder, during her musings Middy had fallen asleep. She opened her eyes a crack to see it was daylight and the room was packed with able bodies. Time to get to work. First, she needed some of the delicious smelling food being cooked.

Fuller was standing at the stove flipping flapjacks and turning bacon. Middy had had no idea Fuller could cook. Occasionally Fuller stirred a pan of eggs, then he deemed everything done and filled plates with the feast. Middy sat down at the crowded table and gave a grateful moan of happiness as she began to heap her plate with food. She stopped only when she saw some of the guys giving her heaping plate sidelong glances. With barely a pause Middy dropped her head and offered a blessing upon their group. "God bless everyone in the room and give them the eyes to see a monster."

There was silence except for a scrap of forks over the plates while everyone enjoyed the feast Fuller had cooked. Finally sated, they all sat back and began to discuss the day's activities. Middy went to the wall where a huge map of the city and the surrounding areas was tacked as well as all the photos the guys had already taken of faces in the areas they had covered. "These are the areas we didn't have time to complete or haven't started yet. If you have a preference, speak up, otherwise, the assignments will be as follows." A loud knock on the door stopped Middy from continuing. Twenty guns were drawn, as each officer reacted to what they deemed may be a threat to Middy. Ritter and Frankie approached the door looking over at the monitor, but all they saw were three badges being held up to the hidden camera.

Frankie opened the door while Ritter and the rest of the room kept their guns leveled. Trust had gone out the window with Albert's finger and Ritter being smashed. One of the men holding up badges spoke up after a brief 'whoa' look flashed on his face at the sight of so many firearms pointed at them. "We are from District 6. We heard about Officer Middleton heading up a bunch of off-duty men in a mad search for the killer and came to volunteer. As far as we know we won't be the only ones showing up to take part in this manhunt. Let's catch this scum," the Officer said.

Frankie turned and looked at Middy as if waiting for orders. "Let them in, the more we have,

the more area we can cover. We were just about
to hand out today's areas to cover. Since some of
these areas are so large let us form three to four-
man teams. For you new guys the areas marked in
blue have been gone over. The photos tacked up
are of likely suspect the teams have come upon. We
are going by this sketch of what the killer may look
like. This was done from several sketches of what
he has looked like in the past. He is called a ghost
because he is so good at disguising himself. The eyes,
however, are something he can only change the color
on. They will always be spaced the same distance
apart as well as having the same general shape.
Don't forget to take a picture of anyone who has the
slightest resemblance to the sketch. By now you all
have a sketch. Okay, now for assignments, speak
now on any preference you may have," Middy paused
and waited for the guys to speak up. The new guys
opted for an area near their district, an area which
was familiar to them. Middy had Ritter, Fuller, and
Frankie following her about on the normal route she
would take daily.

The day seemed to go on and on as one person
after another stopped Middy to talk to her and give
their opinion, pro or con, on her so-called firing as
an officer. They hadn't made it even halfway through
the area Middy wanted to cover when she held up
her hand and called it quits. They were getting
nowhere, it would be better if she stayed locked up
in her home and let the others do the searching. She
opted to cook a decent meal for the guys who were
out searching.

First thing Middy put in the shopping cart

was a huge chocolate sheet cake for the guys. For herself, she had the baker wrap a large slice of double chocolate fudge cake. Already she felt better just knowing she would be eating that slice later. Next, she went all out on steaks and chicken to be grilled. Before dessert, she would serve baked potatoes, corn on the cob and baked beans along with cornbread. It was a meal that would stick to their ribs for the rest of the night. Pleased, she rushed home with her three men to start cooking.

Weary, frustrated men started dragging in later that day. The aroma which greeted them as they entered the house brought a sigh of appreciation to their lips. Suddenly hopes that had begun to sag toughened up. Smiles tugged on their mouths. Soon there was laughter and joking where moments ago lay defeat and hopelessness. It was a defense against all the horror which haunted their lives. Each understood that, and joked to make the other guys have laughter in their life. Coping, coping until the other shoe was dropped, and they had to face the grim reality again.

Looking around at the smiling faces, even Middy's spirits lifted. If this was to be her contribution, then she would do her best to bring these smiles out again. She stood up and began collecting plates. "Cake time," she announced, "My favored part of dinner." That got a laugh from the guys as she cut and dished up the cake. When she sat down with her huge sliced of double chocolate fudge the guys snickered. "Yeah, we can tell." Someone joked.

Middy just smiled and sighed in contentment at the first bite of her prize. She took another large bite of cake and was on the third when the pain hit. Her stomach was a pit of intense pain. Carefully, she put her cake on the table, then tried to stand up. Her body betrayed her as her legs folded and her body jerked with the pain in her stomach. Blackness started to creep in, no matter how hard she fought she couldn't defeat the growing darkness. Soon she couldn't see, but she heard the guys, knew there was panic in their voices, knew it was bad this thing that had hold of her.

"Middleton, Officer Whiting, hold on we are taking you to the hospital."

"Whiting, I'm ordering you, you hear me, Rookie, you are ordered to quit lying on your butt and fight like you have never fought before. You let me down and I'll have you up on charges. You hear me!" That was Fuller.

"Albert, you mad racer, drive." She wasn't certain of that voice. The one voice she didn't hear was the one she wanted to hear, but that voice never spoke up.

It wasn't until the siren died out and Albert braked hard that she began to lose all focus. The darkness was rushing in, she couldn't fight it any longer, and knew she was going to die. When her last remaining conscious fragment began to die away she managed to whisper one word… "mother." As the last of her thinking mind faded she heard the voice she longed to hear. "You die on me, Cupcake, and I'll never forgive you." Then the world was gone.

To the people in the emergency room, it

looked like a hundred cars pulled into the parking area for ambulances. So many people were clustered around the supposed poison victim, they couldn't see her. That is when Dr. Pierce took charge. "Get the hell out of my exam area." The fact such a powerful voice came from the tiny doctor was enough to shock almost everyone into leaving. Only Fuller and Ritter remained. "I said move it!" the doctor said in her most commanding voice. Fuller reluctantly backed off. The doctor gave Ritter a glare. "That means you too."

Ritter didn't even look at the doctor. "She's mine," he said.

"Right at this moment, she is mine. Go fill out the information we need, and sign the permission forms. Back off, now," she said with a determined set to her mouth before she began to bark orders to her nurses.

They invaded Middy's body in so many ways that Ritter wanted to pick her up and take her away. He was too scared to take her from the only hope she had. It was then his mind registered the meaning of Middy's whisper. "Fuller, come here and hold her hand. Watch them closely." Once Fuller took over for Ritter he strolled off so fast it was like his pants were on fire. Stepping outside, away from ears that might overhear his call, Ritter pressed one button on his phone. "Mr. President, Middy needs her mother as soon as possible. We think it is poison," after making certain the boss knew what hospital to go to, Ritter hung up without so much as a goodbye. Now he had to arrange an escort from the airport for Middy's mother. He would take no chances on her getting lost. She had cured his many, many broken bones, surely she could cure Middy her own daughter.

"Fuller," Ritter barked when he once again had his own grip on Middy's hand, "You are in charge of escorting Mrs. Whiting from the airport once she arrives. Lights and sirens all the way, don't even pause for a red light. Understand?"

"Yes, sir. Leave it to me." Fuller turned to the anxious faces watching at a slightly respectful distance. "Listen up. I need volunteers to bring Whiting's mother from the airport. It is to be post haste. I want full uniforms and squad cars, no speed spared. I'll find out the exact time and then we are off. Who wants to go?" Every hand was raised, and for a moment Fuller was choked up with emotion before he shook it off and put on his officer face. At that moment a lab tech came rushing over to the tiny doctor and all the men leaned in just a little trying to catch what was said.

The doctor spoke softly to Ritter giving a worried glance in the direction of the men silently waiting for word. "You are wrong," Ritter stated flatly. Silence fell over the exam room. Nobody moved, some even forgot to take a breath as they kept vigil. It wasn't until Fuller indicated they needed to prepare to go to the airport that the group left leaving Ritter as the silent guardian.

Full uniforms, lights, and sirens, the streets of the city were left quiet and in wonder at the large force which blared down the streets. If some of the patrols were missing squad cars they never reported it. One of their own was in danger, all stops were pulled out.

At the airport were several black cars, this was the Secret Service. They too came to take Mrs. Whiting to the hospital. For a moment Fuller feared they would have to endure a pissing contest to get Mrs. Whiting, yet the urgency with which this little woman strolled through the airport put them all in their place. The SS had her in one of their cars, but the police surrounded them and blared off down the road. Patrol cars kept all intersections open. There would be no delay, of this they were certain.

Chapter Seven

RECOVERY

The SS already had a team at the hospital. One of their charges was down and another was on her way to risk her life. Times like this they were edgy and very bossy. Thankfully the hospital had experienced this before when Ritter had been dying, so the area was fairly clear by the time the first team arrived. Someone had even brought down the barriers used to block sight of Ritter's old room. Dr. Pierce was biting her lip, trying to keep her mouth shut as she was ordered out of the area. At the last moment, she wasn't able to just leave. "I will be staying. This is my patient and I'm going to do everything I can to help her, SS or not," she declared.

"Ma'am, this is a matter for the United States Government. This patient is under our protection. Nobody is allowed to treat her except the person on her way here. This has to be a secure area. That means neither you are any other unknowns are allowed within the area. Now, please exit," explained an SS man. As he was talking, an IV and stand was set up with some strange looking substance inside bag.

"You are not giving that to MY patient," the irate doctor protested.

"No, ma'am. This is not intended for your patient," was the comeback. The SS guard touched his ear. "Say again." Turning, he gave a thumbs up to Ritter, who was still standing holding Middy's hand. "She is here," he confirmed verbally.

"Who? Who is here? I have a right to know who is going to treat my patient," demanded Dr. Pierce.

"The best damn healer in the world. Now leave and do not return."

More black suits were rushing down the hallway as Dr. Pierce reluctantly let a black suit lead her away. She stared at the figure in the center of the suits. A thin woman who looked as if a paper fan would blow her over. Was this woman a doctor? She thought not. Dr. Pierce paused long enough at the door to witness the woman offer out her arm to have the IV hooked up to it.

No sooner had the IV been inserted in her arm than Felith reached out and touched Middy's forehead. "No time to send for Eric and Susan, you are going to have to take the brunt of it. Eat and drink while I start," she ordered Fred.

Immediately Fred grabbed an energy bar and shoved the whole thing in his mouth. He chewed like mad before guzzling a bottle of some evil looking stuff. Ritter had watched him out of the corner of his eye, most of his focus was on Middy. "You have to let go of her hand now," Felith said.

Ritter didn't hesitate to release his lifeline to Middy instantly. From Fred's reaction, he knew this was serious and there was no time left to argue. When Fred reached out and placed his hands on Middy's mom's shoulders, Ritter couldn't help but ask what he was doing. For most of his own healing, he had been out of it. Observing the process now he had to wonder why was this guy allowed to touch her? "What are you doing? I thought nobody was allowed to touch Mrs. Whiting."

Through clenched teeth, Fred answered, "I'm giving her my strength. It isn't like when someone else touches her. They drain her."

"Fred I have to stop and recharge. Open a bar for me and a drink, then turn the IV up. I can't stop for long. It is eating her insides," Felith said.

Ritter blanched, he had heard of this stuff it was highly classified. For someone to be using it here, they would have had to enter a very secure laboratory to steal it. It was unstoppable as far as he knew. He looked with new respect at the skinny little woman eating a bar and drinking the weird stuff. For her to know what it was doing inside Middy... well, it was unbelievable. He had to help. "I want to help. You can use my strength too."

"Nobody except for the family has ever been able to give their energy to my wife," Fred said.

Ritter downed one of the bars they had been eating and guzzled a drink. He nodded. "All I can do is try. It might help. You don't have the other two to help, and this thing is relentless."

"We don't have time for me to faint. It is

determined to live and to live it has to kill Middy. Do it," hers was the final say, and Fred nodded as she touched Middy again closing her eyes.

Fred placed his hands on her shoulders once more and motion Ritter to touch her also. Feeling only slightly self-conscious, Ritter placed one hand on her back and the other on her arm. My strength to you, my strength to you, he thought over and over at Middy's mom. At first, he didn't think anything was happening, then he felt the slightest bit of weakness creeping up on him. He didn't relent, didn't pull back because he knew the impossible odds Middy faced. This was serious, like nuclear bomb serious.

It was only moments before both Ritter and Fred felt Felith tremble. "Stop, stop now. You are no good to her dead, stop." The last plea seemed to reach Felith and she collapsed back into Fred's arms. Gently he laid her out and tried to soothe her with his voice. "It is okay. We are going to save our Middy. She is a fighter, don't forget that."

If he could do that for his wife, then Ritter could do the same for Cupcake. He leaned over her close to her ear and whispered, "I should beat your butt for putting us all through this. You aren't even trying to fight this, damn you, fight."

The three people fighting so hard to save Middy began to eat and drink again. The door was abruptly pushed open and Eric walked in. "Am I in time? I started as soon as the vision hit me. It is bad isn't it, really bad." He gasped as he tried to catch his breath. It was clear he had been running to get there in time to save Middy.

"I'm not going to lie, Eric. This is the worse stuff I've ever seen. We have a fight on our hands. Any ideas?" Felith asked.

"We can either take turns or both of us hit it with all we have," Eric mused.

Felith and Fred shook their heads no at the all-out blasting. "We can't afford to faint. We are the only thing standing between death and Middy," Felith said. "We do it in short burst clearing as much of it as we can. And we have to keep going back over areas cleared because this thing doesn't stay clear. It is fast and evil. I make a little progress, then have to go back and clean it up all over again." It was more explanation than Felith ever gave, that alone had Fred and Eric scared.

"Let's set up your IV, son," Fred said, starting to string another bag up for Eric.

Ritter had watched and listened to the interchange between parents and child. Right off Ritter thought he didn't have a battery. "I'll do him," he stated flatly. His tone of voice said he'd not take any arguing. Ritter was relieved that everyone just nodded.

Eric ate at a frantic pace barely chewing as he washed it down with the strange drink. The four turned as one and approached Middy. Fred behind Felith, and Ritter behind Eric they began. Eric gasped when he first felt the thing inside Middy, but he didn't waver placing a hand solidly on her arm, he fought beside his mother trying to save his sister's life.

Ritter was really feeling it now, the draining of

his strength was so deep it began to hurt him inside. Every moment he spent being this human battery he felt more admiration for Middy and her family. Nobody on Earth was as talented as this family. They should be treated as kings, worshiped, honored. As he mused these unlikely thoughts, he felt his charge starting to sag. "Eric, stop and take a break you won't do her any good flat on your back.

Reluctantly Eric pulled back and with trembling hands tried to open a bar to eat. Ritter took it from him and ripped it open, he then opened a bottle of the drink for Eric before feeding his own weakness. For the first time, he began to doubt they would be able to save Middy. It was like an ugly hole opened in his chest spilling his lifeblood out upon the floor. Filled with the horror of it all Ritter sagged into a chair, allowing his weakness to consume him. No! No, he would not let that monster take Middy from him. He'd give his life essence to Eric to heal Middy with if he needed. He prepared himself to do just that, to give all that was inside him to save Middy, when Eric shook his head.

"We need real food inside us to boost us up," Eric said, his voice so weak they could barely hear him. "Bobby Jay," he called out and almost instantly Bobby was at his side. "Bring us a huge meal, you know the sort." Bobby nodded and was on his phone before he reached the divider curtain. Eric wasn't done with giving orders, "Mother, next break you try to sleep a few minutes, then we switch and I'll do the same. This thing is almost stronger than both of us, we need to hit it constantly, so we will alternate for a while. That way it won't have a chance to undo what good has been done. Constantly attacking it will hopefully wear it away. It is going to be a long night."

With the meal arrived Susan and a young boy. Susan's face was grim as the feelings of her family hit her. They all had doubts they could save Middy. "I want you all to stop thinking this is impossible. I've brought two new batteries, there is plenty of food and my sister is a fighter, so buck up and start thinking more positive thoughts." She watched as they slowly chided themselves for nearly giving up, and took encouragement from Susan's words.

Felith turned Middy over to Eric and turned to face Susan. "You will not risk this child's life," she more or less ordered Susan.

York was immediately in Felith's face, "Susan didn't ask me to do this. This is my idea, and I have the right to help if I want." Tex smirked behind them silently. York had certainly taken to the ability to make his own decisions.

"You, go beef up for when we need relief," Susan instructed Ritter. He was reluctant, it was his job to protect Middy, it just wasn't right he should stop helping. "You won't do her any good flat on your face, go!"

As much as Ritter resisted leaving if only briefly, he knew Susan was right. He bent over Middy and whispered in her ear, "You better start fighting harder. You will never be rid of me if you don't wake up. Wake up!"

"You finally came to your senses," Susan told him, with a nod of approval.

Yeah, Ritter thought, but too late. And maybe he had been too late to save her. I can't lose you,

Cupcake. You have to survive, come back to me...
please. He ate like mad trying to stuff himself so full
he wouldn't have to take a break again. The hot meal,
bars, and drinks went inside him churning as his
own fears tried to take over. He couldn't let the fear
and depression take over. He had to be strong for
Middy's sake.

"York, go eat and rest. Mother you take over
for Eric. We need one of you to take over for York,
and I only have a few minutes left in me," Susan
ordered the forces as she saw fit. Nobody questioned
her. They were her family and knew where her
powers laid. Ritter and Fred were there almost
immediately. Susan didn't chide anyone, just stepped
aside and went to eat.

By one in the morning, both healers were
nearly completely drained despite the frequent
breaks as they alternated. It was apparent in the
whiteness around their lips and the slumping of
their shoulders. Of course, the batteries were in
the same shape, with each session causing them
physical pain now. They all had IVs hooked to their
arms and the supply of bars and drinks was nearly
at end. Desperation and determination were the
only expressions on the faces of those fighting what
mankind thought was a hopeless battle.

Two hours passed in utter agony for everyone.
Fred was on the verge of telling Felith to stop when
she called everyone to her. "Come quickly. I have
it isolated in one small spot. We need to all work
at once to finish it off. Eric joins me, everyone else
supports us."

Fred looked more worried than he had all

night. He knew this was it, they either got rid of this horrible thing or Felith and Eric would pass out and that would mean the end of Middy. Fred held his hand up to stop them all. "Hold a moment. Tex," he called out. Immediately Tex stepped through the curtains. "Get that snooty doctor and two crash carts. She may need to revive several of us after this last attempt."

Almost immediately the snooty doctor was shoved through the curtains to be followed by two crash carts. The doctor swore when she saw the condition of the people in the room, but Tex shut her up. "You are to observe and should anyone drop dead save them," he held up his hand to stop her protest before she could voice it. "You will not interfere in any other way. Stand here." Looking at Tex with eyes like daggers the doctor did as she was told to do, standing there watching what she thought of as a freak show.

Felith and Eric attacked the last bit of horror drawing relentlessly on the two batteries they each had. Felith could feel the darkness starting to creep up on her and pushed all the harder. She couldn't, wouldn't let her daughter die. Eric was just as determined, fighting his own darkness as his strength began to wither away. It was a suicide attempt given by both healers at the same time. Darkness took them over and they fell into the waiting arms of two SS men. York was already out cold, Susan was swaying and went down with a thump. Ritter and Fred just sort of slipped to the floor. It had been an all-out effort by them all. Their last thoughts were 'Middy live'.

Doctor Pierce's eyes went wide, but she didn't hesitate to wade in and start checking pulses. The hearts of the two who had been touching her patient had stopped, the rest were out cold, although the boy barely had a pulse. She needed help, but one look at the SS men standing over her told her nobody else would be allowed in.

Bobby Jay appeared as if out of the blue. He ripped Eric's shirt off and lubed the paddles of the defibrillator machine. Not waiting for approval, he shocked Eric as if he had done this many times before. He started the machine to charging again, even as he felt for a pulse on Eric's neck. Ignoring everything around him Bobby Jay concentrated only on Eric. This was his to do, his part of this partnership was keeping Eric alive. "Come on, Eric, Bruce will kill me if I return without you. Then they will come to shoot Bruce or send him to the gas chamber. You don't want that, do you?" That seemed to work and Eric took a deep breath before rolling to his side falling into a deep sleep. "Blankets, and six cots," Bobby Jay called out to the men in black waiting outside the curtains. They were men used to there being such emergencies. Not only were blankets brought, but warm blankets.

Fred had crawled over to his wife. He knocked the doctor's hand away when she tried to check Felith's pulse. His voice croaked with the deep fatigue, he explained, "Your touch will drain her even more. My touch won't. I'll tell you once we get a pulse." He brushed Felith's hair off her face and began to talk to her. "You promised you wouldn't die for good. The kids are all here, you can't disappoint them. Come on, honey, fight. Fight for me and the kids." He kept on in that same tone of voice encouraging, pleading. At times even threatening.

Doctor Pierce shocked the patient once again, only warning Fred at the last moment. She was relieved when he nodded and said, "Pulse."

Susan and York were both being attended by two black suits. The one treating Susan looked particularly grim. He would pause only long enough to direct the man treating York. Soon everyone was in a cot with warm blankets covering them and hooked up to fresh IVs. Doctor Pierce was slightly impressed with the professional way this team of SS men took care of their charges. She couldn't help but wonder if they had to do this often. Unfortunately, she was removed from the curtain area as soon as her charge was breathing. She didn't even have a chance to ask one question or examine her real patient.

Late into the next day the family slept, no one stirred or indicated in any manner they were becoming aware of the world around them. Black suits paced with worry all except one who slept with his charge. Twice he had proved he would go all the way to save her. Twice he faced down death. There he lay as helpless as his charge, unaware of the care and respect that was given him by the black suits watching over the fallen.

There was another vigil, out in the waiting room of the hospital, an army of foot soldiers in police uniforms kept shifting. Officers came and went unsatisfied, angry, looking for blood without an enemy to beat up. Word had filtered out about the horror which Middy had been subjected to, something unbeatable, a death sentence. So they waited, waited for word of Middy's passing. That is all but a few. The men in Middy's little task force kept busy searching the streets for an elusive killer. Now more than ever the need to find this madman raged in their blood. Vengeance, vengeance for all their fellow officers laying buried in the ground, and most of all for Officer Whiting. They couldn't stop, wouldn't stop, until they found him and made him pay.

The newspapers and news services were full of speculation over the death of the Butterfly Whisperer. People who had never had an opinion before voiced disbelief and grief at the idea she was dead. She was suddenly everyone's golden girl and the man who had fired her was under attack from groups of citizens who now saw the firing of their favorite girl as a crime.

While the world exploded in grief and horror at what they thought was Middy's death, she slept soundly in a private room where all her family had been moved. There was barely room to walk between the sleeping people. As with all hard healing, the healers and the batteries were sapped of all energy. This section of the hospital was shut down to all but the Secret Service.

Like dead bodies they lay on the cots, covered with warm blankets, plugged into weird looking IVs. It was more like something you'd see on a science fiction show than in a hospital. And then the bodies began to wake.

York was the first to open his eyes. For a

moment he seemed confused looking around with fear in his eyes until he saw Susan in the cot beside him. Like a wet noodle, he let his body pour off his cot falling to his knees beside her cot. "Food, lots and lots of food," he said as if to the air, but he knew Tex was listening. He was always listening for any hint of danger. So weak he could not hold his head up any longer York let it rest on Susan's cot. The aroma of french fries, burgers, fried chicken, buttered corn on the cob, and peach cobbler roused York. He let Tex help him back to his own cot and hand him a paper plate filled with so many good smelling foods York was certain he had died and gone to heaven. Never has so much food gone into one young boy so fast. When he at last burped and lay back on his cot, his face held the hugest smile of contentment.

Fred was the next one to raise his head and look for Felith. From then on he had eyes only for her as she slept. Fred ate watching for Felith's chest to rise and fall. Too often he had come close to losing her to the healing. As much as he agonized over what might happen when she went to heal someone he couldn't deny her doing what was natural to her. She hadn't lost a patient yet, but last night... last night he had feared their daughter would be the first person his talented wife could not save. He'd be haunted with the sinking feeling he had felt last night. Lost, he had been lost, unable to help the people he loved more than pouring his life into them.

Susan, Felith, and Eric woke almost as one. Both Eric and Felith wanted to check Middy out first. Fred, Tex, and Bobby Jay together convinced them to eat first and rest.

Susan kept trying to feel any thoughts surfacing in Middy's mind, it scared her that she couldn't find anything. This wasn't like Middy at all, even in sleep her sister's mind was working on problems. Where are you Middy, she wondered.

Almost as if she heard Susan's question an electric shock went through Middy's body. It was as if a bolt of lightning had run the length of her body. She jerked violently as if starting a seizure, then sat bolt upright. "The cake, it was the cake," she cried out before realizing where she was. Her family came and stood around her. Susan's SS man offered her a plate of food. Her mother touched her and she felt the warmth flowing through her as it kept searching, searching every part of Middy for the poison. When finished her mother said one word, "Clean". Such a sigh of relief went up from the others in the room that Middy wondered just what had happened to her. She had figured out the cake was poisoned just before she passed out, but from the reaction of those she loved, it had to have been more. Looking up at her mother, she asked, "What was it?"

Felith sat down heavily on the cot occupied by Ritter. "It was a horror. Almost more than we could handle. I was afraid Mids, afraid I'd lose you."

The grim look set on everyone's face, especially on her father's face was enough to convince Middy that it had been horrible. She looked back at her mother, "Did you... did you die?"

Felith nodded, "And Eric," she stated flatly as if it hurt her to even think of it. "I want to leave Dog with you. He will help you hunt down this killer."

Middy was shaking her head. "No, Dog will

not be happy here, there is no place for him to run."

"Like heck, there isn't. I run with Bruce every night I can. Don't tell me you gave up jogging, Mids," Eric said as if shocked.

Middy shook her head, "You know jogging is not my thing. I'm more the bird watcher sort. Safe on a bench watching birds with a large slice of…," she broke off realizing chocolate cake was forever ruined for her. She laid back feeling broken hearted over something she has loved being ruined forever. Middy was about to turn away. Then, so her family wouldn't see the sorrow on her face, except that is when she saw Ritter sleeping like the dead behind her mother.

Like a bowl of pudding Middy slipped off the cot she was on, and would have crawled across the floor to touch Ritter if Tex and Bobby Jay hadn't lifted her up. "What happened to him," she demanded.

"He is like us, a battery," Eric said. "He did me while Dad did mom until Susan and York arrived to give some relief," Eric turned solemn, "We were losing, Mids. That thing was so strong we began to question if we would be able to save you."

They all became somber, unable to voice the horror which had held them so long in its grasp. It was Middy who broke the silence as she punched Ritter in the arm. "You stupid man, you don't even like me. Why did you do it?"

Middy became aware that her family was looking at her oddly. "What?" She asked, irritated with the whole thing.

Susan spoke in her most no-nonsense voice, "Sweetie, that man loves you so much he'd rather die than let you feel hurt for one more moment. His thoughts were clear to me, practically shouting."

She stood open-mouthed for a moment, then had Bobby Jay and Tex help her back to her cot where she dug into the food as if there was no tomorrow. She had a lot to think over.

Ritter woke while Middy was eating, he felt confused, nothing seemed right to him. It wasn't until his seeking eyes located Middy stuffing her face as fast as she could that it all came back to him. Relief filled him up and he realized he was starving. Trouble was, his muscles wouldn't work right and he kept landing flat on his back over and over. It was Middy's father who came to his rescue, a more serious man Ritter had yet to see.

After propping Ritter up, Fred gave him a plate of food filled to overflowing, then he sat down full of purpose next to Ritter. "I'm going to give you some unwanted advice, son. My daughter worshiped you before you nearly died. I don't know what you said to her to tear her heart apart, but by doing that you may have ruined any chance you have with her. My women are all very stubborn. You'll not find another bunch of women as stubbornly set in their ways as my family. Middy idolizes her mother and copies her in many ways, one is that determination not to show a weakness, to admit to being hurt. The only hope you have is to just be there for her. Let her see on her own that you do actually care about her. You try to sway Middy and you are a dead man to her. Believe me, I know my girls. Have patience, it is all you can do. With that, I'll let you get to the nourishment.

Good luck."

He was gone in a flash, off to attend his wife, leaving Ritter with a great deal to ponder. Foremost was the thought that Middy still cared. Maybe, just maybe, he hadn't lost her after all. That thought went down with the last bite of food and Ritter fell asleep again, his plate clattering to the floor.

Middy picked up Ritter's plate, her face thoughtful as if she was trying to figure out their next step in finding the killer. Perhaps her mother was right and she needed a pet of some sort. Only nothing had presented itself to Middy offering to live with her. Doomed, that is what she was, doomed to a lonely life. She looked around at the people in the room as the color began to creep into their faces. She was wrong, she wasn't alone. These were her family, the people who loved her. The urge for action hit her, she needed to be out there looking for the killer, making the people safe again. The thought crossed her mind that she needed to be legal in some manner, officially able to investigate and bring in the monsters of this world. Turning to her family, she started to tell them she wanted to get a private detective certificate when the door swung open spilling Fuller and Frankie into the room.

"My God! You are alive!" The astonishment in Fuller's voice said it all. They had been kept in the dark milling around without a rudder to direct them, and there she stood whole and apparently well. "But, how? We were told it was hopeless. The men have been keeping a vigil waiting to hear the news you were dead. We said enough is enough. So here we are, out to find out the truth for ourselves. How did this miracle happen?"

Middy gave her family a wary look. "It must have been just that, a miracle. Or it wasn't what they thought it was, we might consider that as the explanation."

"The main thing is you are alive. We need you to plan the next bit of the search. The guys have continued to work on the grid you set up, we have gobs of pictures for you to look at." Fuller blushed in an embarrassed manner. "Oh Damn! I've been so thoughtless. Are you even well enough to go home?"

Middy looked to her mother for the answer, "Mom? Oh, this is my mother, my father, my sister, and my brother. They came to be with me," Middy said, introducing her family to yet another part of her family, the guys. "Meet Fuller and Frankie two of my friends here."

Slowly Fuller and Frankie made their way down the line of her relatives greeting and shaking each person's hand. Last in line was Eric, Middy did not like the gleam of mischief in his eyes.

While he shook Fuller's hand Eric said, "You are my sister's partner and the first person shot. I told my sister I would come help with your healing, but she turned me down flat." Frankie and Fuller, both looked over at Middy, Fuller looking very uncomfortable at the conversation. Eric continued, "I don't know why. I mean, just because I'm a Veterinarian, I know my medicine, believe me, I'm one of the best."

For one moment Fuller looked frozen, then he burst out laughing so hard he had to hold his sides to keep from busting a gut. And the tension in the room with Middy and her family went 'poof'.

"I believe that the doctor, who has been camping in the halls, has to examine Middy one last time before she can leave the hospital," Felith said.

"We'll make certain she comes right away," Frankie said in a businesslike voice. "Leave it to us."

Within moments it sounded as if an army was marching through the hospital. The door opened and the little doctor was escorted into the room with enough men in blue to make any crook shake in their boots. She looked nervously around the room until her eyes fell on Middy. "My God, this isn't possible." She declared. "I know what I saw was an impossibility, but I never expected this!"

Black suited Tex stepped up behind the doctor and spoke in a whisper in her ear, "You are to never mention what happened here again. If you say one more word you will be locked away for the rest of your natural life. Am I clear?"

Dr. Pierce gulped and nodded. There was no doubt in her mind he meant every word. Quickly she examined Middy while mumbling to herself as she realized her patient was more than fit to leave the hospital. "I'll sign the forms needed and you will be out of here as soon as the office processes you through," she told the room in general. A cheer went up from the men crowding the hallway and part of the room.

Very soberly Middy thanked the doctor, "Thank you for all you did for me, Dr. Pierce." The tiny doctor blushed and nodded her head, for once she had no words to say. This was always the best moment when the patient went home.

When Middy opened the door to her home, she stepped back, startled at the sight of dozens of flowers filling every shelf, table, and window sill. She turned around to find pleased smiles on the faces of the flood of men behind her. Frankie was the one who spoke up for them all, "Well, we missed you, so we bought flowers for our gal."

Fighting back tears, Middy opened her arms to the guys. They came one by one hugging her back, some so hard they lifted her off the floor. Frumpy Middy had never received or given so many hugs. When she reached the end of the long line hugging her, a huge beast came bounding through the door and bounced on her giving huge doggy kisses. "Dog, how did you get here?"

Suddenly something flew in the still open door and attacked Dog. It was almost as if an invisible force was all over Dog, here there, everywhere. The large dog jumped, leaped, and rolled on the floor looking like he was having some sort of fit. The attacks were swift, so swift that it was hard to get a look at what was attacking the huge dog. Middy's mother ended the whole thing with one word, "Freeze." Dog's huge body immediately froze in position, his face a study in the woebegone.

The attacker buzzed over Dog's head for a moment before zipping over to hover in front of Middy. She was at a loss for words. Nothing like this had happened to her before, and this, this tiny hummingbird in front of her seemed to be expecting something from her. Middy did the only thing she could think of doing, her voice soft so as not to frighten the little guy Middy said, "Thank you." That seemed to satisfy the little one and it darted off to visit her many flowers.

The room was totally silent as the occupants stood amazed at what had just happened in front of them. Nobody would ever believe them if they spoke of it, so it was sort of made into one of those things a group of people knew but would never speak of except to another group member. It was Susan who broke the silence, "I think you have been claimed, Mids. Mom, you best take him home. I don't think the little one will tolerate him in Middy's life."

Dog, a huge formidable beast of a protector, belly crawled over to and out of the door, where he lay down as if to stop any intruder from going into the room where his family was staying. Once he glanced quickly to see where the little devil bird was before sighing and laying his head down on his paws.

"Poor Dog, he was so excited to have found you. To be beaten by such a little fellow has to be a big blow to his ego," Eric said. A few chuckles came from the men in blue crowded in Middy's place. "And I thought my cat might intimidate him," Eric said, shaking his head as if he found the whole business beyond him. "I think even Bruce would quiver before such a fearsome protector."

They all watched the little bird flitting between flowers, feeding on the nectar still in them. He went to a particularly beautiful arrangement and dropped like a stone to the floor. It was Dog who streaked across the floor first and sniffed the little one's body. His lips curled in such a fierce snarl the officers stood their ground rather than anger the beast. Middy cried out an anguished "No" as she ran to pick up the limp body of the hummingbird. Dog forced his body between her and the flowers. Susan and Felith voiced their concern at the same moment to stay away from the flowers.

Eric had eyes only for the little bird. He placed a finger on the body and spoke in a low voice to Middy and their mother, "Poison, not the same as Mids received. There is a faint chance I can bring him out of it, only faint, Mids. I'll try my heart out." With that, he closed his eyes and concentrated on his smallest patient ever. After a moment he felt hands touching him giving him more power than he could have produced on his own. Clearing the poison wasn't the difficulty, keeping the heart beating took a heavy toll on Eric. The little one's heart beat at such a fantastic rate that Eric felt as if his own heart would beat out of his chest in time with it. At last, the heart caught and beat on its own. Eric stepped back in relief and exhaustion. "I'll mix up a formula you can feed him. He is not to sip from any of these flowers again," he said as he turned to the officers watching intensely. "Go buy quite a few of the hummingbird feeders they sell. Hurry the little guy will need to eat very, very soon. The rest of you clear the flowers out. We can't be certain how many have been contaminated. Don't smell them, in fact, wear a cloth over your nose and mouth."

Middy stirred then, the little bird still cradled in her hands. "Take them all to the CSI Unit and warn them of the danger. Frankie, Albert, you check out the rest of the house for anything that might be out of place or suspicious. Be careful." The little bird

in her hands began to stir. Middy thought of the
terror she had felt when the little bird dropped to the
floor and of Eric's heroic effort in saving it. "Now
you are truly one of us, little one. Welcome home,"
Middy whispered.

As if it had heard her, the little fellow's wings
began to beat like crazy and he was off flitting about
the house like a frantic fairy. York jumped up and
placed himself in front of a batch of flowers, as did
Fred. Susan, however, stood rock still. York and Tex
both watched Susan intently as it was obvious she
was concentrating on something. "He understands
now and won't touch the flowers in here," she said.

"Thank you, sis. You saved us a lot of worries,"
Middy said. The door open and in came two officers
with their arms filled with hummingbird feeders.
Eric came out of the kitchen to take control of the
feeders, setting them up with his special formula
and having the guys hang them around the house.
If anyone thought it was foolish to hang the feeders
inside the house they didn't say anything. It was
as if they had adopted this tiny bird as a mascot or
something.

Chapter Eight

DO WHAT?

Eric couldn't stay as his practice, where he lived, needed him, but he checked over the little bird one last time before leaving and instructed Middy in mixing the formula for the feeders. Middy was sorry to see Eric go, they had always been a team when growing up. Only the fact she knew he would call her, if he ever felt she needed him, made the saying goodbye bearable.

Her mother and father were the next to leave. All it took, was a call for help with a sick child, and her mother was anxious to get to the child. They had a short conversation over Dog staying, but the little hummingbird nixed that idea the first time Dog approached Middy.

That left Susan. She had her dog Goldie with her and entertained the guys with a demonstration by Goldie and her dancing together with York. It was one of the most amazing things Middy had ever seen. She clapped and cheered along with the guys at the wonderful dance the trio put on. It was a shame when their evening was interrupted by the General. Still, the showdown between Tex and the General was a pleasure to watch.

Middy had never liked the way the General would just show up. He thought he could order them around. They were not property, not officially part of any government team, yet the General felt he owned them and they should jump at his barked orders. When one of the guys opened the door and the General walked in, Tex's gun was out so fast it was like a western showdown. The General threw up his hands and Tex's gun was joined by the rest of the armed officers' hardware in the room.

"Oh, damn! Do we have to go through this again? You know who I am. How do you even know I'm here for Miss Susan? I could be here to talk with Middleton." the General protested.

Tex turned to Ritter, "Did this man make an appointment in advance to see Mids?"

"He did not," Ritter said, drawing his own gun.

"But I'm the General, the President personally assigned me as a go-between to the Whitings," sputtered the General when faced down by both Ritter and Tex

"All contact with my subject must be approved in advance. This is a well-known fact. I will not allow her to be put in danger," Tex said. "The standing order is an appointment first and approval."

The General's shoulders slumped in defeat. "I'll be back after you are contacted." With that, he beat a hasty retreat.

As soon as the General left Middy fell over laughing. She looked at Tex and said, "You are my hero." Susan laughed, "It does make my day every time Tex sends him packing. The time he had the General's car shot was a real highlight of my day."

"He stopped trying to order me around about the second time he visited the farm," Middy said.

"That's because you scare him. He isn't foolish enough to tempt having your wrath pointed at him," Susan gasped out between laughs. The entire room turned to look at Middy just as Tex's phone rang.

"Yes, Mr. President. He may come for an appointment. No, sir, I will not allow anyone to approach Miss Susan without an appointment. Tell him tough shit." Mouths gaped open at Tex's words to the highest person in the whole country. Tex hung up. It was clear he was irritated. "Next time I'll just shoot the twerp."

A tentative knock sounded at the door. A uniformed officer was the closest and answered the knock. It was the General. "I have an appointment with Miss Susan Whiting," the General said turning to Susan. "Miss Whiting, you are needed in a rather urgent matter. We will leave immediately."

"They didn't tell you, General? Who thinks you are a security risk?" Susan asked, there was no doubt she knew the answer, she only wanted him to voice it.

"Miss Susan, you know we can't discuss this here. Come with me and you will be briefed by the proper person," the General almost begged.

"General, don't you think it is possible I have plans already? Has that thought entered any of your minds?" Susan asked.

"But, Miss Susan, your country needs you most urgently. What can possibly take precedence over that?" He declared.

"Finding my sister's stalker, a man who has killed numerous people just to cause her pain. I can find this monster, and I will before I leave," Susan promised.

Middy was horrified. Her little sister getting anywhere near this monster was unthinkable. Her thoughts were like a scream inside Susan's mind. Susan turned a troubled face to look at Middy. "Mids? Mids, I've hunted much worse than him. Calm down. I can do this. Tell her, Tex."

Tight-lipped Tex did as he was asked, although he didn't want to put Susan in this madman's sight. "Miss Susan is able to track a dandelion seed in a stiff wind. She is that good."

"You don't understand. Susan, this man is crazy, he kills just to torment the survivors. Look at what he did to my fellow officers, to Ritter, and to me. He is more dangerous than anything you have come up against. You can't defend yourself. What happens to us should he kill you? What about mom and dad, or Eric, or York. We all need you in our lives. It will be the death of me should anything happen to you. I don't know if I could go on. What would be the point of living, knowing I had killed my own sister. Please, Susan, don't do this."

Susan hadn't thought of this, this anguish from her sister, it tore at her heart to think how much Middy cared for her, then she was hit by York's terror at the thought of her leaving him. It was too much, she gave in to their feelings and her resolve caved. "Alright, I'll go be a spy. Let's go, General. Come on York, Tex." It was with a heavy heart, she left Middy, more than anything she wanted Middy to be safe. Having come so close to losing her had left Susan shaken. Of all the possibles in the world, the possibility of losing Middy had been the most real, so very, very real, and so close.

While Middy was persuading Susan to go and not try to find the monster in Middy's life, the public was making the officials sweat. They wanted Middy reinstated, her records wiped clean. The outcry was so huge, that they gave in and the captain prepared to face an angry Middleton.

The day after Susan left to go play spy for the United States, Middy received a summons from her old captain. She started to refuse to go, as the thought was still in her not to endanger anyone else. Too often she had seen what this madman would do, for no other reason than to torment her. She had felt his wicked hand herself, the depths he would go to just to kill her. It was clear, this monster had run out of patience, and wanted her dead. Yet, in the end, she went to see what was going on.

The reception by the guys was more than she could have ever anticipated. There were cheerful greetings, men coming up to pat her on the back. It was the complete opposite of the way she had been treated as a rookie in the department. But then a great deal had happened over the months she served as a police officer. Just brushing against that thought brought the horror back to Middy. She almost turned around and left. It was that stubborn streak in her that made Middy continue on to the Captain's office.

She went on the attack even as she entered the office, "What is this about? We agreed I'd stay away to protect the men. This is bull calling me in here. What are you trying to do, start it up all over again?"

Unfortunately, she had started her rant before the door was closed and the men heard her. There were open mouths and troubled looks passed between the men. This was something they had never suspected, the whole thing of her being fired had been planned? Low conversations were started, heads shook in denial, one or two fists slammed into desks. The whole thing went against who they were, they were the protectors, never should a woman make such a sacrifice for them. It was unreasonable, yet they were angry, angry at Middy for making them feel less than they were, men. And angry at their captain for making them all feel guilty over having let a fellow officer down.

Ritter stood with his back against the office door trying to hear what was going on inside. He had seen the change in the officers who had overheard the truth. Who did they hate more Middy or the system which had allowed such a grossly unfair action as one small woman being branded for the sake of others? He was prepared to enter that office and bodily carry Middy out if needed. Not that he doubted Middy's ability to handle things herself. Who was he fooling? He admitted it to himself, he just didn't want to let her out of his sight. Ritter had almost lost her. The monster had nearly killed her, and Ritter would not stand by and not be there standing over her, watching, protecting his greatest treasure. Only she wasn't his. Not yet.

Inside the office tempers were flaring to red hot. "We are doing you a favor by reinstating you. Don't you understand? This is what the public wants, they are on our backs about this. And besides you won't be coming back as a rookie, you'll have full status, a grown-up cop so to speak. That should make you happy," the Captain argued.

"My lips are moving so I must be talking. Listen for a change, Captain. It wouldn't matter if they gave me your job, I won't endanger the men! Got it?" Her face was starting to show color, a very bad sign. At her side, her fingers began to twitch. Anyone with any sense would have beat a hasty retreat. "You know what happened to my last partner just because he was with me? Fuller was shot, he almost died. I won't be responsible for that happening again."

The Captain didn't take the hints thrown his way, either that or he was totally ignorant of the power in Middy's hands. Since her family did not advertise their powers, he was most likely ignorant. The papers on the Captain's desk began to flutter. Middy was losing it, and she knew it. She took a couple of deep breaths before raising her hand as if pushing the Captain away. The wind pent up inside Middy released and hit him square in the chest, knocking him back into his desk chair. "The answer is no. Don't bother me again," Middy said as she stomped over and jerked the office door open. Still fuming, she continued out of the station and down to the pizza place. She needed some comfort food in the worst way. It had scared her to realize she had been about to blow the captain clear out of the station.

The news media caught up to Middy before she reached Pizza Bums. "How does it feel to be a police officer again, Miss Whiting? Were you surprised?" Questions came from every direction, like bullets flying overhead. Ritter was there before Middy could work up a good berating. "Miss Whiting has turned down the Captain's kind offer. I believe she has other plans which may be revealed in the future. Now please excuse us, as it has been a tiring day and we need to eat some of this fine pizza," he said, inwardly grinding his teeth to keep from slugging a few of the more pushy interviewers. Diplomacy was not a skill in which Ritter was gifted.

Pizza Bums was almost empty when Middy entered. The tables slowly filled up around Middy's table. Middy, however, refused to acknowledge the fact that reporters were surrounding her, instead, getting down to the serious business of ordering. Ritter stood within easy reach of Middy trying to keep back a smile as he listened to her order. "Pepperoni, light on the sauce, double Pepperoni, double onions, double green peppers, double mushrooms, double jalapeno, and triple mozzarella cheese." The waiter didn't even crack a smile as he took Middy's order. The more she loaded the pizza the larger the tip he expected and he knew she tipped well.

The first slice of pizza is always the best, gooey hot cheese would hang from it in long strings, and you caught them with your tongue to pull into your mouth, then bite into the slice of pizza where flavor burst with pure pleasure. Middy made the most of each bite, she loved the different flavors, the mixture was so good that she just relaxed and enjoyed each slice. She didn't offer Ritter any of the pizza so he reached over and took a slice before stepping back to glare at any reporter that dared to even look like they were going to bother Middy. Before he knew it, he had eaten half of Middy's pizza. Middy would have enjoyed at one time having Ritter share a pizza with her, but now, now she didn't know what to let herself feel, so she ignored him. Just like she ignored the reporters who would be a voice to the public.

Well, so much for becoming a private investigator right off the bat. After looking into what it took to get a license the whole thing looked hopeless. Five years as a police officer, or five years with an agency. Middy barely had a year in as an officer, a rookie at that. What agency would take her on with her record? None, that is what. It wasn't as if she needed the money from a job to live. Still, she liked to earn her own way in life. It was a point of honor to her. The thing was she didn't want to be among other people, to put them in danger. So there it stood, the reason she couldn't work for anyone, and the reason she needed to work for someone. It was one of those 'damned if you do and damned if you don't' moments in life.

Middy looked around the place where she lived. It was strange not to have a house full of officers. The grid board was still up, and Middy could see the new pictures the guys had put up while she was busy dying in the hospital. With a sigh, she got up from the computer and walked over to look at the new pictures. No, not the guy parking cars, or the man walking his dog. The little old lady would have been interesting, except Middy knew her. She and Fuller had helped the old woman locate her lost grandson at a store once. Most of the people were either too short or too tall to be their killer. Middy's eyes skimmed pass the fat man in the cowboy hat, then were jerked back to the picture. Something about him had the hair standing up on her neck, like getting a whiff of evil in her nose. She tried to imagine him without the layers of fat, or the hat, but her mind wasn't getting anywhere. No matter how she looked at him, his eyes just didn't quite match the man they were looking for. What she needed was to see the guy for herself. She noted the place and time of day marked down beside the picture before leaving the suspect board.

Some sort of excitement stirred inside her like a spark starting a fire in her belly. For the first time in days, she felt like doing something. She had begun to lose hope of ever catching this killer. Now she had felt evil coming from a subject. It was time for action, and action was what had been missing from her life.

As Middy was starting to feel alive again there came a knock at the door. The monitor showed Frankie and Fuller waiting outside. Ritter went to answer the door, motioning Middy to get way back. He pulled the door open prepared to send the two guys away when Killer went wild. The little bird started dive bombing Fuller and Frankie, and Ritter. The men dodge and cursed the little bird, it was Middy who figured it out. "Gun, down!"

Ritter acted out of pure instinct pulling both men inside, pushing them aside and slamming the door. Two holes appeared in the door where they had been standing. Fuller's face drained of blood as he relived being shot in the squad car. Twice in one year, twice! Only he hadn't been hit this time, thanks to Killer. Within seconds Fuller had processed what had happened and had his phone out notifying headquarters. He was deeply shaken, maybe it was time for him to take retirement. If this shook him up, what good would he be under fire protecting citizens? His confidence in being able to do his job was shaken. Sure, he had recovered quickly and made the call, but what if he hadn't? He couldn't trust he'd be able to next time.

Frankie wanted so badly to get a shot at this guy. His stomach tied in knots, he wanted so much to end this, take the killer down. Still, his first priority was protecting Miss Whiting. He ached, he ached inside with the need to revenge his fallen companions.

Talk about a man's heart leaping into his throat. For a moment that was how Ritter had felt when Middy called out. His greatest fear had become losing her. So close, the damn guy had gotten so close. That little bird had had more sense than any of them. That was a huge blow to his ego. Always he had been the one who spotted a threat to a subject. Now three times he had failed to comprehend the danger until it was too late. Was he getting too slow, not as sharp as he always had been? Three times, three times too late. Maybe he should let another agent take over. Even as he thought about letting someone take over Ritter knew he couldn't. He'd never rest not knowing she was safe.

Sirens finally could be heard approaching, the response time had been slow. They could all be dead by the time anyone arrived. Fuller's shoulders rolled back, he had some choice words simmering in his belly for whoever showed up. Car doors slammed outside and footsteps approached, then they dropped one by one. The sniper had been laying in wait. It was happening all over again, the nightmare was being repeated. Middy tried to get out the door, the bastard was out there, this was her chance to get him. Only three men tackled her and held her down.

Once Ritter was satisfied Fuller and Frankie had Middy in check, he slipped outside. If he didn't get this guy, then Middy would go after him. That thought was like a lump of ice in his chest. First, he checked the two officers, one was still alive, he cracked the door open and motion Frankie to come to pull the officer inside. There was only one spot the shooter could be, that is where Ritter started working his way. But, as in the past, the shooter was gone without a trace. Frustration hit Ritter like a sledgehammer to his chest, taking his breath away. He'd lost his chance.

The S.W.A.T. team showed up, then, along with an ambulance for the wounded and dead. Too late, there was nothing to be found, nothing left, no clues, no witnesses, nothing.

It didn't take but minutes for the word to

spread that the killer was at it again. News trucks were kept well back, still, that didn't stop them from zooming in on the scene of a dead officer being loaded by the coroner, or an ambulance screaming its urgency off on its way to the hospital. Nor were the stern faces of detectives and officers spared. Only Middy managed to stay out of the spotlight. She was fuming, enraged that the Captain had her come to the station. This, this was why she had stayed away. Didn't any of them have any sense? The guys couldn't come to see her anymore, that was glaringly clear. She had to clear them all out and make certain they understood to stay away. It was breaking her heart to have to make such a final break with these guys.

Finally Fuller and Frankie were the only ones left. The crime scene guys had gone, even the reporters left. Middy called both men over to the table and had them sit down. "I want you guys to know I love you, all of you, but none of you can come to see me anymore. One visit to the station, and now another buddy is dead. Make certain the guys all know. I was stupid letting you all come here. Stupid, and careless. I don't know what I was thinking…. Yes, yes, I do know what I was thinking. I was thinking that all you guys had to do was locate the monster and I could take him out. That is all I need, just to set eyes on him. If I see him he won't stand a chance. Then it would have been over, all of you would be safe. I wouldn't have nightmares of yet another fellow officer dying because of me. Now go, go and tell them all to stay away," with that she rose and went swiftly to her bedroom. She didn't want to see them leave her life forever.

Poleaxed, that is what Fuller felt like had been done to him and Frankie. If she had killed them both they couldn't have been more surprised. He glanced at Frankie and both of them looked at the wall of pictures. All the work of getting those pictures had been good for the guys. They had felt like finally they were doing something positive. Nothing was worse than feeling helpless, feeling like you were letting all your fellows down by not finding the creep who had killed them. This, this wall was something positive, a hope for them all. And she was shutting it down out of fear. Fuller stood up and went to Middy's computer. Carefully, he checked to be certain he had her email address. There was no way, no way at all that he would let her give up. She was a woman full of fire, and they couldn't let that fire burn out over fear.

As if he had read Fuller's mind Frankie went and took several pictures of the map they had all been carefully searching block by block. He nodded to Fuller, and the two of them gave Ritter a knowing look as if to say it was up to him to keep her safe now, as they left Middy's home. They had work to do.

The television and radio were off, no sound could be heard, but the zipping about by Killer from feeder to feeder. Middy's place was like a tomb, which suited her present mood. She felt dead inside. Defeated. Ritter watched her with critical eyes. He didn't like this, this passive, beaten side of Cupcake. She was a spitfire, not a passive wilted flower.

The station was flooded with calls of men spotted on top of buildings. The police force was being wasted on checking out false reports, things were worse than the first time this madman had shown himself. The city was on the edge of hysteria coming unglued, and dangerously close to reaching mob madness.

A week went by of unrest and tension. Normal people flared with the tempers of fear, demanding that something is done. The threats to the police department and the city officials were thrown out without a thought of how ridiculous they sounded. That night the first riot took place with cars being burned and people fighting in the streets. Those who seek to protect the people were hard pressed to not only keep the citizens safe but now they had to protect themselves from, not only a madman, but the very people they protected. Mob madness was on the loose, the insanity that people let loose in themselves, when with others who willingly went along with that same insanity. Mob madness, something every city dreaded, every city knew at some time or another.

That day of madness was the day after new pictures were sent to Middy's phone of suspects. She had spent all night printing out the pictures and putting them up on the wall of suspects. It lightened Middy's heart to realize the guys still wanted her to be in the loop and were continuing the work they had started, the search for a monster. She slept late the day of the riot and was unaware of the insanity that was going on in the city until she woke up. For the first time, in many years, Middy had a flashback to when she was an orphan. For a moment she saw in her mind the blackened cars, and the dead bodies that were the last sight she saw of the town

where she had been born. She remembered the
hollow feeling that had been inside her at the sight
of such destruction, and how she had felt it was the
end of the world. But it hadn't been, it had been the
beginning of life for her and her family. They had
avoided the madness, the insane behavior of people
who were once good. Now, now, that madness
was starting over again, all because of one man, a
monster of the worst sort.

With grim determination, Middy began to
study the pictures all over again. She came across the
fat man who had caught her interest before. It was a
place to start.

It can start small and grow into a raging
monster, the mob mentality. It is when good people
allow themselves to be caught up in the hysteria
of others, and become just as mad and crazed as
everyone else around them. Reason, law, honesty,
and honor go out the window. All that is left is
the insanity of the mob. Perhaps they are to be
pitied. Hating them is just joining in on the general
madness, adding to the growing rage of the mob. For
Middy and those of her family, it was like looking
at something so alien that you couldn't even take
it into your mind. There was no reasoning behind
the madness, no logic. Therefore, it was something
unimaginable. She had trained as a police officer on
how to deal with the hate-filled mob, but she was no
longer a police officer. For the ordinary citizen of
the city, it was dangerous to go out. Shopping, going
about the everyday things people did in a day of their
life could lead to death, or, worse, to becoming one

of the mob. Fear fed the mobs and increased the numbers of those not listening to reason.

Through it all Middy paced like a caged lion. She was filled with the urge to do something, anything so long as it was positive. She went through all the pictures the guys had taken again, over and over, comparing the eyes, while wondering if her theory was all wrong. Were the sketches even accurate examples of his eyes? There were so many doubts and so little known. All they really had was his nickname, Ghost. It was frustrating, and the noise wasn't helping Middy think. The mobs needed to go inside and cool down, to stop this craziness. Her temper began to boil and she stepped outside into the not so fresh air. What they needed was a storm, a huge storm to drive them all inside. Without any thought Middy's fingers began to twitch, the wind stirred. Ever since being healed this last time she had felt something, it was building inside her, like something was about to rupture, break loose and devour the world.

Ritter was standing where he could see the length of the road and the surrounding area. He had noticed how restless Cupcake was and thought the fresh air might do her some good. Out of the corner of his eye, he watched over her, letting the cool breeze caress his cheeks and cool his own rising temper. It was the nature of the mob to breed anger and discontent, but Ritter had dealt with it in all its forms. This was a beast he knew.

Gradually the wind strengthens, high overhead clouds began to form and darken, the air sizzled. The storm grew and grew until it darkened the sky. Lightning flashed sending thunderous roars rolling over the city. For once the mobs stopped and listened to a voice louder than their own. When at last Middy's fingers stopped twitching the storm had a life of its own. She stood in the first drops of the rain letting them fall on her skin cooling the anger which had tried to take her over and control her. Her mother's words telling her that only you control your mind ran in her head. I stopped it, she thought to her distant mother. She had been so close to giving in to her own anger because of feeling so helpless. Only she wasn't helpless, she had a power that nobody else had, she controlled the wind. The building of that storm had calmed the growing unease in her.

For hours the storm shook the city, playing out its fury, cooling the citizens, bringing a few hours of peace. Now it was up to those in charge of keeping that peace to do just that, keep it. If they could.

The weather in this area is crazy, Ritter thought as he ushered Middy inside out of the rain and wind. He had allowed her to stand outside for as long as he could stand seeing her pelted by rain and blown by the wind. When the lightning became worse, he motioned to her to go inside. Fortunately, she complied. He didn't know what he would have done if she hadn't just turned and walked inside. He knew her fire burned hot and suspected she didn't forgive what she might think as an injustice. All his adult life he had been the one totally in charge of any subject. How was it he was so uncertain when handling her? Loving someone was full of pitfalls, still, Ritter thought his Cupcake was worth the effort.

The news services were caught in the peaceful lull, unable to sensationalize the captured pictures of the uncontrollable raging mobs anymore. Someone came up with the idea of getting the Butterfly Whisperer's opinion of what was happening to the city. When they called Ritter answered the phone. He refused to let the news services speak to Middy. All the while he kept an eye on her trying to judge her reaction to the request.

Middy started to shake her head negatively, but it came to her that she did indeed have something to say to the people of the city, so she waved her hand at Ritter to hand her the phone. He passed the phone over reluctantly standing ready to snatch it back and lay into the idiots on the other end if needed.

"This is Middleton Whiting, state your business, please," she said.

"Officer Whiting, we would like you to comment on what you think of these riots going on."

Middy thought for a moment before answering, "I do have something to say, but let me make this clear. What I have to say goes for you, the press, as well as the people of the city. When I woke up today this madness had taken hold of all of you. The media were crazy with the story of people gone mad behaving in destructive ways, actually destroying their own city. I have to say I have never been so disappointed as I am now in the people of this city, and the media who did their best to feed fear and anger among all of you. I could hear the madness raging outside. I had to decide what part I was going to take in this day of terror, rained on the city by its people. I could become angry and join the mobs, be fearful and hide away in my home. The choice, as always was for me to make. I walked outside and looked at the city, the cars on fire, the people robbing stores, and hurting one another. I thought about the people of this city, how you pulled together, and how they supported the police when all the killing started. How you cared about each other and strove to help in any manner you could help. And as these thoughts ran through my mind, I knew that you were still good people, only you had given into your fears, allowed yourselves to become as mad as the madman who has held this city and its police force in his death grip. Surely you were still inside, the people making up this crazy angry mob. So I asked for some way to cool your tempers, and allow you to once again be in control of the person each and every one of you is. To be the good people I knew you to be. This strange storm formed and I rejoiced, for now, you had a chance to come to your senses, be the people you were, the people so many officers died trying to protect. Stop the madness, look for ways you can help, make me proud of you once again. That is all I have to say, good night," with that sign off Middy disconnected the call, placed the phone down and walked to the wall of many faces again.

Chapter Nine

LEG WORK

It was time to go out into the city and look for all the people who stood the slightest chance of being a monster. *I'm going to get you, Middy* silently vowed.

Ritter watched with dread the change in his Cupcake. She was a woman filled with a goal, determined to complete the mission she had set herself on. While she slept that night Ritter made a call, "Sir, I need at least two more agents. She is going after this guy, and he is out there waiting to kill her. Send your best, well second best. Send them now!"

In the morning Middy cooked breakfast and allowed Ritter to sit at the table with her for the meal. Ritter was wary of this slight change in her demeanor, but took the seat and ate in silence. She was different this morning and that had him worried to no end. When Middy got ready to go off into the city, Ritter kept his lips clamped firmly shut. It was all he could do not to lock her in the bedroom for the duration of this hunt for a madman.

Killer zipped out the door to follow Middy as she set off by foot towards the first area suspected eyes had been seen. There was an energy to her today. She felt the way she had felt when charging her way through the police academy. Then she had been a frumpy girl they made fun of at every turn. The instructors were quite frank in telling her they didn't believe she had what it took to be a police officer. She had given them her mother's stare and simply said, "We'll see." Today she would bring that determination to the task at hand, finding a monster.

The air smelled clean after the storm that had raged all night over the city. There was something about the fresh clean air that gave people hope of a better day. Middy filled her lungs with the scent of clean she felt. For the first time she stood a chance of finding this monster and stopping him.

At least she is walking slow enough I can scan everything ahead and around her, Ritter thought as he followed Middy in her search for a madman. He even noted the mugger waiting for some helpless woman or man to walk by where he hid in the shadows. Ritter was prepared to shoot the guy if he attempted to mug Cupcake, only an elderly woman rounded the corner of the building and became the mugger's focus.

Mugger, the thought flashed through Middy's mind as her hands reacted. She started jogging towards the man who was twisting the old woman's purse out of her hands. Wham, she slammed him into a wall with a blast of wind then tripped him every time he tried to get up. "Are you alright, ma'am?" she asked the woman who was still holding tight to her purse.

"Yes, he is the dumbest mugger I've ever seen. Look at the clumsy creep," the woman said, turning on the mugger and hitting him with her purse. "You need to go back to diapers and a strong guiding woman to teach you right and wrong. Get up and stand against the wall while I call your ride to jail."

The mugger staggered to his feet and stood against the wall completely bewildered. The old woman was strong enough to shove him away and kick him while he was down. He saw Ritter standing back with his gun drawn and pointed at the mugger's head. The mugger gulped and hung his head, afraid to even look at that gun. What a lousy day.

Inside Middy was laughing to herself. As always, people made up things in their minds to cover her use of the wind. Still, she believed this elderly woman was a force to be dealt with on her own. "Ma'am, you would make a great police officer," she said as she moved away from the pair, mugger, and woman. Ritter still kept his gun trained on the guy until a police officer arrived and took the mugger into custody.

"Damn right," the older woman said, "These young idiots should be scrambling to find real jobs instead of preying on old women."

Middy's phone was buzzing like crazy in her pocket. While she and Ritter walked away from the bustle of the regular cops taking the mugger into custody she answered. "Run! Grab Ritter and run as fast as you can, Mids."

She didn't question why or hesitate in the least bit, but reached out and grabbed Ritter's hand and took out running for all she was worth. Her body wasn't built for running, still, she gave it her best, sides burning, lungs on fire, she ran and ran all the while holding the phone up to her ear with one hand and holding tight to Ritter with the other. It was awkward, although Middy wasn't worried about how silly she must look or what the people on the street thought, she just ran. Eric wouldn't steer her wrong.

The phone at her ear sputtered as Eric started talking again. "Red car, yellow building, stop the car, do it now!"

Frantically, she searched the area for a red car and there it was a little scruffy car to the left. Coming to a halt, she let go of Ritter, her hands taking over, gathering the wind sending it out to stop a car for what reason she didn't know, she just had to stop it. She battled the forward motion of the car, sending a whirlwind to start the car spinning in place. It couldn't go anywhere, just in the circling of the wind. Inside a middle-aged man grimly held onto the steering wheel. It was his face Middy saw the clearest when the car exploded into a million bits sucked up into the whirling wind which surrounded it. Directly ahead was the yellow building with wide windows looking out upon the street. Tiny faces were pressed against the window watching the whirlwind and its cargo of car bits.

"Got it, Eric. You saved a lot of children," She told her brother.

"It took us both, Mids. I'm just glad I won't

have nightmares of tiny kids with broken bodies," He told her. They didn't say any long goodbyes, this was what they did, saved lives.

Gradually Middy allowed the whirlwind to die away. With its death, the roadway became a mess of car parts and the bloody remains of an angry man. Without looking back Middy walked on.

Ritter's mind was in shock. Had he just witnessed his Cupcake take out a bomber? And that dust devil, more of a mini tornado, what the hell? His eyes constantly scanned the area around them as Middy continued walking. Somewhere, out there, possibly watching them, was a madman.

The rest of the day was not so filled with excitement. Ritter was surprised Middy didn't stop to take credit for stopping the man bombing his wife's daycare. At least he thought she had stopped the red car, and now he had an idea what her power was, what she could do. It was as amazing as what her mother did, certainly more deadly than anyone else in her family who he had met. No wonder she resented being made to feel like she was helpless. That was one thing she could never be. His admiration for her went up to new heights, but he kept his mouth shut not hinting that he knew her secret. The only thing that worried him, worried him greatly, was the thought he wasn't up to her standards. How could he make her see him as the man in her life?

Faces, faces everywhere, not one of them the face Middy was searching for. Was this a hopeless attempt to locate the killer? If so, how else could she go about finding the guy? Once again doubt started filling her, she had to overcome it and get her old confidence back. So she looked at faces until they started to blur together. Then she whipped out her phone and took pictures, pictures upon pictures, of everyone, no matter their age, size or gender. That was between being stopped by people who either scowled her, or gave her massive sympathy. It was a strange day for Middy as she saw both the good side and the bad side of the people who lived around her.

They were on the last leg of the area Middy intended to cover for the day when two things happened. A car ran a stop sign, and a little boy decided to dash across the street. Time seemed to freeze for Middy as she desperately flung wind at the car to slow it down. As the wind battered the car Middy ran for the little boy only Ritter flashed pass her to grab the boy dragging him to safety. Horns honked, drivers shook their fists at the driver of the car as they slammed on their own brakes shimmying sideways creating a massive traffic jam. Car doors slammed, and people rushed the car driven by the person who ran into the stop sign. One man slammed his fist down on the hood of the car screaming, "What the hell were you doing? You almost killed that child!" Others joined in expressing their fears for the boy and the anger grew toward the driver.

Middy sighed, they never learn. Her own adrenaline was too high for her to risk another storm. Still, her insides sizzled with that new urgency for release, so she pointed one hand up towards the sky and let it loose. All that weird energy sprang forth and the sky exploded like a thunderclap. People ducked, looking for shelter until they realized it wasn't a massive storm just noise. By that time a patrol car had arrived, Middy slipped away from the scene seeking to make herself as invisible as possible. Soon she was joined by Ritter, neither spoke about the incident.

Foot patrols, Middy thought as she turned to head back home, we need foot patrols, then she realized the thought was impractical in a modern city. Still, she was glad to have a distraction from the manhunt which obsessed her. Bike Cops. No, too easy for rowdy teens and roaring drunks to take them down. All the way home, she mulled over ways officers could patrol not using cars, and didn't find anything useful. Perhaps they were already using the best system for city life. She finally admitted that it wasn't up to her what they did in the way of patrols. She was just a citizen, just a citizen. That didn't mean she couldn't use her storm to cool down tempers, or her wind to stop run-a-way cars, as long as she did it secretly and didn't draw attention to herself. Invisible, that is what she had to be, invisible to the world. How could some dumpy invisible girl draw the attention of a monster? When had it happened? Why had it happened? What had she done that was so wrong, that it caused all the deaths that followed? Middy realized her mind was circling around again. Rambling, her mind was rambling. Proof she was not police material, a rambling mind, crazy.

She felt the breeze on her face before her mind registered the zipping form of Killer. "Killer is saying something is urgent, let's hurry," Middy called to Ritter, already she was running after the little hummingbird.

Reckless, Ritter thought, she is so reckless. He ran after her watching, constantly watching. Because he was watching he saw the body before Middy did. "Stop," he called to her, "let me go first." He knew his error immediately and tried to correct it. "I need you to be my back up, cover me."

At that she stopped, letting him pass her. Her fingers began to twitch preparing to let loose a powerful blast. She was surprised when Ritter put away his gun and dropped to his knees blocking her view. Killer whizzed around Ritter as if urging him on. "He is alive," he said, leaning down, "Call a taxi." Then he stood, the body clutched to his chest.

Middy was at his side then observing the scene, looking for evidence, taking in the tire tracks, the blood on the curb where the body had lain. The rotten creep, hitting a poor dog and leaving him for dead. Eric was too far away to call, so was her mom. Middy would have to depend on the local veterinarians. No Eric, no mom, no heals, not for the first time, she regretted not being able to heal. We all have our roles, she thought. Although finding mine is all mixed up at the moment.

It seemed hours, but could only have been minutes when the taxi pulled up in front of an animal clinic. Ritter still held the dog giving the warmth of his body to help with any shock. It was all he could do besides keep the pressure on the bleeding back leg of the dog. He had to keep alert to everything around them while worry took hold of him for a dog he didn't even know. What had surprised him the most was Killer leading them to the dog. What had the little bird seen? The fact Middy kept a hand on the dog's head also worried him. Was she trying to give the dog her energy?

Middy had thrown a fistful of bills at the taxi driver and he drove away a happy man. The clinic was busy, filled with people waiting to see the doctor when they rushed into it. Ritter didn't pause to answer questions just went past the receptionist desk announcing they had an emergency. He was taken all the way to the back to a metal exam table where he gently laid the dog down.

As the receptionist rushed to get the doctor, Middy started examining the dog. The right back leg was in horrible condition. She had helped treat the animals at the farm, but this was the worst she had ever seen. Mangled, bones in fragments. The leg looked so misshapen that you had to look hard to believe it had ever been a leg at all. Ribs, several fractured ribs on the same side that were causing the dog to labor when he tried to breath. All the damage appeared to be on one side which might indicate the car had either swerved towards or away from the dog. Middy hoped the driver had tried to avoid hitting the dog, still, she couldn't forgive the driver for not stopping to help the dog.

The doctor came bustling in, his face red with something that was not apparent. He carefully went over the dog before sending his helper off to prepare for surgery. There was disapproval in his eyes when he turned to Middy and Ritter. "There is a reason for the leash law. If you had had your dog on a leash, he would not be in this condition. And don't tell me he ran out the door or any other lame excuse. I have to deal with this all the time and they always have some excuse," the doctor said rimming them out with his frustration.

Ritter was getting ready to lay into the guy when Middy stepped forward. "I'm with you on that, there is no excuse for this dog being loose without the proper supervision. Nor is there any excuse for the bastard that ran over him and went on his merry way. He should be locked away for life. Now that we have that out of the way, let's save this dog. I'll foot the bill and take responsibility for his aftercare. I can even assist in surgery if needed. Answer me this, can the leg be saved?" Middy asked.

"No, there is too much damage. The leg will have to go. As for the ribs they will heal, but he must be kept quiet, slow walks, no playing ball or other stressful activity. He will heal faster than you would believe. Believe me, these guys bounce back fast," the doctor said.

Ritter almost smirked, this man didn't know what fast healing was. He caught the tolerant look upon Middy's face and felt sorry for the doctor. "We will wait for him," Ritter stated as fact.

The doctor shook his head, "No, you had better go home and return in the morning. I'll be able to tell you then when he can go home with you."

Now Middy was shaking her head, "We will wait. This dog is under the protection of the United States."

The doctor made a face, more a disgusted grimace than anything. People were so stupid thinking he would fall for any old bull. He'd seen it all, all the crap people put forth in order not to pay a bill or not to have a suffering animal even treated. "Look, don't start handing me a bunch of bull crap. I'll do the surgery and if you are unable to pay for it, we will work something out. You don't have to start dishing out the bull right off like this…."

He shut up when Ritter whipped out his SS identification. "Miss Whiting is under SS protection, which means everyone in her household and family are also under our protection. That includes this dog and her bird," Ritter said.

Middy groaned, "Killer, where did he go? Did he go home or try to follow us?"

For once Ritter chuckled, "I'd say he followed us if that is him buzzing the window." Sure enough, the little hummingbird was hovering outside the window of the exam room as if making certain his dog was being taken care of properly.

"That is your pet bird?" the doctor asked incredulity in his voice, this just got weirder and weirder. "Never mind, I don't want to know. Let me get to work on your dog. You can go to the waiting area for now."

Reluctantly Middy left the dog in the hands of the doctor. She was not use to not being involved in the healing. It just didn't seem right. Before they were even in the front lobby she had her phone out. "Eric, we have a dog here with a messed up back leg the doctor is saying the leg can't be saved. Will you do a phone consult with him?"

"Mids, you don't have to ask, take the phone to the doctor and set it to video conference," Eric said.

Middy did an about face and rushed back to the doctor. "I have my brother on the phone I'd like you to do a video conference with him. He may be able to help," Middy said, offering the phone to the doctor.

"Ma'am...," the doctor began, then saw Ritter tense up behind her, "hand me the phone, then please go back to the waiting area."

Once he was certain Middy was heading back to the waiting area he spoke into the phone, "Look you are just wasting my time and the dog's time with this. There is nothing you can do long distance, nothing at all."

"I can relieve my sister mind," Eric said, "More than that I can advise you on what is best for the dog. Believe me, I'm not trying to take over your patient, but I know my sister. She won't rest until she is certain everything is being done that is possible. Now please show me the damage done."

Idiots. God save me from the idiots, Dr. Clive silently prayed. Still, he moved the phone's camera over the dog's ribs and leg. It was best to get the insanity over with and get on with the job at hand.

Eric studied the injuries longing to be there, to do what his sister wanted, a miracle. "Okay, I agree with you that you won't be able to save the leg. Have you done many amputations before?" Eric asked.

Bristling a little, the doctor said, "Two front legs since opening my practice."

"Okay, set the phone on speaker and set it up in surgery so I can see where you will be working with the dog. I know you have the basics, but since I'm on the phone let me talk you through it as you go," Eric said, "and get Middy back to assist".

Madder than he had ever been with a client or fellow doctor before, the doctor did as he was told. If not for that SS agent in the lobby, he would have dumped the phone in the trash after a few harsh words. But that woman was someone of great importance, so he sucked it up and readied the dog for surgery sending his helper to get the confounded woman. All the while that bird hovered outside his window as if watching him.

Although he grumbled to himself inside Dr. Clive had to admit the video conference was working well. He couldn't fault the person assisting him either. It wasn't until the leg was removed, and he was closing up that things went weird again. The patient had been breathing well up until that point. That is why Dr. Clive was so surprised when Middy said, "Trouble with breaths."

The guy at the other end of the video conference said one word, "Battery."

Middy stripped off her gloves and place both hands on the dog as she repeated over and over in her mind, "My strength to you, my strength to you." She could hear Eric telling the doctor to go on and close up.

Against his better judgment, the doctor stitched the gaping skin edges together while keeping an eye on the dog's chest. Almost instantly after that weird woman touched the dog it seemed to strengthen. Well, this at least he could explain away, the touch of someone who cared for an animal often helped a patient recover, as did the touch of an animal help critical patients in a hospital. That was why hospitals so often had programs with dogs being taken from room to room, bringing smiles to sick and recovering patients. There was no doubt a connection existed between dogs and humans, so he didn't question what he had witnessed.

Middy could feel her energy going, she must have pushed more into the dog than she had thought. She watched as the doctor put in the last stitch before she spoke Ritter's name softly. He was there with a bottle of fortifying drink for her. Middy had no doubt that he had been watching her closely even as she watched the dog. Ritter held her weight as he guided her out of the surgery and into a chair. He could hear Eric say to him to get her a good hot meal as if he didn't know the routine by now. Funny how he now carried those brown drinks and the bars which had helped so much when they were healing Middy.

Cupcake made him wait until she knew the dog was settled in recovery and would be okay. Only then did she allow Ritter to lead her from the animal hospital. The lobby was still crowded with people waiting to have their pet looked at, and though they hadn't seen enough of Middy to place who she was going in, they certainly placed her as she was helped out the door into a waiting taxi. The whispers started then as the people waiting asked and answered their own question, "Wasn't that the Butterfly Whisperer?" That was how Dr. Clive learned who had just invaded his clinic and took over.

Later that night Dr. Clive looked up The Butterfly Whisperer on his home computer. He knew he should be grabbing sleep while he could as he was constantly in a state of exhaustion from the long hours he had put in since opening his clinic. He never looked at the news or even watched TV for there was no time for such frivolous things. His patients were all that occupied his mind. Cynical and sharp spoken had become the person he was now. Too many neglectful people, too many cruel people, and not enough people who cared had made him this way. He knew it, but he didn't care. If it took dressing a person down to get him or her to take care of their pet, then he would dress them all down. Even with his harsh demeanor, his clinic was constantly full of people waiting to see him with their pets. At the moment he was curious about the strange woman who had brought a dog she didn't own in to be helped and wondered why she had called a consultant in to help.

It was like looking through someone else's nightmare, the images on his computer. One site had put together a visual log from the moment she first came to the attention of the public. There she was among the bodies of fellow officers screaming at a madman she couldn't see. They had followed her, the cameras, followed through each death, and it all leads up to the funerals. It was a video of the whole funeral, the camera swings often to the woman officer and her black-suited companion. The film ended with the butterfly landing on her hand and her speaking to it. Hundreds of still shots of that same scene followed. The short frumpy woman officer never looked around for attention, never did more than grieve for her fellow officers, but the press had taken to her and blew her up to be this tragic mystical person who talked to butterflies. Dr. Clive drew one truth from all of it, she couldn't trust anyone. He quickly scanned the remaining articles ending with her losing her job. So this was how she was rewarded, thrown out like so much trash. She was tragic and she had a hummingbird as a pet, how odd was that? He had to face it, for the first time in a long time his interest was caught by a woman, a frumpy woman. Now that was indeed odd.

It wasn't even daylight, and Middy was already up and ready to go get the dog. Killer seemed just as eager as she was to get outside. The little bird flitted constantly from feeder to feeder, taking in so much of his food that Middy was afraid he'd burst open. His nervous energy transmitted to Middy making her pace the wall of pictures looking at all the pictures she had taken the day before. The monster couldn't hide forever, even though he thought he could. She had to find him, but first, she needed to attend to a hurt dog. She saw the night guy's shadow falling ever so often on the cameras which were the extra eyes for her doorway. Middy glanced towards the couch where Ritter preferred to sleep. She knew it was a thing with him putting himself between an entryway and the person he protected. But he wasn't there, she didn't see him anywhere. Could he have taken the guest room that she had prepared for him?

A keycard was shoved into the lock on the door, the security system beeped saying a card had been used to disengage it. The door swung wide and in came Ritter with his arms full of shopping bags. The night guy followed with a fifty-pound bag of dog food. Had he shopped? The idea of Ritter out shopping in a store seemed to bounce around in her head as if it was alien, yet there he was with shopping bags dangling from his arms.

Armed with the new leash and collar Ritter had bought Middy, Ritter, and Killer entered the clinic the moment the doors were unlocked. The hummingbird lost no time zooming to the back to find the sick dog. Middy stopped at the front desk to pay the bill. That was where the first stumbling block, waited for her. "Ma'am, in order to complete our files we need the dog's name."

"He doesn't have a name yet. He'll earn one in the next few days. Why not put its name as undecided at present?" Middy asked, trying to be reasonable.

"Ma'am, it is not possible to leave the name blank. If we did that people could have ten dogs and foster the same rabies tag off as belonging to each of them. You can see the problem. So please give me a name," the stubborn receptionist said.

Slowly Middy counted to get control of her twitching fingers. Thankfully, her phone rang, showing Eric's number. Middy held up a finger to the receptionist as she answered the phone. "Eric, is anything wrong?"

There was a chuckle at the other end of the phone call, "No, Mids, I got a flash of a problem you were having, so got on my gallant charger and came to the rescue. Sherlock, you should name him Sherlock as he is a scent hound," Eric told her. Middy smiled, of course, it fit him perfectly.

After saying goodbye to her brother Middy turned back to the aggravating woman, "His name is Sherlock."

Nodding the receptionist entered the information. The next hurdle was over Middy's credit card, the receptionist thought it was a fake on a fake bank. By now Middy was prepared for a rough ride, and she knew people held animosity towards her because of who she was, evidently this woman was among them. Again she held up her hand in a wait motion and pulled out her phone. She made a call to a local bank, identified herself and requested a rush on cash payment. Five minutes later Middy was handing over six hundred dollars in cash to the dreadful receptionist while trying to keep a smile pasted on her face. As a cop she had had experience with the pasted smile more often than she cared to, being pleasant when she felt more like blasting the guy who had just beaten his wife.

The receptionist's name was Dora, and Dora had grown tired of women with little fluffy dogs trying to forget they had to pay for the doctor having saved their little darling. She hadn't been on duty when this woman had first come in with her critical dog and had formed her opinion on the fancy credit card the woman had tried to pass off as real. She actually felt pleased with herself at having gotten a cash payment out of the witch. Although the fact the snooty woman had walked on to the back as if she owned the place galled her endlessly.

Middy sat on the floor in front of the recovery cage which housed Sherlock. She had carefully opened the door so as not to disturb the IV going

to the dog's front leg as she waited for the doctor
to come to release Sherlock into her care. Gently
she petted the dog who had joined her little family,
while Killer perched on the dog's head. In one of
the exam rooms, a man was getting very loud, and
angry, yelling something about how the doctor had
to put the beast to sleep, it was too dangerous to be
allowed to live. Middy's heart shattered. There was
always hope, the man just didn't know how to reach
the beast he was talking about. She heard the doctor
saying he couldn't do that, not without finding a
reason for such a drastic measure. Now the man was
near hysterical yelling at the doctor, "Are you crazy
don't open the cage! Stop, I won't be responsible for
what it does to you or anyone else! I'm gone. That
thing is not attacking me again." With that, she heard
the man beat a hasty retreat, and the front door
slamming.

"Come on, you don't have to be afraid. I'm
not going to hurt you, come on pretty one," Dr. Clive
coached the growling cat crammed in the small crate.
With a burst of energy the cat rushed out the cage
and up Dr. Clive's body, leaping for a crack in the
exam room door, the cat was through and gone so
fast the doctor hadn't even had a chance of catching
it. Thankfully, the cat didn't head to the lobby, but
towards the rear of the clinic. They would be able to
corner the beast there.

Middy felt, rather than saw, the orange cat fly
past her seeking a hiding place, only it had leaped
into Sherlock's cage. The cat made itself as small
as possible behind Sherlock, it's entire body was
shaking. Middy continued to stroke Sherlock as if

the cat wasn't there while watching it, taking in the nature of the cat. The shaking turned to a trembling and gradually the cat relaxed, assured it was in a safe spot. In the other rooms, Middy could hear things being moved around as the doctor and his assistant searched for the cat. "Ritter, tell them the cat is here, but they are not to enter the room," Middy said in the same tone of voice she was using on Sherlock. The noise ceased, soft footsteps approached, but Ritter was there to block any attempt to enter the room.

Stroking Sherlock, and talking softly to him and Killer, Middy allowed her fingers to get closer and closer to the hiding cat. Her goal was not to grab the cat but to let it become used to her touch. The first time her fingers brushed along the cat, it hissed a warning. Sherlock dropped his head down on the cat almost smothering the poor thing, yet strange as it was, this seemed to calm the cat. Middy took her cue from the dog and the next time her fingers approached the cat's side, she didn't softly touch it instead, she rather roughly rubbed its side in deep streams of touch. The cat is like our cow, Middy thought, soft touches are like flies lighting on the skin. A solid touch is more of a comfort. Each time her hand came close to the cat, Middy gave it a solid touch, as if they were old friends. It wasn't long before she was scratching the cat under the chin, and rubbing the cheek pads

Using that same soft-spoken tone Middy talked to the doctor, "I heard this cat was to be killed. I propose that you let me have this cat. I think I can make a proper home for it. If it needs to be vaccinated or neutered we need to settle that now. I will arrange for another cash payment if you will just tell me the amount."

Chapter Ten

BECOMING FAMILY

It seemed to take forever to wade through everything it took to make the cat legally hers, and by the time they were done Middy was done too. All she wanted was to get home and get her new family members settled into their new home.

They were two blocks away when it became clear that something was happening at Middy's place. Fire trucks lined the street, police cars had traffic blocked off and the stench of burning filled the air.

Nothing, nothing was left, not a picture, not a scrap of clothing, nothing, nothing that spoke of home. Here she sat in the car with two needy animals and all she had to show them was ashes. Killer zipped around and around until he finally had to go eat. Ritter stood staunch, his body rigid with fury, his face speaking of death with a single look to anyone who dared to approach Middy. For the longest moment, Middy sat there in shock not

believing what her eyes told her was true. Then she
closed her eyes for so long Ritter was ready to come
over and shake her.

When Middy opened her eyes she knew what
she had to do. She looked down at the dog with his
head resting on her lap and the cat hiding between
the dog and the back of the car's seat. They needed
a home and, by golly, she was going to get them one
right now, this moment and not a moment later.
The first place she called tried to tell her that what
she wanted took time to find. She responded with,
"Too bad there would have been a nice bonus." and
hung up. Two companies later she had a short list
of properties to go look at. Dodging the questions
the police and fire department were throwing at her,
Middy gave Ritter the addresses.

It was perhaps the fastest purchase of a
house and land in history. Middy was handed over
the keys before dark and brought her mini family
home. True, it was bare bones with only the main
furnishings such as bedroom, sofa, and dining table,
but the rest was easily ordered and arrived within
a couple of hours. Dishes, clothing, food, towels,
sheets, all the little things we never think we'd miss
like toothpaste and soap arrived and were brought in
by amused delivery men. Sherlock's shadow stayed
crouched down behind him where he was laying on
the new dog bed the entire time. The cat's new name
was Watson, and it was clear she was not going to let
her protector out of her sight. Killer immediately
began to feed on the new feeders set up for him only
leaving when anyone approached Sherlock to shoo
them away. Evidently, Killer had adopted both the

cat and dog, and was just as protective of them as he was of Middy.

The night SS man brought several boxes of pizza while the huge delivery truck was still being unloaded. Some happy men sat down with this unlikely family and pigged out on pizza for the first meal eaten in Middy's new home. What a homecoming it was. "Call on us anytime, ma'am," called out the boss of the delivery crew. It was clear Middy had made them all happy with the bonus and the pizza.

She watched them go with a sigh of relief, all she wanted was a hot shower and a bed. But there were beds still needing to be made up with the stiff new sheets and covers, so she put off sleep for a few moments more. At the last possible moment, she realized Sherlock needed to be walked before bedtime. Carefully Middy helped him to his feet while Ritter kept his distance. It seemed Watson did not like men, and threatened Ritter every time he approached.

Slowly they walked in the, as of yet, unexplored yard with Sherlock trying to raise his back leg on trees and nearly falling over, and Watson sneaking off to hide behind bushes, scratching the ground to do her business. Around them, Killer buzzed darting ahead and back over and over as if urging them on.

Finally bathed and feeling almost human Middy headed to the bedroom for her much needed rest. That is when someone knocked on the door. Middy hung her head in defeat, the bed seemed a million miles away as she went to the front door.

Ritter was there before her with his hand warning her off, and that serious look upon his face. Middy sighed and began twitching her fingers ready for anything as Ritter open the door. Three men stood on the doorstep sooty and smelling of smoke. Fuller, Albert, and Frankie took a step forward with Frankie clutching a cardboard box to his chest. "We found a few things you might want to keep in the ruins. The Captain doesn't know we took them, but we wanted to cheer you up a bit so here," he thrust the box at her. They looked tired and haggard and the idea that they had wanted to save a few of the things she loved moved Middy to tears. She opened her arms wide and hugged the three soot-covered men before she could burst out in tears. She had to be the tough one, but how could you be tough when someone did something so wonderful for you.

Stepping back Middy cleared her throat of the tightness that threatened to stop her from breathing. "The wall of pictures is gone, all I have are the ones on my phone. Tell the guys I'm sorry they are lost. I love you guys, but you know you can't come here again, it is too dangerous for you," she said, backing away, her heart heavy with regret. "Thank you, thank you for this wonderful gift."

"Don't you go worrying about us. Watch your email, we saved those pictures, at least most of us did. I put mine on a flash drive to make room. And we love you too," Fuller said as they backed up and shut the door. Then they were gone. An emptiness filled Middy as she carried the box to the nearest table. There were only a handful of items in the box, each looked very dirty from all the ash and soot of the fire, how they had escaped the destruction she didn't know. There were memories of her childhood special bits of love caught in an item. A crystal statue of a dog Eric had given her on one of her birthdays, it had long ears and hints of a wrinkled forehead. It dawned on her that this was Sherlock. Had Eric had a vision of the dog all those years ago? A tiny butterfly necklace her mother had given her when she left home to pursue a job as a cop. It was a reminder that no matter where she was the butterflies would watch over her. A heavy jar in which was a single seashell. A gift from Susan who said thoughts were like the pounding of the waves to her if Middy ever wanted to hear her world she was to listen to the shell. Only one other item was in the box, a pair of crystal hands just opening up with a beautiful blue butterfly rising up prepared to fly away. This was from her father. She remembered him saying he was letting go of her so she could fly into the life she was meant to lead.

Middy broke down and cried, all her treasures few as they may be had survived. She felt stupid for crying over them, for being so happy to see them, for caring so much, and that made her cry harder. A soft nose nudged up under her arm as she held her face and wept. Sherlock had come to offer her comfort. With him were Watson and Killer. Watson wary yet unwilling to let Sherlock out of her sight rubbed against Middy's legs, while Killer zipped around frantic to stop Middy hurting. Middy dried her tears looking at her odd little family, "It is okay guys, it was just an emotional moment. Don't worry, I'm not going into full meltdown. Besides, I think we need to get some sleep." She petted Sherlock and dared to rub Watson under the chin, firmly as taught by Sherlock. Killer seemed satisfied and went back to drinking from his feeders.

Bed beckoned Middy and she told the SS good night going to her new bed. Dressed in pajamas she slipped between the still stiff sheets, wondering what would go wrong tomorrow. Her mind had almost drifted off into sleep, but an ever so slight whine had her looking over the side of the bed. Sherlock looked up at her with the saddest look on his face, as if he felt abandoned and so alone. "Alright, just tonight since this is a new place for you too," Middy said, sliding off the bed to lift Sherlock up onto the mattress. No sooner were she and Sherlock settled down than Watson leaped over Middy, crouching down between her and Sherlock. Okay, Middy thought, as she felt Killer land on the headboard, the gangs all here. It was her last thought for the night.

Morning came amid nightmares of the house burning with Sherlock, Watson, and Killer inside. Middy kept trying to blow the flames out with her wind, but they were too high and too hot. She screamed as the roof collapsed and woke up. Sherlock was licking her face while Watson stood on her chest staring at her. She could never leave them alone in the house, never.

Fetching Sherlock's leash, Middy took her three pets out for a slow walk. She noticed Sherlock had already adapted to only having three legs. He still tried to raise his hind leg when he wanted to mark a tree or bush, but he had figured out how to stand on just his front legs for that moment of marking. Otherwise, he got around fine, if slowly, because of his ribs. Watson continued to be his shadow, eyes hugely rounded while out in the open as if trying to see any threat that may pop up. Killer whizzed about here, there, and everywhere sampling any flower that he could find.

As they walked Middy realize that Ritter was a lot like Watson with her eyes searching everything, tense, ready to shoot any threat to Middy. For some reason that thought gave Middy some comfort in a world that was falling apart. Then what was she if Ritter was the protector? That thought haunted Middy once she thought it, as if it was poking fun at her belief she was a protector of others. She felt her confidence slipping away again and straightened her shoulders, trying to ward off the sinking feeling inside her.

There was a movement to the right, which had Middy turning her head quickly to check for danger. Ritter went on full alert when Middy whipped her head to look to her right. The tension within him stretched like a rubber band approaching its breaking point. Suddenly he could breathe again when he identified the movement, and something like a smile touched his lips.

One of her mother's butterflies flitted from flower to flower before coming over to check out the dog and cat. It touched briefly on Sherlock before switching to Watson, who stood as if in shock, her pupils so dilated you couldn't see any color in her eyes. Watson too was given approval. Lifting into the air, the butterfly flew over to Ritter. Ritter stood still so as not to scare the butterfly, then slowly extended his hand. That was all the butterfly needed as it settled down for a moment on his palm. Lastly, the butterfly flew to Middy who offered both her hands cupped together. There the butterfly danced over her hands, sprinkling color from its wings over them. With the last dance over Middy, the butterfly left.

Wonder filled Middy as she stared down at her hands covered in dust from the butterfly's wings. What had just happened? Had the butterfly blessed her hands? And there was no doubt now, the butterfly approved of Ritter. But her hands? Her power was in her hands. Was this some message to use those hands to make the wind blow more, or what?

Making breakfast Middy's mind was still dwelling on the butterfly. The actions that were taken by the butterfly still puzzled her. Mother had always told her to listen to the butterflies, for they were her guides. How did you understand what they were saying? How? Her mother had always been certain what her guide meant, and so did Susan. For Middy and Eric the butterflies had always appeared in times of great stress, or danger, as sort of a comfort or clue to look out. Yet, they never seemed to do more than that, except, for the funeral when they all gathered to lift everyone's spirit.

This would be their first full day in the new house, and Middy had set aside her exploring of the city looking for the monster until Sherlock could go with her. In the meantime, she had plenty to keep her occupied. On the new computer she had delivered to her, Middy's email program had been flooded with the pictures lost in the fire. Not all of them were there, but most of them had been saved by the officer who had taken the pictures. Middy had set up one room as her office. It was there she filled up the walls with the pictures she was receiving. As Middy worked Sherlock, at first, followed her back and forth from the printer to the wall she was filling up with pictures. Watson tagged along following Sherlock back and forth, back and forth until Sherlock seemed to realize this was going to be a long day of Middy walking back and forth, and settled down near the door going out of the room.

After lunch Middy and the three companions went for another walk. Everyone seemed full of energy so she extended the walk going on until Sherlock began to look as if he was hurting. Briefly, Middy thought about getting Ritter to carry Sherlock back, then scratched that thought since she was certain he would object to having both hands full of a dog. Sherlock never complained the whole walk back to the house. He was a true example of a dog's determination not to let their person down. She suddenly remembered she needed to get Sherlock and Watson certified as assistance dog and cat, and have official vests sent for them.

After she had seen the group settled down Middy made the call to her grandfather. She always dreaded calling him because they were forever bashing their heads together, him with his idea of what she should be doing, and her just as firm in her way of life. For one thing, she didn't think she needed a bodyguard, as she was a powerful force on her own. That argument she had lost, but it still grated on her that grandfather thought she was some helpless little girl. As the phone rang on the other end Middy prepared herself for an argument. "Middleton, how are you my girl?" her grandfather said.

"Grandfather, I have something you can do for me. I know you certified Dog, Eric's cat, and Susan's Goldie, but I need two... well really three certifications, only I don't think Killer can wear a vest. Sherlock is my dog, Watson the cat, and Killer is my hummingbird. Each of them is vital to what I do and so must be able to enter any building I go into," Middy said in her most positive voice.

"Really, Middleton, a hummingbird? Isn't that rather ridiculous?" her grandfather asked.

"Not at all, he has already saved some lives, mine included. I don't know what he could display, which will admit him to buildings. I do know I feel safer when I know he is about," Middy said. She could hear her grandfather sputtering on the other end of the line. She tended to do this to him, something she didn't want to do because she remembered him having a heart attack when she was little.

Finally, the sputtering stopped and Middy heard a sigh from her grandfather. "Okay send me pictures of each of them with their names and information. Are you certain they will behave themselves in any situation?"

"Yes." Middy said while she looked over at Watson hiding behind Sherlock. If she had any doubts it was about Watson, still, she had faith that her instinct about all animals, and natural closeness to them, would win out.

So now her tiny army of animals would be part of a very elite force able to go where no other animal would be allowed.

Later, as she settled into bed with her three companions, she wondered if she was fooling herself into believing she was in control. So far she had produced nothing of any benefit for anyone. Realizing she was losing what little confidence she had scraped up, Middy pushed those thoughts out of her mind, tried to relax and let sleep take her.

It wasn't long before walks in the yard were not enough exercise for active animals, so Middy began to take long walks down the road. The trouble was that cars slowed and people stared at her unlikely trio. Middy did not want to draw attention to herself or her growing family. Still, she would not hide away like some scared mouse. She had had enough of that to last a lifetime.

The week seemed to drag on as Sherlock slowly healed. He was walking so that you had to look twice to notice he only had three legs. By the middle of the week, he was starting to use his nose to find every scent he came across. It was clear Sherlock was eager to be tracking down all the wonderful scents filling his nose. Just what was the question. The thought of using him to track down criminals entered Middy's mind. Still, that would put him and the others in danger, so she wasn't certain that was the best way to use that wonderful nose. Since the thought had entered her mind Middy began to prepare for using Sherlock to follow a scent. First, she ordered a non-restrictive harness so his neck wouldn't be pulled as he strained in harness. She had also ordered a forty foot lead to give him plenty of room to work an area of ground. If Middy overcame her doubts about her companions going into danger, she was ready.

The visit for Sherlock's checkup and to have the final release from Dr. Clive was a test of sorts for the companions. Watson, of course, came with Sherlock and Killer wouldn't be left behind. How they were in the presence of other people and animals would give Middy an idea of how they would react while she went about hunting a monster.

The first test came in the form of a burly man who was rushed out of the clinic by his bulldog as Middy and her companions were about to enter. Middy automatically gave her mother's hand signal for Dog to move aside. It was as if Sherlock was in tune with her as he leaned into Watson to protect her from the bustling pair bursting out of the door. Killer danced a bit as if he was going to go after the man and his bulldog, but quickly settled down. The first obstacle had been overcome for it was very true that not everyone was considerate of people when entering or leaving a building.

Ritter held the door open so Middy and the crew could enter the clinic. Curious eyes took in the three animals and the frumpy woman with them almost with a look of distaste. Some held their cat or dog a little tighter as if afraid they would be contaminated. The moment passed as gradually people began to recognize Middy as the Butterfly

Whisperer. Killer zoomed around the room as if
he was inspecting everyone in turn. Several people
exclaimed over the lovely hummingbird. They grew
silent once Middy checked in and took a seat. Killer
flew back to her, taking a perch on her shoulder.
Sherlock and Watson sat as near as possible to Middy
with Watson between Sherlock and Middy. Ritter
stood where he could see the door as well as the
people in the lobby.

The woman sitting beside Middy fidgeted for
a moment before turning to her and asking in a low
whisper, "ma'am, is that a hummingbird?"

Middy whispered back, "Yes."

"How on Earth did you tame it?" the woman
asked with a sense of wonder and incredulity in her
voice.

"Oh, I didn't, he picked me," Middy told her.

For a moment the woman looked as if she had
been insulted, then the woman's name was called
to go back to the exam room. Middy shrugged it
off. She had learned long ago not to worry about
why other people hated her when they didn't even
know her. People seem to hate anything they don't
understand. She herself certainly didn't understand
other people and their ways. Still, she didn't hate
them for it. That was just them, and she was just
herself. She hadn't lied to the woman, hadn't put on
airs, but had merely answered her question. It was
hopeless trying to understand why people would hate
another person for their looks, the way they talked or
where they had been born, and all the other idiotic
reasons people decided to hate or dislike a person.
Realizing she was letting herself become frustrated

over nothing she reached down and petted Sherlock and Watson to get some objectivity. There was a monster loose in the city Middy reminded herself, and she had to find him before he killed again.

Several people went in ahead of Middy and her crew, new people came in sitting down to wait their turn. It never failed that Middy would receive a long staring look. She did the only thing worth doing and ignored everyone. Relief came when she was called back until the snippy receptionist told her in blunt tones that she only had an appointment for Sherlock. "Yes, I know. These guys have bonded and go everywhere together. Don't worry, I'll not be asking for treatment for Killer or Watson." Middy said as sweetly as she could manage. Middy treated the woman in the same manner she would treat an arrest who was mouthing off. In other words, she was humoring her.

Dr. Clive seemed pleased to see Middy smiling a bit too much, his eyes even smiling. "How is my favorite patient doing? Any trouble walking? Have his ribs acted up at all?" all the while he talked he felt Sherlock's body over and examined the stitch line of the leg where it had been amputated. Now and again he looked up at Middy and smiled again.

"He has really been doing well, so well in fact that he wants to go sniffing along scents he finds. We are both eager to have the go-ahead on that," Middy said, trying to keep things all business.

"Really? If you take it slow and keep him on a leash I think you can indulge him a little. Don't go overboard with it," Dr. Clive said. "It might be interesting to watch him track down something."

"No, it would be too dangerous for another person to come along. If you watch the news you know that," Middy said softly.

There was a long, awkward moment when the doctor seemed puzzled before he removed Sherlock's stitches and pronounced him able-bodied. So, now her dog's doctor thought she was strange too, the thought almost made her laugh had it not been so sad.

Morning dawned with Middy feeling a tingle of excitement. She was looking forward to following behind Sherlock as he sniffed his way to whatever struck him as smelling special. After their morning duty walk and breakfast Middy strapped the harness on Sherlock preparing for their first exploration. Watson was leery of the harness on Sherlock but was unwilling to leave her protector.

They were a strange looking bunch walking off onto the lawn, the frumpy girl, a three-legged dog, wild-eyed cat, and a blur of a hummingbird followed by a dangerous looking man in black. No scent escaped Sherlock's notice, he would stop and bury his nose in the grass for a long moment. Sometimes Sherlock would follow the scent for a while until he was satisfied. Other times he just stood with his nose taking in the scent as he stored the information on it away. Watson would raise her head high and work her nostrils, her ears twitching and eyes staring off in the distance. Killer was the only one who ignored it all. He seemed content to zoom about drinking from every flower in the area. The walk was slow with many a detour as they followed Sherlock's nose.

Mainly Middy wanted to see how good a scent hound Sherlock was in finding things, and people. Dog, her mother's dog, could find anyone anywhere. He took his duty seriously and wouldn't stop until he had the person they were after. It had always fascinated Middy that Dog could and would find people. Dog was capable of ripping a man's arm off, but he loved his people, her mother in particular. She didn't like the idea of Sherlock giving up so often on a scent. That is until she realized he wasn't giving up after all. They had followed along for a while on one, and Sherlock got too close to his goal and scared a rabbit into running in the open. Middy still had her doubts musing over the whole thing on their return to the house. It was a crazy thought, thinking Sherlock could track down a madman. Only Eric had said Sherlock could help me, she thought.

Each day they did a walk with Sherlock in the lead shadowed by Watson. So far, Watson didn't seem to think much of the walks, she always had that far off look in her eyes. Sherlock seemed to settle down and commit more to one or two tracks, rather than being all over the place trying to find everything there was to find. This was working so well that they were able to venture farther and farther into the nearby woods. Middy was becoming in tune with Sherlock and able to read the difference in when he was tracking, and when he was just goofing off. She learned to recognize the moments he raised his head and cleared his nose.

They were traveling along on some track Sherlock was following when he did something which startled Middy. His nose down head swinging slightly side to side, Sherlock was traveling at a fast clip after whatever he was hunting, when suddenly he jumped back like a startled rabbit. What happened next was even more surprising. Watson's fur all stood on end and she crouched down in a charge position. With a snarl that sent a chill down Middy's back Watson rushed forward pouncing, then bounding away, pounce, leap away. She was making these weird sounds as if she were a demon from hell bent on destroying everyone.

Sherlock started bouncing around getting closer and closer to whatever Watson was attacking and barking. Middy prepared her wind, ready to blast some critter far from her friends. It was then that Watson put an end to the game she was playing and bit down on something, holding it down with her front paws as she crunched on it. Only then did Middy see it was a snake. A dead snake now. Middy rushed forward and began to examine Sherlock and Watson for bites. Evidently, the pair had been too much for the snake to get a strike in. Middy's breath escaped her in a swoosh of relief and she plopped down on her bottom on the ground.

Sherlock gave Middy's face a lick before turning to Watson. Watson still held the snake down with her front paws as if she expected it to spring back to life. Sherlock went over to her and place a big paw on her back, squishing her to the ground where he began to lick her all over as if washing away the memory of the snake. Soon Watson relaxed and began to purr, the bond between the two strengthened. They were a strange bunch, but all that mattered was they worked well together.

When they returned to the house, it became clear Watson's personality had changed. The first hint was when she laid a foot away from Sherlock. It was as if killing the snake had boosted her confidence in herself, making her feel as if she could do things on her own instead of needing Sherlock.

Sherlock in return seemed pleased with himself as if all had worked out as he intended. Middy couldn't help but have human thoughts about their behavior. The only one which didn't seem to have been touched by the snake incident was Killer. He zoomed about in his normal manner, as if he had more important things to do than make a fuss over Watson.

Ritter was silent about the whole thing, he was trying to be good, to not push Middy in any manner. But it was hard, and getting harder to maintain that distance. It went against every instinct he had. When the dog had leaped back Ritter had gone into a super agent mode, ready to rip the throat out of anyone threatening Middy. He barely controlled his urge to pull her away from the action. He could see her fingers twitching away and wished he hadn't seen that action. Ritter wished he had never guessed what Middy could do. He wanted her to be dependent upon him, to need him as he needed her. It was a terrible thin tightrope he walked, wanting one thing yet doing another.

One thing Middy missed about being at the farm was having the freedom to practice using her wind. She had perfected the little burst which could turn a page in a book or blow a trash can into a fleeing fugitive, but she needed to practice more of the big winds, those which could down a building or sweep a crowd off their feet. Here at her new home she had room to practice. She just had to get away from Ritter long enough to manage that.

All evening she watched for a chance to slip outside. Trouble was, Ritter was just too vigilant. As darkness fell Middy cooked a huge evening meal for the guys, as all the SS team were staying at the house now. They tailed her during the day, staying out of sight most of the time. She wanted their bellies full and the men contented enough to sleep soundly with only the night man out patrolling the area. Once she slipped into her bedroom and raised the window high enough, she could slip out of it later. Middy didn't like deceiving the guys, but she had to keep her power a secret from the world at large.

When the meal was over and the men sat around for a brief period watching television or playing checkers, Middy went and printed out the latest photos, the way she usually did, putting them up on the ever-growing picture walls. She tried to study them in her usual manner, but her mind wasn't on photos, it was on the wind. Inside her it seemed the force was building again like it had since her last brush with death. It left her feeling restless and on edge, yet that was nothing the guys hadn't noticed before in her.

Gradually the daylight crew drifted off to bed, leaving just Middy up, as usual, pouring over the photos on her office walls. At last, she yawned and drifted off to her bedroom. Having done nothing unusual she felt she was safe sneaking out of the house. Middy waited about an hour to be certain everyone had had a chance to drift off to sleep. Carefully, she eased Sherlock and Watson out the window so they wouldn't raise a fuss when she left. Killer just flew out the window following her.

Going as far as she could from the house and the patrolling SS guard, Middy began to let her wind stir. She built a small force sending it in a narrow line through the trees, watching as the trees bent before the wind as if bowing their heads to the might of the wind. Twice more she sent the wind through the trees being careful not to break or uproot them. She was satisfied that she could break down a door or slam through a wall if needed. Now Middy wanted to work on containment as she had with the red car which was driven by a bomber. Finding a suitable downed tree she moved it out into the open and began.

The log lay still upon the grass not showing any movement to start with, while Middy stirred the air, sending it to twist and grow in power. When she was satisfied she brought the air down, sending the log whirling in place. As Middy studied the spinning log she wasn't happy with it. It had taken her precious time to stir the air up into a spinning whirlwind. The monster wouldn't give her that time. She tried different methods, blowing a wind under the log to lift it off the ground as she had the block of cement crushing Ritter. It was a difficult maneuver taking a sustained effort which drained her body, so that was out. Frustration built inside Middy until she finally just blasted the log with blast after blast of forceful wind. She had ended up blowing the log hard into the nearby trees continually blasting it so it was trapped. Finally, she released her frustration into the air shooting it as high into the sky as she could. A sound like a sonic boom followed as Middy turned to make her way back to her bedroom window with her three companions. Slipping into her bed, she pulled the covers up to her chin and tried to sleep.

Outside Ritter made his way to the front door after watching over Middy. She had managed to cause him to believe in her and her power. Anyone with that much power could cause havoc to the world. They were fortunate that she was on their side. Let's hope she remains there. All the evil she had witnessed has to be weighing on her mind, he thought. Would it turn her into doing something desperate?

Waking to sunlight filtering through the window Middy felt listless and shaky. She should have put something in her room to eat after practice last night. If she had been with her family, they would have seen to it that she ate. Not for the first time she missed them, and the support they provided each other. This was her life and she had to make a monster pay for all the lives he had taken because of her. She straightened up and lifted her chin unconsciously doing the very things her mother did when she was a child, girthing herself against the world.

With determined steps, Middy went into the kitchen and started breakfast for the SS agents. She believed that a person starting the day with a good meal would have a more fruitful day.

Since she was feeling tired Middy only did the duty walk with her three companions. She was worried that she was going about training Sherlock all wrong, so after breakfast, she looked up how to train a tracking dog. Right off it showed she was doing it wrong, now if she was training a dog to hunt game the way she was going might work over time. She studied the charts and suggestions posted about tracking dogs carefully. There was a great deal of dedication and time involved. As she looked over the suggested charts of day to day training Middy realized that a good dog would learn fast. Her strength was returning, as was her determination.

While she still had everything she read fresh in her mind, Middy put a regular collar on Sherlock and short leash. Carrying the tracking harness and long leash she took her bunch of companions out. Ritter, she might as well include as one of her companions, she thought, as he slipped out the door first to check for snipers. He was standing to the side where he had the best view of everything in front of Middy when she walked up and handed him Sherlock's leash. Surprised, and puzzled, he took the leash, never stopping his constant vigil of the area.

"Stay!" Middy told him and walked off. Ritter's mouth twitched just a tad as he suppressed a smile, she was always such a firecracker.

Middy walked out to a spot in the yard. They hadn't spent a lot of time in this area. Bending down, she stuck a fork in the ground to mark the beginning of this first practice track. She had secreted a slice of cheese inside a sock which she had stuffed in her pants near her body. Looking about she saw two distant items which she could line up so moving to either side would show the two separating, a fence post, and a telephone pole. Watching the two guide items she started forward walking about 25 steps. It was farther than the charts had recommended, but she had faith in Sherlock. After laying the sock down Middy turned around, and on the same path she had used walked out. She walked back over to Ritter, taking the harness, and placed it on Sherlock.

Giving Ritter a look that clearly said stay back, Middy and Sherlock approached the fork in the ground. Middy pointed at the ground and said, "Find it." Whenever Sherlock looked to be off the track she had laid, Middy stopped, holding still until he went back to where the track went. Before reaching the sock he smelled the cheese and practically pulled Middy to it. Immediately upon Sherlock stopping and nosing the sock, Middy ran up and took it making a great deal out of praising Sherlock. She worked the cheese out of the sock with him watching to give to him, saving a tiny bit for Watson, who as always was tagging along. Thus, they began learning how to track down a person.

Chapter Eleven

CLOSER

Repetitive, that is what it was to train Sherlock. Every day the tracks became longer until the day came when Middy knew she must now introduce turns. So far Sherlock hadn't let her down and he seemed to have taken wholeheartedly to what they were doing. Of course, that slice of cheese reward helped. Each day they ran tracks no matter what the weather was, in the rain and in the heat they were out running a track.

Soon there were as many as five turns to each track. It was time to introduce other people for Sherlock to find. By now, she had removed the cheese from the item left on the track, and instead, carried the cheese reward in a baggy with her. So now Sherlock tracked for the fun of finding the end of the track instead of for a hunk of cheese. It was going well only, he was used to following her scent. Would he follow someone else?

The guys had taken to watching Sherlock run the tracks and were now familiar with the routine. So, when Middy asked for volunteers the two daytime SS men, whom Ritter referred to as 'spares', raised their hands. Sherlock hadn't had a lot to do with them, he knew them from the meals they all shared, but they hadn't been overly friendly to any of the animals for fear of upsetting the training Middy was doing. Because they were always there out of sight when Middy lay down the tracks they had the idea. She only had a few instructions. She had to be certain they knew how to line up distant objects to maintain a straight line, for it was important that Middy knew Sherlock was actually on the track. She showed the men how she made her maps to follow the track behind Sherlock and be certain she was on the track. Marking her two distant guides for each turn and making a note to indicate to herself where the turn actually was, using a set of bushes or odd flowers that were growing near the turn. Then she took Sherlock and the others and went inside so she couldn't even see where the volunteer walked. This would truly be a blind track for her and Sherlock.

Her nerves were on edge and a chunk of a hot dog, as well as the slice of cheese, were tucked away in her baggy. Middy waited as she timed the aging of the track. She wanted it at least an hour old. So, she and the guys tried to distract themselves reading, or playing checkers. Both attempts at distractions were a total waste of effort as neither Middy or the guys could think of anything but the upcoming track. Finally, Middy rose picking up the tracking harness. The guys and the animals were instantly on their feet, the same eager expression over all their faces. So much so that Middy nearly made a comment about how they all looked alike. Still, she knew some people were sensitive about their looks and wouldn't understand her comment, so she kept her mouth shut chuckling on the inside as she snapped the leash to Sherlock's collar.

The SS man who had laid the track had briefed Middy on the map making certain she knew what landmarks he had used. He had a neat handwriting so the map was easy to understand. Standing well back, he pointed to the starting flag which was one of the flags on a stick that the guys had bought for Middy to use in her training. It was, she had to admit, much better than a fork in the ground.

Just as she started off towards that flag, tires squealed out on the road. Everyone went into SS mode, guns out and cold masks on their faces. The car careened towards the house, shimmying as if the steering was out of whack, with someone waving frantically out the driver's window. Whatever the person was trying to communicate they couldn't hear, watching with horror as the car went into a spin slamming broadside into two trees.

Fuming, as one of the spares practically picked Middy up and rushed her back into the house, despite Killer attacking him and Watson hissing in threatening tones. Middy finally pushed her would be protector away, and whipped out her cell phone to call for an ambulance, and the state police since this was their territory. "Go," she told the SS man, "help them." But a stark "no" was in the man's eyes and his mouth was clamped shut as he crossed his arms and remained with her. Middy closed her eyes and wished for patience, knowing the man was only doing his job.

Ritter recognized the driver of the car despite the fact the car slamming into the tree had done a job on the man's face. Rosco, one of the officers who had been on Cupcake's unofficial team. Amazingly Rosco was still alive. He looked at Ritter through one bloodied eye and tried to say something. "Don't try to speak. Save your strength, Rosco. Help is coming," Ritter said.

Rosco knew he wasn't going to make it. It was that certain feeling a person gets when they just know they are dying. He had to get the information to Middy. Here he was dying in his effort to tell her he had seen the killer, and it looked as if he was going to be a failure. No, he swore, he'd get the info to her… someway. Reaching up, he wiped through the blood on his face and hand shaking with his last strength he wrote on the dash, "saw kill pic cell…." The end came claiming the man named Rosco, officer and friend to many.

The shaky words on the dash had Ritter searching Rosco for a cell phone. Not finding one he went to the other side of the car and opened the door of the car methodically searching the car feeling between the seat backs and under the seats. He even felt up under the dashboard. Nothing. The back seat was just as fruitless as was the area around and under the car. Frustration was reaching a high so tall that Ritter's hands were starting to clump into fists. The world was, however, saved from Ritter's fist by a raised angry female voice.

"The danger is over. You WILL get out of my way before I kick your sorry ass across the yard," Middy shouted at the unyielding SS agent standing in her way.

Her fingers were twitching dangerously when Ritter reached her. He had to defuse this bomb before his spare was blown to bits. "I need you and Sherlock, Cupcake. We need his nose," he said, as he motioned the spare back with a nod of thanks. The man had done his job bucking a dangerous woman and didn't even know it. Thankfully Middy seemed to want to help more than she wanted to make Ritter's spare pay.

Ritter tried to prepare her for what she was about to see. "I want you to know before we reach the car that the driver is Rosco. He didn't make it. The thing is, he tried to tell me he saw the killer and had taken his picture. Only we can't find his cell phone. Sherlock will have to sniff it out if he can," he threw the 'if he can' out to challenge her, to make her want to show him what Sherlock could do. She gave him a look that should have killed him if he hadn't been prepared for it. Secretly he smiled to himself, he had her!

Middy still had Sherlock's tracking harness with her so she simply approached the wreck as the emergency crew pulled up along with the state troopers. Quickly Middy slipped Sherlock's harness on him and pointed at the wreck trying to avoid looking at Rosco dead inside it. Sherlock was all business. He knew his job now and went at it with single-minded determination. After running around the car sniffing inside at the open door on one side,

Sherlock raised his head for a moment before pulling Middy off down the road. Soon it became clear he was following the route the car had taken as it raced towards the house.

Ritter followed Middy and Sherlock with Watson and Killer close behind like small satellites. If the killer had followed Rosco Ritter had to be ready for him. He wouldn't get a second chance, not with this guy's ability to disappear.

Sherlock was running with his nose grazing the road going so fast Middy had to run to keep up with him. This he had never done before, going all out like that. Middy didn't see how he could be tracking, yet he was. Ritter knew the way Rosco's car had swerved along the road, more out of control than under control.

Sherlock was dead on the way the car had traveled, he hadn't wavered the least bit off the scent. Suddenly he stopped and, raising his head, he wind scented, taking great inhales of something blowing across the path the car had taken when it careened down the road. He looked about as if uncertain as to which scent was the most important to his human. The one straight on was the machine scent, but off there to the right was a fresh whiff of man scent. The insides of the car had held that scent. Abruptly Sherlock changed course nearly pulling Middy off her feet in his rush to reach that man scent, the one that spoke urgently to him.

There was an urgency about Sherlock's movements and he seemed to be racing toward something just along the trees lining the road.

Middy was hard put to keep up with the three-legged dog. The hummingbird, Killer, was like a crazed breeze zipping about so fast that he was just a blink in Middy's eye. Watson ran all out to keep up with Sherlock, that was why she smashed into him when he stopped suddenly. All of Watson's fur stood up making her look like a picture of a witch's cat except orange in color. She was tense and poised for battle until Sherlock gave her such a hard lick it nearly knocked her off her feet.

By the time Sherlock had made things right with Watson, Middy had caught up with them. Now for the first time she moaned inside over her lack of athletic ability. Running was just such a pain to do. Still, she had to admit to herself that she needed to get into shape for the type of work she did. Running down a suspect had been so often needed, only… well, she didn't run them down, she just sent her wind after them to trip them up or shove them into a wall where she could hold them down until she caught up with them. She cheated, and by doing so had let herself become run down.

Sherlock looked up expectantly as if to say "I found it". She brought herself back from being angry at herself for not exercising. "Good boy. You found it!" she said making her voice high pitched with praise. And indeed he had found the cell phone. It was clear Sherlock didn't think he was done, as he took off again as soon as Middy had put on a glove, picked up the cell phone and deposited it in the evidence bag Ritter handed her. He went charging down the road again as if determined to follow Rosco's car all the way back to his house.

A stitch began to throb in Middy's side as she stumbled down the road after Sherlock and Watson. Killer came and was a satellite around Middy, as if encouraging her to hurry along. Just as she thought she would have to pull up and stop Sherlock's forward progress he again swung his head towards the trees and took off with that determined look in a straight line to the trees where he stopped and looked back at Middy with his "I found it" expression.

There it was, Rosco's wallet. That posed the question as to why Rosco would throw his wallet out so close to the main road. What was he trying to say? Or do? A decoy? Something to stop whoever was after him? It had to have been a decoy.

Ritter had reached the same conclusion Middy had and quickly shoved her to the ground as he searched for any place the killer might be hiding.

Back at the wreck, the spares had been keeping an eye on the people extracting Rosco's body, and the state troopers. The sudden movement by Ritter did not pass unnoticed. One of the spares began to bark orders at those who had just arrived. "Down, possible intruder" was all he said. The other spare had already commandeered one of the troopers' cars and was speeding like crazy down to where their subject was being held down by Ritter. He skidded to a stop crosswise in front of Ritter and the subject. The subject wasn't speaking, but she was bucking, trying to get Ritter to let her up.

Middy saw a spare opening the passenger's side door of the patrol car and she wasted no time telling Sherlock and Watson to get inside the car. Now that her hands were free she was able to shove

Ritter off her. She stayed down, staring hard at Ritter. It was his expression which held her in place, he looked so determined…, and as if he was in great pain. Instead of blasting him with a how dare you speech she said, "I need my hands free." He nodded and she got up as far as a crouch, looking carefully around. The most noticeable thing she saw was killer, he wasn't acting frantic or alerting on any area. This alone was enough to convince Middy the killer wasn't here. "He has gone. He may have picked up or touched Roscoe's wallet so we need to put it in an evidence bag. Also, have the guys check for tire tracks on both sides of the road and across the main road. He might not have even left his car, but I hope he did and picked up the wallet before he left. We need something with which to track him down," Middy said, dusting her legs and blouse off from Ritter slamming her down to the ground. Ritter was already scooping the wallet up into another evidence bag. She had to admit he was good at doing that not even touching the wallet in the process.

A truce of sorts passed between Ritter and Middy. They moved more like a team than subject and protector as they looked over the area trying to spot anything of interest before they piled into the car and let the spare drive them back to where Rosco was being loaded into the ambulance. The hard part was ahead of them now, they had to inform the department and Rosco's family that he was dead. She would have to leave this for others to do so as not to put Rosco's family in danger. She was so tired of being a prisoner of a mad monster's whim.

It was another hour before the state police

were done with their investigation of Rosco's car. One thing was certain, Rosco was dead because he thought reaching Middy was more important than his own life. Middy hadn't missed the coroner stating Rosco had a bullet in his back. He had driven all the way out to her place, knowing he was dying. Middy hoped the butterflies would honor Rosco at his funeral. He deserved so much more than that, but the rest was up to the department.

The SS guys were quieter than usual as they gathered in Middy's kitchen, sitting around the table. Ritter had Rosco's cell phone hooked up to the laptop sitting on the far end of the table. It was all there, the last moments of Rosco's life. It started with him taking pictures of random people. They were so desperate now that anyone who passed by was suspected of possibly being the monster in disguise. Rosco, like so many other officers, had been snapping pictures of faces, any face he passed that could be a possibility. Then he had snapped the final face, the one which got him killed. He had even managed to take a lopsided picture of the gun firing at him as he ran away. Through his back car window, he continued to snap pictures of being pursued down the road until he could no longer hold up the phone and drive at the same time. Then it became a race to reach Middy. On the computer, there was a perfect picture of the killer. Middy sat long after the guys, except Ritter, had retired for the night. She stared at the killer's picture memorizing every detail, the shape of his ears, his nose and brow. She burned the image into her brain. At last, she stood and walked the dog and cat one last time before going to her bed.

She doubted she would sleep tonight, along with the killer's image was Rosco's bloodied face burned into her mind.

Once they had downloaded all the information they could gain from Rosco's cell phone Ritter called the Captain to report they had found Rosco's cell phone. It was still in the evidence bag as he had only slid the end of the phone out enough to connect it to the laptop computer. There was no need for the Captain to know they had already downloaded all the evidence to Middy's laptop. At least now the police would have an actual photo of the killer to go by instead of doubtful sketches.

Relief and nervous tension went through Middy as the cell phone was passed off to the officer picking it up. To finally have a picture of the killer was uplifting, yet at the same time, she feared for all the officers who would be out searching. If they ran into the killer would they die too? It was unacceptable, she had to find him first and take him down. It was the only way to ensure the safety of others.

The problem was she thought she knew the person in the photo, but he didn't look exactly like anyone she could place in her mind. Perhaps he was in disguise when she saw him, or was in disguise in the photo.

Ritter had slept very little during the night, his mind was too busy trying to find a way to keep his Cupcake from endangering herself. He began to understand her father's obsession with protecting her mother. It was true, they didn't know how to stay safe. He paused in that thought, that he was setting himself up for a life of constantly trying to keep Cupcake from getting herself killed. He'd have to remain strong and dedicated, give her his strength when she ran low on her own. Ritter looked deep inside himself questioning if he had what it took to love someone like Middy. The trouble was Cupcake being a high spirited individual, a force of nature all on her own. What right had he to kill that driving personality? None. He looked over to where Middy was getting ready to take her pets out for a walk. How many more can she collect passed through his mind, the animals, an entire police force? She was like a magnet pulling in lost causes and making them her responsibility. With a sigh Ritter got up ready to do his life's job, his reason for living, keeping Middy safe, a least for a year or two.

Sherlock waited respectfully for Middy to tell him to go out. His whole body was vibrating with the excitement of another day hunting the scent. Middy looked down at Sherlock, "Today we start the real hunt. You are as ready as I can make you. We have a monster to find."

The walk was short with each of the animal companions doing their business right off. There was a tenseness in the air as if the whole world was on edge, waiting to see what happens next. Of course, the rest of the world was completely unaware of what was going on with Middy and her team, so it was unlikely they gave a second of thought about her.

One of the exceptions called while they all ate breakfast. Middy answered the phone to hear Fuller's voice on the other end of the call. "Alright what do you have planned? You are not fooling me gal, you are like one of my grandfather's old hunting dogs once on the track you just don't stop. So let us in on the kill, it is something we need. We need it to finally feel worth going on."

Middy knew he was right, but her heart balked at the thought of them being in harm's way. Then an image of her mother including her and Eric in on not only the chores on the farm but the fun things they did. Everything was always a family event. Except when her mother wanted to take on her personal monster on her own. Had Middy and Eric let that happen? The answer was a resounding NO! She knew that she couldn't leave the guys out in the cold on this venture, this taking down a monster. "Now that we have an actual picture of this monster we need to run facial recognition on every camera there is in the city so we can track where he frequents. Get someone on that and we will phone conference about the best time and place to trap him. Okay?"

"I'm on it. Being confined to a desk job is finally paying off," Fuller said, with a note of cheer in his voice that Middy had only heard before when she had brought donuts and coffee to the men, bribing him to wear his vest. It was good to hear her friend and partner so cheerful.

Still, Middy had to say something about protection, "And all of you wear a vest. I won't be pleased if I find out you guys are not in a vest at all times. Got it!" She actually punched her finger at the phone as if poking him in the chest.

"Ouch, gal, I felt that all the way over here," Fuller said in an aggrieved voice. "I can hear that smile, gal," Fuller said hanging up.

Slowly Middy disconnected the phone call, she missed the guys, missed the joking around and poking at each other just to get a rise out of someone. Not for the first time she wondered what she had done that caused a monster to ruin her life, to kill her fellow officers, and attempt to kill her. She just couldn't think of anything dire enough to have provoked such hate in another person. Who was she trying to fool? Monsters didn't need a reason for hating you, just because you were alive was enough for them to work up a hate. They were so busy working on hating those around them that they failed to live a life.

The phone rang again pulling Middy from her musings. "Hello," she said into the phone. "Soon." There was nothing but the dial tone after that one word. Him. The monster had called her. "Ritter!" Middy bellowed so loud Watson jumped up in the air as if poked. He was there in a flash, the SS man. "He just called my phone. Get them to find out who and where," Middy said. Even the night man got up from his bed as the team went into ready mode. Within minutes they knew the call had come from a disposable phone in the center of the city. It had bounced off every tower around the area and was pinpointed as being at the donut shop where Middy had so often order donuts for the guys. In other words, a dead end unless a security camera had picked up the caller. Now came the tedious job of looking at what the cameras picked up.

Middy had to get out of the house, she felt so

helpless just going over and over the photos taken by the guys. This wasn't her, she was a person of action. This being confined to her home just wasn't right. If nothing else, she could take meals to the elderly as she used to do before all the media storm about her. She called Betty to let her know she was going to make her usual run of delivering meals. Betty was delighted, mentioning how hard it was to get anyone reliable to take meals to the elderly.

After hanging up the phone Middy rubbed the back of her neck upset that the people she had come to love when delivering meals had gone hungry because she had let them down. Sure she could use the excuse that a monster entering her life was the reason she spent less time doing the little things she always enjoyed doing, giving back to people who had so often been forgotten, but she knew that was just an excuse. The real reason she had stopped was fear, and the selfish need to not have another load of guilt placed upon her shoulders by getting the helpless elderly killed. She didn't want to see their deaths the way she had seen her fellow officers killed around her. Who was she kidding she couldn't go back to delivering meals to the elderly, she was still afraid of putting them in danger.

The only thing left to do was find a monster.

It took three days before Fuller finally found a pattern in the movement from the facial recognition program. Each spot indicated by the program was marked upon a map on the computer. Then the frequency of the area being visited was added. Fuller had always thought the computer geeks were just a bunch of wasted space, but now he was one of them and understood more and more each day how valuable they were to the police department. He had always been sharp and able to fathom new methods, the computer, however, was a whole new experience for him. He was a street cop and had always taken pride in his ability to read people, to know when an action was needed. This following a trail of computer images began to fascinate him. Now he realized he could map out a person's entire life just by following them on the computer. What they bought, ate, watched, the medicines they bought, who they called, where they lived, and where they went for entertainment. Every part of a person's life could be found on a computer. In a way that was scary, suppose they were watching him? What if some sick creep was keeping tabs on him waiting for the right moment to take him out? Fuller shook the chills that ran down his back off, this was for Whiting, his partner.

Out patrolling the streets Frankie and Albert were together. Albert was a changed man from the happy gaming young officer he had once been. These days he took everything seriously, every look, every comment or remark by a suspect he weighted and measured as if it was a true threat. He still loved gaming, but now he knew that in real life there were monsters wearing human form. He kept his cell phone plugged in while in the car, running constant downloads of what was around him. He'd not be taken again without knowing who took him or where he was taken. His inability to know where he was when he had been in the hands of a monster had left him feeling wanting, and he was not going to be caught wanting again. Not only did he have his cell phone on constantly but had invested in other equipment for constantly taking video of his surroundings. In today's age, there was no reason a person shouldn't have rings, watches, pins, or chains with cameras, or any other device which would aid them with the world around them. He truly believed in his gadgets and had gone so far as to secretly place surveillance equipment on many items Whiting had, even on the dog's leash. They were not going to lose her to this madman.

Frankie was old school, he believed in legwork and awareness. It wasn't as if he didn't admire the gadgets Albert had, he just didn't think they should rely on them. He knew that, like Fuller, he was up for retirement, and if it was the last thing he did as a police officer he'd help bring down this madman. It was that and the fire in Whiting's eyes which inspired him to work harder than he ever had before. Life was not going to leave his body with him having regrets. He knew a leader when he saw one no matter how they were packaged. Fuller smiled to himself, Whiting would smack him one if she knew he was thinking things like that about her. But he had seen the fire in her, the iron will it took to complete a task, to catch a creep. He only hoped Ritter was able to keep her reined in a bit, just enough to keep her from being killed.

Another day wasted, thought Middy as she took her animal companions out for a final walk for the night. She had hopes that Fuller would come through with the facial recognition program but he still hadn't called. The only plus was, it was another day without anyone being killed, and Middy would take a day like that any time.

Ritter couldn't rest, he should be getting some sleep while the night man was on duty, but all he could do was worry about how to keep Cupcake safe. He had protected everyone from the President to spoiled rock stars, and they were all the same, always knowing what is best for them, or rather thinking they knew. He had stopped trying to convince people that their safety depended on listening to him. Instead, he adjusted, changed his approach so he was always two steps ahead of the brats, the stuck-up rich people, and the ones who thought they owned the world. This assignment had him wanting to tear his hair out in frustration. He doubted himself and for the first time, the stakes were so high that if his subject died he himself would just want to die too. Who would have thought such an unlikely subject would have him tied in knots?

Chapter Twelve

BLACK OUT

A day of double searching the film Fuller had sent her had Middy's eyes tired and wanting rest. She had three more of the cameras' caches to look through. These were all the places Fuller had caught signs the killer frequented. Rising Middy took a break, taking the companions out for the evening walk. She didn't know when night had fallen as she had been so intent on not missing one moment of watching the monster who had destroyed so many lives. A spot was burning inside her red hot with guilt, anger, and pure rage at a foe that hid in the shadows, lurking amongst the innocent people as a normal person.

She thought of all the different ways she had seen him made up in the films from different cameras. He had been a redneck, an old woman, a teenager, a businessman, and even an expectant woman. No wonder they had so much trouble locating him from the sketchs the General had provided. There were giveaways, things she noticed, things Ritter noticed, and undoubtedly Fuller had noticed. There was that fraction of hesitation when anyone who was the slightest bit rumpled came near. Middy would see him bracing himself to act the role he was playing and not flinch away from the person.

As Middy entered the house and released Sherlock, the lights went out. She immediately crouched down and checked outside to see if she could still see the shine of the city reflecting on the horizon. Out. The whole area was dark. Her place wasn't dark for long, one of the first things the SS did when she bought the house was to install backup generators which kicked in almost immediately.

Around her there was the activity of defensive action going into effect. Already they were trying to herd Middy and the animals into what had been set up as a safe-room of sorts. The biggest thing going for it was there were no windows for a sniper to shoot through. Secondly, they immediately set any battery operated item that wasn't already in use, to charging. Extra cell phones were topped off as were talkies for each other. They would not be cut off from communications with the outside world for as long as the generators ran. These men were trained to be paranoid, to think outside the box, and prepare for any outcome.

Even as Middy was rushed into the safe room she saw her computers being downloaded and stored in different areas. No material would be lost, not if they could help it. "Man-made." She heard one of the men say as he received a report on what was going on. Someone had deliberately placed the city in darkness. "The hospitals? What about the elderly on machines? At home care of the very ill? What is being done for them?" Middy asked.

"The hospitals have generators, that should last them for a few hours. Some of the critically ill are already being moved to safety. Since all the horrors during flu years ago, every smart city has made arrangements for emergencies," Ritter assured her. He had been constantly at her side from the moment the lights went out trusting the rest of the team to take care of their assignments.

Ritter was right, any city that realized that the people are its life's blood had begun to take steps to prevent human loss and suffering. It only made sense, without people in the city or town to pay taxes, to buy and sell within the city boundaries, a city was soon dead, or a ghost town. The strange thing had been how long it had taken the bigger cities to understand this simple concept. Small towns with few residents were more apt to join forces to protect each other. They knew that they had to rely on each other if they were going to make it. Whereas the larger cities had come to rely on the things they need to live being trucked into them. They were looking more for profit than the future of the people.

Middy's cell phone rang with the tone for Fuller, she answered thinking he might have more news for her on the facial recognition program's results. "What do you have for me, partner?" she asked.

"You okay, gal? You need me to come chase the spooky guy away?" Fuller's worried voice said in her ear.

"We are fine. You know the spooky guy is afraid of me. He'd pee his drawers if I got near him," Middy said with a laugh. How she missed the banter between them.

"Okay, just be extra careful, gal. I don't want to have to put you over my knee," with that Fuller hung up leaving Middy with the image of him trying to hold her down to spank.

No sooner had she got off the cell with Fuller than Frankie called. "Just want you to put me on speed dial, just push my number and I'll come running. Don't you take any chances as this could be something the killer thought up. You hear me?" he barked into the cell phone.

"Don't worry, the SS guys are like a flock of mother hens all trying to sit on me at once. I feel very secure," she assured Frankie.

"That is when bad things happen, so listen to them. I mean it."

Middy sobered, he was right, she knew it as well as he did that usually when you thought all was well that was when the bottom fell out and all hell broke loose. "Okay, Frankie, I promise to be extra alert. We've seen this guy's handy work and it isn't pretty. So don't worry, I'm going to stitch my eyes open if I have to."

"You promise?"

"Yes, I promise, okay?" Middy replied.

"Okay," said Frankie his voice a bit gruff.

As she disconnected from Frankie someone knocked on the door. The SS went into double protection mode. The door to the safe room was shut and barred from the inside as one agent went to see who was knocking on the door.

In the safe room Middy grew more and more upset that she wasn't in on whatever all the whispering was about outside the safe room. That is until the all-clear was given and a very meek Albert entered the room rushing over to hug Middy. "Frankie and I agreed I should come to stay with you until the black out is fixed. You know how nuts people are at times like this," he stated, not giving her a chance to object.

Middy looked at him and thought to herself how he was all grown up now. It was sad to know the carefree young rookie who had first come to guard Middy was now so sober and down to business. They had all been changed. Death did that, moved you from the young and oblivious to a sober adult in mere moments. "Albert, you know what can happen if you are here with me. If something like that happens to you again because of me…," Middy broke off unable to even put into words the anguish she felt, and would feel.

"Don't you think I thought of that? The thing is… when I'm out there I'm just running in place… unable to go forward. It is like I'm buried alive with the air running out and death just a gasp away. Here I'm doing something positive, and I know that you won't leave me behind if something happens to me.

"The time we all spent with you was the first time any of us felt we were doing something to track this guy down. If you die while trying then you have at least tried. I want to be trying. Don't take that from me," Albert said.

Middy looked away blinking back tears that threaten to spill. Finally she nodded and walked swiftly away to where the bed set where she could break down if she was going to break, free from probing eyes.

It was eating up Middy inside to not be able to protect Albert and the others. She realized their need to do something positive, to act instead of sit on the sideline and wait. They were right she had to include everyone. The trick was to include and still protect. How was she going to do that? How?

It is amazing how one question can dominate a person's mind as this one did Middy's mind. It was more powerful than prison bars, holding her captive. She was a prisoner of love, quite literally, unable to go forward while at the same time unable to stop. She kept running scenarios in her mind on how to make it happen so that everyone was included in taking down this monster. Over and over the scenes ran like flicks advertising a movie. They all ended badly with someone dying. No matter how hard she fought to keep them out of the line of fire someone was exposed. Too many, there were too many people in harm's way. Somehow, someway she had to make it work, had to include them all. And keep them alive.

Middy walked outside with the companions, they were eager for a walk now that the city's lights were up and running. She wanted to see how many items she could hold wind shields around at one time. She walked towards the tree line with Ritter trailing along behind ever alert. For once Middy didn't even care if Ritter saw her making the wind

bend to her will. It was more important to find a
way to protect everyone. While the companions
went about doing their business, Middy arched
and shaped her wind around and around one tree's
trunk and another until she had three going at once.
The fourth one failed and then the other three just
stopped spinning around the three tree's trunks
becoming still air. Failed.

Now that she knew spinning shields wouldn't
work on several people she needed to try a blunt wall
of air, but could she keep it going while fighting?
Middy positioned several people sized walls of air,
that were solid enough to absorb a bullet without
letting it through, in front of bushes. She wanted
to see if the bushes remain still when she blast away
at them. Six walls were up protecting medium size
bushes. Middy began to send single blasts of intense
air at each bush over and over. The results were
amazing, each wall stayed in place for ten minutes
before dissolving.

Eyes narrowing Ritter watched his Cupcake
knowing something was up with her. She hadn't
even tried to hide the fact she was using wind.
Something was seriously wrong. For a whole
moment, he forgot to check for snipers or danger
around his subject as he watched her work. What
was she up to? Like an ice pick to the brain, it came
to him what Cupcake was doing. Protection, she was
practicing different ways to protect those around her.
It had to have been Albert who convinced her to let
them all be there for the capture of this serial killer.
As Ritter watched Middy fire time and time again at
some bushes he noticed how the wind hit an invisible

wall and seemed to bounce off. Those wouldn't work, it would result in the men firing and the shots bouncing back to hit them.

"They would kill themselves right off."

Middy whirled and blasted Ritter with a bullet of air. When he hit the ground Middy realized it was him and rushed to his side. "Did I hurt you? Did anything break? Answer me, you dope."

"Only… only knocked the wind out of me," Ritter said and started gasping and laughing like he had never laughed before. "Wind, get it?" He sobered when he saw Middy's face. "I'm okay, Cupcake. You didn't hurt me, honey. It is okay," he soothed as he stood and rubbed her arm.

Middy frowned, "What do you mean they would kill themselves?

"The shield would make any shots they fired, and believe me they will fire their guns the moment they see this guy, glance off back at the shooters. So something which keeps bullets from coming in will also keep them from going out," Ritter explained as he watched Middy closely for any negative reaction to his advice.

"I see. I can't fit them with wind body armor. My talent isn't going to let me do that. They have to be able to shoot, they deserve a chance to shoot him. So I'm back to square one. I can't let them go, nor can I stop them from taking part in taking him down," Middy's voice drifted off as if she was giving in to not being able to control the situation. A deep dread settled on her shoulders weighing her down. Turning, Middy called to the companions and went back to the house.

A gloom settled on the prisoner of love. Two needs so wanted and so far out of reach. Like a cup of water and a slice of bread set just beyond a prisoner's reach as he slowly died of thirst and starvation.

After the final walk of the day for the companions, Middy went off to her bedroom earlier than she ever had before. The four SS guards looked at each other in question as to what was up with her. Only Ritter knew, just as he knew he had to fix this for her, give her hope again. When he stood, the spares and the night man relaxed, the boss was on it and they all knew he could fix anything, or so they hoped.

The knock on Middy's bedroom door was neither tentative or intrusive it merely demanded that she answer the door. Instead, she said, "Enter."

Ritter walked in taking notice of the bedroom's layout as he did any room he entered. Then he walked over and sat on Middy's bed uninvited. "I've been thinking about our problem with the guys. I think I have an alternative," he said watching her closely. He had deliberately included himself as being teamed with her. She was a loner, and he knew that the inclusion might grate on her.

"Speak," she said, no expression, not even a hint of what she was feeling.

"Helmet and body armor for anyone who wants to help take him down. You used that on Fuller, remember, insisting that he wear his vest. So they already know you are a stickler for safety. It won't seem odd coming from you. They respect you enough to do as you bid, Cupcake," he said the last part very softly as if willing her to accept that one fact.

Her face muscles moved slightly as if she was debating something with herself, finally, she nodded. "Good thinking, Rit."

Rit? Ritter's heart started beating a little faster. She had given him a nickname.

Now she had to persuade the guys to wear full body armor. How was she going to pound that into their stubborn heads? Fuller had been easy when they were partners. He seemed gruff and hard-nosed, but he realized what she was doing by teasing him about driving if he didn't wear his vest, and allowed her to do it. The thing was she didn't have command over the guys. She was a civilian now, a person to be ordered around and protected, not a companion in arms. She'd have to start with Albert.

At breakfast Middy laid down the rules to Albert and the others. Vests and helmets when with her, no exceptions. She told Albert to spread the word that anyone who wanted in on the take-down had to wear a vest and helmet.

Albert started to protest "I can't breath in a vest. And with the helmet, it is just too dang hot…,"

Around the breakfast table, the SS guys started unbuttoning their shirts to expose vests on all of them. Near the door was a table with helmets. The wind went out of Albert and he nodded his acceptance. Middy wondered when Ritter had the guys get the helmets. She gave him a mental thumbs up for coming through for her, and that posed a whole different problem for her. What was she to do about her attraction to Ritter? She just couldn't deal with that right now, there were too many people to try to keep alive.

One down, so many more to convince that Middy knew it was going to be a tough campaign. She would let Albert have a shot at letting the others know what she wanted. Then it would be up to her to handle the complaints and instill in them the need for taking precautions.

Somewhat reluctantly Middy picked up the phone and pulled up her contacts. The phone on the other end rang several times before the owner answered. "This is not a good time whoever you are, call back later," a male voice said.

"Frankie?" It hadn't been like Frankie at all, so abrupt and rude.

"Boss? Is something wrong? You hang tight we'll come." Frankie said. You could almost hear him checking his gun getting ready for a shootout.

"No, no I don't need you yet. I just needed to talk to you," Middy said, and all went quiet at the other end of the phone call for a moment.

"Not now, robbery in process." Frankie hung up on her. Robbery! Had the man been going to leave a robbery to come to her? The whole thing made her feel small, like a little child. Her parents were like that, coming at a moment's notice. At the same time, she had the urge to rush out and help Frankie with the robbery, but she couldn't. A monster was watching her, stalking her, out to hurt anyone she cared about just to hurt her.

Okay then, a change in approach was called for in talking to the guys. Middy sent a text to Fuller to be passed on to anyone who was to be included in the take-down of the monster. *To everyone included in taking out the sniper, please forward. Everyone must wear full protection vest and helmet to take part. Nobody dies. That is an order.* An order, who did she think she was sending them a text like this? Middy berated herself even as she pressed send.

Almost immediately Fuller sent a reply. *Yes, Boss.*

Shortly a text came from Albert. *Yes, Boss.*

What was with this boss bit? They had to be setting her up for a joke of some sort. That would be just like the guys to set up the only woman to make her look stupid. Only she didn't believe they were wanting to make her look stupid any more. A joke yes, but nothing cruel. Their relationship had changed, and changed again as this crisis tried to crush them all. It had gone from being cruel jokes to being protective, then to a need to help out. Where this all ended up she had no idea. And she really only cared that it ended with all the guys alive and well.

Through the night and the next day, several of the "*Yes, Boss*," messages popped up on Middy's cell phone. It seemed the whole force wanted in on this. Well not all of them, but those who had been there the most frequently during the whole sniper bit and, her own private investigation. It worried her that so many would be there if this all came together. That is if they located the monster and could surround him. And there it was, the reason for so many wanting to take part. They could surround any building he was in so he couldn't pull one of his ghostly disappearing acts.

The only thing left to do now was to find this ghost and take him out, well arrest him, maybe stomp on him a bit, throw him against a wall, shoot his kneecaps. No, none of that… not much anyway. Never had she wanted to get to a guy so badly before, except once, and that was the night her parents had nearly been killed. But they had foiled that monster and her mother made certain he was locked away for life.

The thought of her parents had Middy calling them to see how they were doing. As always her mother answered on the first ring. "Middy, do you need us there?" she heard her mother say.

"No, mom. I just wanted to see how you and dad are doing. We need to have a family get together before much longer. I miss you guys," Middy confessed.

"We will make that happen as soon as possible. I'll be done with this round of healing before long. I'm certain Eric and Susan can use a break from everything going on with them too. If you need me sooner you know I'll come," her mother said.

Guilt swept over Middy, it seemed her mother was always having to come to rescue her. "No, mom, I'm good. I love you."

"Love you too, Mids," her mother said as they both hung up the phone.

Time seemed to almost slow down and stop as nothing new was found out about the ghost. He wasn't spotted in any of his disguises, or as himself. It was as if they had gone back in time to when they knew nothing, saw nothing. And the whole thing was wearing Middy's nerves thin.

It was on a Wednesday night when the first call came in of a sighting. The officer was someone Middy didn't know well and therefore she was a little hesitant about just dropping everything and going to the bar where the guy said he saw the ghost. Still, she couldn't discount any chance of finding this monster, so she had her SS geared up and went flying down the roads to the bar.

The place was packed with guys and couples drowning their daily troubles in beer and whiskey, and loudness. It was totally not the sort of place she envisioned this Mr. Neat ghost hanging out in, too many germs for someone like him. But then, the guy was a master at disguises. Suppose the neat freak clues he had left were all part of a misdirection? Middy filled her phone up with pictures of everyone she saw inside the place while dodging groping hands and drunks that seem to all zero in on her. Ritter stayed beside her. Now and then one of the drunks seemed to trip on their way to try to get Middy to go to bed with them. One even gave out an "oof" sound as he staggered away from her. Middy gave Ritter an annoyed look.

"What? I was just helping the bum along. He'll want to thank me in the morning. Well, he should thank me. You would have killed him," Ritter said with a straight face.

He jokes at a time like this? Of course, he does. It is what you do when you are worried about life and death. Middy decided, perhaps they all needed to lighten up a bit. "Nope, wouldn't have killed him, but he might have walked funny for a few weeks," she said, while her eyes scanned the ever moving crowd for a monster.

"Ouch," one of the spares said with a grin upon his face. Pretty soon they were all throwing around raunchy jokes. Their mouths were yakking, their lips smiling, only their eyes betrayed the intensity of their search.

All too soon it was clear they had hit a dry hole. Nothing was going to happen here tonight. Feeling let down Middy called it a night and the four of them went back to the house.

Two days passed before another call came with a suspect being sighted. Once more they rushed out, this time to a shopping mall which posed a problem in size for the four SS and Middy. They decided to split up Middy and Ritter with a spare would start at one end of the mall while the other two spares started from the other end. They would pass each other in the middle and continue on if there had been no results. It was immediately clear they needed to split again each to a side so they could glance into the stores as they passed them, entering if needed. Ritter was firm about Middy staying in sight at all times. For him it was a time spent in constant hell, hoping to see a killer, yet trying to watch his Cupcake at the same time.

Middy's cop sense was in overdrive, he had to be in here somewhere. The thing tripping her up, making her hope that this was just another dry hole, were the families, the families with children doing their weekly shopping. If so much as one child died when they trapped the monster they were after,

Middy would not forgive herself. She tried to just let her eyes slide past the kids running about causing headaches for their parents, only no matter how hard she tried not to think about them, she still saw them and they mattered.

On the very edge of her vision Middy saw a movement. It wasn't anything that had signs flashing on it saying look here. In fact, the movement had been so casual that she doubted anyone else had even noticed it. A woman had reached out and straightened the sleeve on a blouse hanging on a clothing rack in a clothing store. Middy stopped walking and focused on the woman waiting for her to turn towards her so she could see the woman's eyes. When she did look in Middy's direction Middy was certain this was no woman. "I have eyes on. Close in to where the subject is standing. He is inside 'Picky Girls'. Subject has spotted me and is on the move, leaving shop going towards the back of mall exit."

"Back off! Back off and just observe, Cupcake," came Ritter's voice in a growl.

"Agreed, everyone keep eyes on only until we are clear of bystanders," Middy said. The closer they came to the exit door the more the crowd thinned. We are going to get him, Middy thought, but in the next moment they turned a corner and he was gone. How could he have vanished in that one instant? The five of them spread out searching every hallway, every store. Middy even checked out the fitting rooms in two clothing stores. It was in the second store she found evidence the ghost had changed his appearance once again. The dress and a wig were left in the changing stall. Of course, the attendant hadn't noticed someone different exiting the stall than the one who had entered. They had no idea what he had changed into. Was he now a man or a woman, old or a teenager?

To have been so close and have lost him. That thought ate at Middy all the way back home. She had seen him, actually seen him and hadn't taken action against him because of the crowded mall. It wasn't that she thought she should have tried to take him down, no, not that. It was the fact she had lost him. Why hadn't she alerted the rest of the team and surrounded the place? Did she think she had to be the one to take him down? Middy had only wanted to keep them safe, and alive.

Ritter glanced at each of the spares and slid his hand over his throat. It was the sign for we are done here. It was Cupcake he was worried about. During the time he had been her SS guy he had come to understand she took each failure personally. It didn't matter that this guy had outfoxed many a CIA operative, or that this was the first time they had ever been this close to him. What mattered to her was that he was still free to kill others should he want. Ritter could almost see Middy's mind sifting through everything they had done in following the guy. Ever turn leading up to him pulling the disappearing act. She needed to understand the guy had this escape planned as with all the shootings he had done and escaped. It wasn't anyone's fault. Ritter looked at one of the spares, "Get the car. We'll sweep the outside area and circle around to the front entrance."

Looking to the other spare he merely said, "You, left." They separated at the exit going their assigned ways.

Middy was certain the ghost guy had left the area already, there was no reason he should chance being caught by staying around since he knew he was being followed. Still, she couldn't take the chance that she was wrong. They did a sweeping search around the mall with nothing standing out. The ghost had disappeared once more.

Despite her own disappointment in losing the ghost guy once again, Middy decided that since they were out she would treat the guys to dinner. She figured the break from her cooking would be a fun thing for them and she knew it would be great for her own moral. She let her SS guys pick the place to eat, or she started to until they became so silly over the names of places. It was when one of the guys suggested Rosy Hot Dogs that she lost her patience. "Since you guys can't decide where to eat between you, we are going to the first Mexican food spot we see, even if it is a tamale stand on the side of the road. No steak for you guys tonight. Next time be good and I might let you have a huge steak with a baked potato. Now hang your heads in shame, my little boys, and come along." The smirks on their faces didn't make the supposed head hanging look even the slightest sincere.

Middy was remembering that Ritter had started this whole silliness with his joke in the mall when they saw a very nice restaurant which filled the venue very well. Middy was pleased that they would at least be dining in a decent place, but the parking lot didn't offer any place for them to park being filled with cars. "Well we know it is good," one of the spares joked. Yeah, good and full of people, Middy thought, noticing Ritter's mouth had that tight shut intense look to it. Maybe this wasn't the best of plans.

They found a parking space way in the back lot, it was clear Ritter wasn't happy about the spot or the lack of lighting in the area. He didn't say a word, but the guys knew and tightened up around Middy as they stepped out of the car. Middy felt like they had created a wall around her shielding her from even speaking to people as they entered the restaurant. This feeling was why she always dumped her SS guys at the first opportunity, only she couldn't shake these four guys it was like they were super glued to her. When they entered the restaurant there was a waiting list to be seated. Middy had committed to eating at the first place they saw and she didn't like the idea of backing down, so they sat in the waiting area. "From the number of people eating here I'd say this has to be a fantastic eating experience," she said.

The door to the restaurant opened, and a young man and elderly woman walked inside. The man looked around then stopped as if he couldn't believe what he saw. He walked quickly over to where Middy and her SS sat, stopping in front of her. "Middleton? Is that really you?" the man asked.

Middy looked up and a smile spread across her face as she recognized the speaker. Beside her, Ritter developed deep frown lines in his forehead. "Henry Barlow, what are you doing here?" she exclaimed standing to give him a hug.

"Mother wanted to do some big city shopping

for Christmas. It is not like we don't have months and months to shop in," he said, teasing his mother.

"Oh, you. You know Christmas is only two months away," Mrs. Barlow said, giving Henry a punch in the shoulder. "The boy has no manners. Please introduce us to your friends."

Middy gave a crooked smile as she turned to Ritter and the spares. "These are my shadows at the moment, Ritter here is the boss and these three guys do a lot of the legwork for him. Ritter, guys, meet Mrs. Barlow and her son Henry, friends from back home."

Henry put a hand on his chest as if stabbed. "Mids, you know I consider myself more than just a friend. Speaking of which, how about we see a movie or something tomorrow night?"

Silence fell over Middy and the SS. Middy looked up at Henry with such a caring, yet torn look that Ritter wanted to yank the guy's heart out and stomp on it, but he only looked to Middy to see what she would do.

"You haven't seen the news lately, have you? There is a madman out there stalking me. He is shooting anyone that he thinks I care about to cause me pain. I'm sorry, Henry, I want to see you, but now is not a good time," Middy said with regret in her voice. Beside her, a black cloud formed over Ritter, darkening the more Middy smiled at this Henry fellow. She is mine, he thought. Only thinking something was true didn't make it so.

Concern was plain on Henry's face as he took Middy's hands in his own. "Please be careful. If you need me call and I'll come running no matter what,"

Henry said, then leaned in and kissed Middy's cheek. Nodding his head to the SS guys he escorted his mother away from the four of them, to safety.

Chapter Thirteen

NO SENSE FRETTING

Try as he might Ritter could not shake the feeling that Cupcake was slipping away from him. All through their meal out she kept glancing over to where the Henry fellow and his mother were seated. The easy joking that had been going on while they drove to the restaurant had also slipped away as Middy began to speak about Henry.

"He was a sick boy when my family was traveling to our home at the farm. Mother healed him and his family eventually became good friends with our family. There was always that thing of mystery that hung over us which sort of kept us separated from the town folk. But the Barlow family were always kind and respectful. Henry was the only boy who even talked to me when we went to town. He used to tell me all about the school there and the girls and boys in his classes. I thought it sounded like a real pain in the neck to go to school when you could do all your lessons at home and work on the farm instead of wasting all that time in classes," Middy gave a laugh. "And they thought we were weird. I never could understand the waste of time in going to school. It certainly didn't seem like they were learning much more than how to cut others down with words." Middy picked at her food eating slowly, so lost in memories of that long ago time.

Ritter's brooding over Henry was interrupted by the man himself. As Middy and the others stood to leave Henry got up from his table and walked over to catch another few moments with Middy. Ritter and the three spares stood slightly away from Middy and Henry as the pair talked softly about catching up at some point in the future.

That night Ritter investigated Henry Barlow and his family. His grumpy mood deepened when he couldn't find anything wrong in the man's past. He had wanted to find fault with the man and be able to tell himself this Henry Barlow was not good enough for his Cupcake, but he couldn't find fault. The man was spotless, a real good sort according to what he could find out. He should have known, his Cupcake wasn't going to like a guy that much if there was anything wrong with him. So he had a fight on his hands. Somehow, someway he had to get her to like him more than this fresh as the fallen snow Henry Barlow. He had to make a battle plan and win her back. It was his own fault she was no longer interested in him, he admitted to himself.

Flowers, Ritter thought, no flowers just about killed Killer. Cake at one time would have been the easy go to as a gift for Middy, but that bastard had ruined that for his gal with poison. Ritter went to bed still brooding over something he had little control over.

The next day Middy started exercising, trying to get herself into better shape so she would have the strength for prolonged sessions blowing wind. She had to be ready to fight this monster, and protect her people. Her family had faced a monster before, but this time, this time it was her own personal monster. She didn't know if she could be as generous as her mother had been with her monster, and that scared her. To give in and let loose the rage she felt inside her from all those she knew dying. Would she still be herself after that?

Jogging along behind Middy, Ritter was in a foul mood. Nothing he thought of seemed right for trying to woo his Cupcake. He made another sweeping look around while trying not to look at his subject, the woman he wanted, and laughed. She truly wasn't a jogger. Even he felt the pain she must be feeling at her awkward slow jog, more a stumbling stepping than anything resembling a full out jog. Running shoes, he thought, nope she'd be insulted and sock him one. There went his mind jogging off thinking of ridiculous things to give her as gifts. Suddenly his bad mood was gone and the game was on, ridiculous just might work for him. That put him right back into brooding over what sort of ridiculous thing to get her. Who knew courting would be so confusing?

Later that night as Middy headed to bed she stopped just inside the doorway to her bedroom. A box was sitting on her bed. It looked like a shoe box, but she wasn't going to approach it without it being at least scanned. Middy didn't put anything past this monster stalking her. Backing out of the room slowly, Middy first thought to alert Ritter, only this was his sleep time. That left the night man who was patrolling outside the house.

Hogan was on the last leg of his patrol around the house, later he would range out a bit keeping the house in sight as he searched for signs of an intruder near the road to the house and the woods behind the house. He was startled when the subject stepped out in front of him and automatically drew his gun. "Ma'am, you best get back into the house. I almost mistook you for an intruder."

Middy held her hand up to stop him from continuing the lecture about her being outside the house. "There is a box on my bed which I didn't place there," she said certain he would go into that super protective mode the guys all had.

"Yes, ma'am. It has been checked and is safe," he said surprising her.

"You are sure?"

"Yes, ma'am." Came the soft reply.

Somewhat confused and upset over something being done in her house that she wasn't in on, Middy went back inside going to her bedroom. The box was still there sitting like it was waiting for her to come to open it. Her mouth twitched to the side as she approached the box. What could it be? Slowly she lifted the lid off the box, still not convinced that this wasn't a bomb or something ugly sent to her. Her brows shot up in surprise and something like a laugh bubbled deep inside her. Shoes, running shoes that were electric blue with glow in the dark bright yellow poke-a-dots.

There were smirks lingering at the corners of the SS guy's mouths the next morning when Middy came out and prepared breakfast in those comical shoes. Nobody dared laugh as Ritter was giving them the evil eye of death for just thinking it was funny. Within, he too was laughing at the shoes and the frumpy girl who wore them, once breakfast was over, and she started jogging with the three animal companions following behind her, and Ritter. She did look funny doing that awkward stumbling run of hers and those yellow dots flashing brightly in the sunlight. At least he would know where she was at all times in those shoes. Ritter just hoped his next gift would go over as well as this one had.

Middy suspected that the running shoes were a joke from Ritter. The man didn't know who he is fooling with, she thought, her mischievous side springing to life. As the pain started in her legs from jogging she distracted herself by sending a rush of short puffs of air to untie Ritter's shoelaces. Stopping as if to catch her breath she concentrated on tying his shoes together before starting off again. Behind Middy there was the sound of a crash and a thud followed by a softly muttered curse from Ritter. She smiled with renewed energy spreading through her as she sprinted off. Turning, Middy headed back towards the house passing Ritter with his shoes draped around his neck and his look dark. Yet he smiled at her when she went past him. Middy's mouth twitched suppressing a smile back.

That spark was back, the one which had lit the fire inside Ritter for his Cupcake. He hadn't realized how much he wanted to see that mischievous side of her before this moment. When he had realized she had tied his shoes together he had felt it, that burst of excitement, the challenge of overcoming her hard-headed bossy ways. He had almost jumped up and raced after her, but he was on the job. He had to protect her, and nothing would keep him from doing what was needed to keep his Cupcake safe, not even having to jog after her in his socks. His mind was working on what gift to give her next.

But all those thoughts stopped when Middy stopped and stood still, not so much as running in place. What had he missed? Where was the danger? All he saw was Sherlock and Watson staring at a spot on the side of the road, and Killer zipping around them. Nothing, he saw nothing, no sniper in the trees, nobody kneeling in the bushes, nothing. He tried to see what Sherlock and Watson were staring at when suddenly Sherlock leaped back. Watson pounced forward then she too leaped back. Sherlock yelped and took off running towards the house with Watson and Middy hot on his tail. There was a sound he could just barely hear, a sound that sent him off after his subject yelling at the spares, "Open the door! Open it fast get them all inside! Hurry!" Then he too was running full out from the menace.

They all threw themselves through the open door and yelled: "Close the door!" Middy drew a relieved breath and started checking Sherlock and Watson over for damage. Sherlock was the only one of the animal companions who had been stung by the Yellow Jacket Wasps. Ritter had one sting which he downplayed. However, Middy knew how much a sting from a wasp could hurt and insisted on treating him after Sherlock was treated. Her touch was more painful to Ritter than the sting was because it woke all the man inside him, the hungry want and need. That one simple act of her applying the mixture she had fixed on the sting had him tied in knots afraid to move. So he sat and took in her touch, the thrill it sent through him while staring at her watching each flash of a grimace on her face, the little furrow forming between her eyes as she concentrated on him.

It wasn't fair, Middy thought, as she finished up with the sting on Ritter's arm. She wasn't certain this stuff would help the sting, but Doctor Andy said it would. Her mother always had just touched them to stop the pain and take away the stuff put in a person by the stinger. It just didn't seem right putting this on the outside of a person when the hurt was inside them. For one horrifying moment, Middy realized she didn't have any common sense about such things. What if she had children and there she was ignorant of all the things the rest of the world did to cure ills? As she rubbed the pasty stuff on Ritter's sting she watched it begin to relieve the redness and the swelling which had started around the sting until it was gone. This stuff is amazing, she thought standing up and stepping back. "That should do it," she said turning away to keep from looking at Ritter. There was no way she was letting him get to her again. A girl may be foolish once but never again. "Sherlock," she called, and sat on the floor to treat the dog again, only his sting was cured too. "That's a good boy. Let me put some more good stuff on you, big brave fellow."

For a wild insane moment, Ritter considered running out and laying on that wasp nest, if she'd treat him again. He may have been that desperate to get her attention, but he certainly wasn't that stupid. She'd kick his butt if he did something like that. A kick in the butt was better than being ignored, he thought, then shook his head at himself. He wanted her to respect him, not think him dumb. So he did the next best thing and went on-line to find wasp and bee gifts. He didn't want to make a big thing of giving her things so he ordered the smallest, but cutest item he could find and had it sent overnight delivery. Self-satisfied he followed Cupcake into the kitchen and stood in a corner watching the doorway, and her, as she prepared lunch. It was nothing he didn't normally do, the watching out for her, or so he told himself.

Early the next morning two packages arrived at the investigative center where all Middy's mail was now processed. Nothing was let through until it was thoroughly examined, x-rayed and sniffed. Two packages arriving at once had the center extra alert. One or both could be booby-trapped or contain something harmful, like a bomb or something poisonous. So the two small packages had been examined in every manner they could use other than blow them up and examine the bits left over. When the investigators were satisfied the two packages were safe they were sent on to Middy's home, slightly beat up looking, a tad lopsided, but safe. One was addressed to Middy, the other was addressed to Ritter.

Middy sat in her bedroom looking at the lopsided box addressed to her for a long time. She was almost afraid to open it. The last package she received had Albert's finger in it. The horror of that finger flashed through her memories bringing a chill with it. Slowly she reached out and fingered the tape on the box. A small split started in the middle of the tape where a scope had been inserted to look inside. Middy carefully worked her way along that split until the two top flaps were split apart. Taking a deep breath Middy picked up the small box and ripped the rest of the tape apart. Gently she lifted the flaps up to expose what was inside. Bubble wrap. Middy stared at the bubble wrap as if it was some alien material made on Mars. Feeling foolish for having that inner fear that another finger would be in this small box, Middy removed the bubble wrap to find a jeweler's box inside. Now she really was puzzled. Her eyebrows shot up and her mouth scrunched to the side as she opened the box. A butterfly and a bumblebee were sitting upon a leaf their feelers touching. Ritter. Middy wondered if he couldn't find a wasp for the leaf, at least she thought it was from him.

The battered box sat for a long time on Ritter's dashboard. It seemed to be staring at him, maybe judging him. What a crazy thought, a box judging him? He really had gone nuts, hadn't he? With an angry grunt, he grabbed the box and ripped it open. A wasp. A wasp on a keychain. The anger vanished as a smile crept upon him. *She* sent it to him. It had to be her… or one of the other SS. That had him frowning for a moment, but the smile won out and he was convinced that his Cupcake had sent him a gift. Feeling warm inside he sat in his car and transferred his keys to the gift Cupcake had sent him. He was starting to gain ground. Now if he could just keep from ruining things all over again.

Mentally Middy didn't know if she was ready to accept Ritter caring anything for her. She was finding it hard to trust anyone in that particular area except her family. Once bitten they say a person is twice shy. Only for Middy once a trust was broken it just didn't seem fixable again. People were creatures of habit and would display the same mannerisms over and over no matter how much they swore they had changed. Just look at how Julian was still behaving in her snotty manner. Not as bad as she used to be for certain, but still the wicked side of her came out over and over again. How long before Ritter went back to pushing her away, telling her to "go" again? And herself, she was still that person who cared about him. Her own stubborn mind just refused to take him seriously any more. She was lopsided, that was it. For the moment she was leaning towards him instead of away. The next earthquake would send her way the other direction, and that was why she was afraid. It was why she was sitting here in the bedroom brooding over a butterfly and a bumblebee, and how cute they looked together.

The next day seemed like some other person's life to Middy. There were glances shared with the man she was afraid to ever trust again. True, mostly he was in super SS mode, but then there were those rare moments when he would glance her way and no matter how hard she tried not to be looking his way, she was. The only thing to do was to wear herself out so that she was too tired to even open her eyes. So she led Ritter and the companions on a long stumbling jog, which tortured her body and made her want to call for a car to come get her as she turned around to head home. She couldn't help but notice Ritter lifting an eyebrow at her. Let him think she was an insane person, maybe she was, flashed through her mind. She could be insane just imagining he was looking at her in an interesting manner. The whole thing could be her mind setting her up to be pushed away again. Only this time she wasn't going to be the one showing interest. Then stop looking over at him, she told herself making herself look away to concentrate on the road in front of her, to listen to the sounds of Sherlock and Watson, and the slight zipping sound of Killer flying.

Ritter had noticed the abrupt change in Middy, how she turned her head away from where he was jogging. She is fighting me, he thought, what the heck do I do now? Pretend you don't notice, keep on doing little things. Remember you are in a fight to get her back, to make her want you, you can't afford to lose this battle. Do whatever you have to in order to win her over, he told himself. Only he worried that this was one fight he might not be able to win.

The idea popped into Middy's head that if the guys were going to tease her calling her 'Boss', then she was going to act like she was one. She began to think about all the scenarios that might possibly happen when they found this madman. So many things could go wrong and usually did. Then she considered all the men who had responded with that 'Yes, Boss" bit. There were enough individuals to form up teams for certain tasks. Middy spent the rest of the day at the computers making up the different teams which had popped into her mind. Each team had a job to do when the monster was cornered, with each job being vital to keeping this evil contained. She printed out the sheets of paper which listed each team and placed them in a folder on her computer desk with the title 'Game Plan'. She knew that things would probably not go as planned, but a plan can be changed as the need arose. It was what they all did, adjusted, approached each suspect with whatever worked, and if that didn't work then you switched to another approach.

Ritter kept his silence, watching, always watching. Whatever was going on in Cupcake's head had him worried. This calming of her did not speak well of whatever she was planning, and it didn't speak well of his plans to win Middy.

Late into the night, Middy worked on the assignments she intended to press on the guys wanting to take out the monster. She added different scenarios with changes and mixes of the teams to suit each thing they came up against. It could all be for nothing, but she wanted to be as prepared as possible. She wanted the guys prepared too. Losing sleep didn't matter as long as they all survived.

Ritter finally fell asleep out of pure logic and sense. For one of them had to be alert tomorrow, and it didn't look as if that person would be his Cupcake. Whatever had her up so late he'd find out when he searched her hard drive. There was nothing she could keep secret if she used the computer. Her mind, however, was something he had trouble reading. Just when he felt he knew her she'd hit him with something completely weird. Wind, now who would have ever thought his frumpy lady could control the wind? If it hadn't been for all the weirdness he had seen when her family had healed him, then her... his mind stumbled there with the thoughts of her having come so close to dying. He wasn't going to let that happen again, ever.

Jogging, it must have been invented by someone cruel that loves pain, Middy thought. Lack of sleep had her wishing she could go crawl back in bed and let the day fade away to dreams of... Ritter, there she had admitted it to herself, she was dreaming of him. She wouldn't do that, go hideaway. It wasn't something her family did. They faced things, but dang, this jogging was going to kill her yet. Determination drove her on through the pain, she had been inactive for too long it was time to push until she had a monster in her grasp.

The night seemed darker than usual as the moon and stars were hidden by black clouds. Ritter had one of the spares also take the night with Hogan, the usual night guard. There was an uneasiness stirring inside him. He didn't like this sort of night where it was so dark outside you didn't see shadows because there was no light to cause them. Maybe the guys thought he was being too careful, but there was never a time when you were too careful. Things happened regardless of how much care you took to protect your subject. He lay on the sofa for a long endless seeming time before he was able to let sleep claim him. Even then the slightest noise had him jerking awake. They needed to find this joker and put him away before they all went nuts with worry.

The stillness of the morning woke Ritter. He jerked awake leaping to his feet so fast the blanket around him didn't have time to slip free. It wrapped around him sending him sprawling on his face to the floor. Ritter rubbed the lingering sleep from his face feeling slightly stupid for making a fool of himself, and face-landing on the floor. Then the silence seeped into his mind, the reason he had waken so suddenly. Something was wrong! He should hear Middy in the kitchen making a huge breakfast for everyone as she pumped herself up for a run. Sherlock's nails should be clicking on the floor, and Killer darting madly about feeding on the hummingbird feeders. None of that was going on.

In his tee shirt and shorts, Ritter grabbed his gun and started sweeping the house with an intensity which had him locking his jaw to keep from screaming out for his Cupcake. Dread sat like a two-ton weight on his heart. Everything looked normal. There was nothing overturned to indicate a struggle of any sort. No sign that the night patrol had come up against trouble. When the other spare came out of a guest bedroom looking as if he hadn't yet woke up, Ritter questioned his own instincts. Still, he couldn't shake the rising feeling of wrong inside him.

The spare saw Ritter's gun out and didn't hesitate for a second as he pulled his own gun out.

The two of them finished sweeping the house on bare feet. They met up at Middy's room. It was there Ritter held up his hand and motioned his spare back. Nobody was going to see his Cupcake sleeping in bed, her hair a mess and sleep still in her eyes. Nobody. With great care Ritter slowly turned the knob on the door to Middy's bedroom, silently he cracked the door just enough to look inside.

Wham! Ritter slapped the door fully open and entered, his rage and gun both ready to attack. Nothing. The bed's covers had been pulled half off the bed as if they had clung to Middy when she left the bed. The bedroom window was closed. Most damning of all were Watson and Sherlock still upon the half of the covers which laid upon the floor. Middy and Killer were both gone.

A curse nearly passed Ritter's lips, but he held it back. Now was not the time to go into emotional meltdown. With a hand signal to the spare, he retraced his steps opening the front door of the house to check on the night guys. A sweep of the yard located their two bodies. One had his gun out and looked to have been crouching down arms extended to shoot. Only he hadn't had a chance to fire. Why hadn't they raised the alarm? Alert and take down, they all knew how Ritter ran an outfit. The first sign of danger alert the team, then proceed to take out the treat. "Damn!" exploded from the spare. He looked at Ritter and had the good sense to shut up again.

Gently Ritter removed Sherlock and Watson from the bedroom. They were alive but limp and

unconscious. Feeling like time was running away
from him Ritter sent his spare off with Sherlock and
Watson to have blood drawn, and to be checked over
by the doctor who had removed Sherlock's leg. He
also drew his own blood instructing the spare to have
his blood drawn too to check for even the slightest
trace of something which may have incapacitated
them. After seeing Sherlock and Watson off, Ritter
returned to the bedroom to search it for Killer
fearing the little bird was dead, but hoping that the
fearsome little hummingbird had escaped somehow.

Both Watson and Sherlock were very sluggish
and looking lost after their trip to the doctor. Killer
was still missing. Ritter hoped the little bird had not
received a dose of the same gas Sherlock and Watson
had as he knew birds were more likely to die from
even the faintest trace of gas. The blood samples
were already being analyzed to try to determine
what had been used on Middy and the companions.
Ritter knew it had to have been a fast acting gas or
Middy would have used her wind to blow it away.
She sure the heck wouldn't have gone down without
a fight that would have torn the place apart. The big
question was how had he slept through it all? The
blood of Ritter and that of his spare had been sent
off by private courier. He had to know if he had just
allowed his subject to be taken while he slept, or
if he and the spare had been gassed too. If he had
been sleeping while Cupcake had been taken by a
madman he'd never forgive himself.

As soon as Ritter alerted the locals to the
kidnapping and the fact that there would soon be
many SS and other officials in their area, Middy's

unofficial team started arriving at the house. It seemed they had set up a phone tree of sorts to alert each other when the monster was sighted. Only this time they were spreading the news. The Boss was gone!

There was a horrible, frightening rage building inside of Ritter. He hid it from those around him well by appearing to be all business. Business was all that was keeping him sane at the moment. She was gone. He had lost her. Now his whole reason for living was to find her, to get her out of the clutches of a madman. He couldn't let loose of his emotions until then. Control was all he had, control of his team, control of Cupcakes guys, and if he had any say in things he'd have control of the FBI too. They were not going to be allowed to mess up, to get Cupcake killed.

Fuller was the first to arrive. His face was sober and had a look upon it that kept even Ritter from saying anything to him as he made his way into Middy's office. Frankie and Albert were next along with Frankie's new partner. Introductions were not made, everyone knew each other and Ritter. Frankie's troubled eyes rose from staring at the floor to look at Ritter. Ritter knew he had to explain how four SS men could lose their subject. He just didn't know how it happened himself. Still, he didn't drop his eyes from Frankie's eyes, and taking a deep breath he started the briefing. "Sherlock and Watson were knocked out by some sort of gas. I have blood work being run on myself and we are needing those results ASAP. Two of our over the night shift guys were killed. We know it was late or at least after one or two in the morning before the snatch took place. Whatever took Sherlock and Watson down didn't last long. We woke up even quicker than they did."

"What about Killer?" Frankie asked.

"We have no intel on Killer. At the moment he is missing in action," Ritter ran a hand over his face to keep the fear for Killer showing, "I certainly hope he made it out and is tailing the kidnapper. He is one tough and smart little guy." The door to the house was pushed open interrupting Ritter.

The three men who walked in as if they owned the place had FBI stamped all over them. Fuller, Frankie, and Albert looked at each other with a shade of a sneer on their lips as the older looking of the three started barking orders. "My name is Jack Burns. I'm heading up this operation, and all you people need to clear the crime scene. One rep only will we take from the local cops. All others clear the area. I want a rundown from the guy who failed to keep Miss Whiting safe first off, then I'll hear a little input the locals have."

"Not going to happen." Both Fuller and Ritter said at the same time.

The graying at the temples FBI guy shook his head with a look of disgust on his face. "That does it, all of you out of here NOW!"

Ritter held up his hand to keep Middy's guys in place. His own expression often made grown men wet their drawers as he stared the FBI man in the eyes. Only before he could take a step forward Fuller and Frankie were in the guy's face. "You will stand down and lend only what small amount of assistance you are able to lend. First off, this is not your operation. It is and always has been the Boss's operation. She set this all up to catch a killer you guys have failed to catch for too many years. The very fact this idiot was stupid enough to come into her home means he is now doomed. There will be no other talk of you or anyone else being in charge. We go with *her* plan." God help me, I hope I'm speaking the truth, Fuller thought to himself.

Burns looked at all the aggressive face looking his way and did the only thing he could do, bluffed. "I'm afraid you don't understand. If you continue to get in the way of a federal investigation you will be brought up on charges. No one has priority over this kidnapping except for the FBI. I suggest you clear out while you still can go of your own free will."

Ritter had enough of this idiot. They were wasting time pissing up a tree that was too tall for them. Taking out his cell phone he held it up and showed it to the Burns guy. Slowly deliberately he pressed on one contact. Burns' forehead wrinkled up as he watched Ritter lift the phone to his ear. "Mr. President, I don't have time for a pissing contest with the FBI. You need to call these guys off so we can get your granddaughter back." Ritter listened for a moment before handing the phone to Burns.

"Yes, sir. But, sir, you know we handle these sorts of operations. We can't just hand it over to the locals. What?!" Burns' voice took on a note of disbelief and anger before he seemed to deflate, a look of defeat upon his face. Glaring at Ritter he handed the phone back.

"Yes, sir. I will keep you informed," Ritter said putting the phone away before waving Fuller forward to take charge of his men.

Although Fuller was pleased with putting down the FBI, who had a tendency to just swoop in and take over any operation they thought warranted them, he didn't believe Middy had set up her own kidnapping. He didn't think the FBI guys would go along with this whole thing either. Just as he was about to speak his mind there was a knock on the door. Four more men had arrived. On their heels came six more of the guys who had been in on the citywide search they had been doing section by section. All ten of these guys had been there when she had been poisoned and nearly died. Sober faces looked to Ritter, Fuller, and Frankie for instructions.

Ritter motioned everyone to follow him into Middy's office. Sherlock came on wobbly legs to stand between Ritter and Fuller. Watson, more in control than poor Sherlock was himself at that moment, pressed against Sherlock as if lending support. Before Ritter could start talking again, ten more men arrived as did the official team from Middy's old station, and the state troopers. It was crowded in the office by then. Ritter held his hands up for quiet and glanced over at Fuller, before speaking. "Miss Whiting left her game plan here on her desk for us to use. It is up to us, all of us," he emphasized, "to be there for her. We are her back up. You all know, well except you three," he said looking at the three FBI men, "how deadly this creep is. The Boss has instructed all of you to wear a vest and helmets. In this folder are the teams she has formed. Each of you has a part to play in taking this creep down. We will NOT let her down, agreed?"

The noise of so many men crowded into the office and the hallway was deafening as shouts of agreement roared forth from sober-faced, determined men.

Chapter Fouteen

SURVIVING

It felt as if cotton was stuffed in her head keeping her from thinking straight or being able to even open her eyes, but Middy had always been a stubborn girl and she opened her eyes anyway. Then she wished she hadn't as something liquid poured over her face causing her eyes to burn and her nose and throat to feel as if they were on fire. She tried to bring her hands up to block whatever was being poured over her face, but something was wrapped around her wrists keeping her hands behind her back. The shock of realizing that she was tied up went through Middy like a bolt of lightning. Suddenly the cotton was gone from her brain and she knew that the monster had her. Keeping her eyes closed against the horrible liquid that poured over her, Middy felt around behind her to see what was on her wrist. Tape, of all the bad luck. If it had been rope or the plastic ties she could have used her wind to worry the tie loose, but the tape was harder to get off. She'd have to do short bursts over and over on one spot to weaken the material until it was weak enough to tear apart. Possibly she could find the end of the tape and try to pry it up to run air under it. Both options were things she had never tried before when playing with her wind.

What was he doing to her? Middy wondered as water ran down her face, and she was able to breathe once more. The water stopped and she thought for a moment it was safe to open her eyes, then a bristle brush was worked over the skin of her face. She could feel it rubbing her skin raw. The creep was scrubbing her face off. She couldn't smell anything anymore except the disinfectant which was periodically poured over her alternating with water. The skin on her face burned from being abraded and having whatever foul thing he was cleaning her face with being poured on the raw flesh.

It seemed an eternity that her face was tortured before the monster stopped. For one brief moment Middy thought it was over with, then she heard the snick of a knife as it sliced through her clothing. It was too much! She was not going to let this creep see her naked. Fury and panic built inside her as her fingers began to twitch drawing the air around her to her. With her eyes still closed she tried to reason out where she thought the monster was standing or sitting next to her. Throwing her wind would be difficult enough with her hands tied behind her. She was hampered more by the fact she didn't know what was around her, the size of the room, anything. Middy could only guess that she was in a bathroom because of the feel of a bathtub around

her and the liquid that was poured over her had to go
down a drain or something even though it gathered
around her at the moment. She was in a tub then,
in a bathroom, so a small room with raised sides
of the tub all around her. Difficult, hopefully not
impossible.

Risking hurting her eyes again she open
them to see the back of the monster's head as he cut
away the bottom of her pajamas. He shoved her
firmly against the side of the tub to expose more
of her nearer leg. Her hands were smashed against
the tub preventing her from releasing her wind.
Middy could feel the power building inside her
begging to be released. It wanted the freedom to
rip something apart. Middy needed her hands free
that was all there was to it. Freedom to move and
direct her wind, to take down a monster. Frantically
she bucked kicking her feet up and slamming them
down as she tried to hinder the man with the knife
cutting at her clothing. She wasn't going to let him
cut her clothing off if she could help it. Twisting and
trying to draw her legs up so she could kick him,
Middy became a wimpy bucking bull, thrashing and
pushing until she had her legs up in one desperate
move. Not allowing the creep to think on what she
was doing Middy kicked out nicking the side of his
head since he was not facing her. When he finally
looked at her Middy knew who this monster was and
it was so stupid, so dumb that he hated her so much.
What had she ever done to deserve such hate as that
which radiated out of his eyes? At the moment he
looked infuriated with her. She thought he was going
to hit her and braced herself so as not to show any

expression of being hurt. Only he didn't hit her in the face. He picked up a rubber bat like thing and whacked her on the head. Darkness claimed her sending her off into a dreamless void.

Killer battered the glass on the high window of the warehouse with his tiny body. He couldn't get to her. She was being hurt. The one he claimed as his to protect was being tortured and he was helpless to reach her. His energy was fading fast as it had been a long flight following the car in which she had been placed. It had only been luck that he had managed to get out before that thing had made the others go to sleep. There was much Killer wanted to do to the thing. Killer looked one last time to where Middy was being tormented. Very much he would do much damage to the thing. There was nothing else he could do here as he hadn't been able to find even the smallest opening to get into the warehouse. He had to return and try to get Sherlock and Watson out of the house.

His mind made up Killer flew up to take in the surrounding area, letting his homing instinct take over to fly back to the house. Overhead dark clouds were forming as the wind began to whip aimlessly battering Killer and the building. He had to get away from here before he was bashed into the building and killed. Desperate now, the little bird worked his wings as never before fighting against the forces rising around the building. Twice he had to clutch desperately at a tree branch to keep from being blown to his death. When he finally broke free his flight was erratic as he lacked the energy to keep himself in the air.

So weak he could no longer fly the little hummingbird laid upon the ground as if dead. Only his heart was beating so fast in his breast that he thought it was going to burst out of him. The sun was rising before Killer was able to move again. Directly before him was a glass house which held many flowers. The nectar in those flowers called to him like a siren calling to a lonesome sailor.

Sometime later Killer had found a small opening into the glass house. He feasted on the flowers and allowed himself to recover. When he had filled himself a second time he took to the air. Zipping out of the glass house he was immediately battered by the wind again. The storm was getting stronger.

They had delayed long enough, and Ritter was wound so tight that should one more delay be heaped upon him he would tear whoever caused it to bits. Sherlock and Watson both paced in front of the door wanting, needing to go find Middy. Theirs was a constant reminder of how urgent it was that Ritter get to searching. A storm was brewing inside him, growing with each moment that passed. Even the FBI creeps were making a wide circle around him when they walk anywhere near him.

Fuller and the others were studying what Middy had been working on before she had gone to bed and been abducted. When Fuller stood up from the desk, Ritter took a step towards the door. "Listen up. Here are the assignments," Fuller barked handing out slips of paper to each head of the teams Middy had arranged on her charts. "Each of you go over with your team what you are to do when we find the Boss. Remember vest and helmets at all times," Fullers' lips curled almost into a smile at the groans that went up all around him, "Bosses orders." There was a hush upon them then as their minds turned to what she might be going through if she was still alive.

It was during that moment of silence Ritter heard it. It was a constant tapping on the window. He held his hand up to alert the others, everyone crouched down pulling out their weapons. The change in their faces went from moans to intense concentration as they spread out through the house. Then the house seemed to moan as a gust of wind hit it hard. "A branch in the wind. You guys are spooked over a branch," the lead FBI man snarled at them. None of Middy's guys looked at him or even acknowledged he was there, but kept on searching the house as silently as they could.

It came down to Middy's bedroom, which had been sectioned off as the crime scene. Ritter told the others to hold fast, as he approached the door alone. With his hand, he motioned to Frankie to keep the others out of the bedroom and slowly turned the doorknob. Cracking the door open the tapping became clearer to everyone. Ritter entered his weapon ready, his face set to deal the death he was ready to give to this so-called ghost. The color drained from his face when he saw the source of the tapping. Killer. Killer was trying valiantly to stay up at the window as he tried to get someone's attention to get in. "Stand down," Ritter barked back at the others holstering his weapon and going swiftly over to the window raising it to let Killer inside.

Killer fluttered in crashing into Ritter and dropping to the floor. The little one was spent after his flight fighting the wind home. Ritter scooped him up carrying him into the kitchen. "Albert, make up some fresh formula for Killer, that which is hanging might be poisoned by the gas. Poor little guy, he is near dead," Ritter ordered grabbing a kitchen towel to wrap Killer's little body in, the poor little guy was so cold.

Albert and Fuller mixed the formula up doing it the way Middy always did when she was there. Not knowing what else to do they gave it to Ritter in the bowl they had mixed it in. Ritter held the towel wrapped bird close to his body to give Killer what warmth he could while he open a drawer and took out a teaspoon. Carefully he turned Killer so the little one might feed as he scooped up a teaspoon full of the formula. The room was so silent if a hair had fallen from someone's head they would have heard it hit the floor as they watch the hummingbird, who appeared to have died with his beak touching the fluid in the spoon. A group sigh of relief went up when Killer began to feed.

"What the hell? It is only a bird. You guys are nuts," grumbled the FBI guy. It was Fuller's gun in the guy's face that shut him up. Fuller gave Ritter a look and backed the three FBI men out of the kitchen. Grumbles could be heard the moment the kitchen had been cleared of the insufferable Burns again. "Get that damn gun out of my face or I'll have you up on charges for interfering in a federal operation and threatening a federal agent." The men in the kitchen didn't even try to hear what Fuller was telling the guy. There was a tone to the message Fuller was delivering that none of them ever wanted to be on the receiving end.

"Listen to me, you dumb-ass. That little bird is going to help us find the Boss. If you so much as snarl your lip in Killer's direction you will be limping the rest of your life. Now sit your ass down, and shut up," Fuller said letting the muzzle of his gun drift down to point at the agent's kneecap.

In the kitchen, Killer was finally up standing drinking from the teaspoon. Ritter was patient with the little guy even though he was tied in knots waiting to learn what Killer could tell them. Watson suddenly ran over and jumped up so she could put her face over Killer. Something seemed to pass between the bird and cat some silent communication that Ritter wasn't privileged to as a human. Watson looked up at Ritter with her eyes narrowed as if trying to tell him get Killer and let's go. Then the cat was back at the door pacing with Sherlock, impatiently waiting to go after Middy.

"Albert, wash three feeders for Killer and fill them up. It is time we get on the road," Ritter commanded. He was in full charging mode, ready to charge in and get his Cupcake wherever she was being held. He only hoped he wasn't too late. As Albert made up the feeders for Killer Ritter checked his weapon. With hardly a pause he put on his vest and picked up the helmet that Middy had told everyone they had to wear when it came time to get this monster which had her captive now. He slowly turned checking on each man who was there to be certain they understood this order of hers was one they would all follow or be left behind. Only the FBI guys had failed to gear up. "I assume you have a vest and helmet in the trunk of your car. Go get them and wear them. This operation is being done according to Miss Whiting's orders and her number one order is vest and helmets or you can't take part in the operation," His look said there would be no argument. The lead FBI man looked at him as if he would kill Ritter soon, and Ritter slowly smiled back at him with his own eyes so cold the temperature seemed to drop around the FBI man.

The edge of Middy's mind fought the blackness which threatened to devour her very soul. Gradually she entered a dream-like state where she wasn't totally awake but was becoming aware of things around her. Foremost was the noise of the building she was being held in, it rattled and shook. Now and then something banged into the side of the building. Then she remembered… the monster had her.

Slowly Middy woke up, but she kept her eyes closed in an attempt to figure out what was going on around her. Cold. She was so cold, her skin burned as if she was raw all over. That is when she remembered the harsh brushing of her face. Had he done the same thing to her whole body? It sure felt like he had. Horror tried to take over her mind at the idea of this creep seeing her naked, for naked she surely was if the wind being sucked up by her hands brushing over her body was any indication. Wait? Why was the wind so high outside? Suddenly she was aware that her fingers were still twitching, still pulling air to her. Had she done this while she was out? It was a very scary thought. Just thinking that she might bring down destruction on those she cared about in a careless moment while sleeping had her heart near leaping out of her chest.

This was here and now. She had been so upset when this creature started cutting off her clothing. She remembered to strike at the tape on her wrists over and over faster and faster in her panic at what this monster was going to do to her once he had her clothing off. Her head hurt where he had hit her, maybe he knocked something to do with her wind loose. Even now her fingers were drawing the wind to her, it was building up, beyond a mere storm inside her. If she sneezed she might blow the world away. That made her laugh, and it was such a weird moment to laugh with her naked and in the hands of a monster that she laughed again. Suddenly she sobered, fearing her mind had become unhinged. He's knocked me into a state of crazy, she thought. Then a thought occurred to her, something she had seen on a sign somewhere, and she laughed again. "You don't fool with Mother Nature," she tried to say and laughed again at the garbled sound of the words. She really was nuts! A person wouldn't laugh at a time like this, would they?

Cars had to be sorted out among the men. Who was going with whom? That wasn't a problem for the individual teams they all would pile into one car so as to be ready to start their part once they located the madman and the Boss. Then there was the SS and FBI. Ritter would have preferred leaving the FBI behind, but in the real world, he would have to live with the fallout that was already set to come when this was over. So in a grudging move, he motioned them to come with his bunch in their car. That is when the head FBI blew up yet again. You see there was a dog, a cat and a hummingbird included in the lead car.

"The fucking pets can't go," FBI head guy stated as if that was the end of it.

Ritter made a hand signal to one of his men and the guy dashed back into the house to return with three vests, one for each animal. Ritter held each one up for the FBI guy to see before he placed it on first Sherlock, then Watson and the last one on Killer. Each of the companions stood rock still to accept their vest. To their credit, these little ones knew the vest meant they were on the job. Each went to his or her place in the car, with Killer standing on the dash in clear view of the person who would be driving. This was the first time Killer would be inside the car instead of flying over the car, he seemed to have taken the lead spot for it was him who knew where Middy was being held.

"Your two men and one of mine will follow in the FBI car. They are to take their lead from my man. Understand?" Ritter said.

Rubbing his forehead as if he had the hugest headache in the world, the lead FBI man nodded. This was the worse assignment he had ever undertaken so far. Right from the start it seemed he had stepped into some alien world where nothing was under his control. Not one word he said was respected. How was he expected to do his job if nobody cooperated? Now, here he was in a car with people he thought had lost their minds. These people were those the common folk depended upon to be there, to solve the crimes to tell them what to do to survive. Yet they barreled right over him, ganged up on him as if he had no idea how to run a kidnapping investigation. Instead, they were depending on a bird? How crazy was that? He had been so happy to have been the one assigned to this case when it came down to their office. Here was his chance to make a name for himself and his fellow agents. He'd ride in and sweep the local yokels aside right off, then shine in their eyes with his superior knowledge of how to proceed. Now, he sat in the back seat with a dog and cat. A damn dog and cat! So they were service animals, so what? The person they were assigned to help was the one missing. You don't bring the animals along on a rescue mission. It just wasn't done.

Sherlock sensed the anger towards him in the man sitting beside him. He reached his long tongue out and licked the man's face to comfort him.

"Damn it!" The man cursed wiping his face in disgust.

The raging wind caught the car and shoved it sideways flinging Watson into the man beside her. She had her own opinion of this pretender and gave a low threatening growl for his ears only. She stared the man in the eyes daring him to say anything or move.

A spare drove the car while Ritter watched Killer for any hint as to where they should go. The storm which seemed to be growing in strength around the car shoved them from side to side. The fact that they stayed on the road at all was amazing. It wasn't until they entered the outskirts of the city that things became really difficult. It was like being in an active war zone with bullets… rather trashcans and anything lightweight enough to be picked up by the wind suddenly jumping out in front of the car or slamming into one side or the other. A newspaper would block the windshield. Fortunately, Ritter had experience with the newspaper on the windshield, and while his spare drove, Ritter hung out the passenger side window grabbing and pulling paper free from the windshield. They only hit another car once as a result of Ritter attempts to keep the windshield paper free. Other people driving however, were not so fortunate.

The train of cars holding determined men out for blood and worried about the safety of one of their own came to an abrupt halt when an accident happen right in front of them. Car doors slammed and men piled out of the line of cars following Ritter's car. There wasn't any hesitation, no stopping to watch the event before them. These were men of action. Carefully they rendered aid to the people in the three-car accident the wind had caused. Fortunately, only one person had a broken arm from the car that had slammed into the driver's side of his car. Hot tempers were quickly cooled down once the drivers involved realized they were surrounded by police officers.

Along about the third accident they came upon, Ritter considered should they stop or keep going. On one hand, he didn't want to delay getting to Cupcake, while on the other hand, he had a duty to protect and help everyone. Besides Cupcake would have his hide tacked on the door if he didn't render aid. Each stop was agony to Ritter, and to the guys and the animals. Killer would buzz out and fight the wind trying to hurry Ritter and the others along. The last accident had included a small child something that sobered Ritter and had the others looking haunted. They, like him, were wondering if they were going to be too late to save the person they all cared about. Still, he stopped to give aid to the elderly woman whose car had been flipped by the wind.

"Ma'am, we are going to set your car upright. I want you to make certain your seatbelt is secure. That's right just check it. Now Frankie here is going to place a blanket over you. It is just here to keep glass off you in case a window breaks. I think the windows are all going to make it alright, but it is best to be safe," his insides churning with the need to go, to get to Cupcake, Ritter took the time to calm the woman. "Now hold tight, and don't be afraid we are going to set the car up right."

Thankfully they had plenty of muscle to rock the car up onto its tires. "Ma'am, we are going to help you get to that little dress shop. I want you to stay there until this storm passes. You can call your family from there and let them know you are okay. Easy now, I've got you. I'm not going to let you blow away," Ritter continued to talk softly to the elderly woman until he had seen to it that she was safely inside the store. This was eating up too much time, he had to go. That was all that he could think of, getting to the woman he now knew he loved.

The building in which Middy was held prisoner by a madman shuddered. Her skin crawled with revulsion at the thought that he had touched her. Over and over she shot wind at the tape around her wrists, each time she tried to break the tape apart it held her fast. He must have used the strongest duct tape made, Middy thought. Constantly she beat that tape with her only weapon, wind.

Finally, Ritter thought, as the caravan of cars started moving again, he could almost feel the relief coming off the others as they piled into their cars to follow along behind his car. The sky was so dark now with angry clouds that it had darkened the streets enough that the automatic streetlights were coming on. Dread hung over Ritter like a damp blanket in a winter freeze sending chills down his back. He had no idea if they were even heading in the right direction. All he had to rely on was Killer. They drove on. With each second the storm became worse. Now the wind howled around the car, whipping into his open window as if lashing out at them personally. Killer fed often from the feeders they had brought along for the little hummingbird. With one hand Ritter would hold a feeder for Killer to drink from while batting with the other hand anything which tried to block the windshield's view in front of the driver.

We are heading in the direction the wind is blowing, Ritter reasoned, it has to be going to her. If I'm wrong I may have just killed her. He looked over at Killer. The little bird seemed content to continue the direction they were going. Watson and Sherlock were sitting up in the back seat by the FBI man. The pair were watching everything. Watson softly rumbling under her breath with her ears pinned back and her eyes staring straight ahead as if she could see the target. Sherlock was quiet and still as a statue except for his nose. His nose seemed to be sucking in huge whiffs of the air around them and the car. Just find her for me, Ritter silently begged the sad looking hound.

Chapter Fifteen

IN DESPAIR

He, the madman, stood looking down at Middy with what she took to be a grin upon his face. What right had he to grin? He had shot Fuller and all the others she called her brothers in blue, then he cut off Albert's finger. He should be worrying about what she was going to do to him instead of grinning like a fool at the sight of her abraded body. She tried to make eye contact to see if she could figure out what he had planned, but there was nothing in him, nothing inside but madness, cleverness yes, clever madness, the worse kind. "I'll try not to kill you," Middy managed to get out, wondering why she said it.

"She speaks! The pile of filth speaks. I'll have to cut out her tongue, I will, I will. Filth can't talk, everyone knows that."

Fear crawled down Middy's body like the slime left behind from an army of slugs, lingering, creepy. She clamped her mouth shut and flung wind at the tape binding her hands with such force it made her body lift slightly. The madman's eyes widen each time she was lifted up. "BE GONE, DEMON!" he suddenly shouted, striking her body over and over with the rubber bat. Keep him busy, Middy thought, get free, then take him down. She bucked in the tub as much as she could bound and inhibited by the sides of the tub, thrashing about to make it difficult for him to strike her. He kept shouting that "Begone, Demon!" bit and was beginning to froth at the mouth. Suddenly Middy realized the guy was scared. Scared of what was the question, demons, her, or something from his life?

The building shook with a violence that bespoke of hurricanes or a tornado force. Even as Middy felt the shudder of the building she was lost in the call of the wind, of nature, the air, the earth beneath the building. It all called to her like an old friend greeting her after a long trip away. She was lost in the feel of the wind rushing to her hands, caressing her body, feeding her need. Lightning was released from the clouds which had gathered over the building. It crashed with a loud boom which rocked the already shaking building. Dust filled the room in which Middy and the monster were in a struggle of wills. Something new played over Middy's fingers. A tingle went across her fingers it was something she hadn't felt before, yet it had the echo of the untouched power building inside of her since her last near death experience. She tried to harness that tingle and shape it as a force to use against the duct tape on her wrists. It danced wanting to go its own way, wildly unpredictable in its actions. Somehow, someway, Middy harnessed the tingling beast and shot it at the duct tape on her wrists. The tape gave a little offering freer movement of Middy's hands. With a sense of victory within her grasp Middy sought more of the wild tingling trying to use it once more to split the bindings keeping her from bringing her hands around to fight off the madman standing over her. Outside the wind howled shaking the building continually raining dust from the rafters down on Middy and a madman.

"Filth! You bring filth everywhere you go. Demon woman, I must end you," the madman said in almost a whisper as if it had just dawned on him that the only way to end his personal torment was to kill her. He swung the bat down, again and again, bruising her legs and shoulders. The skin split on her forehead from one glancing blow and blood dripped down her face, which only seemed to enrage him all the more. "The dirt, I'll have to clean your body again. You can't be a proper lady all dirty like that."

The madman stopped beating her, kneeling down he poured some of the cleanser solution over her head again. This time she closed her eyes tight before he could get it into her eyes. Middy kept her eyes closed as the monster began to scrub her already raw skin. It took every bit of willpower she had learned about blocking out horror and pain to not cry out in pain as her already tender flesh was scrapped over. It was so much worse this time since her skin was already raw from the first time the monster had scrubbed her down.

Carefully Middy searched for the source of the tingle on her fingers. It had to come from someplace, a hidden spot deep inside her, for she had never had access to it before. You are here somewhere, she thought to that elusive bit of power. Yet it didn't come to her, wouldn't bend to her will and take shape in her hands. This was not the time to experiment with new powers. Middy knew it, accepted the truth of that disappointment, and returned to shooting wind at her bound wrists.

The monster kept scraping that brush over her damaged skin, but Middy hardly felt it now. There was one thing on her mind and one thing only, to get free and take the monster down. She pulled more and more wind to her making the walls around her bow towards her and the monster. The storm outside raged in all it's fury, slamming the sides of the building sending lightning bolt after lightning bolt down to roar in a blast of sound which deafened her with the rebounding vibrations. That tingle began in her fingers again, sizzling along them, sending little shocks up her arms. Without hesitating so much as a tenth of a second Middy gathered the tingle and blasted it at the duct tape on her wrists. The tape gave again, and that was all it took to pop the tape in two.

For a moment Middy laid still evaluating everything going on with the monster, the room, herself. She could feel the toll of using her wind for so long and hard was taking on her body. The feeling of nausea, the little quakes insider her tummy and other parts of her body. Not now, she silently begged. I can't give in now, I'm so close to getting this monster, of ending his terror. Even as she told herself she couldn't stop now, not when her hands were finally free, the darkness of utter exhaustion shut down her mind.

She was dreaming, but it wasn't real, it couldn't be real. In her dream, she had found the monster who had killed so many of the people she had worked with, those she cared about, her on the job family. True she had often wanted to slap them up against the head and yell at them that she wasn't the goof off they thought she was, but then sometimes she was that person. Yeah, sometimes she goofed off, like not jogging, not keeping fit like she should. The thing was, she was more deadly than most realized, probably more than she knew. Hopefully not more than she feared. That fear had always been the secret she held inside herself. What if she killed someone?

Inside her mind, down deep, Middy knew she wasn't awake. Some tiny nagging part of her was screaming at her to "Wake up!". Middy began to fight herself trying to wake up. It was urgent, the need to wake up and get the monster. It ate at her, demanded she ignored all the danger signs which told her body to rest. Rest or die those signs were telling her. Then she would just have to die because this monster was not getting away.

Groggy, barely coherent Middy fought to open her eyes. That effort alone made her want to throw-up. Images of Albert's finger in that package, of Ritter all but dead, smashed and shattered, laying on a hospital bed with IVs hooked to impossible places because he had no viable veins in his arms or legs, flashed behind her eyelids. They were seared into her brain, burned there in all their horror. A whimper tried to work its way up her throat, but she caught it, held it down in a raw throat that ached to let loose. She was her mother's daughter and would not let the monster see her weak, broken.

Somewhere there came the sound of something breaking loose and crashing down making a lot of noise. That sound was enough to bring Middy fully awake. She felt terrible, every part of her body was telling her to just pass out again. Only she couldn't, not yet, not until she saw the monster in custody. Another loud crash nearby made the tub Middy was in rock and tilt to the side. She opened her eyes fully to see what the monster was up to. He stood beside the tub stripped down to his underwear. She gagged, this was not going to happen to her, she had her hands free, and it was time to put them to use, despite all the nausea, the trembling muscles.

As the monster reached for the waistband of his shorts Middy brought her hands from behind her back sending a blast of wind forcing the thin man, who did not look like a monster man, out of the bathroom. Struggling, Middy managed to get to her knees while holding the madman against the ceiling of the next room. She carefully got to her feet after she unwrapped her legs while maintaining the wind pinning the ghost. Thoughts ran through her mind weighing options. She had to figure out how to disable this monster until help arrived, if it arrived. Already the edges of her mind were getting fuzzy. Middy could feel the darkness creeping up on her, threatening to take her down. Just a little longer, she thought, let me hold on long enough to disable the monster. Only her mind wasn't working right. It was starved for the energy she didn't have to give it. Something drastic had to be done, but what? Her brain seemed confused, unable to form a valid thought. Middy knew she had to do something, besides staying alive. The only thought that her mind seemed capable to hold on to was to keep the monster trapped.

A feeling of panic began to gather inside Middy. Her strength was leaving her and she still didn't have the monster confined. Although Middy didn't have enough energy to pull wind to her the wind kept flowing in filling her up. It was as if it had a life of its own. Outside lightning flashed and thunder boomed its loud voice shaking the building. Her arms began to tingle, and that tingle traveled down her arms into her hands settling in her fingers. The air crackled sparks spit off her fingers flowing in erratic forks of energy to where the monster was suspended against the ceiling. He screamed over and over as the sparkling forks of energy hit him.

As the madman screamed the building around them shook violently. One of the walls crashed inward. The building was starting to come down around them. One wall coming down weaken the whole structure. Air rushed to Middy as if it had been denied access to her for far too long and would not be held off any longer. It filled her up, and for the first time gave back to her some of the energy she had pushed out. The roof shuddered and groaned as the wind ripped it off the massive converted warehouse. The sky was shattered over and over with angry lightning. The booming voice of such violent

crashes of electricity drowned out all the moans
and crashes that the building made as it was being
ripped apart. All the while the monster continued
to scream, and scream. Dark splotches were
starting to form in Middy's vision. She had trouble
remembering what it was she had to do, yet she held
the monster who had killed her people. With each
flash of lightening her body tingled and the monster
received shocks from her fingers. Trying to stay
focused on the screaming man, Middy sank to her
knees. Slowly she fell backward until her head came
to rest against the tub. All the while she kept her eyes
on the monster, kept him pinned, punished him with
shock after shock. Nothing else in the world was real
to her only the monster, and the need to hold him, to
make him pay.

Killer erupted from Ritter's pocket and flew
out the window Ritter had open trying to keep the
windshield clear for the spare driving the car. Ritter
didn't even have time to protest before the wind
slammed the little bird back into the windshield. The
car stopped and the spare driving looked ghastly
green as he turned to face Ritter. Ritter tried to open
the door to get out, but the wind was too strong
keeping him from opening the door more than an
inch. Frustrated Ritter dove out the window landing
on his shoulder, not the best exit he had ever made.
Fearing the worse he gently scooped Killer up, then
handed him off to the spare so he could crawl back
into the car. No sooner had he settled into the seat
and reached for Killer when Watson and Sherlock
both leaped out the window.

"What's wrong with them?" the FBI guy asked.

Ritter frowned, looking to where Sherlock and Watson had plastered themselves against a building and were inching forward. He thought he knew what they had in mind. "She is close. And they think it will be faster on foot from here. Tell the others," Ritter ordered.

The spare handed Killer over to Ritter in order to make the call to the others. The little bird trembled, fluttered one wing weakly, before opening an eye to look up at Ritter. "I get it Killer. You need to stay in my pocket this wind is too strong for you to fly in. Okay?" The frown line between Ritter's eyes deepened as he realized he had no idea if the little bird understood anything that people said. He had seen the great heart of the little bird. It was so full of courage and intelligence, but did it understand people-speak?

Securing Killer in his shirt pocket again, Ritter checked his handgun before going feet first out the car window. At the last moment on his way out of the window, he remembered the tracking line for Sherlock. He shook his head at what he was doing, this was a crazy idea, really crazy, he thought as he snatched the tracking line up.

Up and down the line of cars men were crawling out of the windows of the cars. Every one of them wore vest and helmets. Anyone watching the swarm of men exiting the cars might wonder if the area was being invaded. The men were all armed with various weapons as were called for in their part of this attempt to capture or kill a man who had terrorized the city. If a watcher held any hope of seeing an end to the constant fear from an invisible sniper it rested on the shoulders of these men exiting those cars, and a woman who couldn't seem to hold a thought in her head at that moment.

Middy watched the man suspended in the air wondering what he was doing up there. Was this a circus act? No, no, that was just stupid, no one would perform an act in weather like this. She knelt there with her hand thrust forward towards the man in the air thinking how stupid he was to be doing a dangerous act in weather so foul. Then the sky split in amazing flashes of lightning and sparks flew from her fingers to the crazy man. The man screamed and screamed. For some reason, a smile tugged at Middy's face as if she thought it only fitting he should scream. She was tired, so tired. All she wanted was to lay down and sleep until dinner. Middy's eyes started to close, but a little nagging voice inside her yelled at her to keep it together. Swaying, her mind more in a stupor than alert and aware of what she was doing, the wind flowed through her, out her hand to hold a monster in the air. The monster looked puny, a thin pitiful man who didn't look as if he could be a threat to anyone. But wasn't that the way of monsters? They posed as ordinary people, not showing their true nature. Only in their secret hidden ways did they do the horrible things they did to others.

The wind and lightning whipped and crackled over the building bringing down another wall. Soon the whole building would be crashing in on top of Middy and the monster.

"This is ridiculous," the FBI agent grumbled as

he wiggled out his window. "You have no idea what building Whiting is being held in, do you?"

"Maybe I don't, but these guys do," Ritter said, indicating Sherlock and Watson.

"Once this wild goose chase is over I'm going to see to it you never work for the government again. By now Miss Whiting is probably dead, and it is all your fault. If you had let me conduct a proper investigation we'd have her by now."

Ritter hoped with all his heart he wasn't making the mistake this FBI man thought. With everything inside him, he wanted to bring his Cupcake safely home. This storm, it had to be caused by her, it had to be. He couldn't be so wrong in believing that. Hauntingly there was that nagging doubt, the one which told him mistakes were made, nobody was above being wrong. For that reason, he was putting his trust in a dog, a cat, and a tiny bird. Their instincts had to be right. They didn't question themselves just went ahead and did what was needed. So did he.

"Let's go," Ritter called and followed as Sherlock pulled him along. It was a good thing the dog was short-legged as it kept the wind from getting under him and blowing him away. Ritter and the other humans in the group had to fight for every step. That constant fighting to keep on his feet was irritating Ritter. He wanted to go, and go fast instead of this crawling, creeping pace. Looking up at the sky, Ritter's brow developed deep furrows when he saw lightning striking in concentration in one area about a block over. It sounded as if all hell was breaking loose over there. That's my girl, she is letting me know where to come, Ritter silently cheered to himself. "We are off about a block. Let's cut through to the next street."

What little strength Middy managed to pull into herself went swiftly as she instinctively tried to keep the monster pinned. Everything around Middy seemed to be determined to crash and add to the pile of the broken building that was already gathering in a heap over her. So much broken jumble piled up that she could barely see beyond her own hands raised sending the wind and electric shocks at the monster. Her only thought, the only thing she could remember to keep doing, was to hold the monster. Haze was gathering in her mind though and that was a bit scary, for there was a nagging little something telling her she couldn't give in, not yet.

The area they approached on the next street was where the storm was sitting. It was a good thing the warehouses in this area were mostly deserted and unused because the storm was doing a great deal of damage to the buildings. Lightning struck one metal roof and left a gaping hole, black and sooty looking. The wind, having found a hold on the now damaged roof was raising the tin and slamming it down with vigor. The small force of humans and animals crept forward while dodging flying debris.

Killer, from time to time, would poke his head up out of Ritter's pocket. Each time the little bird peeked out Ritter would say, "Not yet, Killer", and Killer would duck his tiny head back down. Ritter was worried about the little bird. This storm could easily strike the bird down, as it had already demonstrated. How the little guy had made it back to the house, after following Middy here, Ritter didn't know. He had given up trying to understand what drove the hummingbird to claim Middy as if she were his own property to care for and to protect. He knew how the little bird felt, he too wanted to claim her, and protect her. Never had he felt the jealousy that had overcome him when Middy laughed with the Barlow guy. He'd wanted to strangle the guy then beat him to a bloody pulp. He didn't, for no matter how enraged he was at another man talking to his Cupcake, she had the right to talk to him. The one thing in his life that he always tried to uphold was the belief that people had to live their own lives. Only, Cupcake, well, Cupcake lived on the dangerous side of life, and that just about killed him.

Albert jumped back into Frankie and some guy he didn't know from one of the other districts when the side of the warehouse which had been hit by lightening, collapsed almost on top of him. Ahead of them, the building they had been heading towards went down collapsing upon itself with the wind whipping stray bits up in the air and slinging things out in all directions.

Ritter bent down and picked up some shredded material. His heart just about stopped beating when he recognized the material as being from Middy's pajamas. Sherlock yodeled a song of 'follow me' and took off running towards the pile of rubble which was left where the building had been. Frankie stepped up beside Ritter looking down at the material in Ritter's hand as Sherlock jerked Ritter forward. "My God! She is in there." Frankie gasped.

Grim faces wiped away the faces of worry. Suddenly the teams were thinking this would be a recovery rather than a rescue and take down. Ritter wasn't having any of them jump to conclusions. "Teams, we know the ghost is in there and that he has our gal. We aren't going to let him keep her. And we damn sure aren't going to let him get away this time! Surround the building. Snipers get ready. We work in from all sides, except I will follow Sherlock to our gal. He won't let me down." Turning Ritter looked for Watson, but Watson was stalking someone, she had no reason to wait, her prey was just ahead.

The remaining parts of the building came crashing down. Middy tried, she gave the last bit of her conscious thought to holding the monster. Then a sound, like an angel, only it was singing in Sherlock's voice. The sound was saying "I'm here, you can let go." So she did. Middy gave into the shaking, the darkness hovering over her trying to consume her. She let it take her knowing deep inside herself that her job was finished.

Watson squeezed herself through two-by-fours, broken sheetrock, and metal pipes. There was one objective in her mind attack the person who was a threat to her happy home. Since she killed the snake the cat had found her slot in this strange family of creatures and people. She was a protector.

Sherlock yodeled again and began frantically digging at the largest pile of rubble. It was at that moment in time, Ritter realized most of the wind had stopped. The only wind blowing now was just from the storm. A pain of fear clenched in his chest as he joined Sherlock tossing rubble aside in a frantic frenzy searching for his Cupcake. Killer launched himself from Ritter's pocket zipping off to who knew where. Ritter barely took note of the little hummingbird's departure.

Fuller was torn between helping Ritter dig his partner out from the rubble, and going after the man who had put her there in the first place. In the end, his partner won out. Going over to where Ritter was throwing things off the huge pile of debris that was heaped in one spot, Fuller bent over and began digging in the same spot as the woeful hound, who was making anxious noises in his throat, throwing in the long yodel of a baying hound in-between. A hand came down on Fuller's shoulder. Looking up he saw the grim, worried face of Frankie over him. "Go, you and Albert are the ones that need to arrest that bastard. It is what the Boss wanted. I'll do this," Frankie said. Fuller rubbed a hand over his eyes and nodded. He hadn't been tearing up, not really.

Albert was advancing slowly over the rubble, checking under pockets of Sheetrock, broken lumber, and furniture looking for the madman they all wanted to find. He glanced often at the other teams to see if they had found anything. A big part of him wanted to be over there with Frankie and Ritter. He tapped down that part, his job, the job assigned by the Boss, was to arrest the killer. Fuller was searching a couple of feet over, they had a line to keep up. A tight line, nobody wanted this guy to get away this time. Ghost or not they wanted him too badly to slip up and leave a gap for him to slip past them. Something whizzed by Albert's head and he crouched down so fast that Fuller, startled, reacted leaping on top of Albert to shield him.

Killer zipped back to check on Albert and Fuller hovering in front of Albert's nose. "Get off of me, old man, it is just Killer."

"Don't old man me. Someone has to look after you."

"Don't baby me. I was just startled when he zipped by my ear. Sounded like a bullet. Can you blame me?" Albert moaned.

Slowly Fuller got up, reaching down he offered his hand to Albert. "No, kid, I don't blame you. I might have wet my pants if he did that to me. We both have reasons to be jumpy." Killer buzzed around the two officers once more, before sprinting off. A quick flick of his eyes assured Fuller nobody was alerting on the enemy yet, so he took a moment to study Killer. The little bird was diving up and down in one area. "There, Killer must have him."

No sooner had Fuller spoken, than a terrifyingly eerie growl came from the same area Killer was diving into. Rushing forward, Fuller and Albert closed in on the spot as a high pitched scream ripped the air. All around the circle of men began to close in on the sounds coming from the pile of rubble that a tiny hummingbird kept disappearing beneath. The teams Middy had assigned adapted to the situation, half of each team had their weapons out while the other half cleared a path for them all to maneuver through the broken building's debris.

Once Fuller and Albert reached the spot, where Killer was attempting to peck the heck out of a skinny man in his underwear, they heard Watson threaten the man again. It was chilling, the cat's scream of warning. Carefully the two officers began to remove rubble seeking the madman beneath. Soon the other teams arrived to help out. Fuller stepped aside and pulled out his weapon, this was his and Albert's arrest. He wanted to look over and see how Ritter and Frankie were doing in clearing the rubble off of Middy, he didn't. This was his job, his last time to arrest anyone. After this, he was taking that retirement.

Water was pouring from a broken water pipe somewhere beneath the rubble Frankie and Ritter picked their way through layer after layer of sheetrock and broken two by fours. A wooden beam blocked progress frustrating Ritter. Putting his shoulder under the beam Ritter lifted up as hard as he could. The water made the sheetrock, which crumbled, all soggy underfoot. It was slick to stand upon that soggy mess causing his feet to slip making traction to lift difficult. Some of the weight lifted from Ritter's shoulder. Glancing back his eyes met those of the FBI man. The man nodded at Ritter and Ritter nodded back. A pact passed between them, all animosity was suspended in favor of saving Middy.

Lifting a large section of wall off of the pile covering Middy, Ritter had his first look at his Cupcake. Only her upper body was revealed, and that part of her was covered in blood. Her blood. There were very few spots on her flesh that wasn't bloodied. Her flesh wept, oozing blood and clear fluid as if the body had tried to heal itself. She was still, so very still. Her chest didn't rise and fall. Her wonderful face didn't scrunch up in that way it did when she was annoyed or mischievous. And… she was naked. "Look away!" Ritter bellowed.

Those helping to lift things off of Middy jumped back. Their faces turned red when they realized the state the Boss was in. Ritter was already ripping his shirt off to cover Middy, as he placed the large shirt over Middy's breasts and shoulders another shirt was dangled in front of him. Middy hadn't drawn a breath the entire time it took for Ritter to cover her up. Grief morphed into a rage inside of Ritter. Slowly his hand reached for his gun. His face became stone as he stood and looked over to where a skinny man in nothing but his underwear stood. One fist clutching his weapon, the other clinched so tight his knuckles were white. Ritter stood the rest of the way up. There was one thought in his head at that moment. Kill the bastard.

Frankie was still staring at Middy, despite Ritter's order to look away, he found he couldn't stop staring at her abused face. He found it hard to believe things would end in this manner. She couldn't be dead. All their efforts to get here, to find her, and him, for nothing? For an arrest, for a skinny wacko? All that seemed so insignificant now as he stared at Middy's body laying there half covered still in the wreckage of the building. She looked so pale, not a hint of motion in her. Then before his eyes, her chest rose slightly and fell. It could have been a trick his eyes were playing on him, but he wouldn't accept that, just like he wouldn't accept she was dead. "She took a breath," he told Ritter reaching out to stop Ritter from leaving.

Ritter's legs gave and he knelt back down feeling for a pulse on Middy's neck. It was there, slow, almost gone, but there. "Blankets and a litter. Call for an ambulance. And tell them we need a glucose drip." Gone was the desire to kill, in its place was the desperation to save his Cupcake. "Let's get her out! See to it that creep is caged."

Spirits renewed, the guys who weren't detaining the ghost began clearing the debris off of Middy. Meanwhile, Ritter tried to revive her enough to drink some of the brown drink he had in his pocket.

Chapter Sixteen

MESSENGER

Ritter wrapped Middy in the shirts given him by the guys and his own jacket to give her warmth. She was so cold. The blood on her concerned him to the point he was not willing to wait for the medics to arrive. Frankie had sprinted off to fetch a car along with one of the other guys. Once in the car, Ritter continued to try to get some of the brown fluid down Middy, only he was afraid of drowning her since she wasn't awake or swallowing. The drive to the hospital seemed to take forever. All Ritter could do was warm Middy as much as possible, send his own strength to her, and pray. He was at the point of calling Middy's family when they approached the turn into the emergency room's entrance driveway. A car nearly hit them as it sped pass screeching up to the hospital.

A man bounded out of the car not even shutting the car door behind him. In his hand he grasped a medical bag. He looked more like a football player than what the medical bag indicated. The man started to sprint for the doors of the emergency entrance to the hospital when his phone rang. Whipping his phone out he stopped dead and shouted, "What?" He spun around spotting the line of police cars which had followed him up the drive.

Ritter was ready to have the football player shot, only Ritter had Cupcake in his arms. And here the idiot came, running towards him as if for a touchdown.

The SS were reacting as if Ronny was some insane madman coming to kill them all. Ronny didn't care how crazed he looked, his mission was to save the life of Eric's sister. Then the cops were on him, smashing him down onto the pavement cuffing him, someone put a knee in his back. "Stop! You are killing her," Ronny yelled, but they weren't listening. These men had just taken down a monster, and nobody was harming their girl again. Desperate, Ronny yelled towards the man carrying Middy, "Eric sent me."

"Let him up," Ritter ordered. There was no hesitation, the cuffs were off and Ronny was helped to his feet. "You have the IVs? She needs them immediately."

Ronny didn't waste time explaining, he knew if Ritter said now, Middy had to be worse off than even he realized. As Ritter knelt down holding Middy to his chest Ronny got his first look at her. "Good Lord, what did he do to her?" But he didn't expect an answer. His concern now was, could he find a vein if her arms were as bad as her face and shoulders seemed to be. Even her legs were raw and bleeding. Fortunately, when Ronny stretched one of Middy's arms out her forearms were clear. What he didn't know was her arms had been taped behind her while the front of her was being scrubbed so roughly.

Ronny looked up at one of the officers standing over him and Ritter. "You, hold this bag up. Hold on, I have another one for you to hold too. Keep them up high so the fluid will flow." Ronny glanced at Ritter to explain what he was doing. "I'm going to piggyback some fluids in with the Andy bag. She is losing a lot of fluid from her skin. If she has other injuries we may have to give her blood too."

Nodding, Ritter watched closely every move of the man Eric had sent with the life saving brown IVs for Middy. He remembered Bobby Jay saying Eric saw things, predictions he supposed. He was relieved Eric had seen this. "Why didn't Eric come?" Ritter asked as it was bothering him that this stranger was here instead of Eric.

"Critical patient. He is having to treat, then rest," Ronny said in a low voice, just for Ritter's ears.

"Understood." That ended the conversation.

By that time, people were upon them from the ER, people who were used to taking charge. One of them was Dr. Pierce. She took one look at Ritter and shooed the others back inside. The scowl upon her face stayed as she had Ritter and Ronny place Middy on a gurney. Ritter kept hold of one of Middy's hands and opened his mouth to speak. Dr. Pierce held her hand up to stop him. "I know. She is yours. But at the moment I need her. You can stay. The rest, go." She hesitated before continuing, "Will the family be coming?"

Ritter locked eyes with Ronny, and Ronny shook his head. "No, but this is one of her doctors. He will be in attendance."

Lips clamped firmly shut, Dr. Pierce nodded. She had learned her lesson. She didn't like it, but one thing she wasn't going to do was get herself locked away where she couldn't help her patients. Then, of course, there was that thing, that impossible thing, which had been done before. It ate at her. She wanted so very much to know how this woman on the gurney had survived something that was not survivable. Only, she kept her mouth shut about that subject or any subject that might be thought of as a breaking the oath on the papers she had been made to sign, swearing never to reveal anything that had happened to this woman.

Not letting the grimace he felt inside show, Ronny ran along beside the gurney with his human patient. He was well aware he could be sued for working on a human instead of an animal, but he hadn't thought ahead of more than hooking up the IVs. Now he had to think ahead as if he were a real human doctor. He ran over in his head now the things he would normally do for a dog brought in with this much skin raw and bleeding. One thing he could scratch right off was shaving the patient. In his mind, he laughed at that. First, he would examine her completely, send off blood work, and start the process of cleaning the affected areas. Then, well, he'd have to apply ointment, and bandage the areas. Her face, neck, shoulders, and legs he knew were raw. Only her forearms on the front side of her had been spared. The backside he had yet to see. Ronny's eyes flicked to Ritter. Worry hit him hard. This man would not like him looking at Middy.

Being careful to keep as much of his patient covered as possible, Ronny began his examination. He was nervous as a cat thrown on a hot tin roof. Foremost in his mind was the fact this is Eric's sister. One slip up and not only would the hulk of a man holding Middy's hand shoot him, probably, but Eric would never forgive him. Drat, the luck. He hadn't thought things through when he told Eric he'd bring the IVs needed to save Middy for Eric. The poor guy was in such pitiful shape healing that Saint Bernard. Ronny had watched Bobby Jay tend to Eric when he was in one of these sugar low comas. Easy he had thought. Only, then there hadn't been an SS agent and half the police force watching, at least not in his mind's version. Then there was sour puss Dr. Pierce watching him like a hawk ready to dive down and rip his throat out.

Systematically Ronny went over Middy's sleeping form. Satisfied there was nothing more wrong with her than the abraded skin on her front side, and the deadly sugar low problem, he straightened. First, he needed to make peace with the woman doctor breathing down his neck. Then he would deal with the lawmen. "Dr. Pierce, since this is your hospital, would you do the honors of cleaning and dressing the abraded areas? I want to set up a second line in her other arm, but let's wait until you have finished taking care of the wounded areas," he said. Turning to Ritter he motioned his head to indicate they should leave. "Let's give Middy some privacy while we talk."

Ritter followed the football player out of the curtained cubicle where Middy was being treated. He had a thousand questions, but only spoke one. "Where can I get a supply of the Andy Bags?"

Pausing, Ronny almost laughed, but then he considered this was a serious question by a man with a gun, so he kept his face serious when he answered. "You call Dr. Andy, he makes them up special for the family. This is his number," Ronny read off the number and watched the SS agent put the number into his phone before continuing. "Eric said that if we didn't get the Andy Bags in Middy…. Well, he was very upset, so I said I'd come since he was in no shape himself to travel and didn't want to leave his patient. Just don't let them know I'm a veterinarian."

"No chance of that. Miss Huff and Puff would have a tizzy fit. What about, Cupcake? Is she going to be okay?"

Cupcake? He called her Cupcake, wait until Eric hears this guy's nickname for his sister. That little slip by the SS agent made the trip and all the stress connected with it worth doing. "Yes, we got to her in time. Do you know what was done to her? Eric will want all the details," Ronny said.

"Not yet. She is the only one who knows for certain. The… uh… the entire building was brought down in the storm on top of her. We caught the killer. She saw to that." Ritter turned away for a second to compose himself. He'd thought his Cupcake was dead when he saw her. That feeling just about ended him. He had been determined to kill the guy who had taken his Cupcake from him. That sense of loss still threatened to take hold of him and send him into a mad rage. It also made him realize he had to declare his feelings for her as soon as possible. Maybe he didn't have long to live, but he wanted that time, those last days to be with the woman he loved. The Ronny guy was fidgeting, there seemed a restless urgency about his swaying. "What's wrong?"

The question startled Ronny, he had thought he was containing his need to get back home. Evidently, he hadn't hidden his concern for Eric as well as he had thought. "I'm worried about Eric. Normally, when he has a bad case like he does now, I take care of the other patients. Eric with Bobby Jay's help will stay in the backroom doing what needs to be done. I'm afraid he'll overextend himself without me there." Ronny motioned to the curtain area behind which Middy was being cleaned and bandaged. This I had to do for him. He was insane with worry over Middy. I think…" Rubbing a hand over his face Ronny continued in a whisper… "that last time scared him more than he is willing to let on."

For a moment Ritter didn't say anything, then his voice held something Ronny didn't want to analyze. "It scared all of us."

Ritter turned to face the curtained area as if willing it to open. Ronny wasn't the only one fidgeting now. Ritter took a step towards the curtain just as Dr. Pierce called out, "You can enter now, the worst has been done." He didn't need to be told twice, immediately ripping the curtain back along its runner, he went to Middy. She had so much gauze covered areas on her face that she looked like a clumsy constructed mummy. He reached out a hand to her face but didn't touch her. Even as she slept in her coma-like state he couldn't, wouldn't take a chance on hurting her. Instead, he grasped the guardrail on the side of the bed holding on so tight his knuckles turned white.

Ronny went over the bandaged areas on Middy's face and shoulders. He didn't look beneath the covers, he didn't dare, not with Ritter across from him bending the guardrail. He was aware of Dr. Pierce watching them closely while she cleaned Middy's legs with antibacterial soap. It was up to Ronny to rein Ritter in, the man looked as if he were about to go into a killing rage. "Take a deep breath, and center yourself. You won't do the team, uh, Middy, any good if you go off half-cocked. Breath in. Breath out. Think calm thoughts. Think of how she is safe now. We have her, you have her." Ronny kept talking while watching Ritter's hands. He gave an inward sigh of relief when those hands loosened and let the guardrail go. Without revealing the tension inside him, Ronny turned to Dr. Pierce, "Good job, Doctor. I think as soon as our patient regains consciousness she can be released." The shocked 'no' he saw in her eyes had him continuing. "I don't think the hospital needs to have a floor shut down in order to keep her here. And I'll be supervising her at home until we are certain she is out of danger. Do you agree?"

"I'd rather keep her here until I know she is out of danger," Dr. Pierce said, noticing Ritter shifting out of the corner of her eye. "However, if you assure me you will stay in attendance until she is up and about, then I'll agree." The SS agent seemed to relax at her words. Mentally she gave herself a kick in the pants. Would she never learn to keep her mouth shut?

Once Dr. Pierce had finished with the dressing of all the abrasions she administered an antibiotic as a precaution. This, she knew, would be all she would be allowed to do with the SS keeping a constant watch on her movements, and a hundred, or more, police officers coming by to check on the Whiting woman. Her own thoughts were not kind about all this disruption in her efforts to care for a patient. She wondered if they were trying to cover up their own mistakes in protecting this woman, or if the woman herself was the cause of all that had happened to her. She'd heard that Miss Whiting was the target of the man who had killed so many police officers. Had a mad killer done this? Whatever the answer, she would probably never know the truth. She, as they had already indicated, was not one of the team. Then she smiled to herself. Well, that new doctor had treated her as an equal at least. The handsome devil!

The phone had been vibrating like crazy while Cupcake was being treated by the woman doctor. His Cupcake was on the second of the brownish IVs now. Why don't you wake up? I need you to wake up, Ritter fussed mentally at Middy. I have something important to ask you. WAKE UP!

"Wake up!" it was like a shout in Middy's mind. She struggled to wake, her body fought her, demanding that she stay in the embrace of darkness until she was recovered enough to wake naturally. That voice still echoed inside her, and oddly caressed her very being. She was drawn to the voice, her mind sought it out, hunted it through the darkness, across the nightmare lands in her mind where the bodies of those she cared about were piled in bloody heaps. Groggy, nausea threatening to take over, she found her way to the light and awoke.

The moment Middy's eyes opened, Ritter fell to his knees beside her hospital bed. He didn't care that anyone on the other side of the curtain walls might hear him. Nor did he care if he looked like a fool on his knees looking into that mummified face with those wonderfully opened eyes. Ritter was not waiting a moment longer to declare his feelings to his Cupcake. There may never be another time to do this. One, or both of them could die tomorrow or the day after. It didn't even occur to him that his actions were those of a desperate man who had thought he would never have a chance to tell the one person he loves how much he needed and loved her. He raised her head a bit so Middy could see him kneeling beside her and watched her eyes fasten on him. "I don't know how to do this, but, here goes. I love you. Please say you will marry me and put me out of my misery. I don't want to spend what is left of my life without being able to hold you in my arms, to be able to show you every day how much you mean to me. So, will you, marry me?" Eyes pleading his case he looked at his Cupcake trying to show her how much he loved her.

Middy couldn't understand what Ritter was

going on about. He seemed intense, wanting her to say or do something, but the nausea and darkness were having their way with her. Giving in to the demands of her body, Middy threw up on Ritter and then passed out.

Ritter wiped a hand across his eyes to clear the mess off his face. Staring at Cupcake's bandaged face he nodded. "I'll take that as a yes," he said. If it wasn't a yes, he was going to turn it into one, somehow, someway.

Ronny had been about to enter the area curtained off where his patient rested when he heard Ritter talking. Thankfully, he had paused before breaking the bit of privacy Ritter had with Eric's sister. Otherwise, he wouldn't have heard the man ask Middy to marry him. The moment had been so personal, that Ronny hesitated another moment before finally going in to check on Middy.

Ritter had just managed to wipe his face clean when the doctor Eric had sent came in to check on Middy. He had stood when he heard the curtain rings being rattled. "She woke briefly. She was sick to her stomach then fell back into that deep sleep," Ritter said still watching Middy's sleeping form. Turning to Ronny his face in protection mode, stern with a real sense of threat broadcasting. "Tell me the truth. Is she going to be okay?"

Before speaking, Ronny went over to Middy and checked her pulse and respiration. He felt the only bit of bare skin he could find, which was her lower arm, then faced Ritter. "She is recovering. The fact she woke up briefly is a sign that it won't be much longer before she will be back with us," he hesitated before going on. "This is by far the worst case I've seen, but then I've only experienced this with Eric. Bobby Jay has always been there to take care of Eric."

"Are you saying you don't know?" Ritter said with a bit of anger coming through.

"I'm certain. I wouldn't say she was doing well if she wasn't, believe me. I've had experience with Susan's SS man, so I'm not stupid enough to tell you something that isn't true," Ronny said. Ritter gave a snort of a laugh startling Ronny.

"Yeah, I like that man. He can be on my team any day," Ritter said. There was the hint of a smile upon his face as he remembered Tex putting the General in his place. He felt a fellowship with Tex, after all, the man was a fellow Texan.

Ronny motioned Ritter to move closer to him. Once Ritter leaned close he whispered. "Eric said we should smuggle the pets in. Any ideas how?"

Finally, something he could do for Cupcake. A mission of high importance in his book. "Leave it to me."

It didn't take more than a phone call to have Killer, Watson, and Sherlock brought to the hospital. Ritter had no idea why Eric had sent word to have the companions brought to be with Middy, but he was taking no chances with his Cupcake's recovery. If a bird, a cat, and a dog would help get her back to herself, he'd make damn sure they arrived.

It was Albert who pulled up to the ER with Watson, Killer, and Sherlock. He had brought the vests declaring Watson and Sherlock as 'companions', and Killer's too. Once the three unlikely companions were outfitted Ritter approached the ER's sliding glass doors. And there was the first bump on the path to Middy in the form of a burly security guard. "No pets allowed," he told Ritter in an 'I'm tired of dealing with jerks' voice. Ritter flashed his ID and kept walking. "Hold it. I said, no pets! What part of that did you not understand?"

"Let's see, oh, the *pets* part. These are 'companions', as you can see by the vests they are wearing. See, right here," Ritter pointed to the words on the sides and back of Sherlock's vest, "COMPANION".

"Bull crap. Anyone can sew up a vest and claim their pet is a 'companion'. And is that bird with you too? That there is a health hazard to the patients. No bird, no cat. And I'm not convinced the dog is legal," the security guard said, looking very put out that he had to deal with everything.

Ritter held up a finger to indicate he needed a moment. Taking out his phone he punched one number on it. When the call was answered on the other end Ritter straighten his shoulders, making a show of giving respect to the person he was talking to. "Mr. President," he paused letting that sink into the mind of the security guard, "I am sorry to bother you, but it seems the three companions are not being allowed into the hospital to see my subject." There was a pause as some very loud shouting was heard coming over the phone. "Yes, sir. She is going to be alright. Dr. Ronny is here supervising her care. However, Eric sent word to bring the companions. He thought they are needed for her recovery. By the way, Killer and Watson helped pin down that serial killer." There was a long moment of silence before the voice on the other end spoke again. "Yes, sir," Ritter said, then extended the phone towards the security guard.

Face turning several shades between red and purple the guard took the phone gingerly in his hand. Slowly he raised it to his ear as if it were a gun being pointed at his head. Apparently, Middy's grandfather was in a foul mood. At least, from the expression on the face of the security guard, Ritter gathered the man was wishing he had never gotten out of bed this day. With a brisk "Yes, Mr. President." The man hung up the phone and handed it back to Ritter. "You are cleared to enter, all of you."

All of them were again stopped by the walk-in desk. "I'm so sorry, sir." A soft spoken woman with gray hair stopped him while standing up at her desk. "We have a policy forbidding animals in the ER."

Immediately, Ritter liked the woman speaking to him. She had that feel to her that is missing in so many people of the modern world. "Yes, ma'am. These, however, are companion animals. They have special passes to go everywhere to be with their person. And, you see, ma'am. Their person is back there in one of your curtained cubicles." Ritter gave the woman his most sincere expression, knowing he was playing on her motherly generous side to give in and let him go to his Cupcake.

Mildred looked at the three-legged dog, the orange cat and the bird zooming around this serious man. They did have official looking vests on, and appeared well behaved. As if sensing her hesitation the cat came over and rubbed its face against her leg. Then, that cute little bird zoomed up and hovered in front of her face as if it were studying her even as she studied it. It was the dog who decided her. The dog sat down directly in front of Mildred and offered his paw to her. "I am sorry, sir, I just am not allowed to let you take the pets. Now if you excuse me I need to find my pen, it has rolled under my desk," she said, giving a motion with her head for him to continue.

Ritter gave the woman a Texas smile and saw the slight uplift of her lips in response as she turned away to bend over to crawl under her desk in search of the alleged pen.

Finally, Ritter thought, as he reached up and pulled open the curtain to the cubicle where Middy was being treated, coming face to face with Dr. Pierce. Inwardly, Ritter sighed. This woman had been a thorn in his side from day one. She didn't have a clue as to what was going on with Middy and didn't seem capable of keeping her judgments to herself.

"Hold it! My patient has too many raw areas to risk contact with animals." Dr. Pierce was in her chicken hen protective mode, ready to do battle, even though she knew this was a fight she couldn't win.

"Just watch. These three are her companions. You know the amount of trauma she has been through this year alone. Knowing that, can you deny she needs her trauma team with her?" Ritter motioned with his head as the three pets zeroed in on Middy. He told himself he had faith in whatever Eric saw as the need for the pets to be here with Middy. No matter how much he couldn't see the reason, there had to be one. He had seen how in-tune with the pets his Cupcake was, and how they seemed to relate to her. Don't let her down now, he silently begged them.

Killer zoomed around and over Middy's sleeping form on the hospital bed. Once he seemed satisfied with what he saw the little bird took up a perch on top of the IV pole holding the brownish fluid being dripped into her veins. The next to approach was Sherlock. The hound had waited until Killer was done with his inspection before putting his paws on the bed. Pushing up with his one hind leg the dog attempted to pull himself up on the bed with his forepaws. Ritter reached down and gave the struggling hound a push up so that the dog could lay down alongside Middy. Sherlock very carefully gave Middy a lick on her forearm, avoiding all the bandaged areas as he snuggled against her. Satisfied, he settled down resting just his nose on the bare skin of her arm.

Watson waited until Sherlock was settled before she jumped up on the bed. She didn't hesitate, instead she carefully maneuvered herself to stand on Middy's chest. She placed each paw down in slow motion, being very careful not to stand on any of the bandaged areas. Once in position, she stared down at Middy's face as if willing her to do something. "What is the cat doing?" Dr. Pierce asked.

"Communicating," Ritter said. At least, I hope so. What had he expected? That she would instantly wake up? Life was never that easy.

Middy's chest rose and fell as if she was taking

a deep breath. Dr. Pierce wanted to go check her, but, Ritter put a restraining hand on her arm. "Let them do their thing."

Middy stirred deep in her mind. She was being summoned as only a mother or pet owner is summoned when one of theirs is feeling badly with the need to help. Slowly she fought the fog which held her prisoner in her own body, that weakness from not having enough fuel in her body to keep her brain alert. Then she was awake, aware that the companions were becoming restless waiting for her to get up and maybe feed them, or let them out. "I'm...mm wake," she mumbled rather crackly. Watson looked over her shoulder at Ritter, a rather smug expression on her catty face. Sherlock's tail thumped with vigor on the bed, and he licked Middy's arm again. "K, let me up." Middy started to sit up, groaned rather unlike a lady, and plopped back down. Memories flooded back into her mind, making her relive those horrible moments when her skin was being scrubbed off her. She opened her eyes searching for Ritter, then he was there taking her hand in his. The heat of his hand warmed her, steadied her, and took away the horror. "We lose anyone?"

Ritter shook his head no because he couldn't find his voice. Looking down at her, so helpless in that hospital bed, he couldn't find his words for all the rage, and the relief conflicting inside him. Then, he forced himself to become the SS man he was and found the words she needed to hear. "No deaths. You caught him, Cupcake. Fuller and Albert made the collar, just like you wanted. Watson and Killer held him after you passed out until they got the cuffs on him. You should have seen Watson, she had her mouth on his throat doing this weird growl. That sent cold chills down my back. She didn't leave a mark on him, but man, he was scared so bad he pissed himself," Ritter chuckled as he remembered Fuller telling him about the takedown and Watson's growl.

An image of the skinny man in his underwear hit Middy between the eyes bringing back the fear of him planning to molest her. Ritter's words sank in and she pictured that skinny man in his underwear wetting himself. Giving a tiny laugh, Middy winched as the skin on her body pulled. She was so raw and sore. "Thanks, I needed that," she said, hoping the look on her face was anything but the haunted feeling she had inside her.

Watson had moved off her chest when she had attempted to sit up, but Killer had taken her place. He poked his beak at the bandages on her chest cocking his head. Swifter than the eye could follow he zoomed up and off to hover first in front of Ritter, then in front of Dr. Pierce.

"Okay, perch and we will explain," Ritter told the little bird. He looked over at Dr. Pierce. "I think he wants us to explain why his person has bandages."

"You are joking, right?" she said.

"Doc, you don't want to fool around with Killer. I've seen him in action," Ritter said, with an amused look on his face. "Okay, I'll tell him, and the others. You may leave now, but send in Dr. Ronny."

The dismissal raised Dr. Pierce's hackles. Not again! No way was this creep barring her from her patient. "No. I stay, and I'll tell the bird what is what. You leave."

"Not going to happen. She is mine. I will never leave her," Ritter countered. Now he was in fighting mode. Nobody was going to separate him from his Cupcake. A tiny breeze brushed his cheek, immediately he turned to Middy. He couldn't see much of her face, but what he saw said it all. "Okay, honey, she can stay and explain. After that, we will see."

Dr. Pierce blinked. What had she missed? Whatever had happened was in her favor. She'd take it. That was when she remembered her patient was awake. How stupid could she be? Arguing in front of a patient, you just don't do that. She could feel her career sliding down the drain already. Never mind that she might be locked up for the rest of her life, to lose the one thing she loved to do was the worse thing that could happen to her. "Apologies, I just don't want to be thrown out of the room again. You can't know what that does to a doctor, how we feel."

It was Middy who spoke, "He knows. Believe me, he knows." Middy glanced over at Ritter remembering how she had kept him out and made him stand across the street. Why hadn't she thought about how he might be feeling? And the crushing blow was he was straight out of the hospital after recovering from a death sentence. She had let her own hurt feelings rule her that day.

Chapter Seventeen

HOME

Doctor Pierce looked at her mummified patient feeling trapped. She was being allowed to stay, she should be feeling elated at having won that battle, but she didn't. Somehow things had been turned around on her, and she felt helpless. Helpless was not a good feeling for a doctor. She cleared her throat. "If all of you will take a seat, I will explain to any who are wondering about the bandages on you, Miss Whiting."

Five minutes later Killer flew at the doctor causing her to shut up. Satisfied, the little bird returned to Middy. "I believe he has heard enough. I'm feeling much better now."

Ronny walked in at that moment, having stood outside the curtained cubicle while Dr. Pierce was going on and on. He couldn't blame the little bird for shutting her up. "Ronny?" Middy asked. She had seen his picture before but had never met

Eric's partner.

"Yes, Eric sent me. He was very concerned. It is good to see you awake, even if looking somewhat like a mummy." Ronny chuckled, trying to set Middy at ease. This was really awkward for him, meeting his best friend's sister like this. "Your fellow here took very good care of you. I just brought the Andy Bags."

Middy glanced at Ritter, who still had a hold on her hand. 'Her fellow,' where did Ronny get that idea? "Thank you. I'm sure they saved my life. I could feel how depleted I was becoming. They have the guy, and that is what counts. No more men in blue are going to die because of me."

"Can that bullshit!" Ritter spat out, jerking her hand to his chest. "He latched on to you. Why he did, we may never know. You are not responsible."

She started to reach up and wipe her eyes because she was afraid she had tears in them. And you don't show a weakness to anyone. Only, the raw areas had begun to tighten, the edges of flesh drawing to the center, or what is considered the center of each area. Middy sat there helpless to hide her pain and the grief, the guilt she felt for each person who had died because she hadn't wiped the cake off her mouth in the coffee shop. It was such a stupid reason for all those deaths, and all of it was on her head, her fault. She caused them all to die. "It was the cake. The cake I ate at the coffee shop. I should have wiped my mouth. If I had, none of them would have died. Families wouldn't have been ruined. I caused it all, every bit of it." Middy took a gasping breath, wanting to be alone. To weep until she was dried of tears.

"No, you are not going to take this on yourself. He could have sat facing another direction while you ate. He could have left any time he saw you were there. There are so many things *he* could have done. All you did was enjoy something you loved. Now he has taken that pleasure from you. *It. Is. Not. Your. Fault.* Now, come here, rest against me while Ronny sees to your release. We are going home." Ritter pulled Middy to him and wrapped his arm around her, letting her lean into his chest and cry. He felt so helpless, not knowing how to fix this for her. How did you take the guilt away from someone as tender-hearted as his Cupcake? Holding tightly to her, he thought of the families without a father or brother, grandchild, or lover. One man was responsible, one man with more hate inside him than should ever be. His Cupcake didn't make the man the way he was, she simply enjoyed… had enjoyed eating cake.

Once she had demonstrated how weak she was, a sniveling crying wreck, Middy was ready to go home. Only, now the bandages on her face were soaked and needed changing. Hurting, more than she would let on, Middy lay back upon the hospital bed so Dr. Pierce could redress her face. She felt as if a burden had been lifted from her shoulders. Ritter was right, at least she wanted to believe he was right. And, he had said he'd never leave her. She wanted to believe him, to believe in him. Still, the image of him in her mind telling her to go kept sneaking in, robbing her of the peace of mind she needed.

Ronny left during Middy's breakdown feeling they needed some privacy. He had also grabbed Dr.

Pierce by the arm and tugged her along with him. "Let's give them a few moments. We can see to the discharge, or rather you can see to it. It has been a pleasure working with you, Dr. Pierce," Ronny said, giving her the smile which had won many a cheerleader's heart.

"I'm just thankful this is over with, barring no problems with her recovery at home. These people scare the crap out of me," she said, then remembered this man was a friend to one of the family. "I mean...." She shut up realizing that anything she said would just make it worse.

Ronny was remembering his own introduction to what Eric could do. The day he asked Ronny to not ride any motorcycles for at least two weeks. Everything that had followed had scared the crap out of him. Now he understood. He guessed he had learned to accept Eric and his family. "You need to look at the good that comes about from them. You do know that a serial killer was caught today. He is the guy who held Miss Whiting prisoner and did all that damage to her. A real madman. But, due to her bravery, and the diligence of the SS and the police force here, that man will never kill anyone again. You can go home knowing you are safe, at least from him."

The frown line permanently creased in Dr. Pierce's forehead deepen, "I guess that is something to remember." Dr. Pierce looked deep in thought for a moment. "She had to have suffered a great deal with all the skin he rubbed off of her. She was very brave. Yes, you are right, that is what I'll remember from now on, instead of the threat to put me in prison for the rest of my life."

Ronny's mouth twitched just a little as he kept the laughter from roaring out of him. Man, he had a lot to tease his friend Eric about when he went home.

It was Ronny who came up with the plan for exiting the hospital. There would be no doubt Middy was leaving if an officer escort were added to the mix, and the three companions and SS protecting Middy all left the hospital at the same time. The plan was simple and executed perfectly. Middy, the companions, Ritter and Ronny slipped out a side door while an officer dressed up like a mummy in a hospital gown and wig went out the ER doors surrounded by protective officers. Headlines read 'Police Take Care Of Their Own'. And they did, only not in the way everyone thought. The stalking cameras were led in a merry chase around the city ending up at headquarters with no Middy among the many men in blue.

In the meantime, Middy was carefully loaded into a paneled van parked as if to deliver linen to the hospital. The van slipped away past the reporters seeking any story involving the Butterfly Whisperer.

When the van finally stopped the thought that ran through Middy's head was 'Finally home'. Ritter leaped out of the van and hurried to her side, then surprised her by scooping her up into his arms and carrying her to the house. Stern eyed cops watched this, some with smiles on their faces, others with concern. In their minds she was theirs, anything involving her was their business. Although they knew this SS man, and liked him, for the most part, they wanted to protect this short frumpy woman from any hurt physical, or of the heart. So, they frowned wondering if they needed to beat up an SS man.

As Ritter hurried towards the house several things had changed in the yard and around the house, Middy found her voice and said, "Stop." Ritter stopped, his heart beating so hard in his chest with worry thinking that she wanted him to leave her be. He felt as if his body quaked with the beat. "Turn, please." He turned in a slow circle.

Behind them, the guys all held shy grins on their faces as Middy looked at the yard where plants of all sorts had been planted in the few hours she had been at the hospital. They had wanted to send her flowers, but the last time they had sent flowers Killer had nearly died. Instead of cut flowers they had each picked a flower, tree, or bush that would be good food for Killer and would look beautiful in the yard. "Surprise!" they all said.

"Don't you guys make me cry like some wimpy girl. I'll have to have these dang bandages changed again. Get your buns over here for a hug."

So they did, lining up they each carefully approach and gave her an awkward hug. Seeing as they couldn't touch much of her body, and weren't about to hug Ritter, who clutched her to his chest possessively, too. The truth was Ritter was so relieved she wasn't making him put her down that he would have suffered even being hugged for her. Still, if he felt her wince, the hugger received a death glare, and if they lingered too long his foot was a quick reminder to move on. All in all, he was pleased with himself, he had her, and was making it clear she was his.

Middy had reached her limit by the time the last of the guys had been hugged and thanked. As if signaling an end of all the happiness one of the bandages on her throat began to seep blood. A grim reminder of all that had happened that day.

Quietly the guys withdrew, smiles upon their lips, lines of worry on their foreheads. They would go now to their families, their job, or to bars to sit quietly and drink away all the tension the previous months of horror put upon their shoulders. Haunted, that is what they all were, haunted with visions of those they knew and trusted with their lives lying in pools of blood. It had been a good day. One of triumph. Not even triumph, however, could take away what they had all lived through. Time. Perhaps in time they would find a way to deal with the demons keeping them awake. In the meantime, they would cling to an unlikely person, a short, frumpy woman with a temper, and a tender heart for as long as she would put up with them.

Inside Middy's house, Ritter placed her in a soft chair, then brought a stool with a cushion to place her legs upon. Once he was certain she was settled, he tended to the companions. He cleaned and refilled Killer's feeders, gave Sherlock and Watson food and fresh water. Now he was at a loss as to what do next. By now he figured Ronny would have arrived to advise about Middy's care. The fact the big man hadn't been waiting at the house when they arrived had worried Ritter. Too many things had happened lately for him to ignore anything unexpected. So it was he sent the spare to find out what had happened to Ronny.

Ten minutes passed before Ritter heard car doors slam outside, and laughter. Relief came like a breath of fresh air washing over Ritter when he recognized the voices of Ronny and the spare. The door opened and the spare looked over to Ritter. "You will never believe what happened," he said laughing. "He had a flat tire right where that nest of wasps used to be. It seems they had started building again and trapped him in the car." He bent over laughing.

"You okay?" Middy asked, worry in her voice.

"Yes, I couldn't risk getting out of the car, being allergic to them. Don't worry, I have a pen, just in case. But, no sense taking risks," Ronny said.

Middy nodded as she thought over all the risks there were in the world besides serial killers. Sherlock came over and plopped his head on her knee as if sensing her thoughts were ones of worry. Absently she rubbed his head taking comfort from her three-legged friend.

Dinner was another problem for Middy. She normally would cook for the guys, but there was no way she would be able to get around without causing her many abrasions to start bleeding again. Then there was the question of how she was going to be able to eat with her face wrapped up like a mummy. Ronny came up with a tolerable solution. Chicken broth, chocolate shakes and pudding with whipped cream, served with a straw. Ronny had trouble not laughing as he placed the straw in Middy's mouth.

Middy spit it out and glared, at least she thought she glared, but that only caused Ronny to actually burst out laughing. "After all the stories Eric has told me of the mischief you caused while a child, this is so funny. You at the mercy of a straw…," he broke off talking as he was propelled backward with a gust of wind. "Point taken, my lady." Ronny bowed and handed the straw to her as a prize for besting him. Now, Ritter was glaring at Ronny, while the spare sought to look anywhere but, at them all.

"She is quite capable. Cupcake is very strong. If I were you, well I think you know, now, to walk carefully," Ritter said, beaming at Middy as if he were so proud of her knocking Ronny back. She, in turn, looked disgruntled at him praising her. Okay, he thought, she is in a bad mood. I'd better walk softly. He went into SS mode, pretending to be a fixture in the room, not a person.

Ronny was delighted at all the information he had to share with Eric when he returned home. It just got better and better. However, Ritter had a point, he'd have to be careful not to become someone Middy disliked. The tales Eric told of his aunt Julian being the subject of Middy's anger were so funny. Now he had witnessed, even felt, some of that vengeance Middy displayed when upset. He picked up a slice of the pizza they had ordered and stuffed his mouth before he lost his good sense and said something to anger Eric's sister. Just watching Middy and Ritter interact was funny. Man, oh, man, as serious as this trip had been, Ronny was having a great time.

Ritter didn't like the look in Ronny's eyes,

they spoke of mischief. When it came time for the companions to go on their last walk of the night he couldn't make himself leave Middy. Instead, he had the spare go out and watch over them, while he kept an eye on Ronny. Middy would have to wait until morning before Ronny would let her take a shower. This discussion led to the awkward talk of her getting ready for bed. She still wore a hospital gown since putting clothing on would have been bothersome to the many abrasions on her body. Just moving to sit up had caused problems.

"I'll come to help you undress for bed," Ronny told her, even though he felt embarrassed just considering helping her undress.

Middy started to shake her head no, then reconsidered that action as the flesh on her throat protested. "No, I'll manage." Turning she went into the bedroom with the companions. Shutting the door firmly, she wondered how she was going to reach the ties behind her neck without pulling something.

A soft knock sounded as someone tapped on the door. "Middy, do you need help?" It was Ronny. What had she expected? Did she think Ritter was going to bang on the door and offer to undress her? Not hardly. Not him for sure. When she didn't answer Ronny she heard him walk away. The ties were beyond her, she just couldn't reach back without pulling the flesh on her chest and stomach. Frustrated, wanting nothing more than to be rid of the bandages, the raw skin, the constant pain, Middy sat down on the edge of the bed. She would just have to sleep in the stupid gown. The bedroom door opened at that moment. Ritter walked in with his arms full of blankets and a pillow. She stared at him, for once lost for words, then she found her voice. "What do you think you are doing?"

"Getting ready to bed down. I'm not taking any chances. You are not safe in here alone," He said, his face was stern. Ritter started making a place to sleep on the floor. He pulled out his gun and placed it beside the pallet, then looked up at her. His voice was so serious when next he spoke. "I think we should elope tomorrow. If we leave in the morning we can be back by nightfall. I can arrange a private flight out and back. Later we can have a wedding with the family and the guys present. You just need to give me the go-ahead and I'll make the calls to set things up. There will be no questioning your honor once we are married." There, he had laid it all out for her, the reason for the elopement. Now, it was up to her to agree or shoot him down.

White static. Her mind was filled with white static. "Are you asking me to marry you?"

Ritter frowned. "You want me to do the knee thing again?"

"Again?"

"Earlier, in the hospital, don't you remember? I asked you, on my knees, and you agreed... sort of. Well, you threw up on me and passed out. I took that as a yes," Ritter said, doubts beating him up inside. He hadn't expected her reaction.

Middy couldn't help it, as badly as she felt, her body aching, frustrated, angry at being so helpless, the whole thing struck her as so funny she started to laugh and couldn't stop. Her body protested the tender flesh pulled and began to bleed again, still she laughed. She laughed so hard and loud that Ronny and the spare came running nearly taking her door off the hinges bursting into the bedroom. The spare had his gun out, and that made Middy laugh all the more.

Ronny glanced at Ritter, down at the pallet, then over at Middy. Seeing blood beginning to stain the hospital gown he rushed over to her, but she waved him off.

Finally able to get herself under control, Middy motioned Ritter over. He looked as if he were walking into the jaws of a shark as he approached her. Middy indicated he should lean close to her. Feeling like he was about to be told to get out of her life and never return, Ritter leaned down waiting for the axe to fall on his neck. She insisted on looking him in the eyes the whole while he had been coming to her, and now his Cupcake held him there with her eyes alone. A breeze brushed over his cheek making his whole body shake with longing. Then, she spoke in a soft low voice just for his ears. "I want a ring. When do we leave." Ritter grabbed her then and kissed her mummified lips. When she winched, he pulled back. He felt so alive, like he could fly, like Superman, and leap tall buildings.

It was supposed to be so simple, just fly off have a quick wedding and back to normal life, whatever that was. Life isn't like that though. Things take a twist and turn in directions you never foresaw. Like Ronny calling Eric to let him know his sister was getting married the next day. Then the phone calls started coming, first Eric saying he had finished his critical healing and they had to delay a day so he could attend the wedding. Then it was Susan wanting to be her bridesmaid. Before Middy and Ritter knew it, they were no longer eloping, but planning a wedding in a week at the house. That, of course, meant all sorts of planning. Somehow the guys got wind of the wedding and demanded to be part of things too. How to fit them all in, and feed the crowd was a huge problem with Middy more or less a helpless mummy. The fact her family would be there for her marriage lightened Middy's spirits. Mother would heal her and she could then wear a wedding dress instead of bandages. Mischief in her eyes she looked over to where Ritter was trying to sleep on his pallet. "You know that you will have to wear a tux now," she teased.

"No damn tux," He stated flatly.

"What? Are you going to make me walk down the aisle and not have a memory of you looking great in a tux? I don't think that is fair," she said.

"Don't worry you'll be looking like a mummy so my suit will be an improvement," Ritter mumbled and rolled so he was facing away from her.

"Mother will be there." She left that hanging in the air and turned off the light. She heard him mumbling under his breath. It sounded like "Oh, damn. I have to wear a tux."

Chaos, utter chaos. Workers were everywhere turning the large side area into something fitting for a wedding. Middy's aunt Emily was flying in, and Middy wasn't able to drive to pick her up. Ritter took care of that problem by having the spare go pick aunt Emily up. The guys all wanted to be part of the wedding, or to attend. The Captain even called to say he was coming. Then, of course, the media learned of the upcoming wedding. That meant the phone had to be monitored for media calls. What happened to a simple elopement? Now they had the problem of who the groomsmen would be, and the bridesmaids. All Middy wanted was to simply say her vows, and have ice cream and ca... no, no cake. She still couldn't eat cake. Therein lay a whole problem in itself. People expected a wedding cake. And a groom's cake. Middy didn't want any cake to be around, none, zero.

The spare pulled up with a grin on his face, beside him sat Middy's aunt Emily. "Ma'am," he called to Middy. "We have solved the wedding cake problem. Your aunt is going to make cobblers, blackberry, and peach. She will use whipped cream as the icing, and we serve each slice with a scoop of ice cream. I can't wait!" he turned and started talking to Emily. She smiled and nodded.

Hugging her aunt to her, Middy whispered her thanks to Emily. "I don't know how the world runs without you, Auntie Em. But, I don't want you working the whole time you are here. I'm giving you orders right now to have some fun too."

Emily blushed and nodded.

Two days before the wedding, Middy's parents arrived. This was a whole new experience for Ritter. Facing his future in-laws was a scary thought. The father was powerful. That power surrounded Fred like a weapon of terrible destruction. Ritter just felt it there, knew it was something he never wanted

to experience. Middy's mother was …. She was
something he couldn't wrap his mind around, not
fully. He owed her so much. She had saved his life.
Saved his Cupcake. And she terrified him. A person
as precious as she was should always be protected
from the cruel world. And yet, how could you even
think to keep her from doing this wonder she could
perform? It boggled his mind. Then, he thought
that Middy was the same in her own way. She
was a weapon. Not a healer. A powerful invisible
weapon. So secret, and so deadly. That she managed
to keep from destroying the world was a wonder
to him. Rage could make people do very stupid
things. Thankfully Cupcake was a gentle person
despite her bluster. He'd have to be certain he never
caused her to distrust him. Crap, he was going to be
sleeping with a weapon. He chuckled to himself and
Cupcake's father scowled at him.

"We need to talk. Not now, Middy needs
healing first," Fred said.

"Yes, sir. Understood," Ritter answered. There
was so much more he wanted to say. Like how do
you deal with it? How many people know the truth?
How much danger is she in? He didn't say those
things though.

Middy was told to lie down upon the bed. Her
bandages were removed, and a sheet put over her
to the neck to hide her body from the men in the
house. Middy's mother sat in a chair beside the bed
and leaned over to touch her daughter. The house
went silent as the healing began. Ritter had come up
to stand near Fred. Carefully he reached out placing
a hand on Felith's shoulder. He gave of his own

strength to help her heal his Cupcake. This he could do. Ritter kept his eyes on Middy's face. This time he could see the healing taking place. Last time it was all on the inside, invisible to the naked eye. Now he watched the flesh on Middy's face heal, the new skin slowly growing to replace the raw abraded and scab filled areas. The scabs fell off. Beneath where they had been now was clear healthy skin.

Felith slumped just a fraction when she was done healing her daughter. Of the recent heals she had done, this had been the easiest. She smiled at Middy. "Now we find you some wedding jeans. Or a dress, if you want." Middy laughed at that last bit. Her mother had been married in jeans.

Fred motioned for Ritter to follow him. They walked outside and away from the house. Ritter waited for Middy's father to start the conversation. His nerves were on high alert. If this man took a disliking to him, Ritter could find himself constantly on assignment at the South Pole. He wouldn't go. His mind made up Ritter broke the uncomfortable silence. "You might be considering sending me off on a long assignment away from Cupcake. I'm just going to say this once. There will be no debate over this. I will stay with your daughter even if it means giving up my job, sir." He shut up then and waited for the blow that would end his career.

"That is what I want to talk to you about. Middy is a lot like her mother. She doesn't think about the consequences of her actions. You can't go running off and leaving her on her own. Your job, from now on, is to remind her that blowing a newspaper on a criminal's car windshield could result in innocent people being hit and property damage. I'm telling you this now because this is a lifetime commitment. You also need to be her battery. She can be drained just like her mother is drained. Think long and hard. Be certain you are up to being there every moment of every day for the rest of your life." Fred didn't pull any punches. Ritter had to know now before he married Middy, what his life was going to become.

"Yes, sir. I agree." Ritter smiled and offered his hand to Middy's father.

The day dawned with natural thunderstorms lashing at Middy's home. Eric called to say his flight was delayed because of storms in his area. Someone thought it was a smart idea to rob a local bank and most of the guys were tied up with that. To top it off Middy still didn't have her dress. It seems that wedding dresses are designed with bean poles in mind. That meant the dress Middy had selected had to be altered. Middy hadn't even given any thought to where to rent tuxes for Ritter and the groom's men.

Middy's aunt Rosemary was to do the bride's hair. That had Middy tied up in knots. She was a simple person and didn't do fancy hairdos. There she sat, leaning back over the sink, with aunt Rosemary washing her hair. Not since she was very little had anyone else washed her hair. She had been brought up to be self-sufficient. A person who could live without having to depend on others. It was something her parents instilled in her. Not by spankings, but with responsibility. Shopping was not an outing as it seemed to be to pampered kids. It was to get the things which were needed to live. And you never, ever, showed disrespect to anyone. Having her aunt Rosemary pamper her felt strange. Sure, she enjoyed having her scalp massaged, but there were so many things she should be doing instead.

When the rain hadn't let up by noon Middy stepped outside of the house. Looks were passed between the men folk in the house. Her mother, who had taken charge in her usual no-nonsense manner voiced a warning. "Leave her alone."

Standing in the rain, with a hood over the curlers in her hair, Middy studied the sky. It didn't look as if the storm was in any hurry to move along. She had had enough of rain for today. She wanted the sun out while the wedding was taking place. After all, they had taken great pains readying the yard for the wedding. They even built a sort of gazebo where the bride and groom would say their vows. Raising her hands she summoned the wind to her. She had created storms, today she would end a storm, or rather, push it on to rain on someone else.

It was like lifting weights. Every muscle in her body pooled its energy to Middy's hands. Holding her hands over her head she used the wind like a knife splitting the storm apart. Then she began to shove one half in one direction. Once the rain clouds began to move Middy switched to the other half of the sky creating wind to blow that half of the storm away. Five minutes for each half of the storm appeared to be enough to assure they were both in the path of natural winds heading away from Middy's house. She felt drained. And the day was just beginning.

Driving up the road to the house was a limo. The wind... uh... the breath went out of Middy. This could only be her aunt Julian. Julian liked to put on airs. She was the one aunt Middy didn't get along with.

Sure enough aunt Julian stepped out of the limo. She was dressed in the latest fashion. Her hair was picture perfect. Middy watched Julian approach, and wondered what else would go wrong.

"What a quaint place you have, Middy. Is this a rented house? What is wrong with your dog? He looks broken. Oh, your cousins send you their love," Julian rattled on, every word sought to make Middy feel bad on this her wedding day. "Surely you are going to have your hair done. I can't believe you would get married looking like this."

Ritter had come out to greet Middy's aunt. He heard all this pointless chatter. Then, he pulled a Tex. His gun was in his hand so fast that if you had blinked it seemed to appear by magic. "Stand back and identify yourself, ma'am. Nobody approaches *her*," he motioned his head towards Middy.

Middy nearly choked with laughter trying to bubble out of her. Only by sheer willpower did she keep a straight face. Julian, on the other hand, screeched and hopped back a pace. "I'm her aunt. Tell him I'm your aunt," she demanded of Middy.

Tempting. It was so tempting to just let her aunt squirm, but her mother would not approve. "Yes, this is aunt Julian."

"Are you certain? When I came out she was being a bitch to you. I'll shoot her if you want. Just say the word," Ritter kept his gun trained on Julian. Out of the corner of his eye, he saw Middy's mouth twitch once, then sober.

"No, it is okay. I'm sure she will control herself." Middy motioned Julian to follow her into the house.

"I have never been so insulted. You need to fire that man. He shouldn't be allowed anywhere near decent people." On and on Julian ranted about Ritter. Middy kept her silence. It occurred to her that once Julian saw Ritter standing in his tux waiting for her in the gazebo she would be punished enough.

Eric and Susan were in the next car to arrive. It was a rental driven by Bobby Jay. The day had brightened. It was going to be a beautiful day after all, Middy thought, as she rushed to greet Susan and Eric. Most of her family would be here for her wedding. Middy realized that this made the day so much better than an elopement would have been. Tux! Middy had forgotten about the tux again for Ritter. She searched him out immediately. "I forgot to order you a tux," she confessed.

"Don't worry, I have it covered," Ritter told her. He watched the confusion on her face and decided to tell her. "Any of us who have been detailed to watch over the higher ups invests in a tux. We never know when we will need one." Middy's mouth twitched to the side. That twitch worried Ritter. He kept his mouth shut though. This thing, this loving someone, was a matter of learning how to live with that person. He sure wasn't going to mess it up before the wedding.

Chapter Eighteen

VOWS

Middy still didn't have her vows figured out. The one thing she thought of when thinking of Ritter was how he was stubborn. And that didn't fit anything she could think of for vows. Or did it? An idea began to form. Whether it bore fruit or not was yet to be seen. Weddings were so stressful, Middy wondered how it was anybody ever went through the process. But then her family was there. Aunt Emily was the best cook Middy knew. Who else would have come up with making a three-tiered wedding cobbler instead of cake? How she loved her aunt for all the times she had given her chocolate cake when she was growing up. And now she was making a wedding memory for Middy.

Watching her mother trying not to organized everyone made Middy smile. If there was one thing, besides healing, that her mom was good at it was giving orders. Walking over to her mother she gave her a hug. "I need to take my bunch out for a walk and clear my head. Will you organize these guys?" she started looking around at all the frantic commotion going on as chairs were set up and decorations were being sorted.

"Go," Felith told Middy. Her daughter was impulsive. Felith understood how she may need a few moments alone to let her mind catch up with her heart.

Gathering her three companions Middy headed towards the peaceful quiet of the near forest. She needed a few moments of quiet, to think.

Ritter started to trail after Middy, as he always did to watch over her when Middy's mother stepped in front of him. "She needs a few moments alone. You need to go see about your clothing for the wedding and the ring. Let her be for a few minutes."

Ritter gave his spare a hand signal to go after Middy, then went to the room where he was to dress. Worry filled his mind. Cupcake could still back out of the wedding. He knew how swift she was to make a judgment. Letting her think things over just didn't seem like a good idea to him. So he paced in front of the window. Back and forth, back and forth, with every moment that passed convincing him that he was losing her... again.

Out of sight of the house, Middy sat on a fallen tree. Watson was busy stalking some critter. Killer flew around zipping through the trees as if on a mission to explore every inch of the place. Only Sherlock remained beside Middy. He sat beside her as still and looking as pensive as she did. "Guys," Middy said to the three of them, "Things will change now. Everything will be different, from the way we sleep to how we think each day. I need you all to be strong for me. Help me to be a better person. I am going to need you to keep me from strangling Ritter. Already I can see that he is going to be a demanding man. You know I don't do demanding."

Middy had closed her eyes as she talked to the companions. When she opened her eyes the three of them were next to her. She nodded at them. "Okay, let's do this."

Back at the house, Eric was watching Ritter pace winding himself up so tight he thought the man would explode. "She is safe. Don't worry so much. My sister is quite capable of defending herself. And I think I'd have a vision if she were in danger," he told Ritter.

"It isn't that. I'm scared. She will have time to think and back out of the wedding. I can't get a breath for worry I won't get her to marry me." Ritter admitted.

Wisely, Eric nodded. He had his own doubts about being able to persuade a girl into marrying him. Of course, he was just a wimpy looking guy, while all these SS men went over the top in looks. Eric heard the breath go out of Ritter.

Ritter went over to Eric looking him in the eye. "Will you do something for me?" Eric nodded again. "Touch me and tell me how long I have left? Doc said one to two years, but I have my doubts. And I feel guilty getting Cupcake to marry me when we won't have that long together."

"You mean that thing that was in your brain? Mother took care of it when she fixed you. You've thought all this time you were going to die?" Eric asked.

Not knowing whether to whoop out loud or hug Eric. Ritter did neither. He just said, "Thank you."

Looking past Ritter out the window he saw Middy with her companions exiting the woods. Ritter turned and looked at his tux as if he had never been about to climb the walls a second before. "I'm off to shower. You will have to help me with this thing," Ritter said motioning to the tux. "I don't think I can tie that damn tie today." With that Ritter stormed into the bathroom. Eric heard the water turn on and very shortly a deep voice began to sing, to actually sing. Eric stifled a chuckle, this would make a wonderful story to tell Middy's children.

Rosemary fussed around Middy placing one of the curls, which spilled from where Middy's hair was pulled up on top of her head, to just the right spot to enhance the whole look. For Middy's part, she was just glad to be rid of the torture curlers. This wasn't her, would never be her, this fancied up hairdo. She never wore makeup or high heels. How the heck was she suppose to walk. Nope, not going to happen, they just had to find her a pair of flats to wear. So what if she was short. The battle of wills began. Middy had no doubt as to who would win.

Feeling like a clown made up for the circus, Middy held her arms up for her wedding dress to be slipped over her head. Stupid makeup, dumb shoes, she wasn't going to wear the shoes even if she had to go barefoot. Aunt Rosemary could just go take a flying leap! How she had ended up with makeup on Middy didn't even know. One moment she was protesting and the next she had stuff on her face. Where was her mother? She needed her mother to take charge of Rosemary and send her packing. Middy's heart was pounding in her chest as the panic built. This wasn't her, she wasn't some poof-girl. As the wedding dress slid down her body and settled in place, Middy stepped out of the ridiculous shoes Rosemary was insisting she wear. She was ready to send a burst of air out to plaster Rosemary to a wall while she ran away. The door to the room opened, Middy's mother entered.

"You may go help Emily," her mother told Rosemary. Just like that the world righten for Middy. Once Rosemary went out and shut the door Felith turned to Middy. "Wipe your face and do it the way you want. Susan was concerned about you." Reaching behind her neck Middy's mother removed the leather butterfly necklace she wore. Carefully she placed it around the hair on top of Middy's head, arranging it as if it were a decoration. "That is your something borrowed. As for blue, and old, this is what your father and I wanted you to have."

Middy watched in the mirror as her mother placed a beautiful butterfly necklace around her neck. It was just the thing to accent her dress with so many colors. There was red, yellow, black and even blue on the butterfly just like the one which had blessed Ritter. Now, with her face looking like herself, her feet bare, and this gift from her parents Middy felt ready.

Ritter stood in the gazebo trying not to jump

out of the place and go find Middy. Everything was ready. The minister was there, his groomsmen were standing beside him, Eric with the ring. Bobby Jay and Officer Fuller stood beside Eric. And here he was in his tux all done up like some pretty boy. He was fretting his life's blood away looking down the rows of chairs, which held so many law enforcement officers that a crook would faint dead away, for his Cupcake. If she had changed her mind they best lock him up. He wouldn't be responsible for his actions.

When the music started playing Ritter straightened up as if at attention. His eyes searching for the procession of women which would indicate his Cupcake was coming to him. After what seemed an eternity a young girl came skipping out with a basket of rose petals over one arm. The child skipped with all the glee of youth down the aisle made between the chairs. Next Rosemary came rushing out, then stopped and began the sedate wedding step, taking way too long for Ritter's jittery nerves. Emily followed in Rosemary's wake a gentle smile on her face. She looked over at someone and Ritter realized it was that Doctor Andy fellow, the guy who did the Andy bags.

There were soft mutters from the crowd when Middy didn't immediately appear behind Emily. Then Killer appeared zipping up and down the aisle with his super speed to flash around Ritter as if being certain Ritter was there. Sherlock and Watson came after him walking side by side. Watson seemed to give the Captain the evil eye as she passed him, but continued on to sit down with dignity at the front. The music's stirring notes signaled the bride was on the way.

She was there on her father's arm, looking so beautiful that Ritter's breath froze in his lungs. Ritter filled his eyes with her as she took the first step toward him. The trees around them suddenly let loose what seemed like thousands of butterflies. They fluttered over to Middy and she stopped walking. No! It was a mental scream from Ritter. He pleaded with the butterflies to let her continue. The butterflies surrounded Middy for a long second. When they moved, some went to make her a butterfly train, others settled on the bouquet she held of different types of Ivy.

Middy looked at Ritter once the air had cleared in front of her. She kept her eyes on him the rest of the way down that forever aisle. She could feel the butterflies keeping step with her. The breeze created by so many tiny wings brushed over her like a caress. Still, she kept her eyes on Ritter. He looked to be leaning forward as if trying to get closer to her. She hoped he was, that this wasn't some pretense of his. That he was really with her forever. When Middy reached the gazebo the butterflies left to cover the gazebo in all their many colors. There was a sound as if everyone finally took a breath after not breathing for a long while. Ritter stepped beside Middy as her father handed her over to him he felt such relief.

Most of what the minister said didn't penetrate the private bubble in which Middy and Ritter stood. They could only see each other. Their hearts seemed to beat as one. Their eyes locked gazing at each other. When it came time for the vows they were still in their private bubble.

Ritter looked into his Cupcake's eyes almost afraid to speak. This was it, the moment he swore his eternity to her. "My life is forever yours. I will always be there to support you, to love you. I will pick you up and throw you over my shoulder when I think you have forgotten how to stay safe. But I promise to let you do your thing. You aggravate me. You make me laugh. You breath life into me. I will never leave you, never lie to you. Never live a moment without holding you in my heart. I am yours forever."

Middy's heart stumbled, lost a beat then came near to bursting with love. "I promise to knock you on your butt when you are too full of yourself to listen. Mostly I promise to love you for eternity. When you are your most aggravating I will try to understand, and try to keep my hands behind my back."

Somehow, some way, they made it through the ceremony. Middy didn't remember much of what was said. She did recall promising to knock Ritter on his stubborn ass when he needed it.

Time for the kiss came. They were man and wife. And the butterflies came surrounding the couple fluttering along Middy's hands and arms. For one solid moment, after the butterflies rose into the air in a starburst of color, Middy could have sworn her arms held butterfly tattoos. Then they were gone. And life resumed. For just a moment Middy stared at one of her arms. Had she seen what she thought she had seen? Or was she just crazy? Ritter cupped her face making her look up at him. "I saw it too," he whispered. Taking Middy's hand he turned them to face their friends and family.

"Let's make a run for it." Laughing they held hands and ran the gauntlet of the people who had come to see them married. Only to be stopped by a blockade of police officers.

Fuller stepped forward holding a bottle of something bubbly. The rest produced glasses. "Before you leave," Fuller said, giving Middy that senior officer look he had down so well. "We want to give one toast." Quickly the glasses were filled. Middy expected the Captain to give the toast, but it was Fuller who raised his glass high. He looked at everyone then concentrated on Middy and Ritter. "To the best rookie partner, I've ever had the trouble of breaking in. And to her fellow. Don't mess this up! Raise your glasses '*To the Boss!*'"

"To the Boss!" everyone shouted. All except the Captain. He looked a little green around the gills.

"You jokers," Middy said. "I love you all. Now let me get my eager husband to the hotel. All of you stay and enjoy the food. Uh… Emily two large portions of that cobbler to go. Heck, make it half of each tier." Everyone laughed at that. Middy was known for her sweet tooth.

Ritter bent down and started raising Middy's gown on one side. His hand slid up her leg. With an "Aha!" he produced a garter. Turning Ritter threw the garter over his shoulder towards the crowd of men. He threw it so hard it flew right over everyone's head and landed on Eric's shoulder. Blushing Eric held the garter up in triumph as if he had won a trophy. Everyone turned to look at Middy.

Grumbling under her breath so only Ritter heard it Middy turned. She didn't look to see anyone in particular before she tossed her bouquet of ivy over her shoulder. She turned just in time to see Tex snatch the bouquet out of the air and hand it to Susan. There was a besotted look on his face, which he quickly covered up with a stern frown. Interesting.

Ritter took Middy's hand and they ran for the car waiting for them. This honeymoon night was last minute in planning, but they had secured a nice room for the night. The main thing was that it would be away from family and friends, so they could be themselves and not worry about waking up anyone. Practically shoving Middy into the car, Ritter then ran around to the driver's side and got in slamming the door. Middy had only seen him like this the time he shoved her to the ground when the monster killed all her fellow officers. They sped down the road to the highway with a squeal of the tires. He drove like a maniac. Middy knew that there was another car hot on their tail. She never went anywhere without someone watching her. For a moment she wondered if some poor SS was going to be called Ritter's babysitter now that he was officially part of the family.

Driving over the speed limit Ritter finally came to his senses. He had it bad, that need to get his woman in bed was raging through his blood making him near crazy. She was his now legally. He just had to make her want to be his, and he planned to love her, give her so much pleasure, she would

never leave him. He just had to get her to the hotel.
The damn tux tie felt like it was strangling him.
Reaching up he yanked it until it was untied then
threw it into the back seat.

"Stop the car!" Middy yelled at him.

What? What was wrong? Had she changed
her mind already? This wasn't happening, it couldn't,
not now. He pulled the car over safely after slowing
enough to maneuver on the side of the road. Dread
in his heart he looked over at his Cupcake. She
looked angry.

"Get your butt in the back and find that tie.
Put it on. Don't you dare to even loosen a cuff link
on your tux. That is *my* job." She poked her finger
into his chest as she scowled at him. Ritter's heart
started beating once again. In fact, it thundered
in his chest so fast and hard he thought it would
explode. Diving over the back of his seat he found
the damn tie. His hands shook in time to the beating
of his heart. She wanted to undress him. That
thought filled his brain up so nothing else could get
in. His mind was filled with white fuzz. He fumbled
with the tie. Finally, he got the thing tied. "Okay?"
he asked. When Middy nodded he relaxed and
crawled over the seat to start the car again. Behind
them, two SS sat in their car wondering what the
heck was going on. Their orders were clear follow,
however, don't get in the way. Protect from a
distance.

The rest of the ride was made in silence. Ritter
couldn't speak for the tension in his body and mind.
She wanted to undress him. How he loved her. All
his fears were laying quiet, laid to waste by the one

thought, she wanted to undress him. Here he had
been worried he had rushed her. A smile he couldn't
contain spread upon his face. This is what happy
feels like he thought.

Middy saw the goofy smile upon Ritter's face.
He looked so relaxed. She'd just have to wind him
up again once they reached the hotel. But, in a good
way.

The End

www.ingramcontent.com/pod-product-compliance
Lightning Source LLC
Chambersburg PA
CBHW071508260626
47170CB00002B/302